"Zombies…" Jannik gasped.

Graf unlimbered his crossbow and started back into the hall. "Aren't you a pretty one?" he growled.

The thing was shambling out from the doorway. Its face was shriveled down to a dried-out skull. Horrible eyes, somehow both vacant and malevolent, glared up at the men. There was an eerie green luminescence about the zombie, a soft glow that made the hair on Jannik's neck prickle with fright.

"We need to run," Jannik urged his partner.

Graf ignored him and loosed the bolt, sending it speeding down into the zombie's forehead.

Jannik had seen Graf destroy many zombies with such shots. This time, however, the results were far different. Both men watched in horror as the bolt simply glanced off the withered skull. With the spectral glow looking even more pronounced now, the undead continued its slow but murderous march toward the stairs. Beyond it, other hideous creatures shambled into view.

More Zombicide from Aconyte

Zombicide Black Plague
Age of the Undead by C L Werner
Zombicide Invader
   Planet Havoc by Tim Waggoner
   Terror World by Cath Lauria
Zombicide
   Last Resort by Josh Reynolds
   All or Nothing by Josh Reynolds

ISLE OF THE
UNDEAD

CL WERNER

First published by Aconyte Books in 2023

ISBN 978 1 83908 213 9

Ebook ISBN 978 1 83908 214 6

Cover art by Dany Orizio

Distributed in North America by Simon & Schuster Inc, New York, USA

Printed in the United States of America

9 8 7 6 5 4 3 2 1

ACONYTE BOOKS

An imprint of Asmodee Entertainment Ltd

Mercury House, Shipstones Business Centre

North Gate, Nottingham NG7 7FN, UK

aconytebooks.com // twitter.com/aconytebooks

For Gwen, who guided me through all the unforeseen pitfalls, thunderstorms, and power outages.

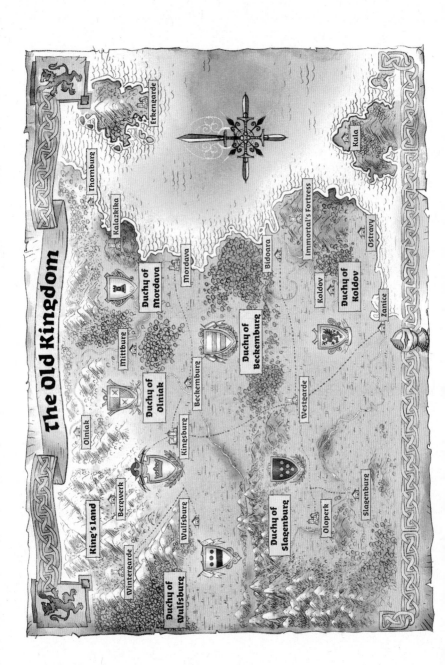

The Old Kingdom

Erkengarde

Thornburg

Kalozkika

Kula

Duchy of Mordava

Mordava

Immortal's Fortress

Ostravy

Mittburg

Bidoara

Koldov

Zanice

Duchy of Olniak

Duchy of Beckemburg

Duchy of Koldov

Olniak

Beckemburg

King's Land

Bergwerk

Kinesburg

Westearde

Wulfsburg

Winterearde

Duchy of Slagenburg

Oloperk

Duchy of Wulfsburg

Slagenburg

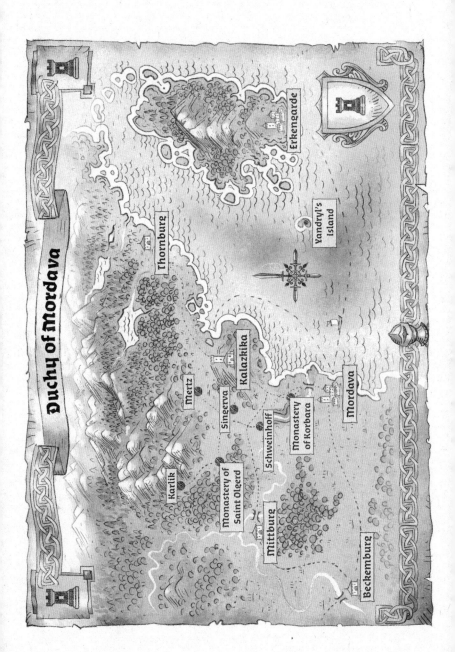

Duchy of Mordava

Erkengarde

Vandryl's Island

Thornburg

Mertz

Karlik

Singerva

Kalaztika

Monastery of Saint Olgerd

Schweinhoff

Monastery of Kortbara

Mordava

Mittburg

Beckemburg

PROLOGUE

Jannik Hassel tucked the heft of his axe underneath his arm while he rummaged through the battered trunk. Clothes and keepsakes were tossed aside, adding to the debris that littered the room. He found his irritation mounting. Why did people hang on to such trash? Where was the good stuff?

Jannik finally spotted a small silver necklace. The pendant was some clumsy portrait of a child, carved in wood. Sentimental value rather than monetary worth. Still, at least the chain might catch someone's eye. He stuffed the necklace into the burlap sack hanging from his belt. It joined a far too meager collection of loot. After all his years driving a coach between Singerva and Schweinhoff, Jannik had expected better pickings at Feig's inn. Angrily, he slammed the lid of the trunk and stove in its side with a kick of his boot.

It would be just like that conniving innkeeper Feig to hide his money in some secret spider hole. Some dark corner it would take weeks to find. Jannik gave the trunk another kick. He hoped the innkeeper had died unpleasantly. From the condition of the place, it looked as though a considerable number of zombies had converged on it. Perhaps one of those piles of badly gnawed meat down in the wine cellar was all that remained of that swine Feig.

"What's all that noise?" a voice growled from the doorway. Jannik spun around, axe at the ready. He relaxed only slightly when he recognized the speaker. Tall, scar-faced, and still wearing a bloodstained cloak, Graf had a compact hand crossbow clenched in one fist. Jannik winced when he noted that the weapon was aimed at him. As a coachman, he knew the deadly accuracy Graf possessed. He'd been the most notorious highwayman in the province. The very best partner to have for a spree of looting. Graf possessed few scruples and sometimes the abandoned places they searched weren't as empty as they seemed. Living survivors or undead marauders, the highwayman would dispatch them by putting a bolt through their skull.

"Just having a look around," Jannik told Graf. He jostled the bag drooping off his belt. "Pickings have been less than I expected." The coachman glanced around the shambles that had once been the innkeeper's bedroom. "I think someone's already been through here."

Graf favored him with a cold smile. "Think again," he advised. He nodded his head at the floor, indicating the rooms on the lower story. "Found two walkers still prowling about in the kitchen. There was another one locked inside the pantry." He had a smaller, similar sack to Jannik's pinned to his coat. With his free hand, he reached into it and withdrew a silver goblet. Jannik recalled that Feig brought the vessel out only when a noble stopped at the inn. Anyone familiar with the place would have known to look for it.

"If someone got here first, they'd hardly have left that,"

Jannik agreed, a sour note in his voice. He gave Graf's report about zombies a brief thought. "Maybe the previous looters were ambushed. Caught out by a bigger pack of walkers than the ones you found."

The highwayman replaced the goblet in the bag. "Whatever happened, I'm sure they didn't leave this place. Either they locked themselves in somewhere and starved, or else the zombies got them. Whichever, any loot they found's still here someplace."

Jannik considered the problem, thinking back to all the times he'd brought passengers to Feig's to wait out the night before pressing on to their destination. To avoid meeting up with men like Graf on some dark road. The Black Plague had changed everything in the kingdom, making desperate allies of former enemies.

"We might try the loft," Jannik said, gazing up at the ceiling. "Not much space up there but if–"

A loud crash from below ended further discussion. Both of the looters instantly snapped to high alert. The initial violent noise was followed by the clamor of splintering wood and heavy objects slamming to the ground. Jannik and Graf shared a frightened look. They knew what they were hearing was the barricade they'd raised to seal off the main doors being broken.

"Zombies…" Jannik gasped. It was always a danger when searching a place that undead in the area would be drawn to them. No matter how careful and quiet the looters were, the zombies seemed to have an innate ability to sense when the living were around.

Graf unlimbered the second crossbow he carried. With a

weapon in each hand, he started back into the hallway. "We'd better go and see. There might only be a few."

"Or there might be dozens," Jannik grumbled under his breath as he followed the highwayman. As he climbed down the stairs behind Graf, his eyes kept darting around, looking for some way to quickly leave the inn. Every door and window, however, was blocked up. Keeping things out also meant keeping things in.

"Aren't you a pretty one?" Graf growled when he reached the bottom of the stairs. From over the highwayman's shoulder, Jannik saw the loathsome creature his partner had spotted. The thing was several yards away, shambling out from the doorway leading into the barroom. Its thinness was almost skeletal and the wispy white cloth that was draped around it might as easily be a burial shroud as the remnant of a proper garment. Its face was shriveled down to a dried-out skull with a tattered pit where its nose should have been. Horrible eyes, somehow both vacant and malevolent, glared up at the men. There was an eerie green luminescence about the zombie, a soft glow that made the hair on Jannik's neck prickle with fright.

"We need to run," Jannik urged his partner.

Graf ignored the coachman and aimed a crossbow at the necrotic creature. "It's only one of them. Show some spine." He let loose the bolt and sent it speeding down into the zombie's forehead.

Jannik had seen Graf destroy many zombies with such shots. This time, however, the results were far different. Both men watched in horror as the bolt simply glanced off the withered skull. With the spectral glow looking even more pronounced now, the undead continued its slow but murderous march toward the stairs. Beyond it, other equally hideous creatures shambled into view.

"Khaiza's Shovel!" the highwayman cursed, invoking the sinister funerary goddess. He aimed the other crossbow and sent another shot at the advancing zombie. Again, the bolt was deflected by the rotten skull, bouncing from the decayed flesh as if it had hit a block of granite. Graf tried to back away, spinning around when he found his way blocked by Jannik. Before he could shove the coachman aside the glowing creature surged up onto the stairway and its bony talons wrapped about the man's head, long nails ripping into the looter's face.

"Get away from him!" Jannik raged as he saw the zombie gouge bloody furrows in his partner's cheeks. Without thinking, he sprang down and brought the edge of his axe cleaving through the air at the creature's head.

The axe bounced back at him, repulsed by the glow exuding from the zombie. Taken by surprise, Jannik lost his grip on the weapon, and it went clattering down the steps. He pitched onto his back and drew his knife.

The walker he'd attacked shoved Graf to one side, leaving him to tumble to the floor where the rest of the undead were waiting to tear the last spark of life from the mutilated highwayman. The zombie on the stairs glared at Jannik, its yellowed teeth bared in a menacing snarl. The coachman scrambled upward, pushing himself along the steps while keeping his eyes on the creature that slowly pursued him.

As he neared the top of the stairs, Jannik noted that another figure had appeared in the room below. A grim shape arrayed in heavy black robes. The face that sneered up at him wasn't that of a zombie. For all its pallor, for all its predatory evil, it was yet the face of a living man. There was a sparkle of sadistic mirth in the wicked eyes when they met Jannik's gaze.

"Don't be too hasty," the robed stranger said. For a second, Jannik thought the man was speaking to him. Then he noticed the man's hand as it pointed at the walker on the stairs. That paleness of the stranger's face had at least a speck of life to it, but the gray clamminess of the hand reeked of the grave. And it was pointing at the zombie closing in on the coachman.

"Let's see if he can hurt you with that knife," the stranger scoffed, and in his tone Jannik heard his own doom pronounced.

The necromancer waved his necrotic hand in a dismissive gesture. "It will be amusing to watch him try."

Jannik slashed at the zombie as it reached for him. He managed to retain the blade after the spectral aura repulsed his blow. He made another futile swing, then the walker was upon him.

The coachman's last thought, before everything transformed into gnawing pain, was whether he and Graf would stay dead or if their ragged remains would rise again to join the necromancer's retinue.

Perhaps, Jannik wondered, the necromancer was scavenging the ruins looking for those he could work his loathsome sorcery upon. In his own profane way, maybe he was simply a looter, too.

CHAPTER ONE

Alaric von Mertz felt a coldness around his heart as he gazed out across the desolate town. From the roof of Vasilescu's tower, the knight could see most of Singerva, or at least the ruins it had become. As far as he was aware, the only people still alive in the town were those who'd sought sanctuary in the wizard's stronghold. The rest of the population had either fled into the countryside or died.

Or worse. Though Singerva was dead, there was still movement in its rubble-strewn streets. Singly or in packs, mobs of zombies prowled the wasteland, shuffling along without wit or purpose until some sound or flash of movement would agitate the malignancy that coursed through their rotten frames. However mindless they might appear, hatred of the living provided the undead with their motivating force and turned them into a relentless army of destruction.

The knight walked slowly about the periphery of the rooftop garden, one hand trailing along the ledge that encompassed the perimeter. The other rested on the dragon-emblazoned pommel of the sword on his belt: the crest of von Mertz, repeated in black and crimson on the tattered surcoat he wore over his armor. A last link between himself and his noble heritage.

The Black Plague had infected many parts of the kingdom, and hordes of the reanimated dead rampaged across entire duchies. Alaric wondered how many other towns had become like Singerva. Was there nowhere that was safe?

Alaric shook his head. Safety? Perhaps that might be possible, if the zombies were the only evil that beset the kingdom, but he knew the situation was far more dire. In this very tower, he'd seen the proof. The wizard Vasilescu had revealed himself to be a necromancer, collaborating with others in profane cabals to control the undead and direct their onslaught. Vasilescu was dead, but his loathsome ally had escaped. Brunon Gogol, the villain who'd brought death to Alaric's family and left his father's domain as lifeless as a tomb.

A stir of motion caused Alaric to turn around, refocusing his thoughts on the present rather than the past. A slim, dark-haired woman, her vestments the night-black brigandine of a witch hunter, leaned against the ledge. She directed her sharp, hawklike gaze downward at the great plaza that bordered the front half of the tower.

"The fire continues to hold them," Helchen reported. She wagged a gloved finger at the scene below.

Walking to Helchen, Alaric looked down into the plaza. It was a far from cheering vista. The streets of Singerva might still be haunted by packs of zombies, but the area around the tower fairly crawled with the undead. There had to be hundreds prowling around the stronghold, with more staggering in to join the necrotic throng from every alleyway and side street that opened onto the square. Some of the bodies in the plaza lay sprawled on the flagstones, returned to a true death by arrows from the tower's defenders. The real defense, however, was the one that had been implemented by Vasilescu himself: a wide moat that circled the structure. Pumps in the cellars below fed an alchemical mixture to the trench, creating a wall of fire that readily consumed the undead that marched into it.

"The fire holds," Alaric agreed. He focused on a bulky zombie, its tattered garb marking it as once a stevedore, and watched the creature lumber without hesitation into the flames. The brute's urge to slaughter the living was greater than any caution yet lingering in its brain, and it pitched forward into the trench without so much as a pained yell. From past experience, the knight knew how hard such brutish undead were to destroy. "The fire holds," he repeated, shaking his head. "But how long can we hold the fire?"

Helchen gave the knight a grim look. "That's the question everyone in this tower keeps asking. Even if they don't dare put it into words. You can see the fear etched into each face. The worry about how long this place will be safe." She sighed and gazed up into the overcast sky. "You know, there's a sect of mystics who believe they can draw prognostications from the shapes of clouds."

"We might make use of such augurs," Alaric commented. "That is, if the Order left any of them alive." He knew it was a cruel thing to say, but however much he'd come to respect and depend upon Helchen, he couldn't forget his distrust of the witch hunters as an organization. Many were overzealous fanatics, perfectly willing to hang a dozen innocuous practitioners of magic just so long as the thirteenth to be executed was a genuine necromancer. The Black Plague had only increased his antipathy, for now there was no denying the extreme menace necromancers posed – a menace that, perhaps, justified the murder of innocents to expose the guilty. The idea that honor and chivalry were inadequate to the task of fighting such evil was a repugnant notion that offended everything Alaric believed in.

"Even at our most indolent, the Order had better things to do than prosecute such fakers," Helchen replied, choosing not to respond to the anger in Alaric's tone. After all they'd been through, she'd learned to differentiate between when something was intended to be personal and when it wasn't. She showed her lack of concern with a little laugh. "Just about now we could use one of those charlatans. He could tell everyone that a particular cloud is an auspicious omen and that the moat will stay lit for many years yet."

The knight swept his gaze across the decayed throng in the plaza, at all the clawed hands reaching out toward the tower and the gaping mouths waiting to sink teeth into living flesh. "But how long will it really hold?"

"Hulmul might have been able to tell us." Helchen's voice dipped as she spoke of the wizard who'd helped them reach Singerva and who'd later died fighting against his former master, the treacherous Vasilescu. She set her hand against a satchel fastened to her belt. Alaric knew it contained one of the arcane tomes Hulmul had saved from the Order's vaults and which he'd entrusted her with protecting.

Alaric bowed his head in respect to the dead. Hulmul had sacrificed everything to fight the sorcerous evil which had laid waste to Singerva; in the end, his efforts had even overcome

Helchen's prejudice against those who studied magic. It was largely due to the courage of fallen comrades like Hulmul and Drahoslav that anyone survived Vasilescu's betrayal. Alaric felt his duty to protect the refugees within the tower to be as much a sacred trust as Helchen's regard for the books the wizard left in her custody.

A hard glint entered his eyes as doubt gnawed at Alaric's mind. Was that the only reason he was determined to defend the tower?

The knight's fingers traced the family crest on his sword's pommel, feeling the dragon and the lance transfixing its body. The noble line of von Mertz, of which he was all that remained.

"These people look to me for leadership," Alaric told Helchen, "but can I say that I am worthy of that trust? Can I be trusted with such responsibility?"

Helchen rested her hand on the knight's shoulder. "You've done nothing to dishonor your duty. Many of us would be dead now, if not for you."

Alaric pointed at the ruined town. "I could seek a way out of here. Find someplace safer to lead these people." He closed his eyes and an expression of anguish flitted over his features. "But there's something inside me that doesn't even want to try. I want to stay here."

"Because you believe Gogol will come back," Helchen supplied. "Necromancers aren't so obliging. When they escape, they keep running. If they didn't, then the Order wouldn't need so many witch hunters."

"Things aren't the way they were," Alaric said. "The king has no dominion here now. It is the undead that hold sway, perhaps over the entire province. Gogol doesn't need to hide."

Helchen had no assurances to counter that argument. Alaric could see it on her face. She knew he was right. The witch hunter looked relieved when she stared past him and saw they were no longer alone on the roof. Two others had arrived from below to relieve their watch. One was a short, spry little man with a genial visage even if his eyes were a bit too cunning to encourage trust. The other was a hulking warrior with leathery green skin and long, wolfish fangs that jutted from his mouth. Thief and orc, the pair formed part of the disparate company who'd wrested the tower away from Vasilescu.

"Ya smash'd dat ginkz flippa," the orc grunted, nodding to Alaric. "Da piker innt gonna lampin' fer da new rumpuz."

The thief provided translation for the savage warrior. "Ratbag feels that since you mangled Gogol's arm, he won't be looking for another fight." Gaiseric rubbed his wrist against the golden buttons on the coat he was wearing, a bit of finery that he'd lifted from Vasilescu's wardrobe. "I can't say I agree with him. We killed his master, ruined his plans, injured him. Gogol knows the threat we pose." He tapped his foot against the roof. "And he knows this tower. Its strengths and its weaknesses."

"We can prepare for him to attack. Make a fight of it," Alaric said.

"Gogol won't risk himself unless he feels certain of victory," Helchen cautioned. "Already we've seen the grotesque ways the Black Plague has preyed upon the land. We've seen the horrible abominations the necromancers have crafted for their purposes. There's no knowing what foul surprises Gogol might bring if he returns."

"When he returns," Alaric corrected her. "Gogol was driven by revenge to make my family his first target. Whatever else might be uncertain, you can be sure he won't rest until I'm dead, too."

Gaiseric shook his head. "All the more reason why we can't stay. Gogol is sure to look for you here. That might suit your personal vendetta, but a lot of innocent people will get caught in the fray." The thief jabbed his finger against his own chest. "Mostly I'm worried that I'll be one of them."

Helchen pointed at the plaza below, with its horde of zombies. "If we did decide to leave, how could we?"

"Da stumpiez ballin' da jack," Ratbag growled, his red eyes gleaming as he glanced at the steps leading back into the tower.

"Ursola has been working on a solution," Gaiseric interpreted. Ursola was the other survivor of their company, a dwarf whose expertise was explosives and demolition. "She's been figuring out a mixture drawn off the moat's fuel. Something that can be portable." He nodded as he warmed to the subject. "Could use it to clear a path through the plaza and get everyone out of Singerva." He cast a hopeful glance at Alaric. The knight could feel Gaiseric silently pleading with him to accept the idea.

"We'd still have the problem of where to take everyone," Alaric reminded them. "Ratbag tells us that the orc lands beyond the frontier are also suffering from the Black Plague."

"There's a lot of ground between here and there," Gaiseric said. "Lot of places that might be a safer refuge." He turned to the orc. "Ratbag traveled a long way to get here and he saw several spots that could provide shelter."

"If'n der rottaz ain't shack'd dere," the orc snarled, his clawed fingers tightening about the grip of his scimitar.

Helchen didn't need Gaiseric to translate. "I agree that any shelter Ratbag saw might be overwhelmed by now. We've no idea how far the Black Plague has spread… or if the necromancers are using spells to expand its reach even further." She shifted her focus to Alaric. "Even such a nebulous hope is less foolhardy than remaining here to await Gogol's pleasure."

"I wouldn't expect timidity from a witch hunter." Alaric shook his head. He knew it was the wrong thing to say when he saw the warning gleam in Helchen's eyes.

"The Order hunts necromancers," she said. "It's important to confront them on our terms, not theirs. Staying here and waiting for Gogol to come back is reckless." Some of the sharpness left her expression. "I don't believe your honor will allow you to be reckless. Not with lives entrusted to you."

Alaric bowed his head in defeat. The urge toward revenge was fierce within him. Gogol had set a horde of zombies against the village of Mertz. His undead were the ones that broke through the defenses of Castle von Mertz and slaughtered everyone inside. His father, his mother, sister and brother, retainers who'd served the family so long that they'd become like family themselves. All of them massacred by the necromancer's minions. Some of them had risen again as zombies themselves. He thought of his father. His last memory of the baron was when his corpse had come stalking toward him with the mindless animosity of a zombie. Yes, he had so many debts to collect from Gogol, debts of wrath and vengeance. The urge for revenge was like a thunder hammering inside his heart. But the onerousness of his obligations to the survivors was stronger. "How long does Ursola need to prepare enough of her mixture?" he asked Gaiseric.

The question caught the thief off guard. It took him a moment to compose his thoughts. "A week, maybe? Certainly not more than a month."

Alaric turned and stared back out across the ruined town. A week or a month? Maybe Gogol would return before then. Maybe he wouldn't have to make the choice between what he desired and what duty wanted him to do.

"It's your watch," Alaric told Gaiseric as he moved away from the ledge. He motioned for Helchen to follow him as he headed for the stairs. "We'll spread word among the survivors. Tell them to be ready to leave."

Almost reluctantly, Alaric put his decision into clear words. "When Ursola is ready, we're leaving Singerva."

The funerary chapel dedicated to Khaiza, Mistress of Tombs, nestled in the shadow of the wizard's tower. Like the treacherous Vasilescu, the priests of Khaiza had required close proximity to Singerva's old cemetery. The doleful tones of the chapel's bell were intended to reach even the most distant grave, to assure the dead beneath the headstones that they were not forgotten and so keep them restful in their coffins.

The black-robed figure who now stood in the bell tower expressed a sardonic grin as he considered the rituals of Khaiza's priesthood. Their sacred precautions had availed them nothing, for when the Black Plague swept over Singerva, the cemetery's dead stirred just as readily as any unburied corpse. Only the very oldest of the crypts and tombs remained intact, those places where the occupants had moldered away until nothing was left except handfuls of dust. Everywhere else the fell magic awakened the dead and resurrected them as the undead. The common pits of paupers now stood as trenches, the soil churned by the bony claws of the things hidden in the ground. The marble tombs of the wealthy, for all the protective spells and orisons gold could buy, stood hollow and empty, silver-handled coffins reduced to splinters as their occupants emerged to new and unholy animation.

Many of the dead disgorged by the cemetery now filled the plaza outside Vasilescu's tower. The man at the chapel took pleasure from the sight, for in it he saw a portent of the future. Struggle as they might, the living could never conquer the undead. They could only delay the inevitable. The zombies of the cemetery had spread across Singerva in a tide of massacre, most of their victims rising again themselves to swell the horde's ranks. Fight as they would, the living had either died or fled, abandoning the town to the children of the Black Plague. Now, in all the town, the only people left alive were those inside the tower… and himself.

Mostly. Brunon Gogol looked down at the ghastly arm hanging from the sleeve of his cassock. It was cold and numb, utterly without sensation. He had to concentrate on it to get it to move and if he lost focus, the limb would stubbornly freeze into whatever attitude he'd last demanded of it.

A thousand maledictions upon Alaric von Mertz and his comrades! Gogol's own arm had been mangled during their battle in Vasilescu's cellars. The necromancer had been compelled to amputate the ruined limb. He'd decided to replace it with one cut from the shoulder of a zombie brute, selecting as his donor a brawny creature that had once served as a judicial swordsman. An arm that could swing a great sword with enough force to behead a condemned criminal promised to make Gogol's next encounter with Alaric very different from their last one. Or it would be if the necromancer could devise a way to use the reanimated limb without devoting his full concentration on it. He was versed enough in the dark arts that the threat of infection from the necrotic arm was minimal, but the problem of controlling it was one that continued to vex him.

Still, Gogol had other surprises for the knight and his companions. A devil's smile worked its way across his face as he gazed down into the plaza. The horde of walkers, runners, and brutes continued to press the tower's defenses. Dozens of zombies stumbled into the fiery moat each hour, shoved to immolation by the masses of undead behind them or driven to suicidal aggression by their innate hatred of the living inside the fortress. Some few were even brought down by arrows from the roof, sentinels shooting at heads and hearts to try and thin the enemy ranks. No, while the moat continued to burn, Alaric's people were at small risk. Even the sorcerously augmented abominations the necromancers had created would fail within the flames. Perhaps the murders of undead crows that soared above Singerva might prove a menace, but they had enough mentality left that they sensed danger from the fire and so kept clear of the tower.

No, it would need something different to break the defenses. Something new.

Gogol closed his eyes for a moment and focused his will. Not into the reanimated arm attached to his shoulder, but into the moldering brains of the undead waiting within the funerary chapel. Exerting his commands, he imposed motivation on the zombies. When he opened his eyes again, the creatures were shambling out through the battered doors.

In their lumbering, unfocused movements, the zombies seemed no different from the multitudes of walkers that infested Singerva. Their bodies, however, were even more decayed and fleshless than the creatures that surrounded the tower, withered down almost to a skeletal condition. The more telling difference required a bit more scrutiny to detect, at least from a distant vantage like the bell tower where Gogol stood. As he watched his undead, he could only faintly pick out the eerie glow that emanated from them. The betraying sign of the fearsome enchantments he'd infused into his creations.

They were time-consuming rather than complicated, these spells that altered the character of a zombie. Gogol was certain other cabals of necromancers would adopt the same procedure. There were two basic conditions when it came to the undead. First, those that were corporeal and bound to the necrotic husks of their bodies. Second, there were those that had become spectral, divorced from all material attachment, entities of a purely phantasmal state. What Gogol had done was to change his zombies so that they were endowed with aspects of that ghostly caste. True, their physical forms were shriveled to a more decayed condition, but his spectral walkers had other properties that compensated for a reduction in speed or strength.

The necromancer watched with rapt attention as his zombies lurched into the midst of the horde surrounding the tower. Gogol noted the occasional arrow that sped into the mob, piercing the skulls of more mundane undead. Then he saw one of the missiles glance off a spectral walker's head, deflected by the sepulchral aura that surrounded the creature. He could imagine the consternation of the archer and a moment later a second arrow tried to strike the same zombie. Again, it was sent spinning away, incapable of penetrating the ghostly energy.

The spectral walkers continued to push their way through the zombie horde, drawing closer and closer to the tower itself. Now Gogol could see the green-skinned bulk of Alaric's orc heave into view on the roof's ledge. Ratbag clutched a heavy spear in his hands. Despite the weight of the weapon, he cast it down as though it were a javelin. The missile sped true, but neither its mass nor the orc's brawn was enough to defy the ectoplasmic protection of Gogol's new zombies. The spear was deflected as easily as any of the arrows had been. The spectral walkers continued their ponderous advance.

Gogol's delight at the impotence of the tower's defenders to stop his creations decayed into consternation once the spectral walkers came to the fiery moat. The zombies advanced without hesitation, impelled by their master's will. Yet as they fell into the flames, they encountered a force they weren't able to defy as they had spear and arrow. The alchemical mixture licked greedily about them, evaporating the phantasmal glow and searing the withered flesh of their bodies. Through his arcane connection with the spectral walkers, Gogol could feel them being destroyed.

The necromancer severed his magical link to the zombies. It would be futile to try and recover them from the moat and, though tedious, he could replace them easily enough. No, it was the discovery that the spectral walkers had limitations that posed a greater problem for Gogol. The targets of his revenge were all inside Vasilescu's tower, but to get at them would mean bypassing the moat.

A cold smile returned to Gogol's face as he considered that problem. There were many ways into Vasilescu's cellar, tunnels linked to the surrounding catacombs and cemetery. He wondered how thoroughly Alaric and his companions had searched for those openings.

And whether they'd found them all.

CHAPTER TWO

Ursola Stonebreaker kept a careful watch on the humans working the complex mechanism that pumped fuel into the moat. Alaric and the rest could talk about how these men were now no different from any of the refugees in the tower, how if they let the fire fail that they'd be killed by the zombies just like everyone else. She didn't accept that view. They had been servants of Vasilescu, stamped with the same brand as their treacherous master. When a dwarf unmasked an oath-breaker, that betrayal was neither forgiven nor forgotten. To put any measure of trust in such people was to re-use a broken rope. It was an unsound judgment and one she felt certain Alaric would come to regret.

A grim gleam shone in Ursola's eyes and one of her calloused hands patted one of the fire-bombs resting on the table beside her. Before the Black Plague descended on Singerva, she'd been an expert demolitionist contracted by the renowned Ironshield and Company. She knew hundreds of ways to knock down, pull down, or immolate some structure that interfered with plans of dwarven engineers. Crafting incendiary bombs from the alchemical mixture that fed the moat was so simple it was more in the nature of a chore than anything she'd describe as work. She had an entire keg of the fuel to work with and could always draw off more from the vats that fed the pumps. The duplicitous archmage had been quite thorough about keeping his cellars stocked with supplies. By her estimation, a company of dwarves could hold up in the tower for years with what they had to work with. Even humans, with their more fragile constitutions, could endure for many months in these conditions.

Of course, that was in ideal circumstances. She felt in her bones that Gogol, Vasilescu's partner in his necromantic cabal, would be plotting something treacherous to complete his plan and destroy the remaining member of the von Mertz family. When the necromancer returned, it would be with some trick to bypass the tower's defenses. And she kept an eye on everything to try and figure out what it could be. Ursola agreed with the view that it would be better to take what they could from the tower's stores and find a new refuge. Someplace Gogol would be less familiar with. If they could find such a place.

Ursola scowled at one of the workers who glanced her way as he worked the pumps. Again, she patted the sealed jar and picked it up. If any sabotage came into play, she'd made it clear to these men that they wouldn't have to worry about the undead. Burning alive was one of the few deaths she could think of that was worse than being ripped apart by zombies.

"You seem determined to make them more afraid of you than they were of Vasilescu."

Ursola started at the words, fumbling to retain her grip on the fire-bomb. She turned her scowl from the servants to the woman who'd spoken. "Beards of my grandfathers!" the dwarf cursed. "Stop sneaking around like an elf, Helchen!" She wagged the fire-bomb at the witch hunter. "What if I'd dropped this?"

Helchen crossed her arms and returned Ursola's scowl. "I suppose I would have helped you wipe the mess up," she said, unperturbed. "There's nothing around to ignite it."

The dwarf let out a nervous laugh. "You think so, do you?" She tapped her thumb against the bulbous neck of the fire-bomb. "I've made some improvements. You don't need an outside flame to ignite them. There's a mechanism, some flint and tinder, nestled inside. When the casing breaks, the pressure the device is under is also broken." She set down the bomb and slid her palms against one another. "All it takes is one good spark."

From the color that drained from Helchen's face, Ursola could see she'd caught the idea… and the magnitude of the accident she'd nearly provoked. It reminded the dwarf of how the engineers working for Ironshield would react when she explained some particularly audacious demolition plan to them. Ursola had come to draw a perverse sort of confidence from the uneasiness of those around her, and her alarm of only a moment before changed into boastfulness.

"I felt it was all too awkward, depending on another source of flame," she explained to Helchen, waving her forward to examine the fire-bombs. "This way everything is contained and ready to work right away. Saves valuable time when you're surrounded by zombies."

Cautiously, Helchen picked up one of the devices and inspected it. "If it's so easy to explode them, I'd say they're more dangerous than the zombies are." She fixed Ursola with her piercing gaze. "And I wasn't deliberately sneaking up on you. It's just that a witch hunter gets accustomed to moving quietly."

Ursola shrugged off the apology, more concerned with the problem of the bomb's mechanism. "I've a few ideas to make them sturdier. Maybe run a wick down the neck, so the spark lights a fuse that drops down into the incendiary." She scratched her chin. "Yes, that would probably work, but I'd have to change the design. Reduce the fuel." The dwarf sighed as she turned back to her design sketches. "I think that could be done, but it would change the effect. You wouldn't end up with a burning pool but just a quick flash of flame. Still strong enough to burn just about anything, but it wouldn't linger the way dragonfire does."

The witch hunter set down the bomb she'd been studying. "Maybe we'll never have to use them." Helchen indicated the spidery array of pipes that fed Vasilescu's alchemical brew into the moat. "We've enough fuel to keep the fires burning for a long time. By then the king will certainly have raised another army and cleared this province of undead."

"You think so?" Ursola grunted doubtfully. "You're forgetting Alaric was there with the first army sent against these zombies. They were almost annihilated... and every soldier who fell only added to the undead horde."

"They underestimated the enemy," Helchen replied. "The king won't make that mistake again. He'll have inquisitors of the Order to advise him, and I think this time he'll pay more notice to what they have to say."

"Maybe," Ursola conceded, her tone still skeptical. It

was a constant vexation to a dwarf, this habit of humans to always insist on finding hope where there was none. It was far more practical to accept reality for what it was. To endure and struggle because it was what had to be done, not because of some pleasing self-delusion. There was just a bit of maliciousness when she reminded Helchen of just how dire things might be. "You forget that the kingdom is threatened from many directions. If Ratbag's right, then the orclands are also beset by this blight. I have no love for orcs and goblins, but even I'll concede that it's better to contend with living ones than zombified ones. There's no telling how many of the tribes have been afflicted, or when the orcish undead will cross the frontier into your duchy."

The dwarf gestured at the complex machinery that defended the tower. "I'd not put too much faith in this contraption either. I've spotted six potential faults in its construction, besides the character of the people operating it." Ursola shook her head. "I don't think it was ever intended to operate for such a sustained period of time."

Helchen nodded, her expression grim. "Vasilescu was probably using magic to strengthen it. An option that we don't have the luxury of copying."

From the melancholy note in Helchen's voice, Ursola knew she was thinking of Hulmul. For all the strife that had existed between them, the wizard's death had made a profound impression on the witch hunter. The dwarf suspected that she felt no small measure of responsibility for Hulmul's demise, as though her suspicions of his loyalty had pushed him to be overbold in his struggle against the necromancers.

"I know Alaric has discussed plans for leaving the tower,"

Ursola said, trying to steer the conversation in a different direction. "That's why I've been bashing up so many of these bombs. They'll be handy if we have to burn our way across that plaza."

The witch hunter's expression was grave when she explained the reasoning behind Alaric's change of view. "Alaric's been talking about leaving by himself. He's eager to take up Gogol's trail and avenge his family and is convinced that Gogol, too, is intent on revenge. Since he believes that if he stays here the necromancer is sure to attack, he's been wrestling with the danger that puts everyone else in. The only thing keeping him here is a sense of responsibility for the refugees. Now that same feeling of duty has him wondering if it wouldn't be better to leave here on his own and draw Gogol's attention elsewhere." A low cough of bitter laughter rose from her throat. "As though a necromancer would give him anything approaching a fair fight if they did meet up. The problem with knights is that they sometimes forget that very few people abide by any code of chivalry. Even other knights. But you can't really talk a martyr out of his decision once it has been made." From the way she clenched her fists in frustration, Ursola could see that Helchen had tried such arguments on Alaric already.

Ursola bowed her head in admiration. Duty and obligation were things a dwarf respected, especially when they were considered more important than individual desires. All too often, in her experience, humans wouldn't subsume their own personal interests to honor other commitments. "Alaric won't leave unless he's sure he's no longer needed here," she said, convinced that whatever notions of self-sacrifice the knight had adopted, he'd not act on them unless he was positive the refugees could survive without his leadership. Ursola's eyes narrowed when she noticed a tightening of Helchen's jaw. "You intend to go with him if he leaves?"

Helchen let out a low sigh. "He'll need help. He's a knight, accustomed to combat and battlefields. He doesn't have the training and experience to track down a necromancer." For just a brief instant, Ursola saw something like guilt in the witch hunter's eyes. "The Order has developed those skills in me. Captain Dietrich tempered my abilities in a hundred investigations... and scores of executions." The momentary doubt receded, and her voice became as firm as steel. "If Alaric has any chance of finding Gogol, he'll need me with him."

The dwarf tapped her finger against the tabletop. "You're forgetting the other scenario. You're forgetting that the necromancer has his own motives for revenge. It was by design that he brought the Black Plague to the village of Mertz and slaughtered Alaric's family." Ursola glanced up at the ceiling and the tower above them. "Gogol's just as likely to come for Alaric as the other way around. And while he stays here, the zombie-master knows just where to find him." Ursola gestured at the bombs on the table. "These'll be very helpful if that happens."

"All the more reason to take up his trail," Helchen replied. "Alaric might be reluctant to admit it, but if something were to happen..."

The witch hunter's words faded from Ursola's awareness. She was fixated on a different stimulus, one that the human was oblivious to. From the moment they were born, dwarves were conditioned to subterranean surroundings. They were acclimated to the pressures of different layers of earth and stone above their heads, able to judge the depth of a tunnel simply by the sense of weight in the air. So, too, was a dwarf sensitive to vibrations that passed through floor and wall, often the only prelude to a collapse that might bring an entire tunnel crashing down. Ursola felt such subtle vibrations now. A mere quiver through her boots, but enough to provoke her instincts. Abruptly she turned away from Helchen and stared off in the direction of the disturbance.

The cellars beneath Vasilescu's tower were more brightly lit than they had been under the archmage's dominion. Torches and lanterns hung from the many supporting columns, bathing the area in a flickering glow. The perimeter walls were likewise illuminated, in particular those places where tunnels into the connecting catacombs had once opened. The passageways had been sealed up with flagstones and paving tiles, whatever debris could be scavenged by the refugees to close off the connection with the necrotic labyrinth of moldering tombs. Ursola had judged the results as crude but stout.

Now the dwarf had a bitter taste in her throat. Ursola's estimation of the construction's robustness appeared overly optimistic. Near one of the sealed tunnels, she could see a torch shuddering in its sconce, a clear indication that something was disturbing the wall.

"Are you listening?" Helchen grumbled when Ursola rose from her bench and started walking toward the wall. Some of the men working the machinery stopped and watched the dwarf as she marched straight toward the edge of the cellar.

"Ursola, what is it?" Helchen asked as she followed.

The dwarf motioned Helchen to be quiet. Her gaze roved across the closed-up tunnel. A cold feeling tightened in her gut when she saw a trickle of dust slipping from the stones. She knew what that meant. Someone was digging at the barrier from the other side.

"Go and get Alaric," Ursola whispered as she urged Helchen away from the wall. The dwarf hurried back to the table and gathered up several fire-bombs.

"What is it?" Helchen asked again.

Ursola glanced back at the wall, a grim smile stretching across her face. "I think we're about to have visitors."

Gaiseric hurried after Alaric as the knight dashed to the cellars. "Belieth's bones," he cursed under his breath as one of the refugees on the steps behind him pushed against the thief. The warning Helchen carried up into the tower had alarmed the survivors. Alaric had been quick to turn that excitement into action and before panic could set in, he had everyone who could fight rushing down into the cellar.

Perhaps it was the best that could be accomplished under the circumstances, but Gaiseric worried about focusing their attention in such a way. Except for a few sentinels on the roof, there wasn't anybody left in the tower capable of mounting a defense should the undead manage to cross the moat. He was far less confident in the ability of the flames to protect them after what he'd seen. Some new type of zombie among the horde, creatures that exuded a ghostly glow. He'd watched in disbelief when Ratbag's javelin simply glanced off the things. With the orc's arm to throw them, he'd seen the same javelins pass entirely through a normal walker to skewer the one behind it. These spectral undead, however, might have been made from solid granite for all the effect the missiles had on them. It was true that the flames still consumed the glowing zombies when they reached the moat, but that did little to mollify Gaiseric. If the dark magic suffusing the undead could evolve to make them immune to steel, might it not further augment them so they could defy fire?

"Ya noodlin' fer der rumpuz?" Ratbag's gruff voice was just shy of a bellow as his question slammed into Gaiseric's ear. Of them all, the orc was probably the only one hoping the enemy had found a way into the cellar. Lobbing spears and rubble onto the undead down in the plaza wasn't the kind of combat he longed for. Ratbag wasn't really happy unless he was swinging a blade at something.

"If there's a fight, you're welcome to take my share of it," Gaiseric advised the orc. He saw the befuddlement in Ratbag's eyes. Either the nuance of sarcasm was lost on him, or he couldn't understand why the thief wasn't eager to dive into a melee.

Of course, if it came to that, Gaiseric wouldn't have a choice. The only chance any of them had was to defend the tower. The zombies couldn't be allowed to gain a foothold or it would be the doom of them all. Everyone would have to fight. Fight against an enemy that didn't know fear, that never tired, that would never stop until every last survivor was dead.

The stairway opened out into the cavernous expanse of the cellars. Far brighter than during Vasilescu's tenure, Gaiseric could see clear to the stone walls that encompassed the chamber. His gaze was immediately drawn to the left. It was from this direction that the cellar connected to the catacombs beneath Singerva, the route by which Vasilescu's ally Gogol had escaped. The route by which, he now feared, the vengeful necromancer would return.

It was a fear that wasn't unique to the rogue. Gaiseric could see Ursola standing watch near one of the blocked-off tunnels, a fire-bomb clenched in her hand. The dwarf had drawn off many of the servants working the moat's machinery and posted them along the wall. Even from a distance, Gaiseric could see the fear quivering through the workers and wondered if they'd even try to use the weapons they'd been given before turning tail and bolting for the stairs.

The moment his feet touched the floor, Alaric raced toward Ursola. Gaiseric rolled his eyes. "Just once it would be nice if he acted like most nobles and delegated the dangerous stuff to other people." Clenching his fingers in an effort to trap some luck in his palm, he ran after the knight. It was splitting hairs to tell where bravery and foolishness parted company, but he knew he couldn't let Alaric take such risks alone.

"...the disturbance has only gotten worse," Ursola was telling Alaric when Gaiseric came within earshot of them. The dwarf set her hand against the wall, then displayed the layer of dust that covered it. "If you put your head up against it, you can hear them digging."

"There's a gamble I'm happy to pass up," Gaiseric quipped. The image of a zombie's decayed fist punching through the wall and snatching him while he was pressed against it was just a bit too vivid in his imagination. He grabbed Ratbag's arm when the orc started to swagger past him. "She wasn't serious," he advised the renegade.

Ratbag shot Ursola a sullen look. "Makin' der funny?" he growled.

"Now's not the time to start that all over again," Helchen stepped between the pair. Though Ursola and Ratbag had gained a grudging respect for each other's abilities, old animosities were always simmering under the surface. Generations of strife between dwarf and orc weren't easily brushed aside, whatever the necessities of the moment.

"How soon do you expect them to break through?" Alaric asked Ursola, drawing her focus back to the crisis at hand.

Ursola shook her head. "I'd expected them to punch through before you could get down here," she confessed. Her face contorted with worry. "They must have five different spots they've been picking away at," she added, gesturing to the places where she'd stationed watchers.

"They're waiting until they can break through everywhere at once," Gaiseric stated. He felt sick when Ursola nodded to confirm his speculation. "Zombies aren't capable of that kind of strategy."

"Then it isn't just zombies," Helchen asserted. She glanced sideways at Alaric. "Looks like Gogol has saved you the trouble of looking for him."

"Loaded dice and marked cards," Gaiseric muttered to himself. It was bad enough to fight the undead on their own, but far worse when there was a necromancer in the mix. Their previous encounter with Gogol had cost the lives of Hulmul the wizard and the duelist Drahoslav. If Gogol was making another effort, Gaiseric thought it could only be because the fiend felt the situation was even more advantageous than before.

There was only one advantage for the survivors. The armed refugees hadn't fought a necromancer before, and that inexperience made them unaware of the increased danger. Gaiseric wasn't the only one who recognized the benefit of this ignorance. Alaric turned away from the wall. The knight swept his gaze across the cavernous cellar and the body of armed townsfolk now amassed in the vaults. Brandishing his family sword, he shouted to the crowd to seize their attention.

"Citizens of Singerva!" the knight called to them. "The undead think they've found a way into our stronghold. They are digging their way into the cellar." Frightened murmurs swept through the survivors, and several glanced back at the stairs. Alaric gestured at the same steps. "That is the only means of ascent. The only way these monsters can reach your families. We won't let that happen. We'll hold them here." He shook a mailed fist at the wall. "Whatever comes from behind those stones, we'll stand our ground and cut it down!"

Ratbag punctuated the knight's speech with a fearsome war cry of his own, slapping the flat of his massive scimitar against his chest. The hulking orc remained a source of fear for the townsfolk, but Gaiseric watched that fear turn in upon itself as the bestial shout echoed through the vaults. The brutal renegade was a frightful killer, but his vicious strength was on their side.

"Those of you on this side of Mueller–" Alaric pointed at a rotund cook armed with a pikestaff "–spread along the perimeter, twenty paces from the wall. The rest of you hang back to act as a reserve. If an attack comes, protect the pumps." The knight waved his sword at the alchemical machinery. "We've got to keep those fires going in the moat."

The refugees met Alaric's orders with solemn nods. Quickly, but with fatalistic resignation, they dispersed to the positions they'd been commanded to take.

"You really think there's a chance?" Helchen whispered to Alaric.

"My father told me of a few sieges where sappers dug their way under the castle walls," Alaric replied in a low tone. "Sometimes the defenders were able to drive them back and close the breach."

Gaiseric was still trying to decide whether that information was encouraging or not when the first stones began to crumble and slip back into the cellar. A foul, necrotic smell spilled out from the catacombs beyond, the reek of rot and decay. As more stones fell away, the darkness of the tunnels beyond was visible. He couldn't discern the shapes of what was picking away at the barriers. In the shadows there was only the impression of movement, somehow more horrible for its lack of distinction.

The watchers posted by Ursola backed away as other weak spots collapsed. Cries of alarm rose from the refugees. A few of the least courageous broke away and fled for the stairs. Then, into the flickering light, hands appeared, fumbling at the edges of the holes, picking away at the jagged stones. They were foul, hideous hands, each marked by the filth of death. In some cases, the flesh was drawn tight over bones that extruded where the skin was too thin to restrain them; in others, hands were so bloated with necrotic corruption that they were swollen into mitten-like paws of meat that could only slap and push the barriers, the fingers too fat to grip anything.

"Fire! Now!" Ursola yelled. The dwarf followed her words with action, lobbing the incendiary she held into the nearest opening. There was a whoosh of flame. For an instant, Gaiseric saw the tunnel opening crowded with zombies, then the animated corpses flared up as though made of kindling. The undead didn't shout out in pain, an aspect that only made them more horrible in the thief's mind. With fire licking around their limbs, they still fumbled awkwardly at the barrier, trying to expand the opening until the very moment when their bodies finally gave out and they crumbled to the floor in smoldering heaps.

The watchers Ursola had posted obeyed the dwarf's order, casting the fire-bombs she'd given them into the other breaches. Again, there sounded the snarl of flame and the stench of burning meat wafted into the cellar. For just a moment, there were triumphant shouts from the survivors.

"It's too easy," Gaiseric whispered. His spine tingled with anxiety, the same sort of nervous dread that he felt when robbing a place while sensing some unseen defense waiting to trap him. There wasn't anything to articulate, no warning to be given, only a nebulous awareness of danger.

The danger manifested only a moment later. They could hear the zombies shuffling around in the catacombs. The light from the burning corpses revealed those further back in the tunnels as shadowy figures. Gaiseric could see them sidling to one side, making room for other creatures to renew the attack on the walls.

"Be ready!" Ursola told the watchers as she hurried to distribute more incendiaries from her satchel. The men gave her grim nods and prepared to repeat the earlier attack.

"You'd better get more fire-bombs," Alaric advised the dwarf, taking one of the incendiaries for himself. "If this is the extent of Gogol's strategy, we can do this all day."

The indefinable alarm vexing Gaiseric's brain made him lunge forward and try to stop the knight's throw. "Wait…"

It was too late. Gaiseric watched in horror as the fire-bomb sailed into the breach and shattered against the creature within. The flames revealed that it wasn't a mob of zombies demolishing the walls, but rather only a single animated corpse, albeit one of such obscene mass that it had the size of any six normal walkers. The thing was so bloated with corruption that it looked more like an over-filled wineskin than a human form. Its decayed face was perched atop rolls of distended flesh that rippled in undulating folds down the length of its obese frame. Its arms were like enormous sausages, all definition smothered beneath sagging mounds of necrotic skin.

Once before, Gaiseric had seen this kind of zombie. So, too, had Alaric. The knight ducked down and raised his shield. "Burster!" he shouted in alarm. The heroes threw themselves flat, needing only that single word to know what was coming.

A tremendous roar shook the walls as the swollen zombie, its bloated frame now savaged by flames, exploded. All the corruption that filled the burster was unleashed in a torrent of destruction. The barriers, merely weakened before, now came flying apart in a storm of shattered stones and billowing dust. The scene was repeated all across the perimeter as the incendiaries thrown by the watchers ignited other bursters in the rest of the tunnels.

Gaiseric's ears were ringing from the ferocity of the

explosions. A quick glance showed him that the refugees had been completely staggered by the discharge. Most of the watchers had been slammed by debris blown out from the walls. The fortunate ones appeared to have been killed outright. The others, wounded and prone, were helpless before the mobs of zombies that now surged out of the catacombs. The thief quickly averted his gaze as a pack of runners began tearing into a bleeding man while he tried to crawl away.

"Stand firm! Wotun watches over the brave!" Alaric rose from where he crouched and met the charge of the first of the zombies spilling from the tunnel ahead of them. He swatted the creature aside with his shield, then removed the top of its head with a slash of his sword. The maimed thing quivered on the ground for a moment, then fell still.

"C'mon, ya mollycoddlin' ginks!" Ratbag roared, swaggering into the conflict. The orc's scimitar caught a wiry zombie as it lunged at him, nearly cutting it in half at the waist and flinging the broken residue a dozen feet to crash into a supporting pillar. Gaiseric could see the mangled zombie futilely trying to regain its feet with its spine severed.

"Wotun spare some attention for the lucky," Gaiseric prayed. He usually didn't like to invoke the god of justice, but in this situation, he felt his past indiscretions might be overlooked. Hurrying to Alaric's side, he slashed the knee of a zombie as it rushed the knight, then chopped open its skull when it collapsed to the floor.

"Hold your ground," Alaric warned Gaiseric. "If we look like we're even thinking about running, it'll start a rout."

Gaiseric chanced a glance back at the refugees. Though

many held weapons at the ready, indecision was clear on their faces. They made no move to advance closer to the walls, not a step to join combat. The fight would come to them soon enough, Gaiseric judged, as zombies lumbered past the butchered remains of the watchers. If the survivors could make a stand in the basement, then at least the pumps feeding the moat would be protected.

A startled gasp from Helchen made Gaiseric look her way. The witch hunter lowered her small crossbow, clearly upset with the inefficacy of the bolt she'd just loosed. She drew the flanged mace from her belt and shook it at the oncoming horde. "Marduum, what does it take to kill them?"

Helchen's words put a sick feeling in Gaiseric's belly. He looked past the runners that were leading the zombie invasion and toward the catacombs where the slower walkers were emerging. Some of them were the typical undead they'd battled so many times before, but around others there was a peculiar, spectral glow. He could guess what the witch hunter had chosen as a target... and why her shot had failed to dispatch the creature.

"We've got to get out of here," Gaiseric told Alaric. He brought the pommel of his sword into the face of a leering runner as the zombie tried to rend him with its claws. The undead stumbled back and he finished it with a thrust to its heart.

"If we break, they'll overrun the cellar," Alaric reminded the thief. A sweep of the knight's blade lopped the head from one of the zombies and sent it rolling across the ground. "We'll lose the pumps, and then the whole tower."

Gaiseric pointed to Ratbag. The big orc had advanced

ahead, pushing the runners before him. His path was strewn with broken and mangled zombies, but now he found himself against one of the undead surrounded by ghostly light. The thief and the knight watched in horrified amazement as Ratbag brought his huge scimitar down in a cleaving stroke that could have split an ox in two. Instead, the blow was repulsed by the spectral light. The orc staggered back, unbalanced by the unexpected resistance.

"Ratbag! Come back!" Gaiseric shouted to the orc. Confused by what had just happened, the renegade suppressed his urge to violence and withdrew from the glowing zombie. "We can't fight against that!" Gaiseric advised Alaric. "We can't hold the tower, no matter what we do. We either stay down here to get slaughtered or try to make a run for it."

The knight hesitated. It was clear to Gaiseric that he hated to flee, especially since this development only hardened the conviction that behind this undead horde they would find Brunon Gogol. The thief caught at Alaric's arm, pulling on the surcoat. "You swore to protect these people," he reminded him. It was a low tactic, appealing to the knight's sense of duty, but Gaiseric knew they didn't have time for discussion. More zombies were streaming into the cellar each moment and far too many of them were suffused by a spectral light.

"All right," Alaric said, pain in his eyes. "Back to the stairs! We're going to leave the tower!"

The refugees turned at the knight's command. They didn't need to be told twice to withdraw. The workers at the machinery lingered only a few heartbeats longer before they joined the exodus.

In response to the retreat, the flow of zombies into the

cellar seemed to quicken. As he backed away across the vaults, Gaiseric thought he saw a hatefully familiar face glaring at them from one of the tunnels. Whatever plan Gogol had devised to destroy them, his prey abandoning the tower hadn't been part of them. Whether that oversight was enough to save them, Gaiseric didn't know.

If the rogue's luck held out, maybe it would be.

CHAPTER THREE

Making her way back across the cellar with the others, Helchen watched with mounting dread as the horde streaming from the catacombs continued to swell with more of the glowing zombies. It didn't need a witch hunter to tell that there was a dark enchantment cast upon those animated corpses. A spell that rendered them immune to weapons that could quickly dispatch others of their kind. She'd seen that sort of greenish-blue light before, but always it had denoted the presence of wraiths and banshees, ghostly entities without physical substance. But these walkers were every bit as substantial as the rest of the zombies, it was the spectral light emanating from them that lent them a phantasmal quality.

"We can't hurt them," Helchen growled. The Order had trained her to recognize many nightmarish horrors that lurked in the kingdom's shadows... and to know which ones were beyond her capacity to confront. A witch hunter needed only courage and skill to destroy the zombies and skeletons typically raised by a necromancer. To put down a wraith required expert knowledge and special weapons, for its lack of physicality presented nothing for a sword to stab or a mace to cudgel.

Unfortunately, such secrets were the province of the inquisitors who led the Order. There had been instances when her mentor, Captain Dietrich, employed such specialists to cleanse some site of supernatural manifestations, but the methods used were a mystery to her.

"The necromancer," Gaiseric pointed to one of the tunnels. Helchen caught his gesture in the brief moment before the thief was fighting for his life against one of the zombie runners. She looked toward the catacombs, over the heads of the cadaverous horde. Just within the shadows she could make out the pale features of Brunon Gogol.

"Counting your griffons before they hatch," Helchen hissed. She restored the mace to her belt and reloaded her hand crossbow. In her two encounters with the necromancer, she'd taken something of the man's measure. He wasn't the kind to expose himself to danger unless he was certain he was in complete control. A bolt through his forehead would show him how wrong he was about his conquest of the tower. "Marduum's judgment be upon you," she invoked the Order's sinister god as she took aim at the villain.

The bolt went speeding across the cellar. Helchen knew it was a long shot, at the very limit of the range she could expect from her crossbow. Even then, she might have hit the necromancer had one of his zombies not stumbled into the missile's path. She groaned as she saw the bolt glance from the glowing undead. His attention drawn by the disturbance, Gogol glared at her from the darkness. He waved a hand in her direction. Instantly, a part of the shambling horde was diverted. Instead of advancing upon the refugees, the undead were now closing upon her.

"A fine gesture," Alaric commented as the knight rushed to her side. His sword chopped down a runner as it sprang at her. The crippled creature crashed to the floor, still reaching for Helchen until Alaric brought the edge of his shield slamming down into its rotten neck and sent its head skittering away into the gloom. "Too bad it only made them angrier."

The witch hunter retrieved her mace from her belt and shattered the jaw of a second zombie as it charged her. "They'd be a lot easier to handle without that jackal giving them orders," she stated.

Alaric's face contorted in an admixture of fury and despair. "If I thought I could fight my way through to him…"

"You'd never make it," Helchen admonished him. A sweep of her mace shattered the hip of a runner, leaving it open for the knight's decapitating stroke. She nodded at the glowing walkers that were coming closer with every heartbeat. "You've seen those things shrug off a blow from Ratbag. What chance do you think you'll have?"

Witch hunter and knight turned aside as they heard someone running up behind them. They found Ursola, a fire-bomb clenched in each hand, an enormous satchel of incendiaries slung over her shoulder. "If steel doesn't work, then how about more flame?"

The dwarf didn't wait to discuss her notion. Arcing back her arm, she sent one of the bombs sailing into the oncoming horde. Helchen saw it shatter among several of the glowing zombies. Fire flared up around the creatures. Whatever fell enchantments Gogol had invested them with, whatever spectral power rendered them immune to physical attack, it seemed their defenses didn't include fire. Her heartbeat quickened as she watched flames consume the walkers, the ghostly light dying as their corrupt flesh crackled into cinders.

The fire quickly died, however, and more zombies trudged across the ashes of their immolated comrades. Helchen made a quick estimation of the arsenal Ursola was carrying. The same idea had occurred to Alaric. "How many of those fire-bombs do you have?"

Helchen knew what the knight was thinking. She gripped his shoulder to stay him once more. "Not enough," she said, indicating the stream of zombies still emerging from the catacombs. "There's no saying how many of these things Gogol has back in the tunnels. You'll never get at him."

Alaric looked like he might still risk it, but at that moment Gaiseric added his thoughts. The rogue was bleeding where a zombie's claw had scratched his face and had lost enough blood that Ratbag was helping to keep him on his feet. "Won't we need those bombs to clear the plaza? To get these people out of here?"

The armed refugees were withdrawing up the stairs now, fleeing before the advancing horde. They offered a visual reminder to Alaric about obligations greater than his own revenge. Still, as he looked back across the cellar, he saw no hope of escape. "We'll be trapped just the same. If we can't stop Gogol's horde here, they'll climb up through the tower and come at us from behind while we're crossing the plaza."

Ursola lobbed another of her fire-bombs, destroying a clutch of walkers as they trudged forward. The heroes continued to give ground to the zombies, retreating back across the cellar. "I might rig up something to keep a fire going at the bottom of the stairs," the dwarf proposed.

Helchen took inspiration from her words. Her gaze turned to the machinery that kept the moat fed with fuel. She looked at the barrels of alchemical incendiary that represented the supplies to keep the pumps fed. A smile spread across her face when she looked back at Ursola. "Why be content with a small fire?" She reached into the dwarf's satchel and took one of the fire-bombs. Still grinning, she turned to Alaric. "Help Gaiseric," she said. "I need to borrow Ratbag."

The witch hunter and the orc rushed over to the racks of barrels. Helchen watched as the others followed the last of the refugees to the stairs. "We'll have to be quick," she warned Ratbag. The glowing zombies were much slower than the spry runners that had led the undead horde, but they were closing in just the same. She tried to evaluate if they'd have enough time to do what needed to be done before the creatures blocked their retreat. Ultimately, it didn't matter. Even if they were caught, they'd at least keep Gogol's minions from reaching the refugees.

"Whatcha noodlin'?" Ratbag grunted, his red eyes glinting as he tried to work out Helchen's plan.

Helchen still couldn't make out much of the orc's brutish jargon without Gaiseric to translate, but what she needed him to do was simple enough. "Push over these racks," she said, leaning against one of them and pressing her back against it. The heavy oak, with its even heavier contents, didn't so much as budge under her exertion. For just an instant a tremor of fear coursed through her. She knew Ratbag was inhumanly strong, but if she'd overestimated just how strong then all she was going to accomplish would be to get them both killed.

"Ya wanna blip off der fizzle." Ratbag shook his head. "Lampin' like ya wanna pull der brodie."

The orc's reluctance was obvious. Helchen could see he understood her plan, but doubted it was anything but suicide. "We run like Darkness itself is on our tail," she hurriedly told him, waving back at the stairs. She held Ratbag's crimson eyes for a moment. "You'll give der bump to lotsa rottaz," she encouraged him, trying to emulate orcish speech.

Ratbag grinned, showing off his yellowed fangs. "Gonna make der whole magillah," he growled in approval. "Bimboz be jawin' long stretch. Even if'n us lot takez der pipe." Satisfied that the prospect of annihilating so many zombies in one go was worth sharing in their fate, the hulking orc set his back to the racks and began to push.

For a terrible moment, nothing happened and Helchen thought her scheme had failed. She watched as the glowing walkers trudged closer, their clawed hands outstretched, ready to rip and tear. Then there was a loud crack from the timber frame of the rack Ratbag was straining against.

Once its solidity was compromised, the rack collapsed rapidly. It pitched over in the direction the orc was shoving it, slamming into the next rack in the line. This one fragmented instantly under the tremendous weight of its neighbor and crashed over into the next. Helchen didn't linger to watch the chain reaction further. Slapping Ratbag on the back, she started him running for the stairs. Behind them, the noise of splintering wood and fractured barrels created an almost deafening clamor. Yet beneath the din, she could hear the sound upon which her plan depended, the slosh and gurgle of the alchemical mixture gushing out of the ruptured casks.

Only a few zombies were in their way when Helchen and Ratbag neared the stairs. The witch hunter brained one with her mace, leaving it with a shattered skull. The orc seized a glowing walker in both hands and heaved it into the air. He launched his crude missile into the rest that stood in their path, bowling all of them over. Helchen wasted no time leaping across the jumble of undead. Ratbag plowed into the midst of them, stomping and kicking as he forced his way through the tangled zombies.

"Ginkz colder'n jotun pizzle," the orc grumbled as he joined Helchen on the stairs. She could see that his greenskinned hands had turned a shade of gray and looked oddly blistered. The notion struck her that it might be frostbite and she recalled the way wraiths and their ilk drained all the warmth from the places they haunted. It seemed these pseudo-specters exhibited a similar chill should one be brazen enough to touch them.

"Let's warm things up then," Helchen quipped. She hefted the fire-bomb and stared down at the cellar. The flickering light of the lanterns on the pillars showed that the alchemical fuel had spread far across the vaults, spilling even as far as the openings into the catacombs. She glanced down at the zombies Ratbag had knocked over. Even as the creatures staggered back to their feet, the viscous tide was spreading to wash across their ankles.

"Marduum, let this work," the witch hunter prayed as she lobbed the bomb into the zombies below. The incendiary whooshed into flaming brilliance and the undead were immediately transformed into smoking pillars of fire. As the flames washed down their moldering bodies, they made contact with the fuel pooled about their feet. A dull snarl wafted up from the vaults as the tide ignited, swiftly spreading to wherever the mixture had spilled. When the fire reached a zombie, whether it was protected by a spectral light or not, the creature was engulfed and consumed.

A vast conflagration was soon burning throughout the vaults, greedily devouring the zombies that continued to mindlessly shamble through the flames. Helchen could even see undead stumbling from the tunnels, their bodies smoking from the fire roaring through their flesh. It was probably too much to hope that Gogol had been caught by the flames, but his zombie horde was most certainly doomed.

"Derez der cookout cure," Ratbag bellowed in approval, his eyes gleaming as he watched the zombies burn.

Helchen nudged him up the stairs. "The moat will go out now that there's no fuel feeding it," she reminded him. "Alaric will have to get the survivors moving fast. If we want to get across that plaza, we'd better be with them when they start across."

The orc didn't argue. Taking a last look at the destruction he'd helped unleash, Ratbag hurried up the steps. Helchen whispered another prayer to Marduum. This much of the plan had worked so far, but if they couldn't clear a route through the plaza, then their doom was certain.

If they were to have any hope of survival now, they had to get out of Singerva.

The flames in the moat gradually subsided and the zombies

surrounding Vasilescu's tower surged forward, pitching down into the trench. Without the fire to reduce them to ash, it was only a matter of time before the undead were piled so deep that those following after them would be able to climb over the heap and enter the stronghold.

Alaric glanced away from the narrow window set beside the main gate. He stared back at the frightened refugees gathered in the hall, their arms wrapped around whatever supplies they'd been able to scrounge. The knight shook his head at his lack of foresight. They should have moved the archmage's stores up from the cellar days ago, but instead they'd simply dipped into them as needed. Now those stocks of victuals and equipment were burning along with Gogol's zombie horde.

He caught Ursola's eye. The dwarf nodded to confirm that the fire-bombs had been distributed to those among the refugees deemed the least likely to panic once they started to cross the plaza. There was a ghoulish irony that many of the men entrusted with the bombs were those who'd been servants of the treacherous Vasilescu. As Helchen had pointed out, such blackguards were accustomed to seeing zombies and unlikely to break and run simply because the undead were near. Besides, without Vasilescu to give the walkers their orders, his former servants were in just as much danger as everyone else.

"All right." Alaric raised his voice so his words would carry to the hundreds in the crowd. "Once the drawbridge is lowered, everyone must keep pace. Don't try to rush beyond those carrying the bombs."

"If you lag behind the rearguard, you're on your own," Gaiseric added. The injured thief had recovered slightly after leaving the cellar, but Alaric thought it was fear more than stamina that was keeping the man on his feet. Gaiseric had refused offers of help to cross the plaza, likely because he worried any helpers would abandon him if things went wrong. It wouldn't be the first time the rogue's independent streak had made things more difficult for him.

"Guards with bombs will be following behind the group," Alaric said, trying to allay some of the fear Gaiseric had stirred up. "They'll make sure we can fall back to the tower if we have to." He felt guilty delivering that particular lie, but he knew from experience that nothing placated people so much as the assurance they could return to something they considered safe. The truth was, once they left the tower there would be no going back. The rearguard's job was simply to keep them from being surrounded once they were out in the plaza.

Alaric drew his sword, brandishing it for all to see. Even those commoners with little affection for the nobility still seemed to take inspiration from the image of an armored knight ready to lead them through crisis. That almost instinctive fealty bore results now. The murmurs from the crowd died down. Alaric could feel all eyes on him. He made a circular motion with his blade. It was the signal to the servants manning the windlass. At his gesture, they removed the restraining pegs and the heavy chains unspooled rapidly.

The drawbridge came crashing down, slamming against the edge of the moat and crushing several zombies before they could topple into the trench. There were hundreds more across the plaza, however, and the noise at once arrested what awareness lingered in their decayed brains. The span was still shaking from the impact with the outer edge when the first undead runners emerged from the horde and charged toward the tower.

Ursola lobbed one of her bombs at the creatures, wrapping them in flames. The zombies staggered on for a few paces, then pitched sideways into the moat below. The dwarf hefted another bomb and advanced, tossing it into a second mob of runners as they made for the bridge. Refugees equipped from her incendiary arsenal took position, forming a spearhead with the demolitions expert as the point. Yard by yard, they worked their way out into the plaza.

"Take courage, and Wotun will watch over you," Alaric encouraged the survivors as he led the main group behind Ursola's vanguard. Most of the ravenous runners fell quickly to the fire-bombs, but the plaza still teemed with the slower walkers and the brawny cadavers they'd taken to calling brutes.

"At least I see none of those glowing zombies," Helchen told the knight. "Gogol must have sent all of them down through the catacombs."

Foul smoke wafted back across the refugees as they hurried across the plaza, the reek of burning flesh somehow even more putrid out in the open than it had been when rising from the moat. Children among the crowd began to cry while moans of despair sounded from those who lost hope as the zombies began to close in all around them. A few became desperate enough to try to flee back into the tower, rushing past the rearguard despite shouts for them to stay. Alaric sickened at the sight as they were overcome by the undead well before they could regain the drawbridge.

"Keep going," Alaric shouted to the crowd, trying to

divert their attention away from the grisly spectacle of their former companions being butchered by zombies. In a sinister fashion, the foolish tragedy was something of a boon. The undead behind them were distracted by the activity and some of them were diverted, lessening the pressure on the rearguard. By the same measure, the gruesome reminder of the threat they were under urged the refugees to pick up the pace. Soon it was necessary to hold them back so that Ursola and her grenadiers could have room to work.

"We're going to make it," Helchen declared when they were halfway across the plaza. The mob of zombies between themselves and the town's winding streets was thinning. While there was still a veritable horde following behind them, the way ahead was almost clear. Certainly, there would be scattered packs of undead still to confront, but Alaric felt if he could keep the crowd moving, they'd have a fighting chance of making it out of Singerva.

And then? The knight shook his head in dismay. Escaping the overrun town was only a beginning. He'd still need to find a new refuge for the survivors, somewhere they could secure against the undead rampaging through the province. Alaric glanced back at Ratbag, the orc's huge frame towering over the humans around him. The renegade had crossed half the kingdom when leaving the frontier. He claimed to have seen places that had been fortified by other survivors. If they could make their way to one of those outposts, then maybe they'd have a chance.

"The road to Mittburg," Alaric said, pondering a solution, as he watched the flashes of fire burn them a path to the streets. He almost dreaded to invoke the city's name, fearful that doing so might draw the Black Plague's attention to it. He'd been there several times. It was difficult to imagine such a place with its towering walls and massive population succumbing to the zombie hordes. Then he remembered that, like Singerva, Mittburg would have a cemetery. One with far more graves than this town. Battlements and fortifications would avail the city nothing when the enemy rose up within its very walls.

"There are many villages along the river," Helchen said. "We'll get boats or a ship and travel on the river. The zombies won't bother us there."

Alaric nodded. That was certainly the plan they'd decided upon, but he had difficulty taking comfort in it. Watching the last of the undead cleared away and Ursola leading her helpers into the streets, he couldn't help but turn his head and look back toward Vasilescu's tower. For all the creatures that had fallen into the moat and the dozens more that continued to burn from the fire-bombs, the plaza was still filled with zombies. Hundreds? Thousands? Against such numbers, how could any of them hope to prevail? Escaping Singerva would simply be trading one grave for another.

The knight scowled behind his helm, loathing his despondent thoughts. It didn't matter if there was hope or not, he would carry out his duty. He would see his obligations fulfilled. And then, he would track down Gogol, avenge his murdered family.

After that, nothing else would matter.

CHAPTER FOUR

"The village is called Schweinhoff," Helchen informed them as she made her way back along the deserted road. The name provoked a few murmurs of recognition from among some of the refugees. Gaiseric scratched his head, trying to figure out why it was familiar to him.

The countryside they'd traveled through was eerily silent, not simply due to the lack of human activity, but an absence of birds and animals as well. The skies were empty barring distant glimpses of crows circling above carrion. The forests were utterly quiet, devoid of the rustle of small creatures moving through the brush. Even the trees, their leaves stiffening and turning orange, seemed frightened, suppressing the normal creaks and groans as the wind teased through their boughs. It felt as though the Black Plague had brought a blight upon the entire kingdom, not merely its human subjects.

"We've passed through a half-dozen villages already," said one of the survivors, a burgher whose once fine raiment was now little more than soiled rags hanging off his corpulent figure. "What makes this place any better?"

Helchen curbed the man's distemper with the sort of look

that made it so easy for a witch hunter to extract confessions from suspects. "Listen," she told him, cupping a hand to her ear. Faintly, the sound of rushing water could be heard beneath the sound of wind rustling through the trees that lined the road. "Schweinhoff's different because it sits on the river."

"It's also different because we're six days from Singerva and need to start worrying about food," Gaiseric pointed out. He was pleased to see the burgher lose his bluster. Many of the survivors nearby adopted sheepish attitudes and lowered their faces. The thief could barely contain his disgust. He'd often been accused of misplaced priorities, risking much to pilfer something that didn't seem worth the hazard to get it. However, he'd never done anything so recklessly stupid as what some of the townsfolk had done. Despite every warning and admonition impressed on them by Alaric, many of them had refused to abandon their possessions in the tower. Instead of bundling up food and supplies, they'd fled the stronghold with gold and jewels. Perhaps they'd been unable to believe the knight and his companions when they were told that the countryside was beset every bit as badly as their town. Six days of passing through desolate, ruined villages and finding nothing but mangled bodies and prowling zombies on the road had done much to remove their delusions. Gaiseric thought the refugees were lucky Alaric had taken the role of leader and instituted a policy of rationing what food had been carried out of Singerva. Had the decision been up to him, he'd have told each person to make do with whatever they had.

"We'll have to go into Schweinhoff," Alaric declared, nodding his head slowly as he weighed up their options.

Gaiseric could understand his dilemma. Every village they'd gone into had offered danger with little reward. Each settlement was devoid of living inhabitants, picked over by either the fleeing populace or by looters who'd been there long before the refugees came onto the scene. There had been little in the way of food or supplies to collect, but always they discovered a lingering undead presence. Several townsfolk had been killed by zombies hiding in some shadowy hovel or creeping down some dark alleyway. Gaiseric knew how personally Alaric took such losses and could see him struggle against risking more lives.

Helchen appeared to sense the same thing. "The place looks deserted," she told Alaric. "I didn't see any evidence of anybody around." She removed her broad-brimmed hat and rolled it between her hands. "It looked like some sort of barricade was stretched across the road leading into the village. They might have tried to fortify the place. I also spotted what is certainly a ship's mast standing beyond the rooftops. Some kind of vessel is docked there."

"But no sign of any people?" Gaiseric inquired. Helchen just shook her head.

"It could mean they're lying low," Alaric mused. "Staying quiet so they don't draw the undead to them." The knight unhooked his helmet from his belt and lowered it onto his head. "We'll have to take a closer look. I'll take Ursola and Ratbag and scout the place. Helchen, I'm putting you in charge of the column. If things go awry, keep them moving toward Mittburg."

"And what about me?" Gaiseric demanded. Despite the rigors of travel, his injuries had improved markedly since leaving Singerva. Even so, Alaric made efforts to see that the rogue could take things easy. It was a situation that Gaiseric was growing weary of. Part of his uncurbed individualism was to always pull his weight and never feel obligated to anyone.

"A pyromaniac dwarf and a pure maniac orc aren't the most balanced comrades in arms to have," Gaiseric added, gesturing at Ursola and Ratbag as the two stepped over to join Alaric. Ursola glowered darkly at the thief, but Ratbag seemed to still be trying to work out whether he should resent the remarks or not. "You'll need a devious mind to spot all the things you might otherwise miss." He snapped his fingers as he suddenly made the connection. "I know why I've heard of Schweinhoff before. I knew a fellow who was tied in with some smugglers who liked to use the pier here. Less chance of running into the duke's excisemen. Could be they left some of their goods stashed around. Salted pork that didn't have a chance to make its way to Mordava, for instance."

Alaric sighed and beckoned Gaiseric to join him. "Come along then, but keep close." He cast his gaze across Ursola and Ratbag. "That goes for everyone. If things go bad, we'll have to get out of there fast."

With a few last, encouraging words to Helchen and the refugees, the knight led them down to where the road forked, one avenue leading down to the river and the village nestled on its banks. As soon as they were clear of the trees, the smell of Schweinhoff struck them. It was a slaughterhouse stench. Even before the Black Plague, Gaiseric imagined the village had been redolent with the reek. The landscape leading down to the cluster of wattle-and-daub buildings had a spattering of fields, but much more prevalent were sties and hog-wallows. Schweinhoff's commerce was focused upon the processing of pigs, both those raised by its inhabitants and those brought into the village by the surrounding farms. Butchered and salted, the meat was then sent along the river, either up to Mittburg or down the coast and, eventually, to Mordava.

Getting closer to Schweinhoff, the smell worsened. Gaiseric could sense a palpable evil, a malignant undercurrent discernible beneath the reek. He might have chalked it up to imagination, but he saw Ratbag's nostrils flare. The orc sniffed the air, then growled a warning to his companions. "Nosin' der rottaz," he said. He ran a finger along the side of his scimitar. "Rumpuz soon," he grinned, anticipating a fight.

Schweinhoff had the appearance of a battlefield. The barricade Helchen had noted was stretched across the main road, a jumble of wagons and carts, splintered fenceposts thrust between them to act as stakes. The buildings beyond the barricade looked desolate. Not a trace of smoke rose from any of the chimneys, but Gaiseric could see many places where windows and doorways had been blackened by fire. The mast Helchen had spotted was there, rising back behind the houses and shops, like some great skeletal finger beckoning them on.

"There's some shoddy construction," Ursola opined, pointing her hammer at the barricade. A great gap had been smashed through the obstruction, and shattered boxes and barrels were strewn all about.

"Likely they didn't have time to do better," Alaric told the dwarf. The knight shook his head. "It doesn't look like it was enough to do the job though."

Gaiseric nodded in the direction of the mast. "Even if no one's still around, we should see about that ship. If the mast is anything to go by, could be it's big enough to carry everybody." He waved his hand to indicate the ruined village. "There might not be any sailors among our entourage, but we'll certainly have an easier time out on the water than traipsing through more places like this." The rogue gave the knight a wry grin. "Find some nets and poles, do a little fishing to sort out the food situation."

The argument won Alaric over. Cautiously they moved past the barricade and into the village itself. Every step they came across further evidence of fierce fighting. It chilled Gaiseric that there weren't any bodies to be seen, only the occasional dismembered hand or limb lying abandoned in the debris. The stench increased the farther into the settlement they went, the buildings blocking off any breeze that might disperse the odor. The whole of Schweinhoff stank like a charnel house.

The nearer they drew to the river, the more Gaiseric noticed buildings that were sagging down into their foundations. Storehouses, fishing shacks, hovels only the most destitute would call home – these dilapidated structures were moldy with neglect. He'd heard it said that riverfolk would expand the banks to increase the size of their settlements. Here, it seemed, the river was seeking to reclaim what had been stolen from it. The idea sent a shiver through him and conjured images of angry naiads and other nature spirits from half-forgotten fairy tales.

The feeling of some sinister presence only became more pronounced as they pressed on. Gaiseric would almost have welcomed the sudden appearance of a zombie mob, if only to release the mounting tension. He could tell that the others sensed it, too. Alaric looked as eager as Ratbag to find something upon which to focus his unease.

As luck – bad luck – would have it, neither knight nor orc discovered the menace hiding in Schweinhoff. That dubious honor was reserved for Gaiseric, and it nearly claimed his life.

The thief paused to inspect one of the shanties. A blemish above its door looked like it might be a smuggler's mark as easily as it could be a patch of mold. Gaiseric wondered if they might find some supplies hidden away. Stealing over to the door, he used his pick to unlatch the flimsy lock. The moment it swung inward, he knew that everything was wrong.

The back wall of the shanty looked like a chariot had smashed into it. The floor was gone, sunk into a stagnant pool upon which broken planks from the wall floated. If Gaiseric had thought the stench was rank before, the reek that wafted up from the pool brought tears to his eyes. While he was rubbing them to clear his vision, he heard a gurgling sound rise from the murky water.

It was the only warning he had. Shouting, Gaiseric leapt back as an enormous, clawed hand emerged from the pool and snatched at him. The blackened talons were as long as halberds and gouged deep furrows in the ground as they raked the spot where he'd been standing only a moment before.

Gaiseric cried out in horror and scrambled back into the street. He barely noticed Alaric and the others rushing over to him. His attention was fixated on the huge shape that climbed up from the pool. Easily twice the size of a man, more massive than an ogre, the thing reached out with impossibly long arms as it waddled out of the shadows and into the light.

"Swamp lurker," Alaric hissed, giving name to the scaly monstrosity.

Gaisieric was happy that the knight knew what the thing was. He only prayed Alaric also knew how to kill it.

Helchen busied the refugees with setting up camp along the road, telling them to spread themselves out so that they weren't concentrated in one place. She warned each group to keep within sight of the next to avoid anyone getting lost. The truth was, in the event of a sudden attack, she wanted to keep their options open. It was callous, but if one spot was overwhelmed the rest of the survivors would be able to assess whether it was better to rush to their aid or simply flee.

Perhaps such a ruthlessly pragmatic appraisal of a crisis was why Alaric had put her in charge in his absence. Then again, Helchen reflected, it might be the natural deference people paid to witch hunters. A knight was an inspiring figure, but a witch hunter garnered respect through the Order's fearsome reputation. She was able to command the townsfolk far more easily and with far less argument than someone like Gaiseric or Ursola.

"Keep them occupied," Helchen whispered to herself as she watched the survivors putting down bedrolls and stationing pickets near the trees. It was an old mantra of Captain Dietrich's that a crowd wouldn't have time to be disobedient if it was busy doing other things. Many times, she'd seen her old mentor give a village magistrate or a town militia some trivial – even nonsensical – task to perform so they wouldn't obstruct the witch hunters' own work.

She looked back in the direction of Schweinhoff. The last

glimpse she'd had of Alaric and the others had been as they were marching away along the muddy road. By now she was sure that they'd found a way past the barricades. Whether that involved breaking them down or negotiating entry from the villagers, Helchen was certain they were in, otherwise they'd have sent word back already. Continued lack of news troubled her, however. If things were going smoothly, Alaric would have told the refugees and advised them on their next move.

"You and you." Helchen pointed out two men who had the appearance of carpenters or masons in their former lives. "Get out past the trees and keep watch on the village. Look for anything remarkable. Especially listen for anything unusual." She tugged at one of her ears to emphasize the point. The two survivors shared a reluctant glance, but they didn't argue with the witch hunter's orders. Gripping the handles of the weapons tucked into their belts, the pair hurried off down the road. Helchen couldn't see how close to Schweinhoff they were willing to get, but even a distant vigil was better than none at all.

What was going on? The question vexed Helchen more and more as the minutes wore on. Surely there couldn't be that much to negotiate. Either the inhabitants would help Singerva's survivors, or they wouldn't. It should be as clear and simple as that. Unless, she mused, the inhabitants were no longer living. She tried to convince herself that her friends were capable enough to overcome any undead contingent hidden in the village, but it was a facile argument. The zombies of the Black Plague were far different from those created by necromancers in the past. It was more than the overwhelming extent of the outbreak; the Black Plague had endowed these undead with horrible changes, made them prone to strange and terrible mutations. What if Alaric ran into one of the nigh-unkillable abominations they'd faced in Singerva? It had taken dragon fire to destroy such monsters, and for all its efficacy against less robust undead, Helchen wasn't confident Ursola's fire-bombs had enough destructive force to put down an abomination.

Helchen was still ruminating on the grim possibilities that might have brought disaster to Alaric when she became aware of a commotion to the rear of the refugee column. She rushed along the road, past curious throngs of survivors. A few of the boldest joined her as she ran to where townsfolk were hurriedly gathering up their belongings and breaking camp. Her eyes settled almost at once on the two coachmen she'd posted as sentries farther down the road. Both men were pale and coated in a cold sweat. She could tell from their ragged breathing that they'd lost no time hurrying back to the column.

"What's this about?" Helchen demanded, pouring all the authority she could muster into her voice. If she didn't exert command now, she knew she was liable to lose it. Whatever the sentries had been telling the others had them on the verge of complete panic.

"Zombies!" one of the sentries gasped. "A horde of them coming this way!"

The other man, shaking with terror, elaborated on what they'd seen. "Spectral walkers! The same as chased us from Singerva!"

Spectral walkers. There was no need to ask him what he meant by that. Helchen thought it was as apt a description of the glowing zombies as anything else. She struck her thigh in frustration. They'd put many days and many miles between themselves and Singerva, but they'd forgotten a crucial point: there were limits to what living flesh could endure before it had to rest. The undead knew no such fatigue. It was too much to believe a mob of these new zombies just happened to be pursuing them. Helchen could feel it in her bones that this horde had been mustered by Gogol for the express purpose of hunting them down.

The witch hunter glanced at the roadway and the trees that flanked it to either side. It didn't need much of a tactician to know this was poor ground to try and defend. They'd have better chances in the village where, at least, the zombies would be hampered by the narrow lanes. Alaric and the others might already have secured the place, utilizing it as something of a bulwark against the undead. Besides, if there was a ship in port, they might even be able to escape onto the river before Gogol could catch them.

"Everyone, take what food you have and start for Schweinhoff!" Helchen shouted to the survivors. Her command was carried back down the column. She could see people already hurrying off toward the village and its seeming promise of safety.

Helchen prayed she wasn't simply trading one disaster for another. If Alaric's reconnaissance had been annihilated by zombies hiding in the settlement, then she might be leading the townsfolk into a massacre.

"Marduum grant that I'm right," the witch hunter whispered as she joined the fleeing refugees.

CHAPTER FIVE

The monstrosity that lurched out of the fishing shack looked to Ursola like the progeny of an ogre and some hideous spike-shelled turtle. There was something orcish about the head that thrust out from between its broad shoulders, its face was squat against its skull and tusk-like teeth jutted from its prodigious lower jaw.

Any possible kinship between the swamp lurker and his own kind didn't prevent Ratbag from bellowing a war cry and charging the creature. The orc's scimitar slashed down at the thing's shoulder, but was deflected by the spiked, shell-like growth. The edge of the blade raked down the length of the lurker's enormous arm, slicing a deep furrow that left a ragged strip of flesh sagging away from the underlying bone.

Ursola felt a chill rush through her when, instead of reeling back in pain, the swamp lurker spun about and struck Ratbag. The hulking orc was sent tumbling through the street by the force of the blow. As it turned back around toward Gaiseric, Ursola noted the empty, vacant gaze in its eyes, the blotches of decay around its mouth and along its throat. The beast might have been a terrible enough adversary in life but now, whether by the Black Plague itself or by injudiciously feeding on the flesh of zombies, the swamp lurker was doubly fearsome. It was one of the undead.

"It's not alive!" Ursola shouted in warning. The alarm arrested the attack Alaric and Gaiseric were trying to coordinate and both humans drew back.

"A zombie," Gaiseric huffed, holding his blade edgewise between himself and the lurker. "That makes things so much better."

"Don't get too close to it," Ursola told the thief as she tried to calculate how far the incendiary in her fire-bomb would splash when she threw it.

"Are you crazy? I'm too close to it now!" Gaiseric sprang back across the width of the street as the lurker tried to grab him with its oversized claws. The monster lumbered after him, closing the distance again.

"Try playing with me," Alaric growled. The knight tried to get the lurker's attention by stabbing it in the leg, but the abomination barely turned its head. When he withdrew his steel, a mush of wormy meat dribbled from the thing's injury.

Ursola tried to circle around the monster. If she could find an angle to lob her bomb from that wouldn't put one of the humans in the way, maybe she could still make short work of the beast. The effort was thwarted when Gaiseric had to dodge another sweep of the lurker's claws. By accident or design, the creature was herding him back against the opposite building. With its long reach, the swamp fiend was limiting the man's mobility.

Alaric darted in to attack, but even slashing it deep enough to scratch the lurker's bones didn't divert the zombie's focus. Ursola scowled and made ready to cast the bomb. Maybe Gaiseric would get lucky and escape the splashing incendiary. In any event, he was as good as dead if something wasn't done to change the situation.

Something appeared in the shape of an enraged orc. "Ya slashy mug!" Ratbag howled as he rushed the swamp lurker. "Figger'n ter fahget 'bout Ratbag!" He sprang at the abomination, bringing his scimitar down in a double-handed stroke that chopped deep into its neck. Ursola could hear the sickening sound of the shell-like armor splitting under the blow and the sucking noise as the blade sank into the meat beneath. The lurker stumbled to one side, wrenching the weapon from Ratbag's grip.

Then the monster regained its balance. Its blank, bleary eyes shifted to the orc. The scimitar stuck out from the side of the creature's neck, embedded in the thick bone. Even with all his brutal strength, Ratbag hadn't been able to decapitate the beast. All he'd managed to do was draw its attention.

"Let it chase you and keep back," Ursola shouted to Ratbag. She felt a twinge of uneasiness, wondering what her ancestors would think about worrying whether an orc got caught in the flames of her bomb, but she waved aside such qualms. If Ratbag was howling at the gates of a dwarf stronghold, it would be different. Here and now, he was an ally, and it would be dishonorable to treat him as anything less.

"C'mon an' leggit!" Ratbag jeered at the lurker. From one of his boots, he drew out a curved dagger, but it was clear from the orc's normal level of aggression his bravado wasn't enough to convince him that he could do any real damage to the abomination with such a weapon. He backpedaled down the lane, snarling insults at his pursuer.

"What're you waiting for?" Gaiseric demanded as he came up beside Ursola. "Throw it!"

The dwarf wouldn't be rushed. "Not yet," she said as she marched in the very tracks the monster was leaving in the road. "Not until I can be sure."

Alaric took position on her other side, his kite shield raised to intercept the lurker's claws should the zombie suddenly turn around. It wasn't nearly as spry as the undead runners, but it had already exhibited more flexibility than the sluggish walkers and brutes that made up much of the graveyard hordes. Ursola spared the knight an appreciative glance, then fixated on the creature ahead of them.

Ratbag was in a bad situation. He had to get far enough away from the lurker not to be engulfed when Ursola tossed her bomb, but if he put too much distance between them, the abomination might turn back upon the others. "When I nod, you go," she called to him. They'd have to coordinate with perfect timing if this was going to work. Ursola braced herself and exhaled the breath she'd been holding. She caught Ratbag's eye and nodded her head.

The instant the orc scrambled down the street, Ursola's arm was in motion. The fire-bomb sailed through the air and shattered against the spiked shell that encased the lurker's back. Flame engulfed the rancid creature, licking about its ghastly body and blackening its decayed flesh. The stench of burnt meat rose into the air and strips of charred skin spilled to the ground.

No cry of agony sounded from the undead beast, however, and a numbness gripped Ursola when she saw the burning abomination continue to lurch after Ratbag despite the flames crackling around it.

"It didn't work!" Gaiseric cried out. "It isn't going to die!"

"What do we do?" Alaric asked Ursola. While he retained his poise better than Gaiseric, she could hear the helplessness that edged his voice.

The dwarf's mind quickly raced through all the variables. There was only one thing that benefited them. Despite being set on fire, the swamp lurker remained intent on Ratbag. That gave the rest of them some freedom of movement. "Keep it following you," she yelled to the orc. It wasn't a situation he had any control over, but it would help if Ratbag understood there was still a plan.

"We need more heat," Ursola grumbled. The only vulnerable parts on a zombie were the brain and the heart. In the lurker, those organs must be so protected by a thickness of meat and bone that the flames couldn't roast them back into lifelessness. To prevail over the monster, they needed to intensify the flames.

Gaiseric took her suggestion. The rogue raced ahead, waving at a hut facing toward the river. It was comparatively dry, and the interior was a confusion of hanging nets and ropes. "When we escaped the abomination in Singerva, Ratbag collapsed a house on it."

"All we'd need is to trap it in there long enough to set the shack on fire," Alaric commented.

Ursola nodded in agreement. She plucked another bomb from her satchel and waved wildly at Ratbag. "Over there!"

she cried, pointing to the hut, frustrated that the hovels closer to the orc looked too damp to suit her purpose. "Get it over there!"

There was peril in the scheme. Ratbag would have to turn the abomination around, and to do that would mean running past it and coming well within reach of the creature's claws.

The dwarf wasn't the only one who saw that particular hazard. Before she realized what he was doing, Alaric left her side and charged the swamp lurker. He struck at the hunched monster's neck, hitting Ratbag's scimitar and knocking the weapon loose. The blow was enough to stir whatever was left of the zombie's awareness. It stopped advancing on the orc and turned toward the knight.

"That's right, you gruesome knave," Alaric said. "Let's see if you can catch me!" For good measure, he slashed his sword across the lurker's jaw and sent several of its teeth spinning down into the mud.

The abomination trudged after Alaric as he ran to the hut, pursuing him with the mindless belligerence of the undead. Gaiseric hurried to aid the knight while Ursola posted herself across the street where she'd have the best vantage to make her throw. "You'll have to move fast once it's in there!"

"And don't get tangled up in any netting," Gaiseric added. The rogue availed himself of a massive oar, holding it as though it were a pike. It made for a clumsy weapon, but at least its reach was longer than the swamp lurker's claws.

Ursola readied herself as Alaric ran into the hut. The lurker plunged in after him, its long claws raking the nets and tearing them to shreds. Yet even those frayed cords proved to be a clutching morass within the shack's narrow confines. The monster was soon entangled in the ropes as it tried to attack Alaric. When its arm became ensnared during an attempted swipe, the knight dove beneath the trapped talons and rolled out into the street. The dwarf was relieved to see he'd made his escape. It would make destroying the enemy even more satisfying.

"That's about enough of you," Ursola declared, hurling the fire-bomb into the hut. At once the interior was a mass of flames, the dried ropes and netting ignited by the incendiary. The lurker, caught within the blazing turmoil, struggled to free itself. When it moved toward the doorway, Gaiseric rushed in and jabbed it with the oar. The lurker pushed back and might have wrested the oar away from him had Ratbag not joined the rogue and added his brawn to the contest. Together, human and orc were able to shove the abomination into the center of the conflagration. Ursola could see it twisting about as the fire swelled all around it. Then all sight of the thing was lost as the roof came crashing down. The shack flared up into a crackling pyre.

"Anyone hurt?" Alaric asked as he looked over his companions. Ursola shook her head while Gaiseric acknowledged the question with a raised thumb.

"Mebbe der big gink," Ratbag huffed as he drew breath into his panting lungs.

Ursola squinted at the burning shack. If the lurker had cried out, uttered even a single shriek of pain, they'd at least have something to evaluate. Like nearly all the zombies they'd vanquished, the beast remained silent even at the heart of its own pyre.

"Now we just have to make sure there aren't any more like

him hiding in the village," Alaric observed as he watched the hut burn.

Gaiseric shoved what was left of the oar into the flames. "If there was anything else in Schweinhoff, it would have already showed up to find out what all the noise was…"

Ursola frowned at the thief and swung around, drawing another of her remaining bombs from the satchel. Behind them, around the bend in the street, the sound of hurried footsteps could be heard. A large mob was running in their direction. From the clamor, it sounded like scores of zombies were on their way.

"Well, Gaiseric," the dwarf grumbled as she nerved herself to meet the undead, "don't say you didn't ask for it."

The sound of a mob storming through Schweinhoff intensified as Alaric prepared himself for the attack. "Make for the river," he told his companions. "I'll hold them off as long as I can."

"Noodlin' Ratbag'd skip der rumpuz?" the big orc growled as he marched over to join the knight. His fingers tightened about the grip of his recovered scimitar, its blade encrusted with bits of charred swamp lurker.

"I can't swim," Ursola claimed, a fire-bomb in one hand, a hammer in the other. "Better to go out fighting than drowning."

Alaric shook his head before Gaiseric could speak. "No, I don't want to hear it. Somebody has to get back to the column and tell Helchen that they have to find someplace else. Process of elimination means you're delegated."

"I've never been more unhappy to avoid trouble," Gaiseric griped. He laid his hand on Alaric's shoulder. "Fortune smile on you and luck see you through to the other side." With a last, lingering glance at his comrades, the thief jogged off toward the river.

"From the sound of it, there must be hundreds," Ursola stated. "Runners leading the pack, to be sure. We'll need plenty of Gaiseric's luck if there's more than a dozen of those coming at us."

Within his helm, Alaric gave a grim smile. "We'll just have to make sure we kill them all."

Ratbag barked his approval of the sentiment. "Dem rottaz gonna rumble onta some fly dockwallopaz!"

Alaric laughed. He didn't understand the orcish jargon, but he caught the violent enthusiasm. Ratbag wasn't concerned about survival, only that he should give better than he got in the coming fray. What warrior could ask for more in a battle?

The chaotic din drew nearer. The trio made ready to receive the undead charge. When the first of the mob rounded the corner, however, it brought with it an anticlimax. Alaric saw at once that the mob they'd been waiting for wasn't some horde of zombies, but rather a mass of very alive and very terrified people. Moreover, he recognized their faces. They were the refugees from Singerva.

Sight of Alaric and his companions standing across the road arrested the panicked rush of the mob. People stopped as they turned the corner, confusion and relief showing in their faces. It was the latter that struck the knight when he saw it. Whatever had caused these people such fear, they still had enough faith in him that they thought he could deliver them from their peril. That kind of trust was a terrible burden to shoulder.

"What's happened?" Alaric called out to the crowd. "Why did you leave the road?" He darted a look at the blazing pyre in which the swamp lurker was entombed. "We haven't finished scouting Schweinhoff to make sure it's safe."

Helchen emerged from the mass of refugees, her dour expression telling Alaric some calamity had occurred before she even spoke a word. "It's Gogol. His zombies followed us from Singerva. I had to get the citizens moving." She removed her hat and ran her fingers through her hair. "I didn't see any other option but to bring them here."

Again, the knight's gaze drifted to the pyre. He shuddered to think of the havoc had the crowd arrived only a few minutes earlier, the carnage the abomination could have wrought among the refugees. "I sent Gaiseric to warn you away," he said. "All the noise you were making, we thought a whole company of zombies was loose in the village." He suddenly spun around, alarm in his voice. "Gaiseric! He's going back to the road! He'll run into Gogol's zombies!"

"No, he won't," Ursola corrected him, tugging at his surcoat. She drew Alaric's attention to the thief scurrying back toward them from the other end of the street. Alaric was relieved that Gaiseric hadn't gotten far but was worried by what might have sent the thief running back so soon.

When Gaiseric rejoined them, he was almost breathless from his haste. He barely acknowledged the presence of the refugees before gasping out a report to Alaric. "I made it to the river. That mast we saw… the ship has foundered. Sunk down to the gunwales." He sucked down a lungful of air, then quickly added some words of hope to his account. "There's another ship standing off in the river. I could see crew…"

The rest of the thief's words were lost in the cheers that broke out when the refugees heard there was a ship. Gaiseric shook his head and tried to say more, but Alaric couldn't hear him over the jubilant throng.

From the side of the street, sudden shrieks of terror silenced the cheers. Through the agitated crowd, Alaric could see the burning pyre lurch upward. One long, blackened claw had already reached out from the flames, now another joined it. Stirred by the noisy cheering, the swamp lurker was rising from its fiery grave.

"To the river!" Alaric shouted, waving his sword in the direction he wanted the refugees to follow.

"Not that way!" Helchen yelled as some of the crowd turned and fled back through the village. Alaric felt cold to see fear overwhelm them. In their haste to escape the swamp lurker they were running straight back to Gogol's horde.

"No use trying to fight that thing," Alaric warned Helchen when she turned to confront the abomination. The charred lurker shoved aside the burning planks lying across it as the huge zombie lurched into the street. "Even Ursola's fire-bombs couldn't stop it. All we can do is try to get to that ship Gaiseric saw."

The thief again tried to say something, but his words were lost as he was caught up in the stream of refugees and borne away by the crowd. Alaric and the others hurried down the street. He tried not to focus on the dreadful screams that now rang out as the lurker caught a straggler in its vicious claws. He felt ashamed that he entertained the hope that the abomination would chase after the group fleeing the village rather than continue on their trail.

Through Schweinhoff's narrow lanes the survivors raced. Tortured shrieks told the fate of those who lagged behind. Alaric felt his heart sicken at every scream, knowing that another life rendered into his custody had been lost. Yet what could he do? A squadron of cavalry might have been enough to settle a living swamp lurker, but against this undead monstrosity even if he could draw upon such a force, he doubted they'd prevail.

The only hope now was the ship Gaiseric had seen. Alaric prayed to Wotun that the crew wouldn't be so callous as to abandon them in their plight. He could still see the thief's head bob up from the midst of the crowd ahead, a desperate look on his face as he tried to shout something to the knight. In the tumult, there wasn't time or opportunity for Gaiseric to convey whatever he was trying to say.

The narrow street opened up and the crowd reached the riverside. The only boat of any size tied to the pier was the foundering cog Gaiseric had noted. Anything else, down to the smallest fishing smack, was gone, doubtless taken by the villagers as they fled their doomed community.

The refugees stared in silence toward the river, mute horror written on their visages. Even distracted by the unfortunates it had caught, the lurker was still only a hundred yards or so behind them, just around the last corner they'd turned. The knight was amazed that anything could have made the crowd pause in their flight. Alaric pushed his way to the fore and looked at the vessel standing perhaps a quarter of a mile from the end of the pier. Hopes of charity and rescue collapsed into a despondent disgust. The knight understood now what Gaiseric had been so desperate to tell him.

There was indeed a living crew visible on the deck. Also visible was the flag flying from the main mast. A black field marked by a grinning skull and crossbones.

The ship was a pirate ship.

CHAPTER SIX

Gaiseric hadn't been able to tell if the ship lying off Schweinhoff was a merchantman or a frigate, but he certainly knew what the flag flying from her mast meant. Pirates!

Looking out across the river, Gaiseric felt as though he was between the frying pan and the fire. Within the village they had the swamp lurker attacking them. Outside there was Gogol's invulnerable zombie horde. And here – here were ruthless marauders whose exploits were so infamous that they curdled even a thief's blood. The Jolly Brotherhood, a cadre of buccaneers and corsairs, had long been a scourge upon the kingdom, pillaging ships on both sea and river. The King's Navy had tried to suppress them, but the royal fleet couldn't be everywhere and for every pirate they sank, two more took to the waves. In the chaos of the Black Plague, it was only natural that these ruthless wastrels would appear, drawn like jackals to the devastated waterways.

If he'd even considered the prospect of running into pirates as a possibility, Gaiseric would have pushed Alaric into taking their chances on an overland route to Mittburg. Fickle fortune had provoked events to the current crisis. Now, they were out of options.

"That settles things for us," Gaiseric told Alaric when he was finally able to reach the knight. "I tried to warn you that it was a pirate prowling offshore."

Alaric doffed his helm and squinted at the black flag on the main mast. "Maybe the Black Plague has made them rethink their lives," he suggested.

Gaiseric scoffed at the idea. "A pirate? A pirate only cares about how much he can steal." He didn't like the amused look Alaric gave him. "No, no. Don't even think that. I'm not anything like a pirate. There's a difference between lifting something that's unattended and holding a cutlass to somebody's throat while their ship's sinking beneath their feet."

"Pirates can wait!" Helchen scolded the men. Renewed screams had the crowd surging toward the shore. Many of the refugees waded out into the river, parents holding their children above the water. A handful charged down the pier and began shouting and waving to the observing ship.

Panic raced through the townsfolk, and Gaiseric could not blame them. Lurching around the bend was the swamp lurker, its body charred and blackened by the flames. With every motion, its skin cracked and exposed the raw meat beneath its roasted hide. Fresh blood dripped from its claws and fangs. Strips of human flesh dangled from its tusks. When the beast lumbered into view, it gripped the still shrieking torso of an old man. As its bleary eyes fixated upon the people fleeing ahead of it, the abomination tossed aside the dying person as though it were a toy in which it was no longer interested.

Gaiseric felt his blood turn to ice. There didn't seem to be anything that would stop the hulking zombie. The abomination would rip through them all. Of course, there was the river, but as Ursola had said, it was a mean choice between drowning and being killed by the swamp lurker.

"We've got to stop that thing!" Alaric cursed.

"A good idea," Ursola responded. "A better idea would be how to manage it." She tapped her thumb against a fire-bomb. "We already know these aren't enough to do it."

A thought suddenly came to Gaiseric. He looked back at the pier. It looked sturdy enough to support many people, but how would it fare with something as massive as the swamp lurker? "I've got an idea." He plucked the fire-bomb from Ursola's hand, making placating gestures when she protested. "I'll get its attention and lure it out onto the pier. See if I can get it to fall in the river."

Alaric frowned at the plan. "Even if it wasn't a zombie, you couldn't drown it."

"Maybe not, but the current might sweep it miles downstream," Gaiseric shot back. "Either way, while it's chasing me, you'll have time to get these people away. Lead them along the shore. Put some distance between yourselves and Gogol's horde."

"It's a lousy plan," Helchen said, then clapped Gaiseric on the back. "There's no time to think of anything else. Good luck with it." She led a hesitant Alaric away to gather up the survivors and get them ready to bolt once the lurker was on the pier. Ratbag followed Ursola.

"It is a lousy plan," Gaiseric said as he found himself standing alone before the advancing abomination. He wondered if he even needed the bomb to hold the lurker's attention. "At least it'll make me feel better," he muttered as he lobbed it at the zombie. There followed the expected whoosh as the casing shattered and the incendiary ignited. The monster was transformed into a pillar of flame. A raging firebrand that continued to lumber toward the thief.

"Never the easy way," Gaiseric hissed as he turned, making noise, and ran for the pier. He felt the planks shudder as the lurker pursued him out onto it. However, his hopes that the structure wouldn't support the monster's weight were the only thing that fell apart.

The survivors at the end of the pier stopped calling to the pirates when they saw the lurker following Gaiseric. Screams rang out as they dove into the river. A few were swept away by the current, but most of them managed to fight their way to the shore. A further blow to his scheme. If a person could manage to defy the current, the abomination would certainly be able to do so.

"At least I bought the others some time." Gaiseric's fist tightened on his sword. Maybe the lurker's hide was so charred he'd be able to stab through to its heart before it could tear him in half. And for an encore, he'd challenge Grifterius, the God of Gamblers, to dice.

Watching the blazing hulk of the monster stomping ever closer, Gaiseric almost failed to notice that the pirate ship was likewise closing in. He was only fully aware of its proximity when he heard a loud crack and felt his clothes rustle as something massive flew past him. The next instant, the lurker was flung back, propelled as though it had been kicked by a giant. It cast a fiery trail through the air before slamming into the side of a warehouse. His mouth gaped in amazement when he saw that the beast was pinned to the timber wall by a gigantic spike. The huge missile had crunched through the center of its chest, obliterating its heart in the process. He watched as the destroyed zombie sagged lifelessly from the stake, its burning flesh dripping from its body.

The thief snapped his fingers, releasing whatever luck he'd held. It was certainly expended now. A moment before, Gaiseric had seen death reaching out for him. Instead, he'd been delivered, rescued in circumstances that, if not miraculous, were certainly providential. He laughed and crossed his fingers, trying to catch a fresh supply of good fortune.

Gaiseric turned back to see the ship drawing near the pier. He spotted a ballista mounted on its forecastle. A team of artillerists were cranking back its string and making ready to load a second bolt into the weapon. There was as little uniform among the ballista crew as there was among the ship's company. Each sailor was arrayed in vestments brighter and gaudier than the one next to him. Beneath each sash and hanging from every belt was a vicious-looking sword, axe, or bludgeon. Gaiseric spotted a group of both men and women on the quarterdeck armed with a motley array of bows and crossbows. One towering figure looked big enough to be an ogre and appeared to have fashioned a halberd for himself from a ship's anchor and a broken rudder.

"Ahoy to shore!" a sharp voice cried out to Gaiseric. The ship was still ten feet from the edge of the pier when the speaker vaulted over the gunwale and landed on the planks. She made for an imposing sight, cutlass and axe swinging from the belts that circled her waist. Unlike the other pirates, her garb was more somber, sealskin leggings and a loose leather shirt. An assortment of gold and silver necklaces hung about her throat and dangling from her ears were gold rings so big they looked like bracelets.

The woman's skin had a dusky, warm brown hue that further offset the grisly adornment that covered her face. For, across her features, the pirate had inked a leering death's head in white dye. Her dark eyes smoldered from the sockets of the painted skull.

"Lucky for you I told my boys to take a hand," the pirate said as she walked toward Gaiseric. Her painted lips peeled back, displaying her teeth beneath the painted skull's smile. "Now I need to know if we were just wasting our time."

Gaiseric reached to his belt. The sudden motion brought the pirate's cutlass flashing from its sheath. Up on the ship, he could hear bows being drawn taut and knew the archers were taking aim. If the skull-faced woman didn't finish him, they would.

"Just seeing what I might have to offer so gracious a lady," Gaiseric said. Before he could retrieve anything from his belt, however, the pirate lunged at him. He only had an impression of motion before he felt her arm around his throat. She spun him around, using him to cover her own body. Facing back toward shore, he saw Alaric and the others approaching with weapons drawn.

"That would be far enough," the pirate declared when they were halfway down the pier. Her eyes roved across the group, wavering between Alaric and Helchen.

"We appreciate you killing that monster for us," Alaric said, nodding toward the impaled lurker. "But if you don't let my friend go, you'll–"

"Now's not the time to be making threats, von Mertz," Gaiseric called out as the pirate brought her cutlass against his neck.

"Your friend's right about that," the woman said. "You've no time at all. My boy in the crow's nest has spotted the undead closing in on this village. If you want to get your people out of here, The Demoness is your only chance."

"Demoness?" Helchen gasped. "Then that would make you Captain Sylvia Samdei."

The pirate laughed and released her hold on Gaiseric. Rubbing at his bruised throat, he staggered a few steps away and grimaced. It went against his grain, and might only be delaying disaster, but for the moment he knew they had to trust the buccaneers. He looked over at Alaric. "Introductions can wait," he coughed. "If she's willing to take everyone aboard, then we're not in a position to argue."

"You said it yourself," Alaric objected. "They're pirates. They'll just rob and murder us."

Sylvia laughed again. "At least we'll rob you first. If you just want to be murdered, you can stay here and wait for the zombies."

Gaiseric thought it was a gruesome sort of logic, but it was hard to refute. "There's no good bet here," he said, "but if we have to gamble, I say we get aboard." He held Alaric's gaze and said something he knew would sway the knight. "This way at least we know we won't be joining Gogol's horde when we die."

"And I might only maroon you," Sylvia suggested. "But

make up your mind fast. I know my people don't intend to stick around and join the undead."

Alaric bowed his head, accepting that he really had no choice. "Get everyone moving," he shouted, his voice carrying back to the refugees on shore. "We're taking passage on Captain Sylvia's ship."

The choice made, some of the tension left the air. The archers on the quarterdeck lowered their weapons and the artillerists aimed their ballista at the street leading down to the pier. Gaiseric watched as the pirates lowered a gangplank and the refugees hurried aboard the sinister ship.

"Loaded dice and marked cards," Gaiseric muttered as he clambered onto the ship. Their only hope now lay in the capricious whims of a pirate crew.

Gaiseric wondered if the Black Plague was still a threat if you ended up at the bottom of a river with a chain around your feet.

CHAPTER SEVEN

Helchen watched as the village of Schweinhoff receded ever farther into the distance. She could see the spectral walkers swarming about the shore. Sylvia had been right about how little time they'd had, but looking at Alaric, she could tell he felt regret that they'd been unable to check for any of the people who'd fled when the swamp lurker attacked.

She was grateful they were out of earshot when a handful of the missing refugees ran out from the village, desperate to escape the zombies. The sight of the doomed wretches brought screams from the survivors who were on the decks of The Demoness. They pleaded with the pirates to go back, to rescue the townsfolk. Helchen knew it was a futile effort. Even if they could persuade Sylvia to turn back, they'd never make it in time to do any good. All any of them could do was watch the wretches be surrounded and overwhelmed. There were some things that the Order's training could never quite inure someone to. Watching a witch or necromancer burn was far different from seeing simple townsfolk ripped to pieces.

The witch hunter turned and climbed up to the quarterdeck

where Alaric was talking with Sylvia. The scene reminded her of times when Captain Dietrich had conducted negotiations with street gangs in Mordava to help track down a suspected necromancer. Each gang leader had brought his own retinue in a show of strength. Alaric, with Ursola, Gaiseric, and Ratbag positioned nearby, faced off with the skull-faced pirate and her own cadre. The hook-handed, wild-haired quartermaster, a man named Korsgaard, kept fingering the collection of throwing knives sheathed across his sharkskin vest. The bosun Raubin had a kraken inked across his bald pate and a brace of crossbow pistols hanging from his belt. The first mate, Mendoza, had as cruel a visage as any Helchen had ever seen and a rope burn around his neck that his colorful scarf couldn't quite hide. Then there was the ogre, nine feet and eight hundred pounds of barely restrained carnage. The way Brog and Ratbag glared at one another, she felt it was nothing short of a miracle that the two hadn't come to blows already.

"Of course, we could take advantage of you if we liked," Sylvia pronounced, lounging in the wicker chair Brog had brought on deck for her.

"You could try," Alaric retorted, his hand tightening about the sword sheathed at his side. "It might not go so well for you."

"Be sensible," Helchen told the knight as she stepped onto the quarterdeck. "If they were going to try anything, they'd have disarmed us when we were coming aboard."

"Then maybe it would be a good idea to stop joking about robbery," Gaiseric said, frowning at the words almost as soon as he spoke them.

"Unless I very much miss my mark," Sylvia commented,

her eyes roving up and down the wiry rogue, "you've not done much honest work yourself."

Gaiseric bristled at her words. "I've never sent a shipload of people to the bottom of the sea," he shot back.

"Neither have I," Sylvia told him. She shrugged. "It's a poor pirate who does that sort of thing, like a milkmaid who kills the cow. A sunken ship brings no more shipments to be waylaid." Her smile grew colder. "Naturally, from time to time it's necessary to remind ship captains that there's worse things than robbery, but when you resort to those measures, you always want to leave some witnesses around to tell others you're not one to be trifled with."

Helchen thought the pirate was being truthful enough. It made a vicious sort of sense, from an economic perspective, that there wasn't a margin in wholesale murder. Profit appeared uppermost in Sylvia's agenda. Cost versus gain. However, she decided maybe the buccaneer needed to consider the other side of that equation. "We're not ones to be trifled with either," she said. "There's a dead necromancer in Singerva who learned that the hard way. So, it would be smart to lay off the threats, even in jest."

Sylvia made a dismissive wave of her hand. "When you live in the shadow of the gallows, you're bound to develop gallows humor." She leaned forward. "The fact remains that we didn't save your bacon from the goodness of our hearts." Helchen didn't like the way her eyes kept lingering over the bulky leather case hanging from her shoulder – the one in which she kept the arcane books Hulmul had charged her with preserving. She hadn't heard of The Demoness being a ship that was connected to any practitioner of the black arts, but even the lowest initiate of the Order knew about The Ghoul, a vessel reputed to be captained by a sorcerer and crewed by inhuman fiends. Perhaps Sylvia had an inkling that she could enhance her ship through dark magic, and make her vessel as infamous as The Ghoul?

Helchen laid a protective hand across the case of books and glowered at Sylvia. "That I can well believe," she told the pirate. "So, what do you expect?"

Sylvia smiled at her officers. "Straight and to the point. Just like one of the Order's dogs." She pointed to the foredeck where some of the refugees lingered. Most of them had gone into the hold to find a spot to rest and to get away from that last grisly view of Schweinhoff. "They're what I expect. All of you really... though I'm not sure about the dwarf and the orc." The statement brought a scowl from Ursola. Ratbag gnashed his fangs, provoking in turn a growl from the ogre. Sylvia brushed her hand across Brog's arm and waved him back.

"I will explain myself," Sylvia apologized. "As you can imagine, people in my profession depend upon a certain normalcy to prevail. Without that, we can't thrive."

"You're saying the Black Plague has made it difficult to conduct piracy," Gaiseric supplied.

"Impossible would be a better word," Sylvia corrected him. "What few ships dare venture out now do so in fleets of such size that only a fool would attack them. Moreover, even if there were opportunities to plunder, the usual avenues to sell what we capture have been cut off."

"I'm not surprised." Helchen shook her head. For a long time the Jolly Brotherhood had offered sanctuary to all manner of outlaws. Many a suspected necromancer had last been seen as part of a pirate crew. When the Black Plague descended on the kingdom, such villains wouldn't hesitate to turn their sorcery against the same criminals who'd harbored them.

"So what kind of trade are you about now?" Ursola asked. "I doubt it's anything honest."

"When the serpent stirs, the shark makes common cause with the whale," Sylvia quoted an old maritime proverb. She sat up straight, puffing herself with pride. "The Demoness is temporarily engaged to gather up survivors of the zombie plague. We bring them aboard and take them back to our employers." She motioned for calm when she saw the anger her speech evoked. "No, I'd sink my ship before hiring her out to a slave ring. We've been commissioned by the templars of the monastery at Korbara. They've established a sanctuary there and are trying to bring as many people as they can find to the stronghold."

"We be gettin' two pieces o' silver f'r e'ry man, woman, 'n nipp'r," Korsgaard chuckled. "By me reckonin', that lot yer brung 'll nab us one hun'rt 'n eighty-five coin. More if'n them templ'rs 'll pay fer the likes o' dwarves 'n orcs."

"So it's only about the money," Gaiseric said. From the way he said it, Helchen wondered if maybe he wasn't taking it a bit personal. Perhaps in the pirates he found a dark reflection of his own lawless proclivities.

"Ratbag saw several places that had fortified themselves between Wulfsburg and Singerva," Alaric informed Sylvia. "We'll try for one of those instead."

Sylvia pursed her lips and played with one of her earrings. "I'm not doubting the reliability of your orc," she said, though her tone put the lie to her words, "but you might consider that many things could have happened. Places that were safe last week might have been overwhelmed or abandoned since then."

"We know Korbara's all right because we made port there only yesterday," Mendoza stated, his voice a dry whisper as it crackled up his scarred throat.

"Impertently, we get paid to brung yer to the templ'rs," Korsgaard emphasized. "We be gettin' noth'n fer dumpin' yer willy-nilly 'pon shore."

Alaric glared at the quartermaster. "You'll understand that we don't precisely find you trustworthy."

Helchen pressed her hand against the knight's chest, pushing him back. "It's her ship and her decision," she said, meeting Sylvia's gaze. "She'll land us where she chooses. Otherwise, if there's trouble, the people we rescued from Singerva will suffer for it."

Sylvia stopped toying with her earring. "I'm glad we understand each other," she said, staring into Helchen's eyes.

The witch hunter favored her with an icy smile. "So that we understand each other, if there is any trouble, know that you're the first one going down."

The quiet mockery in the pirate captain's expression vanished. Helchen was glad to see that Sylvia understood what she'd said wasn't a threat, but a promise.

Spectral walkers lined the shore, their soulless eyes turned toward the river. The zombies had been thorough in their conquest of Schweinhoff. Behind them, the village was as lifeless as a tomb. The few dozen survivors from Singerva who'd tried to hide among the ruins had been ferreted out and slaughtered. With a necromancer's black magic to guide them, there was no hiding from the undead.

The horde of zombies parted with silent, eerie uniformity as their master passed among them. While his legions might be indefatigable, Gogol was still a mortal man with many of the limitations and vulnerabilities common to the living. To accompany his undead in their ceaseless pursuit of Alaric von Mertz and his followers, he'd found it necessary to offset his own need to rest. When the cadaverous throng parted, a gruesome sight lumbered between their decayed ranks. Four immense brutes, among the largest zombies Gogol could find, supported a curious and grisly contrivance. Metal poles pierced the chest of each creature, joining them together into a square formation. Between these poles, a rough framework had been assembled to support a large chair hooded by a thick canopy.

Gogol reached out and pulled aside the black curtains of his crude palanquin. He paid no notice to the undead all around him, but fixed his attention on the ship sailing away down the river. "Forward," he snapped at the brutes bearing him. With lurching, swaying strides, the zombies carried their master out onto the pier.

"You're there," Gogol snarled. His living hand tightened until a bead of blood oozed from his palm. He didn't need magic to know Alaric had eluded him. He could sense the knight's presence on that ship. Had the man been killed by his spectral walkers, the necromancer would have known it. The debt he owed to Baron von Mertz wouldn't be satisfied until the whole rotten family was exterminated. Proper redress for the pious nobleman who'd once condemned Gogol to hang. Next to the father, it was the eldest son he felt embittered against. It was at once both vexing and appropriate that Alaric should be the last of the line, the last to suffer the necromancer's revenge.

"So you still think to escape me?" The zombie-lord shifted his gaze to the water beside the pier and the ship lying there. "Not this time," he vowed. "There is still an accounting to be made between you and I."

Exerting his will, Gogol compelled his undead arm to shift and link fingers with those of his living hand. Curled against his breast, one hand over the other, he drew upon his magic. He had work for his zombies, labor more nuanced than simple massacre.

The spectral walkers surged into motion, their corpse-candle glow casting eerie reflections on the river as they trudged into the water. By the dozens, by the hundreds, they swarmed about the sunken ship. Through sheer numbers, the zombies accomplished a feat that should have been impossible. Gripping the hull, the undead dragged the flooded cog up onto the shore.

Gogol refocused his commands, sending his deathly minions back through the village. Not to seek victims this time, but to bring back tools and timber. They were going to repair this ship that misfortune had so kindly left at the necromancer's disposal.

Then they were going to continue the hunt for Alaric von Mertz.

To the very throne of Darkness itself, if need be.

CHAPTER EIGHT

Fog billowed across the river as The Demoness headed downstream. Alaric's view from the ship's deck was limited to only a few dozen yards, not enough to afford a glimpse of either shore or to judge how far they'd journeyed since leaving Schweinhoff the previous day. It was an unfamiliar thing for the knight, trying to judge distance and speed while sailing when night and fog blotted out any sign of land. He knew, of course, that Sylvia had such navigational skills. It would be a poor pirate who didn't.

"We'd better get where we're going soon," Helchen said as she walked up onto the foredeck and joined Alaric near the prow. Even at such an early hour, the witch hunter was alert, with one hand curled protectively against the bag of books she'd brought from Vasilescu's tower. "She might take a longer view, but I'm dubious how long Captain Sylvia can keep her pirates under control. They might need us alive, but that doesn't mean they won't try to rob us."

Alaric was less skeptical of Sylvia's command over her crew. "I think that's a needless worry. I've watched her giving orders and her men obey without question. You might wonder whether they obey out of confidence or fear, but either way they do what she tells them." He shook his head. "Even the ogre does what he's told. Probably the only reason him and Ratbag haven't killed each other."

"Gaiseric's doing a good job keeping Ratbag away from him as well," Helchen reported. "From what I can tell, with an orc it's very much a case of 'out of sight, out of mind.' As long as he isn't looking at the ogre, Ratbag isn't on edge."

"One thing my father always said about orcs is that they always have to know who's the toughest in the tribe," Alaric commented. He was quiet for a moment, the memory of Baron von Mertz occupying his thoughts. His fingers brushed across the pommel of the sword he wore, feeling the dragon engraved there. The heraldry of his family. A family claimed by the Black Plague, their corpses transformed into undead horrors.

The knight shook himself free of morbid reflections. His attention shifted to the books Helchen was carrying. "I have to say, I expected you to have burned those by now."

"Hulmul charged me to preserve them." Helchen's expression was disturbed, uneasiness in her voice. "It's not just noble knights who can feel bound by a promise. I said I'd make sure the knowledge they hold wasn't lost."

Alaric studied Helchen for a moment, trying to decide if he should raise a subject on which he had more than a few questions. "You've been reading those tomes. Not only to evaluate whether they should be destroyed," he hurried to add. Much of the archmage Vasilescu's library had been consigned to the fires of his own moat, but the witch hunter had continued to look over those she'd decided were "safe" to preserve.

Helchen stared out into the fog. Alaric thought she wasn't going to answer him, but at last she began to speak. "The Order has archivists who spend their whole careers evaluating the books we seize. Some will spend decades upon a single tome, determining whether pages should be excised, passages suppressed, or the whole consigned to flames. In my over-confidence, I've been attempting to do in days by myself what an inquisitor would delegate an entire team to investigate for years."

The witch hunter shook her head. Her hand patted the bag holding the books. "That isn't the only reason," she said, her tone more fitting a confessional than the deck of a pirate ship. "Hulmul sacrificed himself to stop Vasilescu. His sacrifice has made me question everything I thought I knew about wizards, everything I read in The Sword of Sorcerers. Perhaps the Order doesn't know everything." She unclasped the leather flap that closed the bag. Alaric could see the tomes within, their yellow pages peeking out from between heavy bindings. "These books were important to Hulmul. By studying them, maybe I hope to gain a different perspective on wizards." She drew the bag shut again and fastened the buckle that held it closed. "A more balanced view from what I was taught by the Order."

Alaric could sense the turmoil that was coursing through her mind. It was a hard thing to admit that all you'd been taught to believe could be wrong. "Magic, I think," the knight said, "is like steel. It can be used as a tool just as easily as it can be made into a weapon. It all depends on who wields it."

Helchen glanced uneasily at the crew who were working on deck. Little more than shadows in the fog, but there was no forgetting that those shadows belonged to pirates. "That's why I must ensure these books don't fall into the wrong hands. I fear I'll have to break my promise to Hulmul if it means keeping them away from these pirates."

A crisp laugh, more like an audible sneer, rose from the fog at the front of the ship. A hunched shape that Alaric had mistaken for a coil of rope suddenly stood up. A few steps, and the manifestation revealed itself as Captain Sylvia. She brushed her fingers to her forehead in greeting, then smiled at Helchen.

"Three-quarters of my crew can't read," Sylvia said, an edge of mockery laced into her words. "Of the rest, a few might fumble their way through their own wanted posters. Somebody who can make sense of a conjure-man's scribblings? You're on the wrong ship, missy." Again, the stern laugh rang out.

"Besides," Sylvia added, waving her arm at the fog before them, "if we were going to rob you, we'd have done it before we got where we're going."

As though provoked by Sylvia's voice, the fog began to lessen. The knight's hand tightened about the grip of his sword, wondering what the change portended. Through the wispy threads of gray, Alaric could see the shore gradually come into view. A sense of wonder filled him as he saw the vista ahead. Before them was a range of rocky cliffs, their sides a sheer drop into the water below. Directly before The Demoness, however, there was a great declivity in the riverside wall. It took him a moment to pick out the towers and battlements of the structure built there, for it had been hewed from the rock of the cliff itself.

This, then, was the monastery of Korbara, a feat of engineering and architecture that Alaric had heard of but never hoped to see with his own eyes. He noted that a strip of land had been reclaimed from the river at the base of the cliff. Here, in ground rich with silt, fertile crops waved in the morning breeze. Terraces cut from the cliff provided sanctuary for flocks of woolly sheep. A stone quay fronted the scene, about which a confusion of different ships and boats were anchored.

"Looks an ideal refuge," Alaric commented, suppressing the amazement he truly felt. It wouldn't do to show weakness in the company of pirates. He pointed at the sheer cliffs around the monastery, appraising it from a military perspective rather than an emotional one. "An enemy would have to come over water to reach the place."

"Or drop from straight above," Sylvia said, gesturing to the heights that stretched over the stronghold. "I've been told some zombies have done that. Walked right off the cliff to try and reach the people below." A brief shudder rippled through her. "Mostly they overshoot and land in the river to be swept away by the current. The few that plummet into Korbara are so busted up in the fall that the templars don't have any problems disposing of them."

Alaric arched his eyebrow and gave the pirate captain a closer scrutiny. "You seem to speak from experience rather than rumor."

Sylvia smiled awkwardly at Alaric, clearly uneasy by his statement. She clapped her hands and seemed to shake off her discomfort. "Right, let's see about getting you people ashore!" she said, dismissing the mood of a moment before. "You're anxious to get off a dirty, larcenous pirate ship and I'm eager to get paid." Chuckling, she marched off the foredeck and began shouting commands to her crew.

"Wizards, orcs, and now pirates," Alaric said as he watched Sylvia walk away. "We're having to rethink a lot of things we thought we knew." One thing the Black Plague had forced upon him was associating with people he'd never have consorted with before. It made him wonder about many of his preconceptions. Sometimes what he'd been taught proved to be true, but at other times he found himself compelled to an entirely different perspective.

Helchen still had a worried look in her eyes. "In the Order we were always told that an exception doesn't invalidate a rule." Alaric noted that she drew the bag of books closer to her side in a gesture he recognized as reflexively protective. "Don't be too quick to trust a pirate or you're apt to know why they fly a black flag."

The knight's eyes glanced up toward the mainmast, picturing the pennant hanging slack and surrounded by the fog. The black flag was a military tradition so old its origin wasn't even recounted in legends. Its meaning, however, was clear. To fly the black flag meant you'd offer no quarter to the enemy, and they could expect no mercy.

When the black flag was flown, it meant surrender or be slaughtered.

Gaiseric felt uneasy as he walked through the halls of Korbara. The twin lightning emblem of Wotun was never out of sight.

Picked out in gold leaf on curtains and tablecloths, carved upon doorways, sculpted into columns, the god of justice's symbol was all around him. For a burglar, Wotun wasn't a comfortable divinity to contemplate. Certainly, he wasn't as vindictive as the remorseless Marduum, but he still regarded criminal pursuits with divine scorn. Gaiseric couldn't shake the impression of the god scowling down on him.

The templars who lived in Korbara, however, were all hospitality. The monastery's halls teemed with people from every strata of society, all treated with the same consideration. Gaiseric was amazed when he passed a sanctuary that now doubled as a dormitory for refugees. An old man wearing the ermine-trimmed doublet of a count was spreading straw across a pew to make his bed while just in the next row, a wizened char-burner was snoring away with her brood of urchins snuggled in her arms. As he was ushered through the corridors, he found wealthy burghers brushing shoulders with ragged mendicants. He even saw a few outlaws, their ears clipped to denote their status as wolfsheads, trading stories with a woman who had the rugged aspect of a ranger about her. In the sanctuary offered by the templars, it didn't matter what someone had been, only that they'd escaped the Black Plague. Even Ratbag was admitted into the monastery with barely so much as a second glance.

Gaiseric looked on with a tinge of envy as the townsfolk from Singerva were conducted down a side corridor to find accommodation in what had previously been the abbot's solarium. Because of Alaric's insistence, they'd secured a meeting with the provisional council who now governed Korbara, a panel made up of monastery officials and leaders drawn from among the refugees. Helchen had let enough hints slip about their ordeal getting away from Singerva that the templars moved with a sense of urgency. Gaiseric thought that they might have at least been given a chance to eat a meal or wash the grime off. Between them, the knight and witch hunter had sold their story a little too well in his opinion.

Their templar escort led them up several stairways and down many hallways. The higher into the monastery they went, the fewer refugees they encountered. It seemed to Gaiseric that the disciples of Wotun had retained this part of their stronghold for their own exclusive use.

"We're inside the cliff itself now," Ursola whispered. "You can feel the weight of the rock above you."

Gaiseric couldn't tell the difference but decided he'd take the dwarf's word for it. After carving the fortress out of the cliff, it only seemed natural that if the templars needed to expand the structure they'd simply dig deeper into the rock.

"You must've impressed the abbot quite a bit," Sylvia said. The captain of The Demoness had joined them at the insistence of the templars. Her piratical garb and macabre facepaint made a stark contrast to the bald pates and voluminous habits affected by the monks. Only in one respect was there any similarity: Sylvia had weapons hanging off her belt. So, too, did each member of their escort.

"The templars are a fighting order," Alaric commented. "Usually suspicious of strangers."

Sylvia turned in his direction. "I think you'd be the first to agree that many folks have been forced to change their ideas of who to trust and who to avoid since the world upended." She gestured at their templar escort. "The Black Plague has turned the world upside down. Anybody trying to help put things back the way they were is at least a small ray of hope in the darkness."

"You intend to set things right?" Gaiseric asked, incredulity etched across his face.

"We're both thieves," Sylvia reproved him. "To prosper, we need people to steal from and people to sell our plunder to. Without both sides of the coin, we've got nothing." She pointed again at the templars. "If they can protect at least a little of the world the zombies are tearing down, you'd better believe I'll give them all the help I can."

"Der bindle stiffz is der george in der ruckuz," Ratbag grunted. "Lampin' dem in lotsa rumpuz."

"He says these priests have fought orcs before," Gaiseric translated for the others.

"The Swords of Korbara have sent warriors to the frontier for generations," Alaric said. "Anytime the Duke of Wulfsburg declared a new campaign against the orcs and goblins, the Prelate of Wotun would send fighters to support the cause."

Sylvia turned a thin smile on the knight. "Sometimes they'd help the Duke of Mordava, too. There's only so much piracy that can go on before the templars take a hand in the business."

"Curious you'd be working with the templars now," Helchen pointed out.

"Ill winds make for curious shipmates," Sylvia responded. "My father was a merchant who traded with Mordava. I went along with him on many of his voyages. Even the last one. Oftentimes there were a few templars onboard to provide us with protection."

"Let's hope they have sense enough to keep their warriors at home just now," Gaiseric said. "Though it doesn't seem they'd object if they were told to go."

Sylvia smirked at the thief. "That's because most of them have taken a vow of silence. But you shouldn't let that worry you. The abbot might be frustratingly pious, but he's also pragmatic. He knows all the refugees he's taken in need protection, and he isn't taking that duty lightly."

"Just what is the abbot's idea?" Gaisieric pressed.

The pirate chuckled. "Same thing any priest of Wotun talks about: saving the world." She tugged at one of her earrings, her expression contemplative. "Only this time, the world certainly needs saving."

The templars guided them onward to a chamber deep within the fortress. It was a large room dominated by a long table ringed by benches. Gaiseric thought it might be some sort of dining hall, but then reflected that the kitchens they'd passed had been on a much lower level of the monastery. The absence of any sort of altar ruled out the place serving as a chapel. Then he remembered that the templars were a military order. He could just imagine the long table covered in maps as warriors gathered around to plot strategy. A complete lack of windows and only a single set of doors made the room a difficult target for spies and assassins.

"I must ask your indulgence and request that you wait here," one of the templars said, speaking for the first time and gesturing them to one end of the table. He waited for Gaiseric and the others to find places on the benches before withdrawing into the hallway outside with the rest of the monks.

"So, what do we do now?" Gaiseric stared uneasily at their surroundings. The walls were bare, the pillars that flanked the room carved from the same white stone as everything else. He could well imagine that the chamber had been hacked out of the cliff and then gussied up by stonecutters.

"I suggest you wait," Sylvia declared, her eyes sweeping over each member of the group. "The templars seldom make requests, but when they do it's not a good idea to refuse them." She frowned and muttered, "That's a good way to almost lose your ship."

"The voice of experience again?" Gaiseric asked.

Sylvia tapped her cutlass. "Shortly after I convinced the former captain of The Demoness to retire, I decided to ensure the crew approved the change in leadership. We spotted a carack sailing about all by herself. Rich pickings and I wasn't scared of the pennants she was flying." She gestured at one of the twin lightning bolts carved into the walls. "We made a good haul, but the Swords of Korbara didn't take kindly to a ship full of pilgrims being waylaid by pirates. For an entire year, I don't think there was a ship we came across that didn't have a dozen warriors of Wotun hiding below decks."

"How'd you manage to get out...?" Gaiseric started to ask.

"Bribery," Sylvia admitted with a laugh. "We tithed a percentage of our loot to the Prelate of Wotun and made a vow to attack no more pilgrims. After that things settled down and we could get back to normal."

Helchen shook her head in disgust. "A priest falling prey to corruption."

Sylvia's eyes sparkled with amusement at Helchen's naivety. "Anyone can be bought. It's just a question of price.

You might even be able to afford a few members of the council here."

"If they can be bought, then they aren't worth seeing," Helchen snapped and started to walk out of the room.

"We asked for an audience with those in charge here," Alaric said, staying Helchen. "We might be able to tell them things that will help them secure this place against the undead." His eyes took on a steely glint. "And they might know things about the Black Plague that can help fight the zombies."

Gaiseric scratched his head. He didn't like to hear Alaric speak like that. It meant the knight was already thinking about leaving and taking up the hunt for Gogol. Vengeance, the thief thought, was a foolish and expensive business. Few anticipated the cost until the time came for it to be paid. He knew it would do no good to try and dissuade Alaric from seeking revenge. He also knew he felt too indebted to the knight to let him pursue the necromancer alone.

"We'll need help," Helchen admitted, setting her hat on the table and letting down her hair. "The spectral walkers Gogol has are something I've never seen or heard of before, but maybe somebody here has a better idea of what they are and how to destroy them." She looked fixedly at Alaric. "Without a reliable way to overcome his zombies, it would be suicide to go looking for Gogol."

Sylvia gave them a puzzled look. "Who's this Gogol you're talking about?"

"A necromancer," Gaiseric answered. "A human hyena who's responsible for all of us being here. It was his zombies that you saw as we sailed from Schweinhoff."

"He's the murderer who killed my entire family," Alaric

hissed through clenched teeth. He slammed his fist against the table. "A fiend who'll one day pay for his crimes."

Gaiseric could see the strain on Alaric's face, his impatience to visit retribution on his enemy. He felt for the knight's dilemma but hoped that events would steer them to the more prudent course.

Gaiseric couldn't shake the feeling that Alaric would find his doom if he met Gogol again.

CHAPTER NINE

Helchen thought it only a matter of minutes since their escort left them before the doors opened again and a file of templars led a disparate group into the chamber. The provisional council appointed over Korbara looked to be as much a cross-section of the kingdom as the masses of refugees they'd seen throughout the monastery. Of course, the abbot himself was to be expected, a thin and austere man dressed in the same white habit as his monks, though with a black surplice around his neck to denote his rank. He had a strained, weary mien about him. Helchen thought it was obvious why he'd appointed a council to share authority, as the burden of so much responsibility was too much for him. It was difficult to estimate just how old he was, but anything between sixty and eighty was possible.

Others on the council included a stately baroness and a rotund guildmaster, the captain of a mercenary company and a master mason who'd been renovating part of the fortress when the Black Plague struck. There was a nervous, sweaty little man who bore the badge of the Kingswatch, the constabulary who roved the duchies snooping for the least sign of unrest. A dour, dispirited young woman arrayed in the blue cassock of Darsina, goddess of the seas, her fingers never leaving the conch-shell talisman she wore about her neck.

Among the council, there were two who immediately drew Helchen's notice. She didn't need to be told what they were as her training under the Order gave her an almost instinctive ability to discern the arcane taint a wizard exuded. Certainly, a practitioner of magic could conceal that tell-tale aura – otherwise unmasking a necromancer would be easy – but these two hadn't bothered to hide their vocation. One was a man with pale hair and a long beard, his robes a shade of green that Helchen knew was called sylvan and almost exclusively woven by elves. Elfkind had limited contact with humans, preferring to keep to their own enclaves deep within the forests, so she wondered what, if any, connection the wizard had with the fey folk.

The other man was certainly a member of the Wizard's Guild. His crimson robes marked him as one of the battlemages the Guild provided to augment the royal army. He had a more robust build than his pale-haired companion and his hair was of a much darker hue. The black beard that tumbled onto his chest was shorter than the other magician's but was thicker and more voluminous. A heavy hood cast much of the battlemage's face in shadow, but what Helchen could see made him seem both perceptive and severe, the sort of man who was quick to observe and equally quick to judge. His gaze was like frost when he looked at her. It wasn't fear of a witch hunter, but rather resentment. She wondered if he'd have been so open with his scorn were things less chaotic and the Order's authority more secure.

The council listened with grim attentiveness as Alaric

reported the fall of Mertz and Singerva, the treachery of Vasilescu, and the decimation of so much of the Duchy of Mordava. It seemed to Helchen that the leaders of Korbara were already aware that necromancers had banded together into cabals to exploit the hordes of zombies infesting the land. They asked only a few questions about the observation that the infection was being passed on to crows and rats and other animals that preyed upon the corrupt flesh of the undead. This, apparently, exonerated the templars in their policy of burning the corpses of any zombies that reached the monastery, something some of the secular leaders had argued against as a waste of resources.

It was when Helchen took up the discussion that dread began to work its way onto the faces of the council. As she'd expected, the spectral walkers were new to them, a menace they'd yet to face. Learning that there were zombies against which even the butchering strength of an orc warrior was useless devastated their confidence that the templars could protect them.

"And you've led these monsters here?" the priestess of Darsina snarled at Sylvia. "Where's your sense, corsair? The safety of this refuge must be your first concern!"

The pirate leveled a frigid stare at the blue-robed cleric. "My first priority, as charged to me by the abbot, is rescuing as many people as I can from the zombie scourge. I don't stop and interview them first to see if they're being otherwise chased."

The abbot motioned for both women to desist before the argument could go further. "What's done is done. Our concern now has to be how to stop these new zombies."

"The only thing we've found that was able to stop these

spectral walkers was an alchemical fire devised by the traitor Vasilescu," Helchen stated with a nod to Ursola. "Ordinary force of arms was useless."

The abbot fixed his tired eyes on the dwarf. "The only luxury that has been permitted to the Swords of Korbara has been an extensive wine cellar. If I put it at your disposal, do you think you could make more of these fire-bombs?" He gestured to the example Ursola had set on the table while Alaric was describing their escape from Singerva.

Ursola sighed and shook her head. "Even a thick dwarf ale wouldn't burn hot enough. You'd need something as hot as dragon bile to turn the trick."

"Then we are without hope," the man from the Kingswatch groaned.

"We've a duty to the people who've taken sanctuary here," the abbot reproved the other councilor. "While we hold faith with Wotun, hope remains. We'll not cast out those who've come here for succor because of nebulous fears." He lifted his eyes, as though peering into the divine realm. "There's no certainty that these new, awful creatures will ever threaten Korbara."

"There's no certainty that they won't either," Sylvia advised the monk. She nodded at Helchen. "Apparently these new zombies chased people from Singerva down to the river. That's quite a bit of determination and shows that they don't give up easily."

The pale-haired wizard looked over at Helchen, anger in his gaze. "The witch hunters have gone to many extremes to destroy necromancy. The Black Plague shows us how extreme the necromancers have become in their turn." He shook his head and ruminated on the threat Korbara was under. "No, it is too much to pretend the undead won't be set against us here. Eventually the necromancers will take an interest in us and when they do, they'll do whatever they have to in order to kill everyone inside."

"Turn out these newcomers," the sea priestess snarled. "It is they who these spectral walkers are pursuing. Send them away and at least we delay the menace. Give ourselves a chance to devise a plan."

The craven words, spoken by a priestess, infuriated Helchen. Before she could speak, however, a man in the surcoat of a templar captain vented his own fury. "That is the churlish speech I'd expect of a coward, not from someone who has dared long voyages across the ocean and stood firm in the face of water-spouts and sea serpents." The templar's voice cut through the cleric and she meekly lowered her head. The warrior-monk scrutinized the other councilors. "Those who've come here for refuge will be granted it. To do less is to show ourselves faithless cowards and to betray whatever is decent within our own souls."

"Then we'll all be slaughtered," the man from the Kingswatch persisted. "Didn't you hear? These new zombies are invincible!"

"Maybe not." The wizard Helchen had marked as a battlemage, a man named Doran, leaned forward and took up the conversation. He looked over at the witch hunter. "This strange glow you've observed around these zombies, you're certain that it resembles that emitted by a wraith?"

Helchen nodded. "I've played a peripheral role in putting down a few hauntings. There's no mistaking that graveyard glow once you've seen it."

"The phantasmal undead are characterized by such ghost lights, though some of the most malignant learn how to obscure it from mortal sight," the other, pale-haired wizard stated as he ran his fingers through his beard.

"Yet these spectral walkers are undeniably still physical entities," Doran reminded his comrade. "In some manner they've been endowed with some of the invulnerabilities of phantoms while retaining their corporeal shells. A hideous combination."

"The whys and whats aren't important," Gaiseric interrupted, frustration sneaking into his tone. "We need to know how to destroy them."

"Agreed," Doran replied, "but to do that we have to understand what these things are." He looked aside at the older wizard for a moment. Helchen had the impression the two were communing telepathically, employing their magic to converse directly to each other's mind. She'd seen Hulmul do the same with his familiar and had some idea how rapidly information could be exchanged compared to vocal communication.

"I think so, too," the elder wizard said, motioning for Doran to explain his theory to the others.

The battlemage stood up and swept his gaze about the table. "These spectral walkers have been infused with the essence of the spirits that once inhabited their flesh. What obscene magic the necromancers are using to facilitate this process is a mystery, but I think there are some things we can assume." He began ticking off points on his fingers as he explained his thoughts.

"When a body dies, the bond between flesh and spirit is quickly severed," Doran said. "Within a few days, the spirit is completely liberated, free to pass–" here he paused and smiled at the abbot "–into an afterworld over which there's still some debate. More certain is the fact that this division of flesh and spirit does occur. Spirits that remain earthbound manifest as phantasmal undead, wraiths and banshees and their like. Bodies that are reanimated after death become the corporeal undead. In general, the phantasmal undead retain a cruel and malicious sentience while the corporeal undead are mindless or nearly so. Vampires are an exception to the rule, but there is a theory that the personality inhabiting them isn't the spirit they had in life but some other force that is merely simulating that role."

"But what about these spectral walkers?" Helchen asked. She was in no mood for an erudite lecture.

"There is, so far as I can determine from what you've related, only one possibility," Doran continued. "The necromancers have found a way to prevent that dispersal of the spirit when the flesh dies. The tether remains though mind and personality have been broken. By this means, the spirit clings to its old body in the form of a spectral aura, endowing the zombie with an ectoplasm field that makes them almost invulnerable." The battlemage tapped his finger against the table. "To create such monsters, however, the necromancer would need to animate a body very shortly after death, before the spirit has dissipated. The natural process, if such it could be called, would have the victim of a zombie's bite rise up as a purely corporeal undead. Spells must be involved to alter that process and, well, even operating with a cabal, a necromancer can't be everywhere. This means that the numbers of these spectral walkers will be limited by how much opportunity the..."

Helchen leaned forward, her face only a few inches from Doran's. "How do we stop them?" she asked, trying to keep the battlemage focused.

Again, there was that silent exchange between the two wizards. "Magic," the elder finally said. "These creatures are partly physical and partly spectral. What you need is something that can affect both. That means employing magic against them." He pointed to Ursola. "It isn't a question of how hot a fire rages, but whether the fuel that feeds the flame possesses arcane properties. The alchemical brew Vasilescu employed doubtless had enchantments placed upon it. Dragon bile is itself derived from substances endowed with occult affinities."

"I know the answer isn't one that will comfort a member of the Order," Doran told Helchen, a sardonic smile pulling at his beard, "but if you want to fight these spectral walkers, you'll need to rely on magic to do so."

Helchen sank back in her seat. Through her mind ran all the Order's teachings, their injunctions against sorcery and the arcane. Then she thought of Hulmul and his selfless bravery. She thought of her own employment of the profane Dragon's Kiss to kill Vasilescu. The evil weapon was concealed in a tiny iron casing and stuffed in her boot, but she wasn't so easily able to hide from the memory of resorting to its use. Despite all the warnings taught to her by the Order, she'd already employed dark magic to fight the Black Plague.

"Magic isn't so common a thing as iron and steel," Alaric said. He gestured at Doran and his companion. "Even the spells of wizards have their limitations."

An air of resignation seemed to settle upon Doran. The

battlemage nodded his head. "There are only a few of us at Korbara. Too few, I fear, to oppose a determined effort by a cabal of necromancers." He turned a thin smile upon the knight. "However, a weapon bearing an enchantment would serve as readily as a spell in vanquishing these spectral walkers."

"We've a few such weapons," the templar captain said. "Relics venerated by the Swords of Korbara for many generations. But even then, I can arm perhaps five templars against these new undead. Far too few to stand against a horde such as pursued these people from Singerva."

Helchen saw the two wizards exchange another of their mental conversations. When Doran spoke again, it was with a mixture of both hope and dread.

"What we need is a weapon with an enchantment formidable enough to destroy swathes of undead at a time." Doran raised his finger to emphasize his next point. "Yet at the same time it must be simple enough that it doesn't need an adept of the arcane to employ it."

"You know of such a weapon," Helchen challenged the battlemage. It would explain the hope she saw in his eyes if such a thing existed. Now she wanted to know why its existence caused Doran such fear.

"Indeed," Doran admitted. "There is such an artifact." His voice quivered as he continued. "But it is kept in a place few would dare venture." He paused as though trying to nerve himself for what he would say.

"To recover this artifact," Doran said, "means going to the island of the sorceress Yandryl."

CHAPTER TEN

"Yandryl!" Ursola spat out the name as though it were poison. Her eyes blazed as she glared at Doran. "What dealings do you have with that witch?"

The battlemage made a conciliatory gesture with his hands. "Almost none," he assured the dwarf. "The Wizard's Guild drafted a petition to her once and I was one of several who helped to write it." He shook his head. "Yandryl rejected our overtures and sent the messenger back to us transformed into a toad."

"All the ships in the Jolly Brotherhood give Yandryl's island a wide berth," Sylvia chimed in. "I don't know that anyone sails too close. I've only ever seen it as a speck on the horizon before changing course." The pirate leaned back in her chair, folding her arms before her. "You'd need to be really desperate to make sail for that port and have to find a crew who didn't put too much value on their skins."

"Who is this Yandryl?" Alaric asked, clearly puzzled by the mix of hatred and fear percolating through the room.

Ursola illuminated the matter for the knight. "She's an elf sorceress with more blood-debts laid against her than any ten orc warlords you could name." The dwarf clenched her hands, as though she had Yandryl before her and was wringing her neck. "Her catalog of crimes against my people is the greatest in all the spitelaw recorded in the vaults of vengeance. Brigand and murderer, they name her. The dwarf who could visit final reckoning upon the witch would be lauded the greatest hero of the age."

"Terrible as she might be," Doran said, "Yandryl has collected treasures from across the land. It is one of the artifacts in her possession that could be the salvation of Korbara and all those who seek shelter here. I speak of a relic called Mournshroud."

A bestial grumble sounded from Ratbag, an intonation so fierce that Ursola forgot for a moment that the orc was her erstwhile ally and she grabbed for the hammer on her belt. "Mournshroud! Dat's bein' swag wot der warlockz jimmied up ter croak lotsa cadavaz."

Ratbag looked over at Gaiseric, expecting the thief to translate for the rest of them. "Mournshroud was made by the orcs to fight the undead," Gaiseric said, taking a bit more care with how he interpreted the orc's growls than he usually did.

"And they lost it to Thane Jurgan Hammerhand when he conquered the orchold of Warlord Grugnak Bloodtusk," Ursola added to the relic's history. "Restitution for the many raids Grugnak had led into the mines of the Whitestone clan." Anger welled up inside her as she continued the story. "Long was the ancient orcish war drum kept as a prize in the halls of Bragadruum until Yandryl attacked my people and plundered our treasures."

"One elf sorceress was able to wreak such havoc?" Helchen wondered, awe in her voice.

Ursola shook her head. "Yandryl was too craven to show herself, so she sent her pet to do her plundering for her. Without warning, the dragon Flamefang broke into the halls and slaughtered every dwarf who stood against him. But there was no mistaking that the wyrm was bewitched by Yandryl, for the beast acted with a fixation of purpose and maliciousness never seen in a dragon. Flamefang destroyed every trap and ambush laid for him before it could be sprung and wasn't deceived by false doors and empty passageways. He even ignored the gold vaults, a thing unheard of for a dragon, and made directly for the enchanted relics held by the dwarves of Bragadruum. These he took up in his claws and it was these alone he took with him when he flew out of the smoldering stronghold." Ursola could picture the scene as vividly as though she'd been there herself, so often had her grandfather related the awful tale. He'd died in shame after the event, his body scarred by the dragon's fire, his honor stained by his failure to stop the wyrm.

"Wait a moment," Gaiseric exclaimed when Ursola finished her tale. "You're telling me we have to deal with an evil sorceress who says 'no' by turning people into frogs and a fire-breathing dragon who can fight an entire dwarf clan and come out the winner?"

"The enchantments imbued in Mournshroud are the only ones I know of that can suit our needs," Doran informed the rogue. "Beating its ghastly drum skin will invoke its power."

"You've seen for yourself that Gogol won't stop," Helchen reminded Gaiseric. "We need something that will give us the ability to fight back."

"There are dangers," Doran admitted. He darted a look at

Ursola. "But whatever she may be, Yandryl is no necromancer. The menace of the Black Plague hangs over her just as it does every other living thing."

"I'm surprised you haven't tried to contact the witch already," Ursola huffed, not about to be mollified by Doran's reasoning.

"No one has seen her in years," Doran said. "Only the servants she sometimes sends to Mordava for supplies."

Sylvia perked up at that information. "Then no one really knows if she's even still on the island? She may have left or died, and it is only her servants keeping the stories alive."

"I shouldn't put too much hope in that idea," Helchen advised the pirate. "At the best of times, sorcerers keep themselves isolated."

The white-bearded wizard across the table nodded. "If stories are to be believed, Yandryl has lived on her island for a thousand years."

"But if she were gone," Sylvia insisted, intrigued despite the hint of fear that still lingered in her eyes, "then we could be certain of bringing back Mournshroud." She looked aside at Alaric and the others. "No doubt we'd find other magic weapons, too. Ursola said the dragon carried off a clawful of enchanted things, and I'm sure that's not the only time Yandryl had her pet go raiding for her."

Ursola could see the glint that came into Gaiseric's eye. The thief was warming to this idea of wealth just waiting there to be collected. "It might be worth looking into," he said consideringly, clearly still not quite past the idea of confronting a ruthless sorceress and her dragon.

"I for one hope the hag is there," Ursola swore, her mind on a satisfaction greater than riches. "An easy death isn't for

Yandryl." She felt it would be a travesty of justice should the sorceress escape the retribution her crimes deserved. The spirits of the many dwarves killed by her command would never rest if she avoided judgement.

"Dead or alive, we must go to the island," Alaric declared. He looked over at Helchen. "You're right. Gogol won't stop. Not until one of us is dead."

"There's another reason he has to be stopped," Helchen declared. "If Gogol was the one to create these spectral walkers, then we need to keep ahead of him before he can devise other enchantments and unleash still worse creatures upon the realm."

"A pity the cur wasn't hanged years ago," Gaiseric cursed.

"Yes," Alaric said, his voice strangely quiet. "A pity."

Ursola was perplexed by the guilt in Alaric's expression. She could appreciate only in the most abstract way the responsibility that weighed on him, that the mutual vendetta between himself and the necromancer was placing others in jeopardy. For her, or any dwarf, such concerns were insignificant beside the chance to avenge their family or clan.

"We'd have more time to strategize if I wasn't certain that Gogol will be after us," Alaric told the council. "And he's certain to bring his spectral walkers with him." He nodded to Doran. "If you're certain Yandryl has this relic, then we must lose no time trying to secure it."

"Mournshroud was certainly in her possession," Doran confirmed. "It might be useful to have a wizard with you if you have to negotiate with Yandryl. She may be more open to discussing matters with another practitioner of the arcane sciences." The battlemage smiled and let a spark of magical energy crackle from the tip of his finger. "Besides, I'm sure I can be useful in other ways."

Sylvia stood up and looked across at the council. "I offer the services of The Demoness to carry this expedition to Yandryl's island," she said. "My ship is the fastest moored off Korbara and my navigator knows the way to her island – if only to ensure we didn't get too close to it. Well, now, we'll do more than that. We'll take whoever cares to go right onto the beach." She flashed a broad smile at the abbot. "So, you see, we're really the best choice you have."

"I thought you buccaneers of the Jolly Brotherhood didn't take risks like that," the templar captain reminded Sylvia.

The pirate shrugged. "If it's a worthy cause, we make exceptions." She smiled at the warrior-monk. "The Demoness has done a few favors for the Swords of Korbara in the past, even before the Black Plague. Retrieving Mournshroud is certainly a worthy pursuit."

Ursola shook her head. "You're fooling no one," she told Sylvia. "Your pirates are only interested in plundering the witch's treasure if it turns out she's dead."

"You object to that?" Sylvia rounded on the dwarf.

Ursola gave the pirate a cold look. "My only objection is if I'm not the one to remove Yandryl from among the living."

Gaiseric rolled his eyes. "That might make negotiations difficult." He looked aside at Alaric. "What if we just tie up Ursola and leave her here?"

"Then you'd find out pretty quickly what it means to provoke a dwarf's wrath," Ursola warned the rogue. "There isn't a hole dark enough for you to hide in that I couldn't dig you out of."

Gaiseric licked his lips nervously. "It was only an idea..."

The ship's deck swayed beneath Alaric's feet as The Demoness made her way downriver toward the sea. With the current to speed her along, the vessel was making good time. Sylvia was confident that they'd be able to reach Yandryl's island in four or five days, allowing that they didn't encounter a storm. Doran was certain that the weather would hold. It seemed the specialty of his fellow wizard at Korbara was prognostication and he'd declared the voyage would have clear skies.

That was at least one less thing to worry about. Alaric considered that he had enough on his plate already. Sylvia's pirates were keyed up and it was a certainty that they'd heard about the wealth they might find in Yandryl's castle. Greed was a good way to make some people forget about danger, but it would mean trouble if the sorceress was still around. The same divinations that foretold clear weather had been ambiguous in regard to Yandryl's status. All he could say with certainty was that they'd find the castle open to them.

If the elf was alive, then they'd have problems with Ursola. She considered herself honor-bound to avenge the dwarves killed by the sorceress. If there was a silver lining to her determination it was the indignation she'd expressed when it was suggested she might stab Yandryl in the back. Assassination was repugnant to the dwarf. When the time came to kill the elf, she'd know who was executing her and why. Such forthrightness meant there'd be no surprises, at least. It was just a bit too easy to imagine himself in her position. In many ways her grudge against Yandryl wasn't so dissimilar from his own vendetta with Gogol.

Alaric knew in one respect at least he was different. His animus wasn't enough to make him jeopardize the lives of others. Getting Mournshroud and bringing it back so it could protect the refugees at Korbara took priority. He wouldn't let anything interfere with that. Afterward, once it was safely in the templars' custody, then it would be time for him to plan his next move.

The knight studied the shoreline as The Demoness headed downriver. The yellows and oranges of the autumn leaves lent the land a sinister quality, as though the Black Plague were draining the life from the entire province. Perhaps from the whole kingdom.

At Korbara Alaric had been able to put together a more complete impression of how dire the catastrophe was. While there were doubtless some holdouts and pockets of resistance, the duchies to the south had been savaged terribly. As far west as Wulfsburg, hordes of zombies prowled the countryside and there was now more than just Ratbag's tales to suggest that the orclands beyond the frontier were also afflicted. There were only scattered reports of anything happening in the north or in the estates held by King Heinrich, but Alaric worried these lands weren't blessed by a lack of undead within their borders so much as a lack of representation among those who'd taken refuge at Korbara.

"Madness," Alaric whispered, as he struggled in vain to spot so much as the least trace of human activity along the shore. Conquest, plunder – these might be wicked motives, but they at least made sense. The more he saw of the extent to which the Black Plague was ravaging the land, the more it seemed to him that the necromancers wouldn't be content until they'd killed every last person. Vasilescu's claims that he'd create a new society ruled by his occult cabal didn't appear to be shared by his fellow adepts. Perhaps the witch hunters did have the true perspective, that the more powerful the magic someone tapped into, the more likely they were to be consumed by that power.

"Ship ahoy!" the lookout cried down from the crow's nest.

Alaric leaned over the gunwale, craning his neck to see the vessel the pirate had spotted. It would be the first they'd encountered since leaving Korbara, but not for an instant did he doubt the man. Not merely the livelihood, but the survival of The Demoness depended upon sighting another ship before they spotted her. After a moment of focusing, he clambered up onto the foredeck. There he found Sylvia and Helchen already straining their eyes to pick out the other ship.

"If Zando's been drinking on watch, I'll have Brog dislocate his shoulder." Sylvia cast a dark look toward the crow's nest.

"Your lookout hasn't been imagining things," Alaric said as he caught sight of something floating on the river. An ominous feeling coursed through him. Though he couldn't make out any details from such a distance beyond the fact it appeared to be a ship, there was a sinister impression that was conveyed to him.

"Looks like a derelict," Helchen said as The Demoness drew closer to the ship ahead of them. Alaric had to agree. The vessel was dilapidated, with slime and mud caking its sides and jagged rents in its hull. The masts, such of them as remained, leaned at crazy angles, only the merest tatters of sails clinging to them. Moreover, there wasn't any sign of anyone on the deck. It made for an eerie impression, much like the abandoned villages they'd passed through earlier. Not simply the absence of life, Alaric reflected, but the withdrawal of life. The difference between a chipped stone and the withered husk of a fish left out in the sun.

"All hands!" Sylvia's voice rose to a thunderous bellow. "Ready for battle!" The Demoness became a bedlam of activity as the pirates scrambled into action. Archers assembled on the quarterdeck while the artillerists led by Korsgaard manned the ballista. Sylvia scowled at Helchen. "Derelict?" she scoffed, drawing cutlass and hatchet from her belt. She gestured with the axe at the ramshackle vessel. "That ship's moving against the current. A fine trick for something that's abandoned!"

Alaric drew his own sword, regretting that he'd left his shield in his cabin below. He reproved himself for being gulled by initial impressions. His eyes roved across the so-called derelict, looking for anything that was unusual. "Oars," he told Sylvia, sighting poles poking through the rents in the hull just above the waterline.

"An old trick of the Jolly Brotherhood," the pirate nodded. "Pretend to be adrift and helpless to lure in prey." A grim look curled on her morbid face. "Mind, only the most bloodthirsty buccaneers favored that kind of game. I was always more interested in plunder than I was in victims."

"I don't think those are buccaneers," Helchen said, a trace of fear in her voice. She pointed her flanged mace at the supposed derelict. It seemed the other crew realized their ploy was unmasked. Now they stood up from where they'd been crouched behind the gunwales, exposing their ghastly nature.

Withered, almost skeletal bodies draped in the soiled rags they'd worn when they died, the derelict's crew of zombies bent to the labor of rowing their macabre ship to intercept The Demoness.

"Spectral walkers," Doran gasped as he rushed on deck to see what had caused the commotion. The rest of the pirates' passengers were close behind the battlemage, hurriedly strapping on pieces of armor or unlimbering weapons.

The ghoulish glow emanating from the zombies was unmistakable, rippling around the undead like marshlight over a bog. The pirate bowmen, incredulous at the stories they'd been told, loosed a volley at the other ship. Alaric watched some of the arrows slam down into the rotten wood of the other ship, but those whose aim was true simply glanced off the zombies, unable to penetrate the phantom aura. Despite the gravity of the situation, strange joy rushed through him. So cunning a ploy, the difficulty of manning a ship – these were beyond the initiative of mere zombies. There was a guiding intelligence at work. Alaric was certain that Gogol was somewhere aboard the decrepit vessel.

"Loose harpoon, ya' lubbers!" Korsgaard roared at the artillerists. The ballista shuddered as it launched its bolt at the enemy. The impetus of the missile was such that zombies were thrown about the deck as it smashed through their ranks, finally tearing through the decayed wood of the quarterdeck and sending a spray of debris into the river. Several of the undead were thrown into the water by the impact, but those who were merely knocked down by its passage quickly rose again and resumed their place at the oars.

"Even artillery can't hurt them," Sylvia hissed.

Alaric caught at the pirate's shoulder. He rejected the urge to stay and get another chance at his enemy. There was simply too much depending on them to risk it all in combat, especially with the spectral walkers and their master. "We can't fight them! We've got to try and outpace them!"

Sylvia nodded and turned back to bark orders to her crew. "Lay on more sail, scallywags, or we'll all be chew toys for that gallows' bait!"

The Demoness lunged forward like a horse pricked by a spur. As the ship put on speed, Alaric began to hope they'd be able to slip past the derelict before it could intercept them. Even as the idea formed, it foundered. With unnatural maneuvering, the undead vessel lurched sideways, pivoting and plunging straight into their path.

"Time to see if your magic's all you claim it to be," Gaiseric cajoled Doran. The battlemage gave him a grim nod, then drew a scroll from his backpack. Crouching on the foredeck, the wizard began to invoke a spell. Gesturing with his finger at the enemy ship, he sent a crackling nimbus of electricity searing into the undead.

"Yes! By Wotun, yes!" Alaric cheered as a clutch of zombies were savaged by the arcane lightning. Smoke billowed off their decayed bodies, eyes burst in their sockets, ragged clothing burst into flames. The green glow winked out as the charred creatures crashed to the deck, their arms torn from their shoulders as their hands were seared to the oars.

Magic was the answer. Immune to physical weaponry, the spectral walkers weren't invulnerable to arcane attack. There was a way to overcome Gogol's hideous minions!

Doran sent a second blaze of energy into the enemy ship,

shocking several more zombies. The Demoness pulled ahead as the momentum of the derelict lessened.

"Loadsa cadavaz," Ratbag growled, fists clenching impatiently about the grip of his scimitar. On the enemy ship, spilling up from the hold, was a fresh surge of spectral walkers. The zombies moved with a jerky, erratic haste but there was no hesitation about their objective. They converged upon the oars, replacing the fallen undead and augmenting the efforts of those who remained.

"Gogol himself must be on that ship," Helchen spat. "Only a necromancer could give them such focus."

Alaric glared at the derelict as it picked up speed. The escape of a moment before was now in doubt, but he wondered if he really wanted The Demoness to elude her foe. With Gogol down there, slinking in one of the holds, his vengeance might be at hand.

"They intend to board," Alaric yelled, shaking free of his own desire to appreciate the situation for what it was. Gogol wouldn't expose himself unless confident of victory and if they failed now, it would leave Korbara in jeopardy.

Upon the derelict, another wave of zombies emerged from the hold. These carried ropes and grapples, making their intention clear. Doran sent another lash of lightning across the derelict, immolating a half dozen of the spectral walkers. A shot from the ballista knocked several others down, but there were still far too many ready to cast their lines when the two ships drew near.

"Repel boarders!" Sylvia shouted as the first of the spectral walkers swung over onto the decks of The Demoness. It was a command the pirates frantically tried to carry out, but their blades were mere steel, unable to defy the ghostly glow that surrounded their foes. Alaric saw a few of the crew dragged down when their defense failed, the claws and teeth of the undead ripping into their shrieking flesh.

"Try to pitch them into the river!" Alaric shouted. Holding his sword crosswise before him as though the blade were the shield he'd left in his cabin, the knight charged at an emaciated zombie just as it swung onto the deck. He felt a terrifying chill as his armored body crashed against the creature, as though the ghostly light itself were draining his vitality. The edge of his sword failed to bite into his necrotic foe, but the impact of his rush was still conveyed into the zombie. It staggered back, then tumbled over the gunwale and into the river.

Defiant cheers rose as others copied the knight's tactic. Ratbag slammed into a spectral walker with his shoulder and sent it spinning over the side. The hulking Brog used the flipped-over mass of a longboat like a battering ram, driving the bottom against several undead. He had a pleased look on his craggy features when the spectral walkers sank into the river. Others on deck, unable to match the brawn of orc and ogre, contented themselves with simply preventing the zombies from advancing further across the ship. Doran, sweat spilling down his face, unleashed spell after spell upon the creatures, forcing pirates to use marlin spikes to pitch the smoldering bodies over the side.

Everyone was doing their utmost, but when Alaric looked across at the derelict, he realized it wasn't going to be enough. Another wave of zombie boarders cast their lines at The Demoness. He felt the bottom drop out of his stomach.

When these spectral walkers joined the others, there would be enough undead to overwhelm the ship.

Just as the zombies threw their ropes and began to swing across, an arctic cold filled the air. A coruscating spiral of frost washed over the boarders, caking their rotten bodies in ice. The ropes, brittle from the sudden freeze, frayed and sent the undead clinging to them into the water. One of the frozen zombies, unable to arrest its motion, swung back against the side of the derelict and shattered into gory fragments.

Alaric's mind reeled, amazed by the sudden and dramatic reversal. This, surely, was the rare frost spell Vasilescu had taught to Hulmul. He turned about, ready to cheer Doran for his swift employment of the devastating magic. Instead, the knight found a pale, shivering Helchen crouched against the gunwale. Clenched in her hands was one of the tomes Hulmul had entrusted to her.

"Helchen?" the knight gasped, staggered by the implication. She barely acknowledged his voice, but simply stared at the book lying in her lap. He couldn't imagine what it must have taken for a witch hunter to invoke arcane powers. There was an unmistakable expression of horror on her face. Perhaps it was more than simply the act of casting the spell, but the awareness that she was even capable of harnessing magic that terrified her.

Any further questions Alaric had were matters to be resolved later. Helchen's spell had eliminated the reinforcements, but there were still spectral walkers aboard The Demoness that posed an immediate threat. Charging in, he helped Ursola turn away a zombie that was stalking toward the staggered witch hunter. With the dwarf's aid, they managed to force the creature over the side.

Doran's shocking magic continued to take its toll upon the spectral walkers, but even as the decks began to clear, Alaric saw the derelict drawing near again, another force of boarders assembled near its prow.

"Helchen!" Alaric called out as he ran to the witch hunter. Her eyes were glazed, her breath shallow and ragged. For all their seeming frailty, the knight knew it took some manner of conditioning for a wizard to master the ways of magic. A novice trying to wield such powers without formal training no doubt would find the process more taxing than expected. For the moment, at least, she wasn't capable of a repeat performance.

Gently easing the book from her grip, careful to keep it open to the same page, Alaric swung around to find Doran. If the battlemage could conjure the same spell, then they might stave off Gogol's zombies.

Instead, a more mundane solution presented itself. "Mister Korsgaard!" Sylvia's commanding voice boomed across The Demoness. She waved her cutlass at the ballista crew and her quartermaster. "You can't hurt those undead, but I think their ship isn't invulnerable. Put a hole in her hull!"

No sooner was the command given than the ballista sent another massive bolt speeding at the derelict. This time the shot slammed into her side, fairly exploding the decayed planks. Water rushed into the gaping wound. Within a few seconds, the enemy began to list to one side. As the list worsened, the distance between the two ships lengthened. The oars on the portside were lifted above the level of the river, the zombies crewing them mindlessly continuing to row the empty air.

Raucous jeers and relieved cheers broke out across The Demoness. The few spectral walkers left on the pirate ship were either roasted by Doran's spells or hurled over the side by Brog and Ratbag. Soon the derelict was only a dark blot receding into the distance behind them.

"Helchen, you were amazing!" Gaiseric rushed over to congratulate the witch hunter. The look she turned on the thief was every bit as cold as the spell she'd conjured. Hastily retrieving the book, Helchen withdrew below deck.

Alaric could only imagine the turmoil besetting her as he watched her leave. It was one reason he didn't join in the jubilation of the crew. He turned and fixed his gaze on the ghost ship and the necromancer he knew must be aboard her. Despite the closeness of their escape from the zombies, he couldn't help a sense of frustration. Once more, Gogol had slipped from his grasp.

"Let's hope Mournshroud is everything Doran says it is," Alaric prayed as the derelict slipped from view. "Then, the next time we meet, the advantage will be mine."

CHAPTER ELEVEN

Yandryl's island was a spit of land well outside the courses usually charted by merchants sailing between Mordava and Erkengarde. Indeed, it was the only visible land as far as Ursola's eyes could see. It was an unnerving sensation for a dwarf, having all that water around her without even the possibility of good solid earth on which to set her feet. She found it ominous then that instead of feeling relief when the island appeared on the horizon, she felt her blood chill. The hairs on her chin bristled with agitation, something she'd only ever felt before when deep in a mine and there were goblins lurking in the dark.

As The Demoness sailed nearer, Ursola could see that the island was ringed by enormous cliffs of a type of stone she'd never seen before. The closer they got, the more unsettling the stone appeared. It had a weird, porous quality about it and there were strange fossils embedded in it, the skeletons of mammoth fish and gigantic reptiles with flippers instead of feet.

"They say the sorceress lifted her island from the bed of

the sea." Sylvia stood beside Ursola on the quarterdeck. The dwarf could see an edge of fear even through the skull painted across her face. The pirate, she knew, was as comfortable on the water as she was down in a cavern. No, it was the island itself, and the wrongness of it, that made Sylvia anxious.

"A great spell, a ritual that was powered by gallons of sacrificial blood," Sylvia elaborated, reciting a yarn she must have heard a hundred times in taverns and pubs, but which only now assumed a terrible reality for her. "Yandryl cried out to the Great Darkness, and the Darkness answered her. A coral reef, long dead and drowned, lifted up from the sea in a great spire. A bastion upon which the sorceress could build her citadel."

Ursola glowered at the strange cliffs. Yes, she could well believe magic had played no small part in making such a place. "Aye, it's an evil isle." She gestured with her hand at the sky. "Even the birds shun the place."

Sylvia tugged at one of her earrings. "If tales are true, you'll not find a fish anywhere within a league of this island." A grim laugh rang out. "Of course, I wonder at any fisherman who strayed close enough to find out."

The wind suddenly shifted and Ursola caught a hint of odor in the air. She looked up at the mainmast and saw that the black flag had spun about. The breeze she felt was blowing across the island. She gave Sylvia a questioning glance. "You smell that?" The puzzled look the pirate returned told her she didn't. Humans were clever in many ways, but their senses were woefully dull. No dwarf would ever mistake that slight tang carried on the wind. "There's a whiff of musk carrying to us from the island." Her throat tightened with an ancestral emotion that was equal parts hate and terror. "Dragon," she hissed.

For only a moment, Sylvia looked as though she didn't believe Ursola, but the severity of the dwarf's expression swayed her. Hands on hips, she shouted orders to her crew. "Mister Mendoza! Ready oars in case we must move against the wind! Mister Korsgaard! Get your men up here and arm the ballista!" She cupped a hand to her mouth and shrieked to the lookout in the crow's nest. "Keep your eyes open and sing out if so much as a butterfly comes soaring up from that island!"

The pirate ship was a blur of frantic activity. Like their captain, the crew had dulled themselves to the dangers ahead of them. Sylvia didn't need to shout the word "dragon" to snap them from their avaricious malaise. The commands she issued were reminder enough of just what might be waiting for them.

"Seems a poor chance," Ursola opined to herself, gazing across the sea. She turned to Sylvia. "My people are far more familiar with fighting dragons than you humans will ever be. Not the scrawny wyrmlings that are forced down from the mountains and try to fill their bellies raiding pig sties. I'm talking about real, proper dragons! The kind that can rip open a mountain with their claws and melt steel with their breath!"

Sylvia glared at Ursola. "If you want to get to that island, scaring my crew into mutiny is a poor way to do it. Kraken bones, but I'm more than tempted to dump you overboard and sail away."

The commotion on deck brought the rest of the passengers up from below. Ursola noted that all of them were armed.

Even Doran had his sword at the ready, reminding her that the battlemage had more tricks than simply spells to draw upon. Alaric looked up to the quarterdeck and fixed a questioning look on the artillerists loading the ballista, then he shifted his scrutiny to Captain Sylvia. Soon the knight and Helchen were both climbing up to join them.

"And what would you advise, since you know dragons so well?" Sylvia suddenly demanded of the dwarf. She pointed at Korsgaard as he supervised the pirates around the ballista. "Surely even a dragon won't be happy with a shot from that flying down his gob!"

"If you're lucky enough to hit him," Ursola grumbled, shaking her head. "Look around you. All this open space! Flamefang will fly circles around this ship. The way to fight a dragon is to pin it down, force it into a narrow spot where it can't avoid anything you throw at it." A low sigh rattled through her chest. "Then pray to your ancestors that everything you can do to it is enough to kill it before it can kill you."

Alaric's face was solemn as he stepped over to them. It was clear he'd heard enough of the conversation already. "What can we do? There's no way to make Flamefang sit still for us." He cast a hopeful look toward Helchen, grasping at a desperate possibility.

"That frost spell of Hulmul's ... I don't know." She shrugged, discomfort visible in every inch of her being. Ursola could tell the witch hunter was unnerved by the magic she'd invoked, even more disturbed by the prospect of utilizing it again. "Maybe Doran knows some other spell, but if so, he hasn't mentioned it."

Ursola wagged her finger at all of them. "There's a better

way than relying on fickle magic," she asserted. "Dragons are a bit like hawks. Very good eyesight, but not so keen in the dark. That's where they rely on their nose." The dwarf nodded at the distant island. "What we do is fall back and wait for night, then row in against the wind so Flamefang doesn't catch our scent."

Sylvia crossed her arms and scowled. "That won't do," she said, her voice dipping to a whisper so only the three around her would catch her words. "You might've noticed my crew are pirates. Foolhardy enough to match the most blood-crazed minotaur if there's plunder to be had. But these men expect to spend that plunder. Give them too much time to weigh the dangers against the rewards, and they'll demand to look for easier pickings." Her eyes roved across the group. "Wait for dark and we'll have a mutiny. No, we've got to head in now, before they decide they don't want to risk it."

"I've noticed that pirates don't like to take risks," Gaiseric stated.

"No more than a burglar likes to break into a house when everyone inside is awake," Sylvia rejoined.

"It may not matter anyway," Helchen said. "A sorceress like Yandryl is bound to have her own mystical ways of detecting ships that approach her island. If we land at all, I suspect it will be because she allows us to." The witch hunter opened her hands in a gesture of helplessness. "If Flamefang answers to her, she'll keep him docile. At least until she no longer has any interest in us."

Alaric set his eyes on the island. "Time could be of the essence and everyone in Korbara is depending on us. I support Sylvia and say we sail straight in."

Ursola wrinkled her nose, the faint smell of dragon still agitating her. "The difference between a fool and a hero is whether a bad idea pays off. Ancestors grant that we're not fools."

Gaiseric racked his brain for every superstition he'd ever heard about drawing good luck to oneself. He already had an old nail borrowed from the mate Mendoza nestled inside his mouth. Cold-wrought iron was supposed to turn aside misfortune, and the thief supposed a bit of deterrence was just as helpful.

It was all the talk of the dragon, of course. He'd been much like Sylvia's crew – too focused on the possibilities of treasure to really think much on what else was on the island. Now, though, Flamefang was about the only thing on his mind. Ursola's terrifying stories about the dragon – this specific dragon – made him almost want to be back in Singerva dodging packs of hungry zombies. "All things in perspective," Gaiseric reminded himself. "After all, there's only one Flamefang but if something isn't done, there'll be so many zombies they'll overrun the whole kingdom."

The thief leaned back against the mainmast and observed the crew as they adjusted the sails. The pirates were trying to angle The Demoness so that she would present her side to the island for as long as possible. It would let them bring more of their weaponry against Flamefang should the dragon come flying at them. Ursola didn't think the archers would accomplish much, but Gaiseric was impressed with the razor-edged harpoons both Ratbag and the ogre Brog had been issued. He knew the orc's strength and didn't think even a dragon would shrug off a spear thrown by him. He'd never dare say it around Ratbag, but Brog was clearly even stronger. It would be a bad day for Flamefang if the winged lizard got near either one of them.

"Unless, of course, Flamefang just sits out of range and burns the ship around us." Gaiseric tried not to think too much about that possibility. Instead, he focused on the narrow defile in the coral cliffs that served the island as a harbor. Even to his untrained eye, it looked unnatural. The cut was so precise in its outline that the opening might have been cleaved by a titan's axe. There were a few buildings on the shore and a stone jetty that reached out into the water. What little he could see of the island's interior was lush and green. He wondered if it resembled the fabled tropics he'd heard about once or twice from tinkers and other itinerant visitors to Mertz.

Alaric and the others were up on the foredeck, watching as the ship carried them closer to shore. Gaiseric thought landfall would only be the start of their problems. They'd still have to find Yandryl's castle, and from what he could see of the interior, it looked like the island was a veritable jungle. They might wander around for days without stumbling onto the citadel.

Then, as The Demoness drew near enough that the ship was nearly parallel to the cleft, Gaiseric saw a sight that stole his breath. Yandryl's castle was unmistakable, like a great marble spire stabbing up from the greenery. It stood upon a tall hill and from where it was situated, he could imagine it was placed in such a way as to afford a clear view down into the harbor. The tallest tower gleamed and sparkled in the sunlight, making Gaiseric wonder with what kind of material it was roofed to make it shine that way. A thrill went through him as he speculated upon gold or gemstones. Wizards and witches were peculiar, so anything was possible if some eccentric whim captured their fancy.

"I don't like it," Alaric declared as the ship made its way toward the jetty in a serpentine fashion, always keeping one side toward the shore. Gaiseric fell in with the knight as he went to join Sylvia up on the quarterdeck. "I don't like it," he repeated when he was in the captain's presence. "They should have seen us by now, yet there's not been any kind of activity."

"Maybe the witch really has gone away, and the servants have been sampling her wine cellar," Gaiseric suggested.

"We'll see," Sylvia said. "Mister Mendoza, wind the horn. If those lubbers ashore are drunk, wake them up." At her command, the first mate sauntered over to a curled length of ivory some ten feet long that was chained to the railing. Gaiseric thought it must have been taken from a sea serpent, then hollowed out by the pirates. Mendoza set his mouth to a brass ring where the horn tapered to its smallest point.

Immediately there sounded a low, dolorous note. It didn't ring through the air, it slithered with a lazy, lingering manner. Whatever its lack of speed, it certainly had volume. Gaiseric clamped his hands to his ears to temper the noise. Alaric grimaced and it impressed the thief that a knight accustomed to the roar of battle should find the horn's call unpleasant.

"Another blast, Mister Mendoza," Sylvia ordered. Her eyes roved along the shore, paying special interest to the buildings. They looked to be warehouses and some sort of dormitory, each built from the same white stone as the distant castle and ornately adorned with columns and balustrades. The second note, however, provoked as little reaction as the first. The doors and windows remained closed. Not a soul emerged to meet the ship as she approached the jetty.

"Maybe..." But whatever appeasing notion he was going to suggest went unsaid. Gaiseric couldn't deny that there was something eerie about the silence that loomed over the shore. While they were all happy they'd reached the island without provoking Flamefang, the dragon at least would have been a tangible menace. This... this was more unsettling because there wasn't anything visible to account for it.

"It looks peaceful," Alaric said, "but so does a grave." He dropped his hand to the sword at his side. "When we land, keep your wits sharp."

Sylvia laughed at the knight. "Sharp blades are more useful than sharp wits," she jeered. "I'll take a shore party to join you." She looked aside at Gaiseric and winked. "To protect the interests of my crew."

"An' ah'll be makin' it me business ter accompany ye," Korsgaard growled. He stepped away from the ballista, his artillerists following behind him. His cruel face contorted into a threatening leer. "Mindin' yer pardon, cap'n, but as quartarmastar of this here vess'l, ah be uniquely qualerfied ter adjuderkate fair shares all 'round o' whatev'r ye might be findin' ashore." He scratched his chest with his iron hook. "Yes, ye might be sayin' ah'm best suited ter pertect th' interests of this'n bunch o' sea-rats ye be callin' a crew."

Gaiseric could feel the intensity that sparked between the two pirates. Here, he suspected, was an old rivalry that had been waiting for the right moment to erupt. Much as he distrusted Sylvia, he trusted the other corsairs even less. Reluctantly, he took the captain's side. "I mean, somebody should stay with the ship…"

Korsgaard set a withering look on the thief. "Mist'r Mendozer be cap'ble enow an' not so eager ter run off wi'out nobody ter arm th' ballister." He grinned as he held up a curiously notched piece of iron. Gaiseric guessed it was some essential mechanism for the ballista that the quartermaster was going to keep as insurance against being marooned on the island.

Alaric moved to confront the rebellious pirate, but the moment he did, the artillerists started reaching for weapons. Sylvia motioned the knight back. "All right, Mister Korsgaard. I presume you intend to choose the other members of the shore party?"

"Ah'll be th' 'eart o' generoserty, an' let ye pick a few lads o' yer own," Korsgaard said.

Sylvia shot him a look that would have curdled an assassin's blood. "I only need one." She smiled. "Brog!" she shouted. "You're going ashore."

Gaiseric glanced down at the ogre and saw the pirate's brutish face split in a vicious smile. When he looked back at Korsgaard, he thought the quartermaster looked paler than he had before. Then craftiness worked itself onto his face.

"Ye'll be takin' th' orc wit' ye?" Korsgaard posed the question to Alaric in a rough laugh. "Aye, ah'm a-thinkin' ye'd be havin' trouble makin' th' cur stay aboard." He glanced back at Sylvia, amusement still in his tone. "There'll be a fracas twixt thet pair, sure as sure. An' when it happ'ns, Brog'll find

th' orc's got as many friends as it takes ter decide th' matt'r."
Laughing again, the quartermaster turned on his heel and
headed below to gather his gear.

"I thought we'd have trouble with Ursola, now we've this
man to worry about," Alaric stated when Korsgaard was gone.

"Korsgaard was always a scoundrel," Doran opined. "If he
was captain of this ship instead of Sylvia, I doubt the Swords
of Korbara would have engaged The Demoness for such a
critical mission." He scratched at his bushy beard. "Another
reason I'm here. Not just to secure Mournshroud but to act as
the council's representative."

"Don't worry, he won't cause trouble until he sees
something he wants to steal," Gaiseric said. He looked over at
Sylvia for confirmation.

"He'll not try anything until he thinks we're not useful
anymore," Sylvia said. "I could say the same thing for nine out
of ten of my crew. A pirate's loyalty is as fickle as the fullness
of his purse."

"You don't say?" Gaiseric prodded Sylvia, and was surprised
to see a contemplative expression appear on her face.

"I made ten voyages with my father from the Islands of
Dartarr to Mordava," she reminisced. "Our ship was beset by
pirates four times. After that fourth attack, the pirate captain
asked for volunteers from our crew to supplement his own."
A grim laugh rolled off her tongue. "I don't know who was
more surprised, my father or Bloody Pieter, when I offered
to join the pirates." She shook her head. "My father made
me work hard. The life of a pirate looked easier. As long as
you kept from getting a knife in the back while asleep. The
Jolly Brotherhood isn't exactly a healthy family and there are

a lot of branches in the tree who'd slit your gizzard for rum money."

"I know that sort quite well." Gaiseric shook his head. "No thought for anyone or anything but themselves." He gave Alaric a sheepish look. "I was just that kind."

"But you aren't now," the knight said without hesitation.

Gaiseric felt his heart swell with pride to hear Alaric say those words. "No… I'm not like that now." There were times when he wished he was, but now wasn't one of them.

The Demoness hung offshore while the landing party moored their longboat to the jetty. Helchen had worried the boat would founder, so overloaded had it seemed. The ogre alone weighed as much as six men and Korsgaard had crammed ten more pirates aboard before they set off. She wondered at the rivalry between captain and quartermaster. Perhaps it was unfair to Sylvia, but Helchen's chief concern wasn't over who ended up with command of the ship, but how that would affect their own mission. She wasn't sure if either of the pirate officers had the integrity to carry them back to Korbara, even if they did get what they were after. Of course, if Doran didn't come back, those mutinous pirates would have a lot of explaining to do the next time they met with the templars, but the ruffians might take the risk for the reward anyway.

Marching down the jetty, Helchen could feel the disturbing silence wrapping around her like a funereal shroud. "There's something wrong here," she declared, gripping her mace.

Doran gave her an icy look. "The Order teaches their fanatics that even the least manifestation of magic is wrong.

This island has played host to the conjurations of a sorceress for centuries at least. Every twig and rock must have some sort of arcane residue clinging to it."

Helchen scowled at the battlemage. "I've tracked enough witches and renegades back to their lairs to know what they feel like. This is different." She racked her memory, groping for the nagging similarity that vexed her.

The first of the party to reach the shore was Ratbag. Helchen wasn't sure if the orc's senses had picked up on something outside the human range or if he was simply impatient for a fight... any kind of fight. Certainly, Sylvia was of the latter opinion, doing her utmost to keep Brog away from Ratbag.

Helchen looked on as Ratbag prowled the shore. Suddenly his hands tightened about the grip of his scimitar. He turned toward a boathouse that stretched away from the other buildings. Exhibiting a surprising degree of silence, the orc stalked his way to the building.

"Ratbag's spotted something," Gaiseric explained, as though no one else could see for themselves.

"Be ready to help him," Alaric ordered. The knight only received amused smirks from the pirates. Muttering a curse under his breath, he jogged down the rest of the jetty, Gaiseric and Ursola following close behind.

"Come along, spellslinger," Helchen snapped at Doran. "They might need some of your magic."

"Or some of yours," Doran chided her as they hurried toward the boathouse. Helchen gave the man a dark look, then scolded herself for rising to the bait. The battlemage knew precisely what to say to get under her skin.

Ratbag had the door to the boathouse down after only a

couple of kicks. Helchen was close enough when it crashed inward to be sickened by the stench that came billowing out. She was reminded of Singerva after they'd made their way down into the subterranean vaults of Ironshield and Company to find the place strewn with corpses. This was the same sort of reek, the revolting odor of a forgotten massacre.

Muffling her face against the stench, Helchen followed Ratbag into the boathouse. Alaric joined them, taking a defensive stance near the door should they need to make a hasty escape.

It took a moment for Helchen's eyes to adjust to the darkness that filled the building. Any light streaming into the place was limited to the door behind her and a jagged breach in the wall across from her. The shimmer of light reflecting off water rippled along the ceiling, and she could hear the sea sloshing about in the narrow channel that ran though the boathouse.

Then, as her gaze became accustomed to the murk, Helchen spotted the first of many bodies. A woman… at least she thought it had once been a woman. The corpse was hideously clawed and chewed. All the hallmarks of a zombie attack, but the magnitude of the damage disturbed her. They'd seen more than their share of slaughtered victims, but nothing like this. As she turned, she spotted other corpses, all of them equally mangled. It was hard to take comfort from the idea that their killers had been so violent that they didn't leave enough intact to rise again as a zombie.

"Da cadavaz work," Ratbag growled, kicking a severed arm into the water.

"I'm not so sure." Doran stepped into the boathouse, a

nimbus of magical light shining from his hand. He gestured to a shadowy corner, the arcane glow illuminating what it held: a corpse, taller and more massive than that of any human. Helchen had only to glance over at Ratbag to see a living specimen of the creature lying there with a marlin spike through its skull. The boathouse had been attacked by orcs. That explained the extensive damage inflicted on the corpses. Doran turned and shone his light across the rest of the interior, revealing more dead orcs mixed among the butchered humans.

"This doesn't make sense," Alaric said. "What would a warband be doing here, so far from the frontier?" He jabbed the point of his sword at one of the green-skinned bodies. "How'd they even get here?"

"Maybe you should ask your friend," Doran said, drawing his own sword as he fixed his gaze on Ratbag. "There's been rumors that the orc tribes have started to cross the frontier. Ready to take advantage while we're fighting the Black Plague." He pointed at a dead orc lying near Ratbag. "Tell me, what tribe does that one come from?"

Ratbag spat on the dead orc. "Cadavaz," he snorted. "Alla dem cadavaz."

Helchen thought about what Ratbag had said before about how the orclands were also besieged by the undead. Coming between Doran and Ratbag, she compelled the battlemage to shine his light more fully on one of the dead orcs.

"There's your answer, Doran," she said. The light revealed that the orc's skin was mottled with splotches of gray and yellow, that the hide had split and burst in places to expose the rancid meat within. A scum of dried blood clung to the lips and fangs. It was obvious the orc had been dead for a long time. As she directed Doran's attention back to the human bodies, it was clear why there was a problem. Death had come much more recently to the victims than it had to their killers.

"Undead orcs," Doran gasped. "I've never read of such a thing before."

"Nor is there any record of zombie orcs in the Order's archives," Helchen stated. She nodded at the monstrous body. "But there's all the evidence you need. Maybe the orcs have been dealing with these things for a long time, only nobody bothered to ask them."

"Ya noodlin' good, bluenose," Ratbag barked. The orc slapped Helchen on the back, almost knocking her down. "Lotsa cadavaz muckin' up der turf." His red eyes glowered at Doran, and Helchen was reminded once more that while they couldn't understand everything the orc said, he didn't have that problem with what they said.

Doran tapped the flat of his sword against one of the dead orcs. "Zombie orcs," he said, a shudder in his tone. He shifted his worried look to Helchen and Alaric. "We should be on our guard. There's bound to be more on this island."

"We've fought more than our share of zombies," Alaric reminded the battlemage. "Both human and otherwise."

Helchen shook her head. "From everything I see here, these appear stronger. Besides, you're forgetting your own questions."

"What am I forgetting?" the knight wondered.

Helchen removed her hat and wiped a cold sweat from her brow. "How these things got here. Zombies wouldn't just happen on this island. They were led here."

"Bonecalla," Ratbag snarled, hate fairly drooling off his tongue.

It didn't need Gaiseric to translate. "Necromancer," Helchen said. She looked back at the dead orcs. Dread pulsed through her heart. It was bad enough to consider a rabble of undead orcs, but to think there was a necromancer commanding them was far worse. Yet she knew it had to be the truth. "A necromancer must have brought them here. Maybe to find the very relic we're after."

The witch hunter mulled over that possibility. It couldn't be a coincidence, to be looking for an orcish relic enchanted against the undead only to find orc zombies on the very island where the artifact was kept. An orc necromancer knew it was here. Her voice was dire as she pronounced the zombie-master's purpose. "Yes, to find Mournshroud... and destroy it."

CHAPTER TWELVE

The forest was more rank than lush, in Gaiseric's opinion. He was hardly an expert on trees and flowers, but it seemed to him that there was something unpleasant and unnatural about the woods that stretched all around them. There wasn't any physical deformity to the trunks, no uncanny color to the flowers, nothing so tangible upon which he could cement the disturbing sense that the place was off. He wondered if it was simply the carnage down at the shore and the thought that even now the forest might be harboring orcish zombies, remorseless monsters eager to tear him apart.

"This is an evil place," Gaiseric commented while he marched down the trail. It was the only one that led away from the desolate harbor. The only route that presented an obvious path to Yandryl's castle.

"It's the dragon," Ursola said. The dwarf turned her head and spat into the bush she passed.

"You've been blaming everything on the dragon since we sighted this island," Doran reproved her. "Not all the ills of the world are the fault of dragons."

Ursola scowled at the battlemage, then looked over at

Gaiseric. "The reason the forest bothers you is because it's dead. Oh, I don't mean the trees and such. They're lively enough. But a forest should sparkle with birdsong, rustle with the scampering of little things in the scrub." She nodded at the canopy overhead. "Without a breeze to stir it, those boughs are as still as the shoring of the Underking's grand hall." She gave Doran a sharp look. "That's the dragon. Animals have sense enough to shun any place marked by a wyrm's musk. Yandryl must keep a tight leash on Flamefang otherwise his spoor would've withered all these plants." The dwarf nodded, more to herself than her listeners. "The elf witch probably keeps him somewhere in her castle, or maybe gave him a cave somewhere in the cliffs to make his lair."

Gaiseric lifted his head to stare up at the cliffs when Ursola mentioned them, but the branches that spread above the path were too thick to provide any but the most fragmentary glimpse of the heights that ringed the island's interior. He thought it was the better part of an hour since they'd last been able to see the castle through the trees. It seemed to him, however, that they should be getting close to the hill.

"Dragon or not," Sylvia said, "there's been no trace of anyone since we left the harbor." She kept close to Brog, her eyes continually roving along the edge of the path.

"It's only natural for anyone fleeing zombies to seek shelter in the castle," Gaiseric suggested. He regretted the words when he saw Alaric wince. It was obvious he was thinking of Castle von Mertz and how its fortifications had offered no shelter to his own family.

The knight shook his head. "If they have, then the zombies

must have followed them. They'd keep after any survivors until there wasn't anyone left to kill."

"There might still be people in the castle," Helchen offered. "It would explain why we've only seen slain undead. The active ones could be surrounding the castle. That would also explain why none of them have been drawn to us."

"There's a cheery thought," Gaiseric said, picturing in his mind the view from Vasilescu's roof as the undead infesting Singerva kept trickling into the plaza.

Doran smiled at the thief. "Here's a better one. Yandryl is a powerful mistress of the arcane sciences. She might not have acted fast enough to save her servants at the harbor, but it's more than possible she used her magic to annihilate the undead invaders when they came near her citadel."

A warning grunt sounded from the path ahead. Prowling away from the main group, Ratbag had been scouting the trail for them. Now the orc came jogging back, an expression of violent impatience in his eyes. "Ya don' know fer nothun, dewdroppa," Ratbag told Doran. "Der fay yegg ain't bumped alla der cadavaz."

The orc pointed his scimitar at the path ahead. Gaiseric could faintly hear rustling in the brush, then a foul stink seeped into the air. It was a rotten smell, but not like the stench of a normal corpse. It had a mildew quality about it mixed with the unpleasantness of spoiled milk.

"Steady," Alaric called out, his voice firm and unwavering. Gaiseric had heard that commanding tone before, the voice of a leader anticipating battle.

The source of the sounds and smell suddenly sprang from the thick undergrowth. It was a thin, wizened creature, slightly shorter than a human and wearing the tatters of a leather hauberk. The face had a pinched appearance with a low brow, long nose, and a sharp-toothed mouth that seemed overlarge for its head. Its skin had a leathery look to it and retained a light green complexion where it hadn't given way to splotches of grayish decay.

"Goblin," Doran named the creature. A spark of electricity shot from the battlemage's finger and seared a hole through the monster's forehead. It crumpled to the ground without so much as a squeak of protest.

Gaiseric gave the twice-dead creature a closer look. The goblin didn't seem particularly threatening. Not compared to an orc. Things could be much worse, he thought, when Ratbag dashed his hopes.

"Even cadavaz, goblinz never do der lone hand," Ratbag snapped at the humans around him. The cause for the orc's warning quickly lunged out of the forest. Six more goblins, all of them invested with the decayed animation of the undead, charged toward the living flesh they sensed on the path.

Ratbag's scimitar tore one of the wizened creatures in half. A bolt from Helchen's crossbow punched through another goblin's eye. The rest of the zombies took no notice of their losses but plunged straight ahead. Gaiseric saw one of them clawing at Alaric's shield, frenzied in its efforts to sink its teeth into the knight.

An undead goblin plowed into Gaiseric, knocking him off his feet. He hit the ground hard, the breath rushing out of him in a single gasp. More by instinct than thought, he caught at the zombie as it dove on him. The edge of his sword pressed against the creature's belly, spilling rotten entrails over the thief. His attacker paid no heed to its injury, but only became more vicious in its efforts to rend his flesh. Gaiseric could feel the clawed fingers scratching at his armor. He locked one hand around the goblin's throat, defying the repugnance its greasy, moldering skin provoked. He had to keep those sharp teeth away from his own face.

Dimly, Gaiseric was aware of the sounds of battle all around him. From the corner of his eye, he could see a zombie lumber out from the forest shadows. It was far bigger and bulkier than the goblin. With a sinking feeling, the rogue recognized it as an undead orc. Seeing destroyed examples of this horror in the boathouse didn't fully prepare him for the experience of watching the necrotic monster shuffle onto the path.

Then, Gaiseric's entire world narrowed to the broad, fear-inducing grin of the goblin. He was losing his struggle against the zombie's frightful energy. Inch by inch, it pressed closer toward his face. It champed its teeth together only a hairsbreadth from the tip of his nose and he knew that the next moment he would feel those teeth tearing into his flesh.

Only in the next moment a shining blur whipped across the zombie. The top of its head, everything above the bridge of its long nose, went spinning away in a spray of rancid blood and brains. The wizened corpse collapsed across Gaiseric, the fell magic animating it broken. He shoved the loathsome thing to one side and scrambled to his feet.

"Poor way to start a fight," Doran said, the goblin's blood spattered along his sword. "If they're close enough to drip on you, they're too close." The battlemage spun about, sending another crackle of lightning speeding along the path. It scorched the skull of a zombie orc, dropping the creature before it could come at Sylvia from behind.

Gaiseric tightened his grip on his sword and made a quick assessment of the state of things. The goblins, as fast and frenzied as the zombies they'd identified as runners back in Singerva, had merely been the advance of a much larger mob. Twenty, perhaps thirty orcish undead were converging upon the path. They moved with the sluggish, clumsy manner typical of zombies. However, when one of them caught hold of the pirate fighting beside Korsgaard, Gaiseric saw that the brawn of an orc yet lingered in these decayed monsters.

The man's arm was wrenched from its socket, the flesh tearing under the zombie's powerful grasp. The corsair fell in a screaming welter of blood, the orc's claws continuing to rip into his body. Korsgaard blanched at the revolting scene but retained enough of his own bloodthirsty mettle to hew through the zombie's neck with his cutlass and send its head rolling off into the trees.

"There's too many of them!" Sylvia cursed. Both her axe and sword were dripping with the tomb-filth hacked from zombie bodies. The hulking ogre beside her was spattered with rancid undead blood. Around them no less than a half dozen of the orcish creatures were sprawled in a final, true death.

"And more on the way!" Alaric shouted back, caving in the skull of a zombie whose legs he'd cut out from under it.

The knight's dour assessment was only too true. From every side, it seemed, the bushes were rustling and more of the ghastly horde lumbered into view. Gaiseric glanced back the way they'd come. "Maybe we can make it to the ship before we're surrounded." It was, he thought, a better plan than trying to force their way ahead for who knew how far in a forest infested with orc zombies.

"Yer talkin' true sense, pocket-pick'r," Korsgaard declared. "Lads! Beat a course back to The Demoness an' leave th' blasted island to th' lubbers!" The quartermaster's words roused the pirates. In a moment, Gaiseric knew, they'd disengage from the zombies and flee back to the harbor, not caring if anyone else followed them or whether they would be overwhelmed once the buccaneers were gone. Inadvertently, he felt that he'd brought about a disaster.

The disaster descended from a far different quarter than Gaiseric expected. The first warning was a thick, cloying smell that blotted out even the rotten stench of the zombies. Then there was a notable warmth that crept into the air. The branches began to wave from side to side, buffeted by a strong breeze.

Ursola put a name to the thing Gaiseric already knew was soaring above the forest. "Flamefang!" the dwarf hissed with a strange admixture of awe, hate, and fear.

Gaiseric had no such confusion of emotion. When the sunlight flickering through the boughs was abruptly blotted out by a vast body that flew between the trees and the sky, the thief only felt terror. He was rather proud of himself that he didn't scream… until the branches overhead crashed down and a gigantic, scaly shape plummeted onto the path.

Dragon! He'd grown up seeing the wyrm on the von Mertz coat of arms, listened as a boy to fables where brave knights rescued beautiful princesses from fire-breathing lizards. Gazing on the beast that had descended upon them, Gaiseric realized only a child could have believed such stories. It would take an entire army to fight something like this.

Flamefang was enormous, fifty feet from his blunt reptilian snout to the spiny barb at the end of his long, tapering tail. His scaly body was crimson, gradually fading to a dull yellow on his underside and belly. Ribbed horns curled back from his somehow snake-like head. The jaws looked strong enough to crush a millstone and the fangs that lined them were like swords. Four powerful legs, muscle rippling beneath the scaly hide, pawed the ground, gouging deep craters in the path. Two wings, leathery pinions each as big as The Demoness's mainsail, were now curled against his undulating back between the spiked spine that ran in a ridge down the body. The eyes, slitted like those of a serpent, considered the combat raging around the dragon with vicious contempt.

So awed by the mighty wyrm's presence was Gaiseric, that he almost didn't see the zombie until it was on him. He scrambled back, stabbing his blade with all the force he could muster. Somehow, he penetrated the thick orcish skull and pulverized the brain within. He scrambled away from the body. "Keep your wits," he chided himself, "or you won't need a dragon to finish you off."

Flamefang loomed over the fray for a moment. His descent had obliterated several zombies, crushing them to pulp under his claws and stopping the flight of Korsgaard and his comrades. When he lashed his tail and mangled a pair of orcish undead, Gaiseric began to hope the reptile was there to help them, perhaps sent by Yandryl. His eyes widened in alarm when he saw Ursola getting ready to lob a fire-bomb at the dragon.

"No!" the thief shouted. He reached the dwarf just before she could throw the incendiary, catching her arm and preventing the attack. Before he could explain his reasoning, Ursola gave him a weary smile.

"You're right, it'd be a waste of a good bomb," she huffed. "It'll need more heat than this to tickle a dragon." Gaiseric started to voice his idea that Flamefang was there to help when Ursola grabbed him around the waist and pushed them both to the ground.

"Dragonsbreath!" she shrieked in warning.

Dimly, Gaiseric noted that Flamefang had reared up onto his hind legs, his horned head tearing apart the canopy above. Then, swift as a thunderbolt, the dragon threw his torso forward. From his gaping maw, a blast of rippling flame exploded. Gaiseric's skin prickled as the heat seared the air above him. He twisted his head aside, away from the source of that immolating spume. By doing so, he was witness to the carnage wrought by the dragon's fire. Two pirates were doing their best to fend off several zombies when everything around them was engulfed in the reptile's fury. The blast reduced mortal and undead alike to charred husks that lay steaming before a blackened and smoldering swathe of forest.

"Quick, before he attacks again!" Alaric was smashing sword against shield to draw all eyes to him. He gestured to the path leading deeper into the forest. It was the only real choice, Gaiseric realized. Flamefang was blocking the way back to the harbor.

"So much for the wyrm helping us," Gaiseric snarled as he ran along the path.

The dragon continued to vent his fury upon whatever

was closest to him, uncaring whether he killed pirates or destroyed zombies. With their slow, plodding movements, there were far more of the undead that fell within Flamefang's reach. The living survivors of the wyrm's assault hurried to follow Alaric's lead. Doran cast hasty spells at the zombies which stood in their way, hoping that his attacks were lethal since many of the undead orcs did not rise again.

"The castle!" Alaric goaded them onward. "We have to make for the castle!" He swung his sword to crush the skull of an orc zombie that staggered out from the underbrush. It was obvious to Gaiseric that the further inland they went, the more zombies there were.

"We don't know if it's safe!" Sylvia shouted back, whipping her axe across the arm of a zombie that reached for her from the forest. Brog finished the mangled creature by crushing its head in one burly fist.

"Maybe not, but we know it's not safe back there!" Helchen pointed out, indicating the forest behind them. Smoke billowed up the path from all the vegetation Flamefang had set alight.

Gaiseric rushed along with the others, his mind racing. There were so many ways things could get worse. All the zombies in the forest might indicate an even bigger force laying siege to the castle. Or it might be that Yandryl was aware of the shore party and had sent Flamefang to destroy them deliberately. It didn't need an undead army to bar their way into the citadel. The sorceress and her guards were just as capable. If they did find the entrance closed, he knew he'd be the one everyone would look to to get them inside. He wouldn't know for sure until he actually saw the place, but he suspected it wouldn't be so easy as getting inside Vasilescu's tower. He shivered at the memory of that perilous climb above a plaza filled with zombies.

"Marked cards and loaded dice," Gaiseric muttered. At some point, his luck simply had to get better.

Abruptly, the greenery of the forest gave way to a grassy hill flanked by deep ravines. Upon that hill stood the citadel of the sorceress. From the sea, it had looked to Gaiseric to be a majestic palace of marble with jeweled turrets and gold-capped roofs. Now that he was closer, he could see that what splendor the castle had possessed was now blackened and fouled by the stamp of violence. Great chunks had been knocked out of the walls. The facade was scored around many of the windows and doors by raging fires. The hoardings, once indeed capped in gold, were now flattened and twisted, marring the precision of the construction by leaning out across the battlements in tangled snarls of wood and metal.

"No sign of any guards," Sylvia said as they all looked up at the fortress. Indeed, for the past few minutes they hadn't even been bothered by any zombies in the forest.

"That's not a good sign," Gaiseric decided. He'd almost have preferred one of the dire scenarios he'd imagined to this deadly silence and brooding devastation. He nodded at the main gates, ponderous steel-banded portals that were now splintered and drooping from their hinges. He looked over at Alaric. "We're not the first ones to pay Yandryl a visit."

The knight digested that obvious fact. "How do you suggest we proceed?"

Gaiseric frowned. As much as he appreciated the

confidence and respect that question implied, he didn't like the responsibility that went with it.

Especially since he wasn't sure how to answer.

The decision was taken away from him when Ursola pointed up at the sky. While the rest of them had been studying the castle or watching the forest for more zombies, the dwarf had only one thing on her mind. The creature her sharp eyes had spotted was flying a circuit above the island's interior. "Flamefang!" she cried.

The dragon was too distant to have possibly heard the shout, but the reptile must have spotted them in the same instant. Flamefang's flight suddenly diverted. The wyrm came winging straight toward the citadel and the band of intruders gathered at the base of the hill. Gaiseric's heart hammered inside his chest when he saw how quickly the beast covered the distance.

"How do we proceed?" Gaiseric yelled. "I say we run and put what's left of those walls between ourselves and that monster!" The thief put his words into action, charging up the hill toward the broken gates.

His companions lost no time following his example.

CHAPTER THIRTEEN

Helchen raced for the gateway. Every step she expected an arrow from a hidden guard to strike her down. Whatever the appearances, she wasn't convinced Yandryl's citadel was deserted. A steel-tipped arrow or some malefic spell would kill just as quickly as Flamefang's fiery breath. It was a certainty that the latter would be her fate if she tarried. If the castle's denizens did cut her down, then at least she'd die trying to save herself rather than idly awaiting destruction.

The witch hunter kept turning her head as she hurried up the hill. As though drawn by a magnetic force, her gaze instantly found the dragon. First, he was several miles away, little bigger than a hawk in her sight. A second glance and the beast was slightly more than a mile away, curled horns and lashing tail removing any delusion about what she was looking at. She was just scrambling up onto the hilltop when the musky, ophidian smell of the wyrm struck her nose. Flamefang was less than half a mile from them now and she could see the jaws opening wide, the flicker of light deep within the dragon's throat.

Plunging forward in a desperate lunge, Helchen brushed

across one of the leaning doors before tumbling through the entrance. She turned her dive into a roll as she struck the polished floor. Her jarring retreat ended when she slammed into an armored body.

"Lampin' whut yeh about, abercrombie," Ratbag grumbled as he pulled her off his back. The orc shifted onto his side and stared back toward the gateway, his eyes widening with alarm.

Helchen didn't really want to know what could frighten an orc, but she felt compelled to turn and look at what had seized Ratbag's attention. She gagged. It looked like all the fugitives had reached the castle in that mad, frantic scramble. It also looked like it hadn't done them any good at all.

The walls shook as Flamefang slammed against them, his wings making a hollow sound when they slapped the masonry and arrested the dragon's momentum. The reptile's head was just outside the gateway, his jaw agape. That light deep within his throat expanded into a blinding inferno as the wyrm spewed his fire at the gateway.

The witch hunter expected annihilation, wondering at the irony that after consigning so many suspected necromancers to pyres she should die by immolation. She clenched her eyes against the searing light. When a moment passed and she didn't feel the burn of flames licking across her flesh, she wondered if Marduum had simply drawn her soul directly into his divine keeping and spared her a fiery death.

Cries exploded all around her, but they weren't the agonized screams she'd expected. Helchen blinked at Sylvia as the captain threw her hands up in an exultant cheer. Alaric was beating sword and shield together in jubilation. A glance at the gateway showed her why.

Expecting a hideous death, they instead had been delivered from the dragon's power. The gout of fire Flamefang spewed at them was blown back into the reptile's face. The wyrm was immune to his own breath, but the effect broke his attack. As the cascade of billowing flame was choked off, the dragon glared at them from outside the citadel.

"A ward! A ward against the wyrm!" Doran shouted, gesturing with his sword at the keystone in the arched gateway above the broken doors. It glowed with a silvery light, some sort of elven sigil etched across its surface.

Flamefang's angry hiss was like the quenching of steel. The dragon stamped his claws into the hill, gouging deep pits in the ground. He made one effort to thrust his head through the gateway but recoiled as if he'd smashed his face into solid stone.

"Looks like the witch wasn't completely confident she could maintain control of her pet," Ursola laughed. The dwarf jeered at Flamefang with an obscene gesture.

"Let's not press our luck," Alaric said, laying a restraining hand on her shoulder. He looked over at Helchen. "It's certain we're not leaving the same way we came," he told the witch hunter.

"That…" But Helchen didn't finish her response. As though he'd understood the knight's words, Flamefang withdrew from the gateway. He cast a last withering look at them, then his leathery pinions were beating at the air and lifting him back into the sky.

Gaiseric sprinted to the smashed doors, sword clenched in his fist for all the good it would do him. "He's leaving!" the thief reported as he stared into the sky. The joy that flickered onto his face crashed into despondency. With a shout, he scrambled back inside, almost falling over himself in his haste.

"Scratch that." Gaiseric shook his head. "He's sticking. Circling around up there like a vulture."

"You can bet he's just waiting for somebody to try making a run for it," Sylvia said, her painted face drooping into a scowl. "We'd be ashes before we reached the trees."

"Only if we're fool enough to meet the dragon on his own terms," Alaric said. Helchen heard the sternness in his voice. The knight was trying to quench the despair that was creeping over them. "Any fortress worth being called one has a back way out so those inside can escape a siege." He looked over at Gaiseric and Helchen recalled how the thief had used a hidden tunnel to slip out of Castle von Mertz several times.

"Ye be ov'rly optermestic, steel-shorts," Korsgaard challenged Alaric, shaking his hook at the knight. "Th' witch might be usin' hexes an' spells t' magic herself away."

Helchen stared down the defiant quartermaster. There were few who could hold the witch hunter's gaze when she was trying to cow them. Korsgaard wasn't one of those few. "If Yandryl used magic to leave the citadel, we'll find out," she told the pirate, faking more confidence on the point than she felt. She let her imperious mantle slip into a reassuring smile. "Why do you think we brought along a wizard of our own?" she asked, nodding at Doran. The battlemage just stared back, neither denying nor supporting her bluff.

"In the meantime, don't forget where we are," Sylvia told them. She turned to address not just Korsgaard, but all the remaining pirates. "This is where we wanted to be. The elf's palace." A greedy glint shone in her eyes, and she clenched her fist as though closing it around a handful of gold. "And it doesn't look as if anybody's going to contest our claim on any of her treasure!"

The appeal to greed and the promise that there was another way out was enough to re-invigorate their flagging spirits. Rallying to their original purpose, the shore party fanned out across the entry hall. There wasn't much in the sprawling chamber that Helchen considered remarkable. It was elegantly constructed, with a high ceiling and ornate columns flanking the archway at its other end. Much of the effect was marred by the blood and bodies strewn about. There were a few orcs and goblins, the creatures bearing all the necrotic evidence of having been undead. Most of the corpses, however, were those of humans, their bodies every bit as mauled as those they'd seen in the boathouse. The fragmented mail and crumpled plate they wore hadn't been enough to guard them from the brawn of zombie orcs.

They headed out through the archway, deeper into the castle. Signs of combat made it clear that Yandryl's household hadn't meekly submitted to the undead invaders. It was jarring to see the finery of the rooms they passed and the halls they moved through contrasted with the gore that marred them. Rich rugs fouled by pools of blood, beautiful tapestries hacked apart by blade and claw. Furnishing that would have been too lavish for a duke's household lay shattered beneath the carcass of a twice-dead orc or charred by fires set by retreating defenders.

"Loot?" Korsgaard howled when inspecting the shards of what had once been a crystal statue of incalculable value. "Th' grave-cheatin' scallywags 'ave turn'd th' place inter a junkyard!"

The other pirates grumbled in agreement, frustrated by the ruination of these rich fixtures.

"As long as Mournshroud is still intact," Doran said, oblivious to piratical anxieties. "Korbara's safety depends on finding it."

"But where do we start looking?" Alaric asked.

Helchen gave that question some thought. "Were Yandryl a human sorceress, I'd suggest heading up," she told the knight. "Wizards often consult the stars, using the constellations to augur the future." She glanced over at Doran and the battlemage nodded his head in confirmation. "For convenience, they keep what they consider their most useful – and coveted – possessions close to these stellar observatories."

Ursola added a further thought. "Yandryl has been raiding dwarf strongholds for generations." The use of the last word impressed Helchen, for she knew a single generation of the long-lived dwarves represented many human generations. "She's stolen far more than just Mournshroud from my people. Whatever treasury she's keeping her plunder in, it'll have to be big."

The pirates forgot their own griping as they listened to the conversation. "What are we waiting for?" Sylvia asked. She looked over at her corsair crew. "Forget the meager pickings down here! Let's find where the witch keeps all the good stuff!"

The suggestion brought avaricious smiles to the other pirates. In their excitement, they roved ahead of Ratbag as they navigated the halls. Such was their enthusiasm that the pirates failed to notice that one particular gallery was occupied until they'd already turned the corner.

Helchen stopped short as she came up behind the surprised pirates. Ahead of them was a long, narrow hallway, its walls cut into niches where ornate statuary stood upon marble pedestals.

Or at least had stood. For the gallery was now infested by green-skinned monsters, hulking undead orcs that were busy throwing down the statues and smashing them on the floor. The zombies practiced their vandalism with a chilling precision, devoid of the bestial glee Helchen had always associated with orcish raids. Like anything undead, the creatures simply did, they didn't feel. That distinction made it all the easier to spot the one exception to the rule.

Far down the gallery, beyond the twenty or so zombies destroying the statues, a lone figure capered about in obscene, malicious delight. He was arrayed in a crude mantle of flayed hides, the leather stitched together with wide bands of gut. Though somewhat shorter and far leaner than Ratbag, the creature was obviously an orc – a living orc, for no zombie could display such an expression of deliberate wickedness on its features. His skin was a pasty greenish gray, what Helchen presumed must pass for pallor among orcs. Fearsome tattoos were inked over much of that gray skin, tribal patterns that lent the creature an even more malignant aspect.

A necklace of fingerbones hung around the orc's neck and about his waist, tied together by their hair, was a collection of human heads. In his hands he gripped a gnarled staff topped by the thick skull of a dwarf. If his association with the zombies wasn't enough, the palpable evil Helchen sensed in the creature's accouterments marked him for a necromancer; confirmation that the foul arcane practice wasn't limited to evil humans but was also employed among vicious orcs stunned the witch hunter. The authors of The Sword of Sorcerers had insisted necromancy was known only among human adepts, to whom its vile energies were in peculiar sympathy. Whether by ignorance or invention, the instructional tome adopted by the Order had misled generations of its adherents. Helchen wondered what else she'd been taught had been wrong or outright fabrications.

The orc zombie-master noticed the mortals who'd stumbled onto him almost in the same instant that they spotted him. Surprise shone in his beady, piggish eyes. Helchen noticed that his gaze was fixated on Ratbag.

Ratbag glared back at the necromancer. "Skargash," he snarled, spitting the name across the gallery.

"Ya scarper'd off, gink," Skargash snarled back. He brushed his hand across the fingerbone necklace, lingering over a gap in the morbid collection. "Now ya get der bump!"

The orc necromancer pointed his staff. Helchen expected some deathly spell to leap from the dwarvish skull. Instead, something behind Skargash lurched to its feet. The gallery had a ten-foot ceiling, but the horror rising to the conjurer's command was so large it had to bow its head. The thing exhibited the roughest semblance to a human form. Its legs were short in proportion to its dimensions while the arms that swung from its shoulders were so long that the knuckles brushed the floor. Its misshapen head jutted forward on the merest stump of a neck. The face was almost a caricature, dominated by a huge bulbous nose and a wide gash of a mouth. The monster's flesh was a deep green speckled with blue and the wiry hair that sprouted from its scalp was a dull black. Vapid, bleary eyes set their empty gaze on the people at the end of the hall.

"Croak 'em!" Skargash commanded the monster. "Croak alla dem mugs!"

Helchen expected a roar or a bellow, but when the giant beast started charging down the gallery, the only sound was that of its feet slapping the floor. It was then that she realized both what the thing was and why it obeyed Skargash.

The monster was a troll. And it was one of the necromancer's zombie abominations.

CHAPTER FOURTEEN

"Burn it!" Alaric shouted as the undead troll charged down the gallery. His mind raced, trying to remember everything he'd ever heard about trolls while serving in the king's army. Fire was especially potent against these monsters. Living or dead, he prayed that the same vulnerability held true.

Doran stepped forward, one hand extended, an arcane scroll held in the other. From his outstretched palm, a billowing spurt of flame rushed toward the enormous zombie. The magic fire washed across the warty green hide, charring the skin and the few rags the troll wore. That was all. The battlemage gawked in disbelief as the creature kept barreling down the corridor, uttering not so much as a grunt of pain from the searing spell.

"Wizards." Ursola scowled. The troll only gained a few yards before she lobbed one of her bombs at the monster. The thing was swathed in fire from head to toe, the flames licking around its misshapen body. Still the undead made no cry of pain. Still the zombie's charge didn't falter. A moving pillar of fire, looking more like an elemental than anything of material substance, the creature continued to advance.

"How about we run now?" Gaiseric asked. The thief had his sword ready but didn't seem excited about using it.

Alaric could see the orc necromancer gesturing to his other zombies, sending some of the creatures to support his troll. Just dealing with the abomination looked questionable, now the odds were getting much worse. "Withdraw!" he shouted, pointing his sword at the corner behind them. "Regroup in the conservatory!" The room was chosen more at random than from any tactical insight. With its beds of exotic flowers and strange plants, he was also sure that everyone would remember it and not confuse it with any of the other slaughterhouse chambers they'd passed through.

"Ya noodlin' sumthin'?" Ratbag growled at Alaric as they rounded the corner and fled down the connecting hall. His face burned with barely repressed hate. It struck Alaric that if the orc had thought there was even the slightest chance of getting to grips with Skargash, he'd have stayed behind and tried to smash his way through the zombie mob.

The knight felt a strange kinship with Ratbag in that moment. Alaric wondered if the renegade had lost family because of Skargash the way his own had been massacred by Gogol. Strangely, it had never occurred to him that orcs might have such connections among their own. From his father's accounts of fighting on the frontier, Alaric had always imagined orcs as a brutish horde only interested in making war.

"Just trying to buy us time so that I can think of something," Alaric told Ratbag. He risked a glance over his shoulder. The troll loped after them with its clawed hands outstretched and its jaw hanging open in a hungry leer. Fire no longer licked around it and most of its skin was burned to a crispy black. With each plodding step, some of the burnt crust flaked away, surrounding the monster in a sooty haze.

"It's still after us!" Sylvia shouted, her tone conveying the cold precision of someone suppressing panic. She was leading the retreat, her corsairs dutifully falling in behind her. In the current crisis, even Korsgaard wasn't questioning her orders.

"We need to slow them down," Helchen said as she sprinted after the last of the pirates.

"I'm open to ideas!" Sylvia retorted.

Alaric glanced back, judging how much distance lay between themselves and the troll. How much time that distance meant. "What we need is a barricade," he said. From previous battles, he'd seen how poorly zombies reacted to changes in environment. A good obstruction in their path and what remained of their awareness became confused. They might hunker down to wait for the barrier to open, or they might try to find another route and lose their focus as they wandered in search of one. Either way, it would slow them down.

"Brog!" Sylvia called to her ogre. She gestured with her hatchet at the ornate columns flanking a doorway ahead of them. The other pirates hurried through as the hulking Brog set down his weapons and clapped his hands on one of the pillars. Alaric could see the mighty thews straining beneath the giant pirate's jerkin as he pulled and strained against the structural ornamentation.

"Don't stare, run!" Sylvia snapped at the knight, trying to goad him into hurrying. "If this comes down, it'll come down fast!" Even as she said the words, Helchen's black hat was pelted by dust trickling from the archway as she jogged beneath it.

"Don't wait on me," Alaric huffed as he forced his body to extra effort. He knew it was a useless admonition. Brog couldn't stop the process he'd started, all he could do was abandon control of when the archway would buckle.

Ratbag moved faster than Alaric had believed possible for the orc. The suspicious glance he threw at Brog as he passed him made the knight suspect the renegade didn't trust the ogre not to drop the whole mess right on top of him if given the chance. A moment later Doran and Ursola plunged through the stream of dust and rubble clattering down from the ceiling as Brog succeeded. The troll was only a dozen yards behind them, its mouth snapping in anticipation of the living flesh it would soon tear into.

A notable groan shivered through the air and Alaric could see the ogre's entire body tremble as he tried to absorb the incredible weight that now settled upon his shoulders. The knight threw himself forward in a lunge that ended in a sprawl just beyond the doorway.

"Let it go," Sylvia ordered Brog. The ogre might have done so anyway, for he seemed at the limit of his endurance. With a grunt, Brog dove to one side and released his restraining grip on the column he'd fairly wrenched free from the wall.

The pillar toppled sideways into the hallway they'd just fled. The column opposite buckled, exploding into powder and pebbles as it tried to absorb the immense weight now pressing down on it alone. With its obliteration, the entire archway fell, spilling tons of rubble and dust into the room. Alaric could see the troll just beyond the crashing masonry, staring back at him with its dullard's malice. Then the monster was obscured entirely by the collapse.

Alaric coughed and spat the choking dust from his mouth. Helchen helped him onto his feet. She was coated in gray from all the dust billowing around them, but otherwise looked no worse for the ordeal. As the gritty cloud settled, Alaric looked across the bedraggled figures around him. Everyone had made it through and, except for a few cuts from sharp pebbles, the worst injury was a gash in Brog's arm. Doran ministered to the ogre by clasping his hand on the wound and reading from a yellowed scroll. In a few moments, the bleeding abated, and the big pirate actually looked heartier than the rest of them.

"That should stop them," Gaiseric laughed, clapping Ursola on the back and pointing at the mound of rubble. "Take a good engineer to clear that away, eh?"

A grim doubt nagged at Alaric. "Or workers who don't care if they get crushed," he said, walking toward the blocked doorway. He could hear the clatter of shifting stones, but it sounded to him far too regular and persistent to be the rubble settling. Peering through a gap in the pile, he recoiled in alarm.

"What did you see?" Sylvia demanded, a wary look in her eyes.

Alaric didn't feel like describing the sight of the troll's burned claws digging at the rubble only a few feet from his face, stagnant treacle oozing from its wounds. "They're already trying to clear it," he stated.

"They?" Doran demanded, turning from his medical ministrations. "They aren't that smart. They're dead." The concept of zombies formulating plans of their own, showing mental initiative, clearly rattled the battlemage.

"Tell that to them," Sylvia admonished Doran, looking away from her inspection of Brog's injuries. "Maybe zombies are a bit smarter than all your books give them credit for."

"Der bonecalla'z still above snakes," Ratbag spat, patting his scimitar as he glowered at the rubble. "Skargash be noodlin' alla der gimiks fer der cadavaz."

Gaiseric interpreted when Doran just gave the orc a confused look. "He says the necromancer is still alive and still giving orders to his zombies."

Skargash! Alaric had been counting on the necromancer simply delegating the attack to his zombies and then continuing whatever it was he'd been doing when they stumbled onto him. He'd neglected to consider that Skargash was still an orc. Of course the villain would want to be near the fighting. Perhaps he was even after Ratbag in a similar fashion to Gogol's vendetta against the von Mertzes. Certainly, the two orcs knew each other.

"The conservatory!" Alaric shouted to the others. The way the rubble was shifting, the knight guessed the barrier would last only a few more minutes. He intended to make the most of that time.

The conservatory presented a very different prospect to the rest of the castle they'd seen. Foremost, it was a big room, providing them with space to maneuver around the sluggish zombies. The beds of plants were arranged in tiers, one platform rising above the other. That would enable them to climb above the reach of the undead if things went sour. At the very worst, the roof offered an escape route. Composed of transparent crystal slabs, the ceiling let sunlight pour down upon the indoor garden. Alaric hoped it would be easy to smash a hole and climb out should they be forced to flee. Even with Skargash directing them, he didn't think zombies would be agile enough to follow them if they did that.

"Captain Sylvia, who's the best shot among your men?" Alaric asked as they came into the conservatory. While escape was something to consider, he preferred to think offensively.

Sylvia looked across the remaining buccaneers and huffed in amusement. "None of these," she stated flatly.

Korsgaard bristled at the disdain. "Ye be givin' these 'ere lads a ballist'r t' sight, an' they ain't a c'rsaire this side o' Nauctil's Vault what be th' bett'r shot."

"I need bowmen, not artillerists," Alaric told the quartermaster. He turned and nodded apologetically to Helchen. "I'm afraid the role falls to you," he said. He pointed up at the highest tier of flowerbeds and waved his hand at a stand of thick, lush ferns. "Hide yourself up there and don't make a sound."

The witch hunter studied the position, already figuring out what the knight was after. "You want me to pick off Skargash?"

Alaric nodded. "Whatever happens, however bad things get, you sit tight and keep quiet. Wait for your shot." He knew how Helchen would resent staying out of the action, but she was also practical enough to appreciate the necessity. "Our best chance of winning is to eliminate the necromancer."

While Helchen climbed up to her post, Alaric gave orders to the rest of the group. "Ursola, Doran," he said, getting their attention. "That troll wasn't much bothered by what you did to it before, but maybe if you coordinated your attacks, it would be a different story."

Doran shared a look with the dwarf and nodded. "We'll synchronize. The beast is sure to fall to the combined flames of sorcery and alchemy."

"Good. Keep back and make sure you get a clean hit." Alaric motioned the pair up onto the lowest tiers.

"What about the rest of us?" Sylvia wanted to know.

"That's simple," Gaiseric offered. He pointed his sword at the floor, drawing a rough line with it. "We stand here and keep the zombies occupied. One way or another," he added with a worried expression.

"Gimme der chanc't fer bumpin' Skargash, an' dat'll be aces." Ratbag's mouth stretched into a murderous grin.

"It sounds like your chance is on its way," Sylvia grumbled at the orc. She motioned her pirates to fan out, deploying them across the conservatory in a crude battle line.

Alaric held his shield high, peering over its brim as he watched the hallway. The zombies were visible now, the charred troll leading the pack. He couldn't tell how many orcish undead there were lumbering behind the abomination, but it was certainly a lot. Maybe too many. He'd already seen for himself that even a zombie orc was stronger than a human, somewhat dulling the advantage someone alive had over the slow-moving creatures. His real hope lay in Skargash being so bloodthirsty that he showed himself and gave Helchen a shot at him. With the necromancer down, at least the undead wouldn't have a brain guiding them.

"Brace yourselves," Alaric warned. The troll ducked its head as it reached the doorway. Its eyes narrowed as it appreciated the presence of living flesh in the room ahead of it. Had it been alive, the abomination might have paused, anticipating a trap. Instead, it simply lumbered forward, its gangling arms rubbing against the floor.

Before the troll had gone even a few yards, Alaric realized he wasn't the only one who'd readied a trap. Concealed by the abomination's bulk, several goblin zombies came whipping into the conservatory. The smaller monsters were far faster than the plodding orcs or the lumbering troll. They rushed at the shore party in a wave of grasping claws and gnashing teeth.

"Hold them back!" Alaric used his shield to throw one of the goblins as it leapt at him. His sword split another from shoulder to belly, bisecting its heart in the process. The slain zombie tripped up one of its comrades, spilling the creature to the floor where Brog's stamping foot exploded its head.

For all their frenzied energy, the goblins weren't able to break through the line of defenders. There simply weren't enough of the creatures to achieve that goal. But Alaric didn't think they were meant to. The goblins were merely a distraction, pinning the survivors in place while the rest of the undead advanced. The troll wasn't deployed by itself this time. As it prowled into the conservatory, it was flanked by orc zombies, enormous brutes bigger than any Alaric had seen before. They moved with a precision alien to a mere shuffling mob of animated corpses. Cutting down another goblin, Alaric peered past the advancing undead and spotted Skargash in the hallway. The necromancer was just beyond where he needed him to be. Another couple of yards, though, and he'd be in the conservatory and in Helchen's range.

"Fall back," Alaric hissed, keeping his voice lowered. He didn't know if Skargash could understand human speech the way Ratbag could, but he didn't want to take the chance. "Let them follow you. Lead them on. Doran, Ursola, be ready!"

Step by step, the survivors retreated deeper into the conservatory. The last of the goblins went down with Sylvia's hatchet in its skull. Now it was the orc brutes who were closing in on them, still keeping company with the scorched troll. Beyond them, other zombies were shuffling into the room. Following on their heels was Skargash himself. Only a few more feet and he'd be in Helchen's range. Just a little longer and at least the undead horde would be without a leader.

"Look out! Get away!" Helchen's scream rang through the conservatory. The instant she shouted, Alaric saw Skargash's eyes widen, and the necromancer retreated several steps.

"Belieth's bones!" Alaric cursed. What had possessed Helchen to spoil the trap? He lifted his head to glare at the witch hunter, then froze. There wasn't any need for her to explain that terrified warning.

Through the clear roof of the conservatory, a gigantic shape was hurtling down at the castle. It was only a moment after Helchen's cry that Flamefang's shadow threw the room into darkness.

"The dragon!" Gaiseric screamed. The rogue ducked his head and scrambled for the door at the other end of the conservatory.

"Everybody get out!" Alaric yelled. It was a command given just a moment too late. One of the orc brutes swung at him with a beefy paw, denting the face of his shield and pitching him to the floor. He stabbed up with his sword, opening the creature's belly. A mortal wound for anything alive, but the zombie was well beyond such things. It loomed above Alaric, pressing itself further onto the sword as it tried to reach him with its claws.

Before it could, the zombie's head was twisted to one side. Alaric saw a crossbow bolt sticking out of its brow. Automatically he glanced up to where Helchen had been posted. She was already making for the opposite door, recklessly leaping from tier to tier and crushing Yandryl's garden as she went. She'd paused in her hasty escape to help Alaric, something that left the knight feeling humbled. Once again, he was indebted to her.

Repaying that debt would depend on getting free of the zombie she'd wounded. The bolt hadn't penetrated deep enough to pierce the thick orcish skull and reach the creature's brain. It needed more force for that. Rearing up from the ground, Alaric slammed his helm against the bolt. Between cold steel and tough bone, it was the bone that gave way. A shudder swept through the brute as the bolt was driven into its brain to disrupt the fell magic animating it.

Alaric just had time to shove the heavy carcass aside before the entire room shook and a rain of shattered crystal cascaded downward. Zombies were slashed by the shower, but except for one that had its head cracked open, they continued to lurch onward despite the shards embedded in their flesh. One of Sylvia's pirates, however, lay in a puddle of gore, grasping at a leg that had been severed at the knee.

No one had time to help the mangled man. The cause of the shattered ceiling was leaning his head over the room, serpent-like eyes scanning the battleground. Flamefang's wings beat the air as the dragon hovered over the roof, his reptilian musk overwhelming the aroma of flowers.

Alaric scurried across the room, desperate to reach the hallway. It was a race against what he knew was coming. His only prayer of survival now was that Flamefang would start his attack at the opposite end of the chamber.

"Wotun be praised," Alaric gasped when he heard the whoosh of the dragon's breath and wasn't instantly immolated. Flamefang had indeed started his fiery sweep where the zombies were concentrated. It would only be a matter of seconds before the same inferno was brought across the room, but by then, the knight would be in the hallway. Ursola seized him by the waist and dragged him deeper down the corridor.

The next instant, the dragon's breath crashed against the doorway. Fingers of flame rippled into the hall for several feet before dissipating.

"If you think you're safe from a dragon, keep moving," Ursola advised. She glanced back at the door to the conservatory and the thick, black smoke billowing from it. "Matter of fact, if you think you're safe from a dragon, make damn sure it's dead first."

"I'll keep that in mind," Alaric said. He looked over their bedraggled group. They'd lost two more of the pirates, either to the zombies or Flamefang's fire. His gaze lingered on Helchen. He started to thank her, but she shot him a reproving look, embarrassed by his gratitude.

"Ye gotter be ribbin' me!" Korsgaard exclaimed. The quartermaster pointed his cutlass at the doorway. Through the smoke, a hulking, fiery shape emerged. In shape, it was clear the apparition was the abominatroll. With mindless fidelity to Skargash's commands, the monster had pursued them through Flamefang's fire.

Before the survivors could either fight or flee, the flaming zombie collapsed to the ground. A filthy, greasy smoke curled away from its immense body.

"Guess it finally found a fire too hot for it," Ursola commented.

"That'd be more comforting if the dragon wasn't trying to serve us the same way," Sylvia said. She waved at her men. "My crew's shares are starting to get bigger than they can spend."

"Share o' what?" Korsgaard rounded on her. "Ain't been eno'gh 'ere ter be payin' me bar tab at th' Cutlass an' Anch'r, an' that's th' plain trooth."

"It means the sorceress kept all the best treasure somewhere safe," Alaric advised the pirate. "When we get what we came here for, we'll find plenty for all of you." The knight thought of his few dealings with mercenaries. Pay was a powerful incentive for the larcenous, but it could only be promised for so long before something tangible had to be offered.

"We have the same plan," Helchen said. "We find our way up, we'll find where Yandryl kept Mournshroud and her other valuables."

Doran had a pensive look on his face. "If we can get there," he said.

Alaric didn't like the battlemage's dour tone. "We're rid of Skargash and his zombies," he stated. "Whatever wasn't turned to ash now has a burning room to cross if it wants to reach us."

Doran fixed the knight with a steely gaze. "I'm not worried about the zombies. I'm worried about the dragon." He glanced over at Ursola. "A dragon attacks a thing until it is satisfied. It doesn't linger around after the fact, nor does it bother itself overlong with prey it can't get at. That's why so many dwarf strongholds have hidden boltholes for their inhabitants to shelter in during a wyrm's attack."

Ursola glowered suspiciously at the battlemage. "You learn all that in a book, or do you have more practical experience with dragons?" she challenged Doran.

"Dragons have menaced communities of men much more often than those of dwarves," Doran countered, frustrated by Ursola's jabs. "They might raid your people for gold, but when they get hungry, they start looking at human farms and human villages."

"You have a point?" Alaric asked the wizard, trying to head off the resentment crackling between Doran and Ursola.

"Flamefang is behaving more aggressively than any dragon I've heard of," Doran said. Ursola gave a reluctant nod of agreement. "I'm disturbed by that. The way he's acting. He appears crazed."

A chill swept through Alaric. He thought of Singerva, of the crows and rats. The animals hadn't been afflicted by the Black Plague until they'd started eating the carcasses of slain zombies. After that, they'd become undead themselves. How long, Alaric wondered, did that process take? The transition from living being to undead monster.

"You mean infected," the knight said, his words conveying the horror curdling his own blood. He shared a knowing look with Helchen.

"What has Flamefang been eating since Skargash brought his zombies to the island?" Helchen shuddered.

There weren't many things that could strike terror into a witch hunter, but Alaric considered it reasonable that the idea of a dragon gradually being corrupted by the taint of the undead would be one of those things. It would explain why the wyrm was hanging about even when Yandryl's magic prevented it from entering the castle. A hunger for living flesh that was stronger than any thought or instinct.

The hunger of a zombie.

CHAPTER FIFTEEN

Even after finding the stairs, Gaiseric wasn't sure they were headed in the right direction until they entered a long hallway, its floor covered by purple carpet edged in gold. The walls were paneled in a light, fine-grained wood. Most remarkable of all were the gilded light fixtures utterly unlike anything he'd heard of before. Glass globes gripped in jeweled sconces, a crisp yellow glow shining steadily within them.

"Amazing," Doran commented as the battlemage inspected the lights. "She's trapped lightning within these globes, sustaining them by means of these wire veins." He pointed his finger at a thin string of copper that descended from the sphere and vanished into the floor. "The priests of fabled Ankhorem were said to harness such powers to illuminate their temples." He glanced around, sweeping his gaze along the walls, floor, and ceiling. "Somewhere there's an alchemical heart that pumps vitality to the globes, but I don't know where it might be hidden."

"Now th're be a fine thing," Korsgaard said, stepping to the wall and examining the globe. "May be fetchin' a purty fee, were we ter lib'rate it from this'n backwat'r." The quartermaster reached out with his hook to see how firmly the copper string was fastened to the wall. Doran drew him back.

"Might be unwise to meddle," the battlemage cautioned. "You don't know if Yandryl laid any protective spells on this mechanism." A chastened Korsgaard stepped away, his enthusiasm for plundering the glass globes notably diminished.

"I know one thing," Gaiseric said, trying to repress his own anxiety over Doran's warning. "This area here is a lot richer-looking than those rooms below."

"That's obvious," Helchen said. She might have indulged Doran's lecture, but she didn't look in the mood for one from Gaiseric. "If you have a point, make it."

Gaiseric just smiled at the witch hunter's distemper. "I've a lot of experience visiting the homes of the well-off. I've always found that however big the estate, whatever the condition of their finances, someone of means always sees that their own apartment is as lavish as possible. Yandryl might neglect entire wings of her castle, but she wouldn't skimp on making her own surroundings lavish."

"That sounds just like an elf," Ursola acknowledged. "Never heard of one that didn't revel in decadent finery. I've heard in their own lands they have taverns where all they do is uncork bottles and sniff perfume. Not even a stein of malt beer to be had in the whole building!"

Gaiseric shook his head. "Whatever the proclivities of elves," he said, "I expect we'll find Yandryl's rooms around here." He raised his finger to emphasize a further point. "If Mournshroud was something she had immediate use for, I expect it'll be around here someplace, rather than sealed up in some vault."

"It's worth looking into," Alaric decided. He gestured to the ornately carved doors that opened into the corridor. "Fan out and see what you can find."

"And watch out for traps," Gaiseric added. The pirates, eager to be about the task just a moment before, now became positively timid.

Helchen leaned close to the thief. "Did it occur to you that if a sorceress were to protect her rooms, any traps she left would be magical? There won't be anything to see."

Gaiseric shrugged. "Just trying to help."

Ratbag scowled at the malingering pirates. "C'mon, letta big gorilla show ya der rumpuz." The orc slammed his shoulder against the nearest door, fairly tearing it from its hinges. He reached over the portal and pulled out a fistful of colored cloth. "Nuthin' 'cept der buncha frippery!" he cursed.

Not to be outdone by the orc, Brog lumbered away from Sylvia. The ogre stepped to the next door. He didn't use his shoulder, he simply drove the flat of his hand against the panel and exploded it at the center. With his hand through the wood, he clenched his fist and pulled, wrenching it loose and lifting it into the corridor.

"I think this used to be something important," Sylvia said when she peeked inside. She shuffled to one side and waved a curious Gaiseric to precede her into the room. The thief hesitated at the threshold, stunned by the sight before his eyes.

The chamber was an extensive one and its far wall curved outward, a sure sign that it was built out into one of the cylindrical turrets that projected from the castle's facade. Narrow windows looked out over the island greenery, but the view they afforded was eclipsed by the one offered by the enormous hole that had been gouged in the exterior wall. Gaiseric imagined it was what would happen if a trebuchet hurled a boulder into the castle. A moment's consideration made him appreciate why that analogy was wrong. There wasn't any rubble inside the room. The wall hadn't caved in, it had been pulled out.

The condition of the rest of the room left no doubt what was responsible for making the hole. Nearly the entire chamber was a blackened ruin. An immense bed, situated atop a raised dais, was merely so much charred wood and ashen cloth now, the stringy remnants of its canopy hanging over it like the tatters of a shroud. Other appointments were even less recognizable. A twisted bulk in one corner might be a wardrobe or a wine rack.

Sprawled among the wreckage was the husk of a body. Helchen was the first to approach the corpse, prodding it with her mace until she was able to turn it onto its side. The body had been lying face down and, to Gaiseric's surprise, the front wasn't burned like everything else in the room.

"This must be Yandryl," Gaiseric said as he looked at the dead face. The features were inhuman in their definition, lean and chiseled in their contours so that the visage was endowed with qualities of such beauty that they were frightening. An elf, surely, and from the elegance of that part of the gown and jewelry that had been shielded from the fire, obviously no mere servant in the witch's employ.

"She was already lying here dead when Flamefang paid his visit," Doran stated. He pointed at the lips and the open, staring eyes, then glanced at Helchen. "Necromancy. Somehow or another, Skargash must have laid a hex on her."

The witch hunter leaned closer and cautiously inspected the body. She covered her nose against the wretched odor that rose from Yandryl's mouth when she pried the blue lips apart. Looking over her shoulder, Gaiseric could see that the inside of the elf's mouth resembled rotten meat. There was just a hint of the same effect at the corners of her eyes. "Some necrotic spell," Helchen confirmed. "She must have fled here when she felt it taking effect, but died before she could help herself."

"Then the dragon came along to make sure of the job," Sylvia said, lifting up the burned shreds of a rug with her boot.

"I think whatever spells Yandryl used to guard her castle only serve to keep Flamefang out," Helchen suggested. "She knew enough to place a stronger ward so the dragon couldn't breathe fire through the open gates, but she didn't think the beast would make his own holes in the building."

Doran shook his head. "There might be another reason. Whatever magic she used to command Flamefang had to be very strong. She might never have thought it possible for that control to be broken."

"Maybe she didn't lose control," Alaric suggested as he stared down at the body. "At least not while she was alive."

Gaiseric only partly listened to the discussion about spells and dragons. His eyes were sweeping about the room, displaying the almost innate knack for evaluating the worth of its contents that he'd developed over his burgling career. Most of what he saw was utterly ruined by the dragon's fire, but his attention was captured by one item that had defied Flamefang's fury. Intrigued, he rushed over to the charred rack that held it. The wood crumbled away as he lifted a fat-bladed sword from its resting place.

"Well, here's something at least," Gaiseric said. Only as he held the sword in his hand did he worry about its obviously magical nature. He tried to reassure himself that even a witch wouldn't keep something that was cursed in her bedroom.

Pushing her way past Sylvia and Korsgaard, Ursola tugged the weapon from Gaiseric's grasp. She peered at it intently, a calloused thumb tenderly tracing the runes etched into the blade. "So that's what became of it," she said, reverence in her tone. She made an experimental swing with the sword, smiling at what she judged to be its precision of weight and balance. Her eyes met Gaiseric's. "Small wonder it survived the heat. This sword is of dwarf-make. The runes name it 'Cryptblade' and it was used by Thane Regin when draugyr stalked the halls of Snogarr Stonefist's steading." She turned to Helchen. "I think this was what the elf witch was trying to reach when she ran in here. Cryptblade was forged specially to destroy the undead." The dwarf handed the sword back to Gaiseric. "Make good use of it, human."

Now aware of some of the weapon's history and qualities, Gaiseric felt uneasy taking it back. He felt unworthy of such a trust. "Cryptblade was meant to be carried by a hero," he protested. He tried to hand the sword to Alaric. "By rights, you're the best of us…"

The knight held up his hand and shook his head. "I'll not set aside the sword of my fathers, no matter how noble a weapon I'm offered in exchange," he declared. "Besides, you've proven your mettle to be of the highest quality. Even if you don't want to admit it," he added with a smile.

Gaiseric glanced over at Ratbag. The orc scowled back at him. "Ya nah gonna foist der midge-cutta on Ratbag," he snarled. He brandished the massive scimitar, letting light play across its serrated edge. "Dere's der gat fer der propa ruckuz."

The thief forgot his notion to hand off Cryptblade to one of his companions when he noted that the light reflecting off the orcish scimitar was abruptly cut off. At the same time, a musky stench billowed into Yandryl's chamber.

"Flamefang!" Gaiseric shouted, already diving for the hallway and praying the others had the sense to do the same.

Ursola stared across the room as Gaiseric rushed past her. The gap in the wall through which sunlight had been pouring into the chamber afforded a brief glimpse of the dragon swooping toward the castle. The next instant, the opening was completely covered by the wyrm's scaly body. The turret shook at the impact of Flamefang's mass against the facade. She saw cracks snake through the stone as the reptile's claws dug into it. Like some gigantic lizard, the beast clung to the exterior wall and craned his head so he could face the room. There was a horrible, decayed aspect to the scales around his mouth. The ugly patches reminded her of a sunburn, although Ursola suspected what afflicted the dragon was much worse.

"Dragon!" the cry went up. There was a frantic scramble for the hallway, a press of bodies that Ursola knew she couldn't win her way through. Instead, she looked to the one spot that hadn't been charred by Flamefang's previous visit. The wall to either side of the hole was unmarked.

"This way!" she yelled, taking hold of Alaric's arm and pushing him toward the wall. Doran spun about and seized on the same idea, pressing against the stones on the other side of the gap. However important their quest, they'd achieve nothing if the dragon reduced them all to cinders. Survival – then they could worry about finding Mournshroud.

The rest of the shore party hurried for the hallway. Ursola saw Korsgaard stumble against Sylvia and knock his captain to the floor. The quartermaster didn't hesitate, but kept moving, buffeting another pirate from his path as he flung himself over the threshold. The dwarf saw Helchen gain the hallway as well, the witch hunter risking a despairing glance back at the people still in the room.

Then the air sizzled as Flamefang expelled his caustic breath into the chamber. The heat was so intense standing only a few feet from the dragon's maw that Ursola felt blisters form across her face. Her chest felt as though she'd sucked a lungful of steam.

In the room, the ogre Brog reached down and seized Sylvia. Holding her by the back of her jerkin, he threw her through the doorway and into the hall. Then the dragon's fire washed across the hulking buccaneer. His brawny frame crisped, muscles bubbling from the bones as his flesh was immolated. Brog managed a single, stumbling step, then crumpled to the floor, a burning heap. Ursola was impressed by the ogre's sacrifice. She could hear Sylvia out in the hall shouting to the dead pirate, bemoaning his loss.

"Try to make a break for it before he breathes again!" Alaric shouted to Ursola, reminding her that the doom of Brog was one in which they all might share. The knight raised sword and shield, ready to spin out from shelter and set himself before the wyrm.

The dwarf seized Alaric and swung him back against the

wall. One sacrifice to the dragon was enough. "Don't be an idiot," she snarled. "He'll roast you before you can blink!"

Across from them, Doran was hastily rummaging among the scrolls he carried. The battlemage looked over at Alaric once he found what he wanted. "Same idea, different strategy," he said before quickly unraveling the scroll and perusing what was written on it.

Ursola didn't know enough about magic to understand what Doran was planning, but she knew enough about dragons to know that whatever it was, they'd have to act fast. She looked across the room, what remained of its contents crackling as the dragon bile spattered across it sizzled. The doorway to the hall was blackened, but it looked like the flames hadn't reached the corridor beyond. They should be safe as long as they could get over the threshold.

Doran looked up from his reading and gave Ursola a grave look. Without further preamble, the battlemage uttered an invocation and clenched his left hand into a fist. Holding it up and away from his own body, he swung out from cover and stood revealed to Flamefang.

Ursola clenched her eyes tight at the blinding flash that followed. It wasn't light that exploded from Doran's hand when he opened it, but rather a darkness so intense that it burned like ice. The effect was intense enough just on the periphery, she could only imagine how staggering it must be for the beast against which it was directed.

The turret shook as Flamefang howled in pain and confusion. The cracks in the wall widened as the beast released its grip. Ursola could hear the wind as the stunned wyrm fell away from the castle, shocked by Doran's spell.

"The un-light will only stun him!" Doran shouted. He swung away from the gap and raced for the hallway, his hood falling back from his face as he ran.

"Move!" Alaric yelled. The knight's arm curled around Ursola's waist as he half-carried, half-dragged her through the scorched ruin of Yandryl's chamber. She bit back any protest at the indignity. At the moment, the human's long legs and consequent longer gait were more important than dwarvish pride.

Behind them, Ursola could feel the turret shake as Flamefang flew back. Even if the dragon's sight was still bedazzled by Doran's magic, the reptile had other senses by which to find his enemies. The trio were just plunging into the hallway when they felt the withering heat of Flamefang's exhalation. They scrambled behind the walls as a little finger of fire stabbed past the doorway.

"Marduum be praised! I didn't think you'd make it!" Helchen dropped the dour rectitude of a witch hunter as she clasped Alaric in her arms.

"You don't even want to know the odds…" Gaiseric began, relief fairly dripping from the man's brow.

Ursola grinned at the thief. "How would you have collected the bet if you won?" She curbed her humor as she noted Sylvia. The pirate captain was crouched on the floor and agony contorted her face. Her eyes were riveted on the doorway. But Ursola knew she wasn't focused on it, but rather the unseen bulk of the ogre whose loyalty to her was such that he'd died to save her. From what she'd seen, that kind of fidelity was rare among buccaneers.

Except for Brog, everyone had made it out of the room.

The pirates made for a tense spectacle. Korsgaard's eagerness to get himself out of danger had, it seemed, shaken the confidence of his artillerists in him. The buccaneers kept close to Sylvia and gave the quartermaster dark looks. Their captain, for her part, kept looking at the doorway as though expecting the burned ogre to reappear.

Oddly, Ratbag looked equally disturbed. The orc ran his palm against the edge of his scimitar and let beads of blood drip to the floor. "Wouldve been der propa bustup," he grumbled. "Der mug wouldve been der ace scrappa."

Another tease of fire from the doorway told Ursola that if Ratbag wanted a tough fight, there was something still clinging to the turret that would more than oblige. Assuming Flamefang even let him get within sword-swing before turning him into cinders.

"Persistent, isn't he?" Alaric nodded at the room they'd just fled.

Doran drew the hood back over his head. "Too much so. He knows he can't get inside and he knows how far his fire can reach. A dragon isn't stupid. Not one as big and old as him."

Ursola nodded. "There's truth in that. A dragon knows when to call it quits and try something else."

"You think it's the zombie corruption?" Helchen wondered. "That the wyrm's brain is already decaying?"

The battlemage looked uncertain. "Maybe…"

"Well, maybe we could discuss this someplace where it isn't so warm," Gaiseric interrupted as they felt heat radiate from Yandryl's room. Flamefang's searing distemper was anything but spent and he seemed intent on venting that anger on the chamber, occupied or not.

The group withdrew down the hallway. At the next turn, Ursola caught at the battlemage's sleeve. "You think there's more provoking Flamefang than just whatever infected meat he's eaten?"

The wizard glanced back down the corridor, then at the paneled walls around them. He seemed worried that the dragon would follow, rip a new hole in the facade through which to spew his flame. Ursola was shamed that she, a demolitions expert, hadn't considered the possibility. The citadel was very strong, and by rights nothing should have been able to pull apart that turret the way Flamefang had.

"I think it safe to say that the best defense Yandryl had on this island was her dragon," Doran stated, looking up from Ursola to assure himself that the others were attending his speculations. "When Skargash's undead attacked, it's certain she activated whatever spell gave her command over Flamefang. I believe that spell was still active when she died. The abrupt severing of such a beguiling enchantment can have severe consequences." Somehow, the battlemage's visage became grimmer. "I think when the spell was disrupted, it confused and enraged Flamefang."

"That's why the dragon is so aggressive," Ursola said. "Why it's so unrelenting."

Helchen raised an objection. "What if it's more than that?" she posed. "I may not be a practitioner," she said, glossing over her actions on The Demoness, "but the Order taught me much about the methodology of magic. Any spell of lengthy duration usually depends on some sort of focus to facilitate it and lessen the strain on the wizard to maintain it."

Ursola hadn't considered that aspect before. The idea

struck her that it might even apply to the Black Plague. Perhaps that was why the necromancers operated in cabals and they needed to share the load of perpetuating the magical scourge.

Doran's eyes gleamed as he listened to Helchen. "You've a keen insight. A pity the Order recruited you instead of the Wizards' Guild." He waved aside her objections. "It remains a fact that you've approached the question in a way I hadn't considered, but which I think now must be right. Yandryl was using an enchantment to control Flamefang, but that spell wasn't broken when she died. As you theorize, she used some sort of focus to maintain command. Her death disrupted the spell, but it didn't end it. Flamefang is lingering here because he's waiting on – no, more like depending on – orders that will never come. A beguilement creates a dependency in the victim for the dictates of the enchanter, a need as consuming as hunger or thirst." He sighed and shook his head. "No wonder the beast is crazed. That alone would be enough without whatever corruption he's ingested by feeding on zombies."

"So you're saying this dragon isn't going anywhere?" Alaric asked. He looked over the rest of the group. "We all saw the condition of the castle when we left the forest. All the holes gouged into the walls." The knight pointed in the direction of Yandryl's chamber. "We've plenty of proof that Flamefang doesn't have to get inside to kill us. With the way the walls are compromised, he has plenty of places to strike from."

Sylvia followed the knight's train of thought. "There are entire sections of the citadel that will be too dangerous to search."

"We came here for Mournshroud," Helchen stated. "We're not going back without it."

"Ye be a might much palaver th're," Korsgaard said. "I be all fer plund'r, but nawt when it'll be costin' me own neck ter get."

Ursola glowered at Korsgaard. "We've already seen how much value you put on your own neck. And how little you put on anybody else's."

Doran interrupted before the pirate could rise to Ursola's remark. "It might be possible to drive Flamefang away," he said. "I think I have some idea about the sort of dragontaming magic Yandryl used based on my observations and Helchen's theory. Yandryl would need a large crystal to focus the spell. If we smash that, the enchantment will be broken." He sighed and looked over at Gaiseric. "Then we depend on luck. Hope that once he's free, Flamefang will want to get as far away as possible from the spot where he was beguiled."

"The other likelihood is he tries to tear down this castle stone by stone," Ursola cautioned. "Dragons don't tend to forgive any injury dealt to them."

"Where do we find this crystal?" Sylvia asked. There was a gleam in her eyes that Ursola wasn't sure she liked. It looked just a bit too much like the goldlust that sometimes afflicted dwarves.

"The kind of magic I think Yandryl used would need great height and a wide open space," Doran answered. "I'd start by looking on the roof of the tallest tower."

Gaiseric gave the battlemage an incredulous look. "Excuse me, but that sounds like exactly the kind of place that suits the dragon. Up in the air with nowhere to run. Would even a witch's spells keep Flamefang from knocking the place over?"

Ursola slapped the thief on the back. "Just try and convince your Luck Devils they should make Flamefang leave after we smash the crystal." She smiled at Gaiseric's dismay. "You only die once."

"I used to believe that," Gaiseric retorted. "Then everyone started coming back as zombies."

CHAPTER SIXTEEN

Helchen had her qualms about letting Ratbag lead her group through the desolate halls. It was true that the orc's senses were sharper than those of a human, but so, too, was his propensity toward violence. The warrior was intent on killing Skargash and unlike Alaric, there wasn't any consideration that would restrain Ratbag unless it was the possibility of failure.

Gaiseric had put the orc's motives into simple terms for Helchen. "You're mistaken if you think he wants revenge," he explained. "An orc doesn't care overmuch about such things unless it is a hurt done to himself that he's trying to avenge. The times the son of a defeated warchief has tracked down his father's killer has nothing to do with the dead warchief. It's the loss in status, the diminishment of his own position that's pushing the avenger on. Kill the killer, preferably in some hideous manner, and it instantly makes the child greater than the sire to others in his tribe. We might not be able to fathom it, but Ratbag doesn't care about the other orcs Skargash has killed. He cares about the tribal belief that by killing the necromancer, he'll draw the power of Skargash's deeds into himself." Gaiseric had shrugged then. "Of course, if all the orcs across the frontier have been turned into zombies, there won't be anybody to care. I don't think Ratbag has thought that far ahead. Orcs aren't known for that sort of foresight."

The witch hunter was unsettled by the explanation. It was a reminder that whatever commonalities existed between humans and orcs, there were even more differences between the peoples. The callousness of Ratbag, his indifference to the decimation of his own tribe, it spoke of an absolute absence of empathy. Helchen tried to imagine how harsh orcish society must be, conditions where helping another meant reducing one's own chances of survival. She'd seen for herself that Ratbag preferred to be self-sufficient, but at the same time had a knack for appreciating the utility of those around him. She wondered if that was the only bond any of them had with the orc: utility. Whatever help he gave, was it from actual concern, or merely the desire to retain something that might be useful to him?

Helchen didn't have the answers any more than she had the answer to where in this blasted citadel Yandryl had hidden her arcane treasures. To ensure the search wasn't disrupted while they sought a means to drive off Flamefang, she'd advocated dividing their resources. Alaric had taken a group including Ursola, Sylvia, and some of her pirates to find the central tower. Doran had gone with them, for he alone could say with certainty if the dragontaming crystal was there and could react if it was discovered Yandryl had placed protective wards upon it. She regretted the necessity of parting company with the battlemage. There might not be any affection between them, but the witch hunter recognized the benefits of his eldritch knowledge. If they did find Yandryl's vault, Doran's insight would be valuable.

Still, she couldn't shake the impression that time was of the essence and it was necessary to divide their forces. Helchen had a persistent feeling of impending doom, some unexpected disaster that was on the cusp of engulfing them all. The last time she'd felt like this was on the way back from the village of Gevina, after burning the witch Kassandra Mergen. On the trail they'd been ambushed by the witch's werewolf lover, a frenzied slaughter that saw five of Captain Dietrich's attendants killed and her mentor himself disfigured by the lycanthrope's claws.

Helchen brushed aside the crimson memory and looked over the small group she now commanded. She had Gaiseric and Ratbag, the quartermaster Korsgaard, and two of the remaining pirates. It was a far from heroic team to draw upon, but it was possible that the survival of everyone in Korbara depended on their success.

Ratbag motioned the rest of them to wait when he found a flight of stairs leading down. Clenching his fists around the heft of his scimitar, the warrior began his descent. The orc was scarcely out of sight before Korsgaard, with typical distrust, darted over to the head of the stairs and peered down.

"Seems like th're be nice pickin's yon'r," the pirate said as he gazed at the polished paneling and purple carpet that ornamented the staircase. "Ye'll be mindful ter keep an eye on th' orc's pockets when ye seein' 'im agin."

Helchen fixed a withering look on Korsgaard. "There's others around I'm already keeping my eye on," she told him. She could see from the way he started that he understood her meaning. It was one of the first tricks the Order taught witch hunters. When conducting an investigation, those making the loudest accusations were usually the ones with the most to hide.

A short time later, Ratbag came stalking back up the stairs. "Lampin' der boffo grubhut," the orc reported.

Helchen looked over at Gaiseric, but the thief just shrugged. "Your guess is as good as mine."

Cautiously, the humans followed Ratbag down the stairs. Helchen soon saw for herself what the orc had tried to describe. The steps opened onto a wide hall with a vaulted roof some thirty feet over their heads. An enormous table, wings extended off from its center to form a kind of cross, dominated the room. Long benches flanked the table, but at the very top of the cross were several chairs with tall, padded backs. Helchen realized that the room was a dining theater, larger and grander than even those she'd seen in the Arch-Prelate of Wotun's palace in Mordava.

Korsgaard and the other pirates lost no time rushing to the table and pilfering it of the candlesticks and silverware set out at each place. Gaiseric's warnings about possible traps fell on deaf ears.

"You may as well save your breath," Helchen advised the rogue. "They've been looking for something to steal since they left the ship. Maybe this'll take the edge off." She marched along the length of the table, inspecting the room with a wary gaze. There were four sets of doors opening into the hall, in addition to the stairway leading up to Yandryl's apartment. She also noticed a far less opulent set of steps that went down to a lower level in the citadel.

"Kitchens," Gaiseric suggested. He indicated the smoothed surface of the steps. "These have seen a good deal of use. Lots of people going back and forth."

Helchen nodded. She was already turning her attention elsewhere. The dining hall was fitfully illuminated, but the candles in the chandeliers suspended from the ceiling had long ago been reduced to clumps of wax. The light, she saw, came from numerous holes in the roof.

"We need to get out of here," Helchen whispered to Gaiseric. Suddenly the least sound felt to her like the crash of thunder. She glowered at the pirates and the racket they were making as they ransacked the room. "Quiet," she hissed. Korsgaard spun around, a sneer on his face, but the quartermaster fell silent when she pointed up at the roof. Hurriedly, he got the other pirates to stop.

"We'll go that way," Helchen said when she'd drawn her team close. She indicated an open doorway to their right.

"Jus' so's it be puttin' somethin' solid above our noggins," Korsgaard muttered. "Me 'eart ain't so keen ter clamp eyes on th' drag'n agin."

As quietly as possible, the group stole across the hall. Helchen couldn't help lifting her eyes and watching the roof. Any moment she expected the sunlight streaming down to be blocked off by the dragon's wings. She didn't know how keen Flamefang's nose was, or how sharp the monster's ears. What she did know was, like the pirates, she'd feel much better with something firm over her head.

Ratbag loped ahead of them, leading the way as they trailed into a broad corridor. There were none of the ostentatious touches they'd seen in Yandryl's part of the citadel. Indeed, the walls were so bare, the connecting rooms so utilitarian, that Helchen decided almost at once that they were in the servants' quarter. As they proceeded, the rotten smell of decaying flesh hit their senses. The rooms they now passed bore evidence of having been hastily barricaded. For all the good it had done the occupants. In each one they found butchered remains.

A vicious leer split Ratbag's face and the orc quickened his step. Helchen didn't understand the sudden eagerness until she detected another smell, one that was almost drowned out by the stench of human decay. It was that sour odor of dead orc. The question now was precisely how dead the source of that stench was.

"Ratbag, wait," Helchen commanded the renegade, but it was already too late. Rushing ahead, the orc threw his shoulder against what was left of a set of double doors. The branch of hallway the servants had closed off was thrown open by his violent advance. Past Ratbag's shoulder, Helchen could see what looked like a dormitory of sorts. From the racks of weapons and stands of armor on display, it seemed a barracks for the castle guards.

Whatever the room had been, it was a shambles now. The dismembered remains of bodies were splashed about the walls, the shattered frames of beds and chests strewn across the floor. The culprits were still busy about their destructive task. Arrayed about the room were a dozen or so orcish zombies, their rotten skin stained red from the men they'd killed. The undead turned when they noticed Ratbag.

The warrior didn't hesitate. His scimitar swung out in a gleaming arc to decapitate the closest zombie. Its head went rolling across the gore-slick floor as the rest of its necrotic brood threw aside the furnishings they'd been demolishing and prepared to meet Ratbag's challenge.

"Help him!" Gaiseric shouted. The thief charged into the room after Ratbag, Cryptblade clenched in his fist. He delivered a glancing blow to one of the orc walkers as it turned to meet him. Helchen had seen the undead shrug off such wounds before, but this time the zombie shuddered and collapsed, its flesh bubbling as it was reduced to wormy mush.

The sight inspired the corsairs to take up the fight. Fanning out, they moved to guard the flanks as Ratbag and Gaiseric held the center. Even Korsgaard joined the fray, tearing open the face of a goblin as it leapt from where it had been hidden among the debris.

Helchen lingered in the doorway, chilled by a sense of wrongness. It took her a moment to realize what it was. The zombies had been making a search of the room when they entered, an activity far beyond the reasoning of such lowly undead. She turned her attention away from the fighting, staring past the combatants to the doorway at the other end of the barracks.

Skargash met her gaze. The orc necromancer had an almost human smirk on his visage. A look of contempt mixed with impending triumph.

The witch hunter swung around, every instinct alert. There was another set of double doors across the hallway, only a dozen yards away. She saw them buckle as a second mob of zombies responded to Skargash's summons. The necromancer's plan was clear. He intended to trap his foes between the two groups of undead.

"We're going to be surrounded!" Helchen shouted in alarm. Her warning caused the pirates to back away, but Ratbag had also spotted Skargash at the far end of the barracks and was determined to reach his enemy.

"Skargash! Ya fer der bump, ya boozy yegg!" the orc howled, hacking through the skull of a zombie and kicking the walker's corpse to one side. "Ya croak'd alla der mugs in der mob! Now ya der bimbo wotz fer der ride!"

"You'll be killed," Gaiseric snarled at Ratbag. Cryptblade continued to wreak a virulent toll upon the undead, but the thief appreciated that he couldn't dispatch the zombies fast enough to hold them off. "Think about it – if Skargash kills you, you'll just become another of his zombies!"

That point appeared to penetrate Ratbag's fury. When the orc crushed the skull of a decayed walker, he made no move to advance further. Perhaps he might have done so in the next moment, but it seemed he'd come close enough to worry Skargash. The necromancer drew back a pace into the doorway. In his place, an immense shape lumbered into view. A creature Skargash had been keeping in reserve.

"Marduum, another troll!" Helchen gasped when she saw the thing. The monster Flamefang had immolated in the conservatory wasn't the only one of the abominations Skargash had brought to the island.

Before the necromancer could send the monster charging at Gaiseric and Ratbag, Helchen opened the grimoire Hulmul had given her. A sour feeling churned in the pit of her stomach. It was all she could do to keep from retching as she once more drew upon forces she'd been taught to despise as profane and obscene. Biting back her disgust, she invoked the icy power of the spell she'd taken such pains to teach herself. The troll and the orc zombies around it were immobilized as layers of frost enclosed them. "Move!" she shouted, a tremble in her voice. She knew the spell was only a temporary measure and Skargash might have a spell of his own to make the effect even more transitory.

Thief and orc didn't need to be told again. Spinning around, they sprinted into the hall. Helchen turned to confront the second group of orcish zombies now stalking toward them. She fought through her repugnance and the fatigue that threatened to overwhelm her and gestured at the necrotic horde. Again, there was a withering chill as the frost washed across the foremost of the zombies, freezing them in place.

Her companions stared at her in amazement. Certainly, they'd seen her invoke the spell on The Demoness, but it must have shocked them to see her resort to it again. Perhaps they appreciated how grave the situation was for her to employ magic to save them.

"Back," she gasped, leaning on Gaiseric for support. Helchen grimaced when steam came billowing out of the barracks. The zombies in the wall ahead of them, those not frozen by her spell, strained to force their way through the ones blocking their path. She saw a creature coated in ice snap at the ankle and shatter as it hit the floor. It would only be a matter of moments before the rest were likewise destroyed and a path cleared for the ones behind them.

"Back?" Korsgaard growled. "Back where?"

Helchen waved her hand. "To the dining hall." An idea was forming in her mind, a plan so audacious it terrified her. But she knew it was the last thing Skargash would expect.

"If this scum decides to chase us, maybe we can beat him the same way we did before." Helchen didn't explain further.

If she did, instead of withdrawing, Helchen thought her companions would stay and take their chances with the zombies, no matter how bad those chances were.

Fleeing back to the dining hall, Gaiseric was too focused on escaping the zombie horde to spare much thought for what Helchen had in mind. It was only when they rushed into the room that a horrible notion occurred to him. He turned his head, looking at the woman he'd helped through the corridor. A shudder passed through him when he saw that she was staring at the ceiling.

"You're not thinking..." he gasped.

Helchen shook her head. "No, I've already decided."

Korsgaard noticed that the pair of them had stopped. "Shouldn't we be about makin' tracks afore them rot-buckets catch up?"

Gaiseric thought the pirate had an excellent point. He cast a longing glance over at the carpeted steps leading back to Yandryl's apartment and the upper sections of the citadel. "We could lose the zombies somewhere up there," he suggested. If his luck held, Helchen would agree.

"We can't search for Mournshroud while dodging Skargash," Helchen stated, dashing the thief's hopes. She looked across the pirates, then let her gaze linger on Ratbag. "The rest of you can go," she said. Gaiseric could tell it was a bluff. She knew Ratbag wasn't going anywhere if the witch hunter was staying behind to fight the necromancer.

Gaiseric groaned. Helchen had taken his measure, too.

He had just enough integrity that he wouldn't leave his companions in the lurch. "Our chances are better if we stick together," he said, unsure if he said it to convince himself or the pirates.

Korsgaard was still hovering on the verge of leading his men away when the buccaneers found the choice had been taken from them. "Black cats and broken mirrors," Gaiseric hissed when the spoiled stench of decayed orc flesh struck his nose. Like the rest of them, he'd expected Skargash's horde to pursue them by the same route they'd taken to withdraw from the barracks.

Instead, a mass of orcish zombies emerged from a hallway opening on their left. The hideous troll was in their lead, moving with greater speed than the walkers following it. Exhibiting an intelligence that was surely dictated by Skargash's magic, the abomination didn't mindlessly rush at them, but instead lumbered into the middle of the room. In one fell swoop, the troll blocked off any escape from that direction.

A second mob of zombies appeared from the other side of the room. Of course, Gaiseric thought. The necromancer had been ransacking the castle for who knew how long. It was natural Skargash would know the layout and how to cut off his enemies.

Helchen, for her part, looked unfazed. Gaiseric knew there was only one possible reason and he braced himself for what was coming.

The orc necromancer jeered at them from over the shoulders of his undead. "Who der gink wot getz der bump now," Skargash snarled, shaking his morbid staff at Ratbag.

"Big palav'r fer der runty bonecalla," Ratbag snarled back, knuckles cracking as he shook his scimitar at his enemy.

Helchen looked over at her companions. "When it starts, everyone run for the hallway we just left." With some reluctance, she drew the arcane tome from its satchel. Hesitation evaporated into a steely resolve as her fingers shifted through the pages.

"You don't have to say it twice," Gaiseric affirmed. It was all he could do to keep from clenching his eyes shut when the witch hunter read from the grimoire and invoked one of the spells written there. Her hand, pointed upward, crackled as an orange flame billowed into existence around it. A moment it clung there, flickering about her fingers, then it went shooting up at the ceiling.

"Ya missed, ya rummy moll," Skargash howled in amusement. The necromancer gestured with his staff and the zombies surged forward, orcs and goblins ambling toward them in a hideous mob.

Ratbag grinned back at Skargash. "Ya a dumb yegg," the warrior laughed. There was a keen glimmer in the orc's eyes, reflecting the arcane flame that had flared up into the rotten roof. Ratbag had gleaned the intent of Helchen's mad scheme.

Gaiseric felt his insides churn as he watched the flame widen a hole in the roof. The bright orange fire flared about the edges of the fissure, blazing brighter than the sun. An unmissable beacon for something he really didn't want to see again.

The zombies marched closer, their monstrous faces curled into expressions of feral hunger. A few fleet-footed goblins charged in from both directions. Ratbag cut one from shoulder to hip, then stove in the face of a second with the hilt of his scimitar. Gaiseric sprang in with Cryptblade, withering two of the creatures as they tried to reach Helchen. The pirates formed a loose ring as they fended off the goblins.

"We be thinkin' it were time ter be leggin' it!" Korsgaard cried out, looking back the way they'd come.

"Not yet," Gaiseric told the pirate. "We try to break now, they'll pull us down."

The quartermaster started to ask what they were waiting for, but the stench of dragon musk made that superfluous. The sunlight streaming down into the dining hall was choked off as enormous wings sailed above the roof. Helchen had sent a signal to Flamefang, and the vicious reptile was answering.

The dragon's fire blasted down into the already burning roof. The ceiling exploded, showering the hall in fiery debris. Several zombies were crushed in the destruction, their rotten bodies crumpling under heavy timbers. Gaiseric spotted Skargash as the necromancer hurriedly retreated, abandoning his undead mob in his haste.

"Run! Now!" Helchen shouted. The witch hunter was already sprinting for the hallway the zombies had been blocking before the ceiling crushed them.

Gaiseric forced himself to run faster than he thought possible. He outdistanced the fleeing pirates, even passed Helchen. He risked one look back as he reached the doorway. The dining hall was burning in dozens of places. Paneling crackled as flames licked up across the walls. The long table smoked as its frilled cloth was ignited. Zombies stumbled about in disarray as fire consumed their flesh.

The thief's gaze rose to the roof and the immense hole at its center. Past the burning beams and shingles, he could see Flamefang's horned head staring down. It felt as though the wyrm's hateful gaze was directed at himself alone. An awful paralysis seized him, holding him fast where he stood.

Their hurried escape from the room drew the dragon's attention in a way that the shuffling movements of the zombies didn't. Gaiseric saw Flamefang's open maw and the infernal light pulsing into life at the back of his throat.

"Blow ya wig or git torch'd!" Ratbag growled as he caught up and ran past. The orc's huge arm curled around Gaiseric, lifting him off his feet and all but throwing him into the hallway.

The instant his gaze broke contact with Flamefang's eyes, Gaiseric felt in control of himself again. He scrambled down the corridor, pausing just long enough to cut down a zombie goblin that was chasing him. He saw a few more of the creatures rushing for the hallway, but before they could make it, a sheet of consuming fire swept over them. He could see their bodies disintegrate in the immolating fury of Flamefang's breath.

"To fight a monster," Helchen said as they hurried away from the burning dining hall, "sometimes you need a bigger monster."

Gaiseric shook his head. "I was talking about Ratbag when I said that." He gestured with his thumb at the orc warrior. The renegade appeared to take it as a compliment.

"It worked, didn't it?" the witch hunter countered.

The rogue crossed his fingers, trying to trap a bit of the luck he was certain they'd all just used up. "Helchen, when someone like me tells you you're playing risks with long odds, I hope you'll take it as a word of friendly caution."

"Have some faith," she advised him.

Gaiseric looked back at the smoke billowing into the corridor. "I have faith that if we keep running into the dragon, bad things will happen." His boot caught an uneven tile and he stumbled. He uncrossed his fingers to catch at the wall, setting loose whatever luck he'd managed to grab.

"Bad things," Gaiseric grumbled, "and I'm afraid I'm the one they'll happen to."

CHAPTER SEVENTEEN

Rancid blood bubbled from the torn neck. The guard staggered back, ripped flesh visible above the steel gorget. Alaric didn't give his foe an opportunity to close in again. With a thrust of his blade, he drove the swordpoint through the soldier's eye and into the brain.

"More of them!" Sylvia cried out. Wielding both weapons, she darted between the undead guards trying to surround her. A sweep of her hatchet nearly severed the leg of one while a slash of her cutlass shattered the arm of another.

Alaric cast his gaze up toward the circular stairway that was their objective. Shuffling down the worn stone steps toward them were three grisly figures clad in gore-stained mail. Only one of them was armed, a hand curled about the shaft of a halberd that it dragged along the floor and was jounced each time the guard descended another step.

The knight withdrew his sword and let his opponent crumple to the ground. Raising his shield, he poised himself to meet the new arrivals. There'd be no mistaking them for anything but what they were: zombies. When Doran used one of his spells to blast open the barred door into the guardroom,

Alaric had been surprised to see humans ambling forward to meet them. In the dim light, he'd thought they were survivors who'd barricaded themselves inside the room. Doubtless it had been true, at one time, but someone must have been bitten while fighting the undead, bringing the Black Plague inside with him.

Alaric had grown just a bit too used to the zombie orcs and goblins, forgetting for a crucial instant that the undead corruption wasn't so limited in its reach. The decayed guards would have overwhelmed him had Doran not quickly invoked a wind spell that tossed the zombies back. Such hurried, frantic casting left the battlemage debilitated. He was now slumped in a corner trying to recover his equilibrium while Sylvia's corsairs kept watch over him.

"Leave them to me," Ursola said. She gestured with the spiked end of her hammer for Alaric to step back. "The dragon's not the only one on this cursed island who can breathe fire." The dwarf waited a few moments more, biding her time until the first zombie reached the bottom of the stairs. Sweeping her arm forward, she cast a bomb at the creature. The incendiary burst into fiery life, engulfing the creature in flame. The guard following behind it was likewise splashed with the caustic material. Both pitched down to the floor, a smoldering tangle of burning limbs.

The third zombie, however, was shielded by those ahead of it. Only a few random patches of its body were ignited, and whatever pain the crackling flames might have dealt a living man went ignored by the decayed senses of the undead. Shambling down the stairs, the creature trampled the corpses of its former comrades and reached out for Ursola with a clawed hand.

"Missed one," Alaric quipped as he pushed ahead of the dwarf and lashed out with his sword. The blade raked across the zombie's neck, parting the putrid flesh as though it were wet paper. The head lolled back on a strip of rotten skin, dangling obscenely between its shoulder blades. The creature took one more staggering step before the vibration of its own motion completed Alaric's task. The thin strip of skin tore away, and the head crashed to the floor, severing the arcane link between brain and body. With the spell animating it disrupted, the zombie collapsed backward into the still-burning carcasses of its comrades.

"I could've dealt with it," Ursola huffed, her fingers curled around the casing of another fire-bomb.

Alaric shook his head at the dwarf's indignation. "Setting yourself on fire might have made things worse." Frowning at the bomb in her hand, Ursola returned it to the satchel hanging from her shoulder.

Sylvia cautiously stepped around the burning zombies and began to climb the stairs. She went as far as where the curvature blocked her sight of the guardroom. "I don't see any more of them," she said. "It's possible that was all of them."

"Or we're just not near enough to draw their notice," Alaric speculated. He tried to put himself in Yandryl's place. How many soldiers would the sorceress employ to guard her castle? A glance at Doran was enough of a reminder that drawing upon magic was a risky endeavor, one that could leave the practitioner vulnerable. The elf would certainly have been aware of such pitfalls and clearly appreciated that guards with cold steel were a useful contingency. So, the question again: how many soldiers would she have stationed in the castle?

How many of those had been able to reach the tower and barricade themselves against Skargash's zombies?

Counting the three that had come down the stairs, the recent melee had accounted for ten zombies. Alaric studied the bodies more closely than he had before. All of them wore a chain shirt, but only about half of the corpses were equipped with helmets, gorgets, vambraces, or other armor. Scrutinizing one of the dead, the knight was disturbed.

"Something wrong?" Sylvia asked him as she returned to the room. His uneasiness was pronounced enough that the pirate was able to pick up on it even with his face hidden inside his helm.

"Look at him," the knight told Sylvia, nudging the body with his shield. "Does he look like a warrior to you?"

Sylvia's gaze roved across the twice-dead corpse. She wasn't disturbed by the grievous wounds the body had suffered. It was when she perceived what Alaric had spotted that her skull-painted face drooped with worry. "I'd say that man was a clerk or a scribe. Some manner of administrator who didn't need to exert himself much." She stepped on an arm and turned its hand over with the heel of her boot. "Those palms are as soft as a child's. This fellow never trained with a sword."

"It's destroyed now," Ursola said, bewildered by the gravity of the conversation. "Hardly matters what it was doing before it became a zombie."

Alaric shook his head. "It does matter," he corrected the dwarf. "If this one and some of the others weren't soldiers, then it means the guards posted here gave shelter to other denizens of the castle."

"It means there could be a lot more of them up above us," Sylvia explained. "And if the people down here were infected, any in the rooms above might also have become undead."

"We'll have to chance it," Doran interrupted. The battlemage slowly walked toward them. Color was gradually returning to his face, but his breathing remained a bit too ragged for Alaric's comfort. "The dragontaming crystal Yandryl used has to be up high. This spire is the tallest in the castle. Even if she placed it in a different turret, we'll be able to spot it from the roof."

Alaric stood silent a moment as he evaluated the risks. He remembered his first view of the castle and the spire that rose above it. It had certainly been topped by some sort of roofed space. Whether the astronomical observatory Doran proposed or something else, it would have provided refuge for anyone fleeing Skargash's zombies. All indications, however, were that these people hadn't escaped the Black Plague, rather they'd simply brought the curse inside with them. Trying to deduce what sort of garrison had been in the tower was one thing, but there was no way to determine how many refugees had been taken in.

Against his worries that any rooms above were infested with the undead, Alaric had to balance the threat of Flamefang. The dragon was menace enough to their search for Mournshroud, but if the wyrm stayed near the castle it might make it impossible to get back to the beach. Even with some secret route out of the castle, there was a very real chance the reptile would spot them. No, he decided, whatever the potential danger, if there was any possibility of getting rid of the dragon, they had to take it.

The knight met the gaze of each of his companions. They were waiting on his decision. Looking to him to make the call.

"We go up," Alaric said. "Keep well apart. At least a yard between each of us."

"So if there are any surprises, they only happen to one of us." Sylvia nodded. The pirate captain appeared much too comfortable with such callous calculation. Alaric wondered how many times she'd been forced to employ such strategies with her own crew.

"Who goes first?" one of the buccaneers asked, his weathered face filled with suspicion.

"I go," Alaric said, but the moment he did he was confronted by angry protests from Ursola.

"That makes no sense, high-knees," the dwarf objected. She patted the satchel of bombs. "I'm the one who should take the lead. Any zombies try to surprise me, I can surprise them." Ursola nodded at Alaric's sword and shield. "You can only hold them off if you have some warning, I can cook them even if they sink their teeth in me. Give everybody else a chance…"

Alaric shook his head. "I make the plan, I take the risk," he insisted.

"Sure, and then if something happens, I have to wait for you to drag yourself out of the way before I toss one of these," Ursola said, tapping one of the bombs so that a metallic ping sounded from its casing. "Besides, if there are too many up there and we must retreat, I'm the slowest one. I should be in the back if we reverse course."

Alaric sighed. His sense of honor rebelled against the idea of letting Ursola take what he felt was his place. At the same time, the pragmatism his role as leader demanded of him wouldn't be silenced. The dwarf's position made sense. Too much sense.

"Be careful," Alaric enjoined Ursola as she started toward the stairs.

Ursola looked back at him with a sullen expression. "Careful would be to set charges and just knock the whole tower down." She nodded at Doran. "That would settle this crystal you're worried about. But I don't have the explosive I need to do that job, so we're stuck doing this."

"A leader does the best he can with what – and who – is available," Sylvia advised Alaric as they watched Ursola climb the steps. They waited for a few moments before following her. "In the end, it's the results that matter."

Alaric felt a chill when he heard the ruthlessness in Sylvia's voice. A pirate, he reminded himself, who spent the lives of her crew always with the conceit that the fewer of them around at journey's end, the greater the shares for those who survived. It was a mindset that found value only in utility.

A sentiment the knight prayed to Wotun that he'd never become desperate enough to adopt.

For all her bluster, Ursola was wary as she ascended the winding stairway. The flourishes of ornamentation, even in the stairwell, only managed to aggravate her, a continual reminder that the castle had been the stronghold of an elf. Yandryl's death, whether it could be blamed on Skargash or Flamefang, didn't erase the outrages she'd perpetrated against the dwarves. Indeed, if there was one corpse on the island Ursola could wish would rise again, it was that of the witch. That way a dwarf could be the one to destroy her and exact some restitution for the unquiet spirits of so many murdered ancestors.

Ascending the tower, Ursola became aware of a change in the air. The atmosphere felt less oppressive than it had in the lower castle. Sensitive to differences in pressure after a life spent in the underground mines and halls of her people, the dwarf knew the cause was more than merely the height of the tower.

The explanation was revealed after only a few more turns of the stairway. The dark passage brightened, sunlight pouring upon the inner wall. The outer wall, Ursola could see, was pitted and gouged, exactly as it had been in Yandryl's chamber. Whether or not the controlling crystal was housed in this spire, it was certain that Flamefang had vented some of his fury upon the structure.

"Trouble," Ursola softly called down to her companions below. When the others joined her, she gestured to the sunlight and the pitted walls that let it in.

"The dragon," Doran hissed.

"Of course it was the dragon," Sylvia told the battlemage. "What else could do this?"

Doran pointed through one of the holes. "No, I mean the dragon. There."

Ursola followed where the wizard indicated. She felt her stomach lurch, as if she'd been dropped down a mine shaft. His red scales glistening in the sun, Flamefang soared above the forest not too distant from the hill. The horned head, she noticed, was always turned toward the castle and she could imagine the serpentine eyes watching for any sign of prey.

"He's seen us!" Alaric exclaimed as the wyrm pivoted in

his flight and flapped his great leathery wings. The reptile ascended toward the tower, his fanged maw opening wide.

For a hideous moment, Ursola could only look on as Flamefang flew at the spire. She'd heard of the phenomenon the dwarves called dragon terror but had only half-credited it with being real. Now she experienced that debilitating fascination, a paralyzing mix of awe and horror, and knew it was deadly fact. She could only look on as the wyrm drew nearer, unable to join the hurried scramble as her companions fled down the stairs.

"Ursola!" Alaric shouted. The knight swung back to help her, even though it would be a useless gesture. They both knew that when Flamefang sent his fire searing into the tower, they'd be cremated in the blast.

Frozen in place, facing the hole in the wall, Ursola saw a flare of fire suddenly shoot up from another part of the castle. A section of vaulted rooftop, wooden rather than stone, was ignited by the strange flame. The dragon noticed it as well and was attracted by the light far more than the movement he'd spotted inside the tower. Flamefang pivoted in midair and dove down toward the burning roof.

When the dragon broke away, Ursola found herself able to move again. "He's gone away!" she yelled. "Quick, while the dragon's busy!"

She gave no further thought to zombies lying in wait on the stairs. Taking long, plunging strides, Ursola charged up the stairs. She could hear the clatter of Alaric's mail as the knight hurried after her. She took it on faith that the others were following behind him.

Two more circuits of the stairway were cleared before

calamity of a different sort reared its head. Ursola passed another section of ruined wall. She only absently noticed that they were now high enough to see beyond the island and out into the bay. Her interest was principally on Flamefang and the immense relief to find that the dragon was directing his fire at the rooftop far below.

Sylvia, coming abreast of the hole and being afforded a view of the harbor, noticed something very different. "Gutless scugs! Craven sea-rats!"

Ursola paused in her ascent and looked back to see what had provoked Sylvia's fury. Gazing out into the blue sea, there was no need to ask questions. They had a perfect view of The Demoness. The pirates had raised sail and were moving away from the island with unseemly haste.

"When I get another ship, I'll keel-haul the lot of you!" Sylvia threatened, waving her cutlass at the fleeing vessel. The other abandoned pirates joined her in cursing their former shipmates.

"They had good reason to run," Alaric said. He removed his helm and glared down into the bay The Demoness had recently surrendered. Hate blazed in his eyes as he stared at the cause of the pirates' retreat.

Ursola followed the knight's gaze, fear tightening about her heart when she saw what had caught his attention. There was a ramshackle, dilapidated ship making for the shore. A ship they had last seen sinking into the river near Schweinhoff. It was the ghost ship crewed by Gogol's spectral zombies. Somehow the undead had repaired it and continued their pursuit.

"Gogol followed us," Ursola stated, only half-believing the evidence of her eyes.

"We can't let him stop us," Doran warned. "If he knows about Mournshroud, he'll try to destroy it."

"Whether Gogol knows about Mournshroud or not, he came here to get me," Alaric growled.

Ursola didn't like the determination she saw on the knight's face. She caught at his arm before he could start back down the stairs. "You'd never get close to him," she said, reminding Alaric of something his mind knew if his heart didn't. "If Flamefang didn't burn you the second you left the castle, the spectral walkers would rip you to pieces. We must stick to the plan we agreed on in Korbara."

"And to do that, we have to get rid of the dragon," Doran added. "Once we are free to look for Mournshroud, we can use it to destroy the undead." The battlemage wagged a finger down at Flamefang. "Besides, the wyrm doesn't care whether he attacks the living or the undead. Wait a bit, and he might take care of Gogol for you."

A cold rage smoldered in Alaric's eyes. "Let's finish what we came here to do, then." Ursola could hear the fury laced into every word. "Gogol has escaped my vengeance too long already. I'll not have the dragon denying my sword an introduction to the necromancer's heart."

CHAPTER EIGHTEEN

The little hairs on the back of Gaiseric's neck continued to prickle as the small band of survivors picked their way through the gloomy citadel. He kept turning around, staring into the shadowy corridors behind them. Over a career of thievery, he'd come to trust his instincts when he felt there were eyes on him. Too many times that nebulous sense of danger was his only warning before some sentinel or watchman sprang out from hiding.

Try as he might, however, Gaiseric couldn't see anything definitive. Sometimes there was a vague impression of movement, but never enough to be sure it wasn't just his imagination playing tricks on him.

Gaiseric finally had to repress the impulse to keep glancing over his shoulder. It was proving a distraction from undeniable threats. Four times since they'd escaped the dining hall the survivors had encountered small mobs of zombies. Only a handful at a time, but even so it only needed one bite to contract the Black Plague. Moreover, the orcish undead were too strong to take chances with. One of the buccaneers had nearly been mauled when a hulking brute crumpled the buckler he carried with such force that it encased his hand. It had taken Ratbag's brawn to peel back enough of the twisted steel for the pirate to extricate himself.

Even more, Gaiseric found that he was losing his focus. Typically, the thief had a pronounced sense of direction, but after almost an hour ranging through the castle halls, he couldn't tell if they'd backtracked and were near the main gate or dining hall. Losing a feel for where he was in relation to where he'd been was something no burglar could afford.

"Seems ter me that thar be mor' fancy gewgaws in this'r wing," Korsgaard said. The quartermaster drew Gaiseric's attention to the corridor they were traversing. Certainly, the fixtures were of finer quality than what they'd seen in the servants' wing, golden candlesticks standing on alabaster plinths, their stems carved to resemble the folded wings of swans. The floor was tiled in alternating mosaics of blue and green, conspiring to create the imagery of flowing water.

"I should think this would be another part of the castle Yandryl maintained for her own use," Helchen suggested.

"Maybe she brought guests through here to impress them," Gaiseric said. His eyes roved across the elaborate illusion of a slow-moving creek. "At least it doesn't look like Skargash's zombies have been through here."

Ratbag continued to range ahead of the group, but the orc looked back when he heard Gaiseric speak. "Der stiff-snatch'r ain't lamped dese digs." There was a surprising eagerness in the warrior's tone rather than the irritation the rogue expected to hear. "Long'rshort, Skargash gonna drift here," Ratbag grunted, patting the blade of his scimitar.

It was an obvious conclusion, Gaiseric realized. They'd already seen that Skargash was searching for something.

Perhaps he was looking for Mournshroud, the same as they were. Whatever his purpose, it was clear he had his zombies ransacking the castle. The untouched appearance of this corridor suggested the undead had yet to come through this part of the citadel. Ratbag was confident that it would only be a matter of time before they did.

"Killing the necromancer isn't our quest," the thief reminded Ratbag. "We need to find Mournshroud and take it back to Korbara." Seeing his words made no impact on the orc, he turned to Helchen. "It's obvious the zombies haven't been here yet. That means if there is anything to find, we'll be the first ones to find it."

The witch hunter pursed her lips as she considered the matter. "There's a fair chance an orc necromancer would know what Mournshroud is and what it can do. Even if he didn't come to Yandryl's island looking for it, he certainly wouldn't pass up the chance to destroy it if he stumbled over the relic." Helchen nodded, her face grim. "You're right. Our best bet is to search where it doesn't look like the zombies have already been."

"Ya bimbos lampin' der tomtom, Ratbag'll give Skargash der rub," the orc snarled. He slashed his heavy scimitar at one of the plinths, chopping the candlestick from its setting and sending it clattering across the floor. "Swish an' der gink's melon goes fer der stroll." There was no arguing with the murderous gleam in Ratbag's eyes or the vicious grin on his fanged face.

"Ratbag says we can look for Mournshroud and he'll keep watch for Skargash," Gaiseric translated, trying to put the best spin possible on the orc's intentions.

"A good idea," Helchen said, as if any of them could compel

Ratbag to do otherwise. She waved Gaiseric to go forward. "Take the lead. Ratbag might miss something if he's worried about Skargash."

It was on the tip of his tongue to mention his own distraction, the feeling that they were being followed, but Gaiseric kept his peace. There wasn't any good that could come of expressing what was likely just paranoia. It would only worry the others to no purpose. Besides, Helchen was right, he was the one who should be leading the way. The ostentatious surroundings didn't mean there might not also be something hidden. Yandryl would either exhibit her treasures in a grand showplace or she'd have them locked away in a secret vault. Gaiseric didn't foresee any middle ground between the two extremes, and if it was the latter, he was better capable of noticing any betraying signs than anybody else in the group.

"Just keep close," Gaiseric told Helchen, then swept his gaze over the buccaneers to include them. "I'm not like Ratbag. If I run into trouble, I expect help… and in a hurry."

The rogue continued down the simulated creek. When he found doors opening onto the hallway, they were carved to resemble the trunks of great oaks, their boughs stretching out above the corridor. It took him a moment to find the latches, for they were disguised as knotholes, and several minutes to satisfy himself that there weren't any traps. At least the kind of traps he could spot.

"Helchen, if you could," Gaiseric said, backing away from the portal and motioning for the witch hunter to take his place. He watched with the keenest interest as she withdrew a small silver icon from one of the pouches on her belt. Pricking her finger, she smeared its surface with a bead of blood. Briefly a symbol flashed across the silver, one he recognized as the icon of Marduum, God of Vigilance. Whispering a prayer to the patron deity of witch hunters, Helchen held the icon to the door and swept it lengthwise in several passes.

"I think it's safe," she said. She brushed her fingers reverently across the icon. "If there were some hostile magic laid upon this portal, the Eye of Marduum would become hot and give warning. Unless the wizard who set the trap knew stronger spells than the Eye can detect." Returning the icon to her belt, she turned the latch and threw open the door. Helchen paused for a moment, as though waiting for some secret ward to transform her into a toad. Gaiseric realized that was precisely her mood when she suddenly sighed in relief and stepped across the threshold. "Come along." She beckoned to them from inside.

Gaiseric stared in undisguised wonder at the chamber within. There wasn't any question what purpose the room served, for the walls were lined with towering shelves, every inch of them stuffed with books of every description. He saw leather-bound tomes with gilded letters on their spines, the product of book binders from Oloperk and Kingsburg and the other great cities of the realm. There were volumes with strange, swirling script enclosed in snakeskin covers. Yellowed scrolls fastened to ivory cores, inscribed with weird picture-writing. One entire bookcase groaned beneath the weight of dwarven volumes, their backs forged in steel and their pages cast from astonishingly thin sheets of bronze.

Korsgaard scrambled about the room, rushing from one shelf to another, his eyes wide with avarice. "Thar be a king's rans'm 'ere!" he crowed. Spinning about, he fumed at the indifference of the other pirates. "Blast yer bones! Can't ye eyes spy a f'rtune when ye see it?"

One of the buccaneers made a cursory study of a volume that had been left sitting on a table in the middle of the library. His visage was one of confusion. "A bit of silver in the clasp. Hardly worth prying off," he said.

"Damnation drag ye ter them drown'd cities o' th' fishy folk!" Korsgaard cursed. "It ain't what be on 'em but what be in 'em as makes 'em precious." He ran his hand along the spines, smiling as he felt them under his touch. "Them conjure-men an' prayer-spitters in Korbara 'll off'r plenty fer this 'ere corlection."

Gaiseric smiled at the quartermaster. "Looks a bit heavy to box up and carry off," he said. "Or were you just going to pick and choose?" The question obviously bothered Korsgaard and a sullen look came over him. "You do know how to read, don't you?"

Korsgaard scowled at the thief, then turned back to the other pirates. "Lads, judge 'em by th' cover. If'n it looks ter be worth cartin' off, liken not, it prawberly is."

While the pirates started rummaging about the shelves, Gaiseric noticed that Helchen was making a closer study of the books. Already she'd drawn three down and had them resting on a table. Unlike Korsgaard, she was familiar with precisely what the volumes were. The thief could see that, left on her own, the witch hunter would spend hours scrutinizing the library. All it needed was a glance at Ratbag standing near the door, every muscle of his being on the alert, to remind anyone that they didn't have that sort of time.

"We need to get moving," the thief told Helchen.

"I still belong to the Order of Witch Hunters," Helchen snapped at him. She gestured at the shelves of books. "By rights, I should burn all of these. The knowledge they contain could be dangerous."

"Then why don't you?" Gaiseric said, his own irritation mounting. There wasn't time for Helchen to have a crisis of conscience now. He could appreciate the contradictory influences that pulled at her, the admonitions of the Order balanced against her promise to Hulmul and her own use of magic. None of that, however, was going to help them right now.

"Because I have to be sure." She removed one of the books and added it to the bag with Hulmul's grimoire. "Canticles of the druids in Greenshire," she explained. After glancing around the library, she carried the other two over to the fireplace and set them on the hearth. "These are more in line with subjects that would interest the likes of Gogol and Vasilescu. I hesitate to even pronounce their titles or their thrice-damned authors."

Gaiseric caught her hand before she could put fire to the tomes. "You're forgetting the risk," he said, looking up at the ceiling. "What if Flamefang notices the smoke and decides to see what's causing it? Are you positive the dragon can't reach us here?"

The witch hunter gave him another reluctant nod. "They need to be destroyed," she said, shaking her fist at the condemned books. "But as you say, we've sworn to find Mournshroud and bring it back."

"Then let's get out of here and see if we can." Gaiseric

steered Helchen toward the door. As he did, he thought he saw a hint of movement in the hall outside.

Helchen felt Gaiseric's body grow tense. "What is it?"

Gaiseric shook his head. "Nothing... I hope."

The chambers branching off from the artificial creek were the sort that would be found only in a wizard's castle. As Gaiseric led her to each new door, Helchen was alternately amazed and disgusted by what they revealed. Yandryl might have built her citadel in isolation, but she'd done nothing to conceal the aberrant nature of her activities. Quite the contrary, the opulence of each chamber made it clear that she'd been proud to show off these horrors to such visitors as she entertained. Of course, the only guests likely to be hosted by the sorceress would themselves be adepts of the arcane. Precisely the sort to "appreciate" what was on display.

They'd passed through an alchemical laboratory, a room of particular excitement for Korsgaard and the buccaneers when they learned that the gold ingots stacked on one of the tables had a dweomer to them, making it more likely it had been created rather than mined. The occult studies wizards engaged in were expensive, drawing as they did upon obscure texts and exotic materials. Most of them could afford their research only by putting themselves at the service of a wealthy patron, but some few discovered magical means to achieve their goals. Transmutation of base metals was a critical pursuit jealously guarded by the alchemists who achieved it lest the very sharing of the secret render gold so common as to be worthless. It was clear to Helchen that Yandryl was one of the select few who knew that secret. Despite Korsgaard's most frantic entreaties, however, she couldn't tell him which of the many hundreds of potions and elixirs in the room was responsible for the transmutation.

Other rooms had been far less savory, the obscenest of which was a vivisection theater where the sorceress had conducted experiments upon living rather than elemental matter. However long it had been since Skargash's zombies broke into the castle, a few of the subjects of those experiments were still alive in their cages. At least until Helchen ordered the tortured, crazed things put out of their misery. After seeing what she'd done, it was just as well Yandryl was already dead. Otherwise, Ursola wouldn't have been the only one calling for the witch's blood.

At last, however, Gaiseric led them to a place that had all the qualities of a show room. A long, crystalline casket stretched across the ceiling, exuding a dull light that flared into brilliance when they walked beneath it. Helchen could see wispy shapes flickering behind the crystal, recalling to her faerie emanations reported from certain glades and copses she'd investigated with her mentor Dietrich. She wondered at the sort of magic the elf sorceress had employed to entrap and bind such fey spirits.

The room the faerie light illuminated was wide and long, dominated by rows of marble pedestals and golden racks. Glass cases edged in gemstones held small artifacts. Helchen had an uncomfortable moment when she saw an ancient athame in one of the cases that bore an unmistakable similarity to the cursed Dragon's Kiss, the dagger she'd used to kill the archmage Vasilescu. Certainly, the blade in Yandryl's collection was the product of the same inhuman culture as that which had made the fossil knife discovered by Unger Ravengrave.

It was an effort for Helchen to turn away from the athame and refocus on the other exhibits in Yandryl's show room. Like the trophies of a huntsman, the sorceress had arranged this hall to boast of the arcane treasures she'd gathered. Each pedestal presented some unique relic, whether fabulously ornate or hideously grotesque. Any conventions of beauty or ugliness hadn't mattered to Yandryl. A cherubic harp carved from pearl and strung with silver thread reposed beside a mummified skull wrapped in the shed skin of a monstrous serpent, raw chunks of malachite driven into the sockets as substitute for its missing eyes.

"Ratbag noodlin' this'r der Mournshroud," the orc warrior called out, his bellow echoing through the room. Helchen and the others hurried over to see what he'd found.

The object Ratbag stood before exuded a sense of evil. A huge drum, its frame ringed with bones, across which had been daubed orcish sigils in what Helchen was certain could only be the dark blood of orcs and goblins. Skins had been stitched together and stretched taut over the ovoid framework, dried hides that were all too clearly those of humans. Beneath the crude, monstrous face that had been painted over the skin of the drum, she could see other countenances, withered and drawn by the tanning process yet still retaining a suggestion of the agonies of death. She could pick out fingers and limbs sewn together with dried gut, little blemishes that exposed some faded tattoo or birthmark. Mournshroud – a device only the cruelty of orcs could produce, Helchen tried to assure herself, though other relics among Yandryl's trophies put the lie to such claims.

"Let's get that… thing… ready to take back," Helchen said, a quiver in her voice. The pirates, hardened as they were by years of brutality, made no move to obey the witch hunter's order.

"Lug ya own junk," Ratbag growled when she turned a questioning eye his way. Frustrated, Helchen looked around for Gaiseric.

Oddly, the thief was the only one who appeared to have lost interest in Mournshroud. Instead, he was scurrying between the rows of trophies, anxious excitement on his face. Helchen thought he was looking for some particular relic among the trophies, then she realized he wasn't paying attention to the pedestals and racks, but rather the spaces between them. He was chasing something. For just a moment, a twinge of suspicion gripped her. Did Gaiseric know of some other treasure held by Yandryl? But no, it was certain he wasn't looking for something. It struck her that he was looking for someone.

Once she had some idea what to look for, the witch hunter quickly spotted the dark shape scurrying between the exhibits, trying to elude Gaiseric. The black, crusty appearance threw her off for a moment, but then Helchen understood what it was the thief had spotted. The thing was a zombie goblin, charred by Flamefang's fire but not quite destroyed. It was clear the undead had been following them ever since they escaped the dining hall. What wasn't clear was why the creature had only followed instead of rushing to sink its fangs and claws into living flesh. That could only happen if some controlling influence was suppressing its natural instinct to attack the living.

Skargash!

Helchen whipped up her crossbow and dashed between the rows of trophies. With Gaiseric pursuing the goblin from one side, the creature was forced back toward her. When it was in range, she didn't hesitate but sent a bolt smashing through its skull. The impact flung the zombie back, tipping over a stand that supported the snowy robe of a nomad shaman. The undead lay inert among the mess, its profane animation extinguished.

"Sm'rt as paint, that shot," Korsgaard laughed as he peered down the row at the dead goblin.

Helchen ignored the compliment. "It's been following us," she said, looking over at Gaiseric for confirmation.

"I think so." The rogue nodded. "Looks like it was one of those that tangled with Flamefang." His eyes were worried when he expressed the same thought Helchen had dogging her mind. "Why didn't it attack us? Why did it try to run?"

Korsgaard laughed again. "Th' lubber were a goblin! Goblins n'v'r stick to a fight lessen' they got suprortee o' numb'rs on thar fav'r. Cow'rds in life, thar be cow'rds in death."

The witch hunter scowled at the goblin corpse. She knew it wasn't so simple as that. In all her encounters with zombies, Helchen hadn't seen evidence that such lowly undead retained anything of their former mentality, especially an awareness of self-preservation. The creatures were mindless in nearly every way, the most basic instincts rotted out of their brains. No, all that was left was hatred for the living and obedience to the necromancers.

"Skargash told it to watch us," Helchen stated, an icy tingle creeping down her spine. She was thinking again of Hulmul, and particularly the connection between him and his familiar. The wizard had been able to see and hear through the senses of his familiar. Perhaps Skargash could do the same if he focused on one of his zombies.

"We have to hurry," the witch hunter said. Even if her fear was a mere possibility, they needed to act as though it were much more. She pointed at the orcish drum. "Get that secured and ready to move."

Korsgaard glared back at her. "Belay that palav'r," he snapped. He gestured with his iron hook at the rows of trophies all around them. "Thar be plenty o' 'spensive gewgaws 'ere. Meself an' th' lads jus' ain't gonna leave…"

The quartermaster's speech broke off. A foul, rotten smell swept into the show room, a stench with which they were all too familiar. Helchen spun around just as a mob of orc zombies shambled through the doorway. Most bore hideous burns, the legacy of their meeting with Flamefang, flesh crackling away from their bodies each time they moved. Behind them, his face twisted with murderous glee, she could see Skargash. The necromancer, obviously, had been keeping closer tabs on the goblin spy than she'd expected.

"Bump 'em! Croak 'em! Giv 'em der works!" Skargash howled, shaking his staff. In response, the zombies surged forward.

"Get Mournshroud!" Helchen shouted. She chided herself for engaging the weakness of all wizards, leaping to magic as her first choice in a crisis as she opened Hulmul's grimoire and turned to the page she'd consulted so many times before. Sickness churned in her stomach as her eyes raced down the cabalistic script and her lips invoked arcane words. She struggled to concentrate on the unnatural sensations, biting back their primal repugnance. Later, she could beg Marduum's forgiveness. Right now, she needed to draw upon the might of magic.

A spiral of frigid wind streamed from Helchen's out-stretched hand, inundating the oncoming zombies with a tide of frost. The orcs lumbered on for only a pace or two, their decayed bodies hardening as ice swiftly encased them. In a matter of heartbeats, they were frozen solid, as though they'd been buried in a snowdrift in the deepest part of winter.

For an instant, Helchen felt relieved, then she lifted her eyes and saw the huge, demented shape that rose above and behind the frozen orcs. The undead troll seemed to have escaped the worst of Flamefang's fire, its scaly hide merely blackened by the flames. The giant beast swung its gangling arms, its claws swatting aside the ice-coated zombies in its path.

"Leggit!" Ratbag snarled at Helchen before charging at the troll. The undead monster struck out with its claw, smashing the renegade with the back of its hand and sending him flying. Ratbag hurtled through several of the displays, scattering precious artifacts in every direction.

The troll then turned upon the horrified pirates. Before any of the buccaneers could move, the creature seized Korsgaard in both hands. Lifting the screaming quartermaster into the air, ignoring the slashes of his hook and the swings of his cutlass, the troll held the man over his head. Then, in an exhibition of strength as awesome as it was savage, the abomination tore Korsgaard in half at the waist. It let the pirate's torso flop to the floor, then, oblivious that it retained hold of the legs, the beast shuffled forward once more.

"Protect Mournshroud!" Gaiseric shouted as he rushed between Helchen and the advancing troll. A swing of Cryptblade lopped two of the clawed fingers from the monster's hand, causing it to drop the dismembered legs. The flesh around the fingers began to wither, but with far less effect than when the thief had employed the sword before. Whatever terrible magic animated the abomination, it appeared stronger than Cryptblade's enchantment.

"Croak 'em! Bump 'em! Giv 'em der works!" Skargash cheered on his undead horrors. More zombie orcs lumbered into view, trampling the frozen creatures to close in upon Gaiseric and the remaining pirates.

Helchen swung around and raced to the pedestal where Mournshroud stood. Gaiseric had told her to protect the ghastly drum, but she intended to do far more with it. She'd put it to use. Whipping the relic away from the stand, she set it on the ground before her. It needed only a glance to tell her that the orc warlocks had used their bare hands to sound the morbid instrument. Pulling off her gloves, she hoped there wasn't some occult melody she had to perform, that the power of the relic was innate to the drum itself.

Ignoring her disgust of the relic, Helchen brought her bare hands slapping against the skin stretched over its frame. A doleful, grisly note shuddered through the room. Well had the relic been named, for there was a piteous, mournful property to that booming intonation. Looking up from the hideous matrix of flayed skin, she gazed up at the zombie horde. It appeared there had been no change. Gaiseric was being backed into a corner by the troll while the last pirates struggled to hold back the orc brutes.

As she looked upon the zombies, however, her hands continued to beat the drum. By accident Helchen discovered Mournshroud's secret. It required the performer to look upon whatever was to be subjected to its power. Gazing at an orc brute while she pounded the drum, she was shocked to see its decayed visage contorted by emotion. Even on the rotted features of an orc, there was such a quality of despair that the witch hunter was moved to pity. She knew, in that moment, the zombie was aware of what it had become.

The flash of awareness swiftly fled, and the orc's body collapsed to the floor, as dead as any of the zombie's victims. Helchen quickly turned her gaze upon the abominatroll. The monster's body was a patchwork of withered spots where Gaiseric had slashed it with Cryptblade, but it was when Helchen's eyes turned the power of Mournshroud upon it that the undead met its end. Just as the creature was raising both fists to smash the thief, a dull awareness, an expression of horror, came over it. Gaiseric scrambled out of the way as the huge zombie came crashing down, its lifeless mass exploding a glass-topped display case and knocking over several stands of glittering armor.

Turning her attention to the orc brutes, Helchen brought them down, one after the other. Dimly she was aware of Skargash just beyond the faltering zombies. The necromancer glared at her. She could feel him drawing on his black magic when he pointed his staff at her.

A ferocious roar brought Skargash whipping around. Helchen saw Ratbag leap over the shattered bodies of the frozen zombies. The orc's scimitar came chopping down before Skargash could redirect the spell he was conjuring.

The serrated blade ripped through the necromancer's arm, severing it at the elbow.

"Ya aughtn't be fergetin' Ratbag!" the orc warrior bellowed.

Shifting his grip, Ratbag drove the blade through Skargash's belly with one hand while with his other he seized the necromancer by the throat.

"Dere's der whole shootin' match," Ratbag snarled. His fingers tightened and with a vicious jerk he tore out Skargash's throat. The necromancer spilled to the floor and made one feeble effort to crawl away. Ratbag's boot crushed the villain's spine. A kick to the head broke his neck and put an end to Skargash.

"I guess that ends that," Gaiseric quipped, dabbing a rag at a cut across his forehead. He looked over the zombies felled by Helchen's drumming. "Looks like they weren't lying about Mournshroud," he said, casting an anxious glance at the fallen troll. Like the other fallen zombies, the abomination was swiftly disintegrating into pulpy slime. Hardly something a necromancer would be able to call back into animation. "They'll make good use of it in Korbara."

Helchen stepped away from the relic, feeling as though every inch of her skin were acrawl with loathing. Being powerful didn't make Mournshroud any less abhorrent. She regarded the drum for a moment, then turned her attention to the other survivors.

"Nothing's over," Helchen said. "We still have to get this thing back to The Demoness. Only then can we be quit of this cursed island."

CHAPTER NINETEEN

A severed hand turned under Ursola's foot, nearly sending her tumbling back down the stairs. Her reaction was to try to steady herself against the wall, but when she did, she found only empty space under her hand. The dwarf pitched forward, saving herself by jamming the peen of her hammer in the crumbling masonry at the edge of the hole. She swung out over the side of the tower, dangling for a horrible moment hundreds of feet above the rest of the castle.

Biting her lip against a scream, Ursola strained her muscles and pivoted in midair, spinning herself back inside the tower. She slammed against the solid core of the stairwell and slid down a few steps. She could see Alaric and Sylvia up ahead of her, slashing and hacking at the zombies descending toward them. There seemed no end to the undead and the steps were becoming foul with their butchered remains.

Nor were all the creatures that came tumbling out of the fray as extinguished as was hoped. Before Ursola could pull herself to her feet, a zombie with its chest split open by Sylvia's hatchet reared up and snatched at her with its claws. She held it back with the heft of her hammer, but from a nearly prostrate position, she couldn't manage to throw the thing off completely.

"Thought we'd lost you," Doran said, his sword lashing out to cleave the top of the zombie's skull. Decayed brains and rancid blood splashed across Ursola as the creature went limp.

Ursola kicked the carcass aside. The battlemage's eyes went wide with fright and dropping his sword, he caught at the body, pulling it back before it could fall through the hole in the wall. "Sorry," the dwarf grumbled in apology.

Doran carefully leaned the corpse against the inner wall, his face one of unspoken reproach. Ursola felt guilty enough already. It needed only a glimpse at the jagged hole inflicted by Flamefang's claws to know why they had to be careful. Anything plunging from the tower was apt to draw the dragon's attention back to them. Indeed, she'd surrendered her place at the front of their advance to accommodate the revised tactics Alaric had suggested. They wouldn't fight the zombies anywhere close to the spots where Flamefang had pulled away sections of the wall, instead letting the undead follow them down to where they could more safely be engaged.

Only now that strategy had run its course. Alaric and Sylvia had reached the top of the tower, with the turret right above them. Their objective, if indeed Yandryl's crystal was on the spire, was too close to turn away now. Moreover, the magnitude of the hole just beneath the turret was itself a risk. Animated or extinguished, the danger that one of the zombies would fall and beckon Flamefang was too great. So knight and pirate fought their way to the landing just beneath the upper room and were striving to cut down each zombie as it climbed down to engage them.

"Help me back up," Ursola told Doran. "I've got to help."

"There isn't enough room," Doran said. "Scarce enough for two of them to use their blades."

Ursola turned her head, glancing back down at the two buccaneers. It was obvious from their expressions that they were content to keep themselves in reserve or to bolt for the guardroom below if things got that bad. She returned her attention to Doran. "Well, what about you? Don't you know a spell or something?"

Doran let a weary smile cross his face. "The sort of magic a battlemage learns embraces power over subtlety and finesse. I'm not so sure I'd be helping if I conjured a thunderbolt that shocked everything and everyone on that landing."

Frustrated by the wizard's tone, Ursola drew away from him and started back up the steps. She risked a look through the hole in the wall. Flamefang was still there, far below, poised above a section of roof that was burned away. The dragon's attitude was like that of a cat watching a mousehole, his full attention riveted on the spot where he expected prey to appear.

Cautiously, the dwarf tore her eyes from the imposing image of the dragon and started back up the steps. She swung her hammer into the heads of the zombies sprawled at her feet, battering them until she was certain the animating force had been driven from the undead. She stopped just below the landing, a few steps beneath where Alaric and Sylvia struggled to reach the stairs leading to the room above. From her vantage, Ursola could see the undead trying to push their way past their comrades to attack the survivors. She also saw that the slain zombies were piling up on the landing, turning the floor treacherous and threatening to trip Sylvia and Alaric each time they moved.

An idea came to Ursola. Shifting her hammer around, she used the spiked hook on the back of the head to spear one of the corpses. Her dwarven brawn served her in good stead as she pulled the body toward her. "Doran," she hissed down the steps. "Get those two sea-robbers to help clear away these carcasses as I hand them down." She turned and called up to the two fighters. "Just keep killing them, I'll see they're cleaned up."

After Ursola had successfully removed three of the corpses, she noticed that Alaric and Sylvia were able to maneuver better. She saw the knight's sword punch through the torn mail of an undead guard, raking down its chest to split the heart within. Sylvia decapitated another zombie with a sideways sweep of both hatchet and cutlass, then caved in the skull of another creature as it stumbled over the headless body.

The gruesome bucket brigade quickly shifted the corpses downward, moving them as fast as Ursola could hook them and drag them off the landing. The slaughter ahead of her continued. Descending the steps, the zombies could come at Alaric and Sylvia only a few at a time and only from one direction, eliminating the threat of surrounding the fighters. The undead fell like wheat before the scythe as sword and axe wrought a gory toll upon them.

Ursola struggled to keep up with the numbers being felled on the landing. Many times she'd start to drag a corpse only to have another suddenly drop on top of it. The muscles in her arms began to feel like someone had set hot pins into them as the dwarf continued to push herself to greater effort.

A cry of alarm rang out from just below her. Ursola hooked another body, then twisted her head around to see what was wrong. She blanched at the sight of Doran struggling with the zombie she'd just sent down the stairway. The creature, obviously, hadn't been as dead as she'd thought and had revived as the battlemage dragged it away. An almost crippling blend of guilt and horror pulsed through her. "I've got to help Doran," she called up to the landing. Reversing her hammer, she smashed the head of the last body she'd hooked, obliterating any chance there was a spark of animation left in its decayed brain.

Lunging down the steps, Ursola thought for a ghastly moment that the zombie had its teeth in Doran's throat. Only the absence of blood told her otherwise. The undead had merely managed to bite the battlemage's cloak, but in its savagery, it was shaking its head from side to side, trying to worry its catch. With each shake of its head, the zombie was drawing the garment tighter around Doran's throat. The wizard's hands were locked about the walker's wrists, trying to keep it from gaining a better grip on him.

"Get off of him," Ursola snarled. Her hammer stove in the side of the zombie's skull and sent it pitching downward. Doran smiled and drew a deep breath as the creature released him. Before the battlemage could express anything more, they both heard a scream from below.

Ursola turned the bend in the stairs just in time to witness the catastrophe. Hearing the commotion above them, the buccaneers had started up to help. When she knocked the zombie off Doran, she sent the creature hurtling down at the pirates. Unaware that the creature was truly dead now, the men had assumed the undead had broken through. They turned to flee.

The sight of Ursola was enough to check the pirates' action, but it did nothing to arrest the corpse's tumble. She made a fumbling effort to reach for it, but she already knew she'd be too late. The dwarf's hand caught only a shred of ragged livery that came away in her fingers. The rest of the zombie hurtled through a hole in the tower wall.

Time seemed to slow down as Ursola watched the body falling through the air. The angle was the worst possible. It plummeted onto Flamefang's spiny back, glancing off the crimson scales before clattering across the roof.

The dragon shifted his horned head and stared at the body for just an instant. Then he turned his eyes upward, looking to the tower. Flamefang was no longer fixated on the room below the burned roof.

"The dragon's coming back!" Ursola shouted. She turned away from the hole, deliberating which way to go. Down or up?

"Alaric! Sylvia! Grab onto something!" Doran yelled. In the face of the crisis, he'd decided to unleash his magic, whatever the danger. Ursola could understand his thinking. Next to being roasted by a dragon, almost anything gave a better chance for survival.

Ursola felt the air suck in around her. It was nothing compared to the effect ahead of the battlemage. Forward of an invisible line defined by his outstretched hand it was as though a hurricane had been unleashed. She could see the bodies of zombies being buffeted by powerful gales, sent smashing over and over into the roof above the landing. Those zombies trying to climb down the steps were thrown back, sent crashing into the room above. Nor did any others appear to replace them.

Alaric was sent sprawling but managed to wedge the bottom of his kite shield into a crack at the base of the steps. With this to serve him as anchorage, the knight kept himself from being sent flying by the magical tempest. Sylvia leveraged herself with her hatchet, sinking it into the mantel of the doorway and holding onto its handle with both hands. The pirate was lifted off her feet by the fury of Doran's storm but managed to defy its strength.

The battlemage absolved the spell almost as quickly as he conjured it. "Move! Into the turret!" Doran was already moving, bounding up the steps like an unleashed hound. Ursola was close behind him and she could hear the buccaneers hot on her heels. Already the musky, reptilian reek of dragon was wafting into the tower. How many seconds before they could expect to feel Flamefang's fiery breath?

Alaric ripped his shield free and charged up the steps. Doran caught up to Sylvia and pushed her ahead. They were just slipping through the trapdoor-like opening when the dwarf started up the final stairs. "Hurry!" she shouted to the pirates. The two men nearly trampled her as they raced across the landing and scrambled up the steps.

There was a hideous impression of heat all around her as Ursola mounted the last few steps. Sylvia and Doran reached down and grabbed her arms, jerking her up into the room. The buccaneers slammed down the iron-banded door at the top the very second she was clear. As it closed, she could see little fingers of flame snake up from below.

"That was close," Ursola said, choking back an urge to vomit. Never had joining her ancestors been so near.

•••

Alaric couldn't give much attention to what was happening behind him. He noticed the tower room only in the vaguest sense, an impression of a waist-high stone embrasure on all sides with thick pillars supporting a roof. Any other details were lost on him. His focus was upon the tangle of bodies pressed up against one section of the battlements.

The knight didn't know how many zombies had been blown over the low wall by Doran's spell. What he did know was that he shouldn't give the ones that hadn't been blown away a chance to disentangle themselves. After the tempest he'd endured, his body felt as though Ratbag had been using him as a punching bag, but he forced his protesting muscles into action. His sword clove through the pate of a walker as it started to rise from the heap of squirming undead. Its brains spilled down the front of its rotten face and it tipped back, plunging over the side.

What followed was butcher's work. Every notion of chivalry and honor nagged at Alaric as he played his sword against his foes. Had they been living enemies, even the most scabrous of ratlings, he'd have been moved to mercy. But against the undead, there could be no mercy. These weren't thinking creatures anymore. They couldn't truly be killed, simply destroyed. Hacking them apart was more akin to breaking a stone or shattering a glass. It was who the zombies had been that evoked any manner of pity, not the malefic things they'd become.

At least such were the arguments Alaric made to himself as he split skulls and stabbed hearts. His awareness withdrawing into a red haze, his swinging sword felt as though it were held by another hand. Only when the last of the wretched undead had been dispatched did anything like normalcy return to him.

"You can stop. They're all dead," Sylvia assured him. When he swung around, he saw that her face was pinched with a wariness he hadn't seen there before. The cutlass was held defensively across her chest, ready to block his sword should he strike at her. Dimly, Alaric realized his arm was raised to do just that.

"I beg your indulgence," Alaric said, quickly sheathing the blade. He compelled himself to look at the mangled wreckage he'd made of the zombies. He couldn't indulge any weakness. Not when he might be called on to do the same thing many more times before the Black Plague was finally turned back.

If it could be turned back.

"At least the dragon's forgotten about us again," Ursola called from where she stood beside the battlements. The dwarf was peering over the wall, pointing at something far below them.

Alaric walked over and joined her. Far below, on the hillside, Flamefang was eating his fill of the zombies that had been thrown from the roof by Doran's spell. Some of the creatures, their brains and hearts still intact after the fall, continued to crawl about on their broken limbs, but even if they had the wit to try, they were too slow to escape the dragon's teeth.

"Your magic worked better than you expected," Alaric told Doran as he turned away from the wall. Now that the knight had the chance, he could see that the turret had indeed become a refuge for the castle's survivors. Crude pallets with scavenged bedding were strewn everywhere. He could see the shreds of pennants and flags turned into blankets, spears and halberds that had been repurposed to act as bedframes.

Whatever the tower's original furnishings, only two things looked to have remained intact. Upon a large turntable stood a massive ballista, a weapon so stoutly built that even the desperate survivors had given up trying to dismantle it.

The other item looked to have been shunned by the refugees. Alaric suspected the flag lying at its base had been covering it before Doran removed it. Resting within the flanged notches of an obsidian pedestal, a crystal the size of the knight's shield smoldered with a sinister light. A yellow glow pulsated from within the facets, sending weird shadows crawling across the floor.

Repressing his uneasiness, Alaric stepped toward the pedestal. "I said your spell was more beneficial than you planned," he repeated. Doran barely looked up from his scrutiny of the crystal. "The wind sent a lot of zombies hurtling from the tower. Flamefang went after them and forgot all about us."

The battlemage shook his head. "I'm afraid he'll remember soon enough," Doran said. He waved his hand at the crystal, not quite touching it. "Whatever magic Yandryl used, whether she found this crystal in some primordial ruin or created it herself, its power is incredible. From its dweomer, I believe it controls Flamefang completely. Dominates the dragon the way you would a dog." His voice dropped to an awed whisper. "Alaric, I think she actually fused her own soul with Flamefang. Bound him to her as though he were her familiar."

Unversed as he was in arcane theories, Alaric had seen for himself how profound the link between wizards and their familiars was. When Hulmul's familiar Malicious died, the severing of that connection had left the man almost insensate for hours. His mind had been so afflicted that he'd nearly been killed himself.

What then, was the effect upon a familiar, if that's what Yandryl had made of Flamefang, when the master died? Alaric didn't know, but he could see that Doran had some idea.

"Even in death, the dragontaming crystal binds Flamefang to Yandryl," Doran explained. "Perhaps with study I could find a way to break the enchantment."

Alaric shook his head. "We don't have that time," he declared. He was thinking not only of the dragon, but also the arrival of Gogol's ghost ship.

Doran drew his sword. "Then our other choice is to break the crystal." He held the blade to one side. "One of two things will happen. Either Flamefang will exult in his freedom and fly far from this island, or he'll be consumed by a need to revenge himself. If it's the latter, he's likely to come straight here to ensure the crystal – and everyone around it – is destroyed."

"We've no choice," Alaric said. His gaze drifted back to the ballista. It was a curious thing to see in such a place. Unless, of course, Yandryl herself had been worried Flamefang would try to destroy the crystal and had set the ballista here to defend against the dragon.

"Maybe," the knight mused, "we can give Flamefang something to worry about if he wants to fight." Alaric turned to Sylvia. "Can you shoot that thing?" he asked, pointing at the ballista.

"I can't," Sylvia answered. "But I know people who can." She set a finger to her mouth and gave a sharp whistle. The noise disturbed the two buccaneers as they rummaged through the bedding in search of any valuables the refugees had hidden. "I have work for you scallywags," she told them. "Get that thing armed and ship-shape."

The buccaneers made a hurried inspection. "Seems fine, but there's a problem," one of the artillerists reported. "There's no ammunition."

Alaric groaned. The ballista itself might have been too stout for the refugees to scavenge from, but its ammunition wasn't. The over-sized bolts would be just as readily turned into bed frames as any spear or halberd. "Look around," he ordered the pirates as he turned and dismantled one of the pallets. He scowled as he found one side composed of a pikestaff from which the head had been broken off. "Just hope there's still something usable."

"Better make it fast," Ursola called out. The dwarf remained by the wall watching the hill below. "Flamefang's finished the zombies… and now he's looking this way." Her last words came out in a gasp as she scrambled back from the battlements.

"Nothing to be lost smashing it now." Alaric turned to Doran.

The battlemage shook his head. "Only our lives." Doran raised his sword and brought it crashing down upon the crystal. There was a loud clamor, like the demolition of an entire wine shop. A yellow cloud billowed outward as the crystal exploded. For just an instant it retained the shape of the facets that had confined it, then with startling rapidity, the gas dissipated.

Alaric's ears were still ringing from the noise, but he could see Sylvia mouth the word "Here" as she rose from one of the dismantled pallets, a bolt the size of her leg cradled in her arms. He rushed over and helped her carry the missile over to the ballista. Relief tingled through him when he saw that the bolt retained its head of barbed steel. It was as cruel looking an arrowhead as he'd ever seen, with three bladed edges that narrowed to a keen point. He imagined it was the stability of the triangular shape that had caused the refugees to utilize it as it was rather than just the shaft itself.

"Is he leaving?" Alaric shouted to Ursola.

The dwarf's visage was dour as she turned from the edge and shook her head. "No. If anything, he looks even more angry."

Nothing for it, Alaric realized. Their one chance now of eliminating or at least driving off Flamefang was the ballista.

The musky reek of dragon rushed into the knight's lungs as he assisted Sylvia in loading the ballista. The artillerists cranked back the heavy steel wire, swinging their own weight to pivot the pedestal on which the weapon was mounted.

Now Flamefang appeared, swooping up over the tower. The wyrm's eyes glared at the survivors on the roof. The leathery wings bore it through the sky with an erratic, bat-like flutter.

"You've only one shot!" Sylvia reminded her men. "Make sure you hit him!"

"How can we when the lizard won't stay still?" the buccaneers shouted back.

It was clear to Alaric that Flamefang was well aware of the threat posed by the ballista, but equally obvious the wyrm intended to make certain of the crystal's destruction by attacking the tower. He kept dipping and bobbing, never allowing the pirates a clear shot at him. At the same time, he could feel the dragon's mesmeric influence scratching at his mind whenever he met that cold, ophidian gaze. Briefly he would be unable to move, then abruptly his body would lurch as the sensation passed and the reptile juked through the air once more. The dragon's power required him to hold his victim's gaze, like a serpent fascinating a bird.

"Why doesn't he use his breath and be done with it?" Ursola growled. Immolation was one thing, but the dwarf was incensed by the idea Flamefang was toying with them.

"To draw his breath, the dragon must concentrate," Doran said. "He can't do that and keep flitting about the way he is." The wizard punctuated his explanation by loosing a bolt of electricity up at the beast. The crackling beam narrowly missed Flamefang as he dropped below the level of the turret. It explained much, Alaric thought. The dragon's gaze, his fiery breath, they were much after the manner of a spell, demanding complete focus to utilize. While the ballista kept Flamefang at bay, they denied him use of his most potent weapons.

Unfortunately, the dragon had other tactics to draw upon. When next he rose above the level of the turret, the powerful tail struck at them. Flamefang couldn't reach past the walls of the castle, being repulsed by Yandryl's wards. But he could scratch at the surface, the way he'd attacked the facade of the tower. If he couldn't reach the ballista or Doran, then his tail could slash across the columns supporting the roof, gashing one of them so deeply that it buckled.

"He's going to bring the roof down on our heads!" Sylvia cried out as debris pattered down around her.

Alaric hefted his shield and dashed through the shower of rubble. "Ursola, your bombs," he cried to the dwarf.

"They won't burn a dragon," Ursola scowled as she placed one of the fire-bombs into the knight's hand.

"They don't need to," Alaric assured her. "When I shout,

we throw. Aim for his face." He lingered only long enough to see that she understood, then hurried to position himself well away from where Ursola stood. "Doran, try to drive him between us." The battlemage gave him a nod, then sent a bolt of lightning searing up at the dragon as Flamefang attacked another of the columns.

The wyrm darted away from the path of the spell. "Now!" Alaric shouted, lobbing his bomb at the reptile. His throw went long, the incendiary falling past the dragon's wings. Ursola's cast, however, struck true. Flamefang's muzzle was ignited as the caustic material splashed across his face.

Though the fire licked harmlessly at Flamefang's thick scales, the dragon was taken by surprise. His erratic flight faltered, his pattern becoming regular. Predictable.

"Shoot!" Sylvia emphasized her command with a downward chop of her cutlass. The corsairs crewing the ballista were no strangers to aiming at a moving target, having sent bolts slamming into fleeing ships dozens of times in their piratical careers. When Flamefang made the mistake of not maneuvering, the artillerists were easily able to follow the dragon's flight. And anticipate where he'd be when their shot hit him.

Alaric heard the snap of the steel wire as it was released and slammed into the enormous bolt. He saw only a blur of motion as the missile rocketed from the ballista. Automatically, his eyes turned to Flamefang. He missed the moment of impact, but he saw the grisly results. The lance-sized bolt jutted out of the dragon's chest on his right side. Steaming blood gushed from the torn scales, sizzling like motes of fire as they dripped from the reptile's body.

Flamefang threw his head back and a deafening roar thundered across the island. He struggled to stay in the air, but his leathern wings lost all semblance of strength and simply folded back against the scaly body. Like a meteor, the stricken dragon plummeted from the sky. His plunge was at a steep angle and when Alaric rushed to the edge of the turret, he saw the enormous beast crash into the side of the hill. The giant reptile rolled down the slope, careening amid the avalanche precipitated by his violent descent.

The last Alaric saw of the wyrm, Flamefang was sliding into the forest, his body snapping the thick trees as though they were twigs. Even in the moment of his destruction, the dragon displayed his awesome power.

"So, that's our dragon problem resolved," Sylvia said, a grin of supreme relief drawing back her lips. The buccaneers were dancing a jig together, celebrating their accomplishment. It wasn't every pirate who could boast that he'd slain a dragon.

"What do we do now?" Ursola asked. The slaying of Flamefang made her as jubilant as Alaric could ever remember seeing the dwarf.

Alaric felt like a knave when he doused the blaze of celebration. "Now that Flamefang's dealt with, we return to our quest. We start by finding Helchen and the others. Then, if she hasn't found it already, we look for Mournshroud."

The knight ran his mailed fist along the side of the ballista. "The dragon might be gone, but the battle has only started."

CHAPTER TWENTY

A stillness hung over the island. Everything was as quiet as the grave. An appropriate analogy, Gogol thought as he stared at it from across the harbor. His undead arm, its skin exposed after he'd pinned back the sleeve, was draped in pomanders and little rings of flowers. The necromancer scowled at it for a moment, irked by the oddities of the senses. He could walk among hundreds of decaying zombies and inhale their rancid aroma without the slightest twinge, yet the necrotic odor of his substitute arm agitated him. He'd need to collect some living specimens and perform a few experiments to figure out why that was.

Gogol leaned against the rail that circled the ghost ship's quarterdeck. Below him, the emaciated spectral walkers awaited his commands. The vessel wasn't quite near enough to shore for them to employ their poles to bring them onto the rocky quay, so they'd have to rely on the sails they'd stolen from a fishing village on the coast. The community had been most forthcoming. Not only sails, but good timber to reinforce the hull. And, of course, having been spared the attentions of the Black Plague until then, the village provided him with plenty of recruits for his crew.

"More than enough to deal with you, von Mertz," Gogol hissed, clenching the fist of his undead arm. "You and your rotten companions."

The necromancer was certain his enemy remained on the island. Had Alaric finished whatever business he had here, then there wouldn't have been a ship waiting for him in the harbor. It bothered him that he'd been compelled to let the other ship sail away. There was a chance that slippery thief Gaiseric was on board, or perhaps the brutish orc who'd almost killed him in Vasilescu's cellars. He was confident, though, that the knight would've disembarked. Likely that murderous witch hunter as well. The Order's killers weren't exactly known to be trusting people and Gogol didn't imagine she'd be an exception. No, he was positive she'd have gone with Alaric. That put at least the two of them ashore.

If he only had some clue where Alaric might be, it would make things so much simpler. Gogol could land his zombies and surround the knight if he only knew where to attack. After his enemy's previous escapes, he didn't want even the smallest risk the man would slip through his fingers again. He had to make certain of his prey before he struck!

Off and on, Gogol had noticed a dragon flying around the castle that stood at the center of the island. The wyrm's presence was a complication he didn't need. He knew his spectral walkers were immune to mundane weapons and could withstand natural fire. He was less certain of their invulnerability to dragon's breath. The disaster under the tower had shown him that alchemical mixtures derived from the reptiles' bile could burn the phantasmal zombies as readily as purely physical undead. He couldn't imagine that the direct source of such power would be less potent.

However, the necromancer's qualms about the dragon were suddenly quashed. Gogol didn't know why the beast was hovering about the castle. It could have something to do with the inhabitants as easily as an expedition led by Alaric. When the wyrm suddenly wheeled about in midair and went careening down into the forest, his opinion changed. Obviously, the dragon had been struck down. Gogol was certain Alaric was responsible. He could feel it in his bones.

"Now I know where to strike," the necromancer laughed to himself. "Make for shore," he commanded his zombies. Exerting his will, Gogol prodded the creatures to greater effort, putting on more sail so they would hurtle toward the quay. He wasn't concerned about stoving in the hull on unseen rocks or a submerged reef. His crew couldn't drown and there would be plenty of time to repair the ship.

Once Alaric von Mertz was dead.

CHAPTER TWENTY-ONE

Alaric led the way back down through the spire. An inexplicable sense of urgency gripped him as he encouraged his companions to greater haste. Flamefang may have been disposed of, but there was still the threat of Skargash's orcish zombies to worry about. Even this, however, didn't explain the premonition of crisis that spurred him on.

Then, as he turned a corner in the winding stairway, Alaric was afforded a clear view of the bay by one of the holes Flamefang had made. He could see Gogol's ghost ship, only now the vessel was right up on the shore. He could see movement and knew the necromancer was disembarking his zombies. Soon the island would be infested with spectral walkers.

"Gogol's here," Alaric said, a note of defeat slipping into his voice. "His zombies are already moving for the castle." He pointed to the file of undead marching through the harbor buildings and into the forest.

"Maybe they're just normal zombies," Ursola suggested as she studied the scene. From this distance it was impossible to make out the eerie glow the spectral walkers emitted.

Doran shook his head. "That's too much to wish for," he stated. "I've met unsavory wizards with the same sort of personality as this Brunon Gogol. That kind lacks full confidence in their own abilities, so when they exert themselves, they do so with all the force they can muster. Overwhelming force if it's available. No, we know he has command over spectral walkers, so that's what he will set against us."

Alaric ground his teeth in frustration. He was thankful he'd let Gaiseric keep Cryptblade and sent the thief along with Helchen. The enchanted sword should be potent against the spectral walkers. Between it and the magic the witch hunter had gleaned from Hulmul's books, it at least gave their party a chance if they ran into Gogol's zombies. They'd need that edge. Unlike Alaric's group, Helchen's might not even be aware the necromancer had followed them to the island.

The knight frowned as he looked at the sword of the von Mertzes that he carried. Unlike Cryptblade, he'd already seen for himself that his own weapon couldn't harm spectral walkers. He looked over at Doran. "Maybe your magic can make the difference."

The battlemage bore a dour expression as he measured his answer. "Magic takes a toll upon those who wield it. My spells can affect the spectral walkers, but I can only do so much for so long." He gestured at the undead as they continued to leave the ghost ship. "I think by sheer numbers, there are too many for my powers to destroy. At least in a straight fight." Doran perked up as an idea came to him. Alaric was reminded that the man was not only a wizard, but something of a soldier as well. "We might try hit and run tactics. Whittle down Gogol's horde bit by bit."

Sylvia came forward. "Maybe I think too much like a pirate," she said, "but if we can get around the zombies, we might not need to fight at all." She turned an inquiring look on Alaric. "This Gogol, do you think he'd have sense enough to leave a guard on his ship?"

"What are you suggesting?" Alaric asked.

Sylvia shared an eager smile with her buccaneers. "Isn't it obvious? The necromancer wants us to fight his zombies, but we don't have to accommodate him. It's like when the King's Navy is trying to catch you out. They want a fight. You don't. So, when you see an opportunity to avoid meeting them, you take it."

Ursola gave the pirate a bewildered look. "I'm sure you've some scheme you're hatching, but by my ancestors, I can't see it."

"It's simple," Sylvia explained. "Even with the necromancer goading them on, the zombies are slow on the march. We go through the forest, slip past them, and steal their ship!" The pirate seemed proud of her devious plan.

Alaric shook his head. "Well and good… if we could leave now." The knight jabbed his thumb at the floor, indicating the citadel beneath them. "We've still got to find Mournshroud and rejoin Helchen's group. We can't just leave them behind."

From the expression on Sylvia's face, it seemed like she would have argued the last point, but recovering the relic was still the paramount concern. "It was a good idea," she said, "and maybe we'll still get our chance." She thrust her cutlass at the distant vessel. "That's our way off the island now that Mendoza's stolen The Demoness. Whatever else happens, we're going to have to make a play to take that ship from Gogol... and hope the blasted scow is seaworthy enough to get us to the mainland."

Alaric conceded Sylvia's point. They would have to take Gogol's ship, whether that meant sneaking past his zombies or fighting their way through the horde.

But first they had to find Mournshroud. And their friends. Allowing that any of them were still alive.

"Der bimbo not goin' bellyup!" Ratbag's angry bellow echoed through the halls. His scimitar was buried up to the grip in the chest of the biggest zombie orc Gaiseric had seen yet. It was an enormous monster that made even Ratbag look like a runt by comparison. The thing's arms were thicker around than the thief's leg and each of its fingers ended in a claw that could gut a bear with one swing.

The thief swung Cryptblade, withering a goblin runner that was trying in its frantic way to sink its teeth in his throat. Though Skargash was gone, the castle corridors remained infested with mobs of the necromancer's monstrous zombies. This pack was the third they'd encountered since recovering Mournshroud and it was by far the most formidable. Helchen and the buccaneers had all they could cope with in fending off the orcish walkers and brutes that surrounded them. With their backs to the wall, they plied sword and mace in a desperate defense. Gaiseric had been similarly trapped, but Cryptblade's deathly enchantment was far more lethal against orcs and goblins than it had been against the zombie troll. He was able to extricate himself quickly after the monsters burst into the hallway.

Of course, Gaiseric felt there was another reason he'd been able to slip away. For every zombie that converged upon the rest of them, it seemed like three had gone after Ratbag. Maybe, in some dim way, they knew the orc had killed Skargash, but Gaiseric thought it was the drum strapped to the warrior's back. Ratbag was the only one among them big and strong enough to carry Mournshroud, so the gruesome relic had been lashed to his back. Somehow, he felt, the zombies knew the power it possessed and so were striving to destroy both it and the renegade carrying it before the drum could be used against them. Helchen had tried a few times to reach Ratbag only to find her way blocked by zombies.

When this mob of zombies emerged from the shambles of a sitting room, it struck Gaiseric that most of them made straight for Ratbag, cutting the orc off from the rest of them... and making it impossible for anyone to reach the drum. He was giving a good enough account of himself but pushed back against the wall and now menaced by this freakishly huge abomination, Gaiseric didn't see how Ratbag could survive without help.

"You've really got to stop doing this kind of thing," Gaiseric scolded himself. Ignoring the remaining zombies near him, the rogue hurdled the corpses sprawled on the floor and ran toward Ratbag. He felt the claws of a zombie rake against his armor, heard his cloak tearing as one of the undead snatched at him as he sped past.

Then he was through and hacking away at the creatures surrounding Ratbag. The first few walkers fell before they were even aware of his sword slashing into their rotten flesh.

The orcish walkers wilted to the floor, their bodies rapidly withering as the animating force was extinguished. A massive brute, its swollen gut drooping over its loins, swung around to meet this new attacker. Gaiseric brought Crytblade sweeping across its face, cutting away its lower jaw. Behind the mutilating wound, the zombie's leathery hide took on a desiccated texture. Soon its prodigious flab of green skin was shrunken back against its bones and the creature collapsed at his feet.

"Ratbag! I'm here!" Gaiseric shouted. He thought the cry might distract the abomination the renegade was fighting, but the monster stuck to its enemy with the mindless fixation of most zombies. A huge, clawed hand whipped across Ratbag's body, shredding his armor and sending torn rings of chain dancing across the hall. Bleeding, the orc stumbled back, losing his grip on his scimitar.

"I said 'I'm here'!" Gaiseric howled as he lunged at the abomination. Cryptblade caught the orc monster just beneath the elbow, biting deep into the green flesh. Much like the troll, it didn't seem the sword's enchantment was enough to destroy the monster outright. He watched as the skin drew taut and withered about the underlying bone. The stricken arm fell limp at the creature's side, but otherwise the beast retained its abominable vitality.

The orc abomination rounded on Gaiseric, slashing at him with the claws of its other hand. The thief narrowly ducked the deadly assault and a retaliatory swing of Cryptblade merely trimmed the tips from the monster's talons.

Gaiseric dodged a zombie walker as it grabbed at him, then spun about and brought his sword's edge cleaving into the abomination's face, splitting its nose and ruining one eye. The withering enchantment caused half of the beast's face to curl close to its skull, lending it an almost mummified look.

The abomination glared down at Gaiseric. "It was worth a try," the rogue quipped as the monster brought its hand sweeping down. The trimmed claws flashed only inches from Gaiseric's face as he jumped back.

Powerful arms closed around him, crushing the breath from his body. From the corner of his eye, Gaiseric could see an orc zombie leaning forward to bite his throat. Hurriedly he reversed his grip on Cryptblade and drove its point into the undead behind him. He could actually feel the strength evaporate from the grappling arms as the creature withered. When he looked up, he saw that the brute's attack had done enough damage in any event. The orc abomination loomed over him and this time he wouldn't have the chance to avoid its claws.

Just as he gritted his teeth and braced himself for annihilation, Gaiseric heard the dull, booming notes of Mournshroud reverberating through the hall. The abomination froze in place, a flicker of awareness in its remaining eye as its undead flesh began to putrefy and drip from its bones in a stream of necrotic ooze. He turned his head to see Ratbag crouched on the floor with Helchen behind him, beating the drum with her bare hands. The witch hunter's steely gaze shifted from the dissolving abomination to take in the rest of the zombie horde.

"Luck," Gaiseric muttered, crossing his fingers. He rose and hurried away from the pool of putrid slush that had been the orc abomination. He joined his comrades, helping the buccaneers stave off the few zombies that had yet to feel Mournshroud's power.

When the last zombie in the hall had been dealt with and Helchen stopped sounding the drum, Ratbag rose to his feet. The big orc ignored the dark blood oozing from his torn skin. His attention was fixed on the scimitar lying in the abomination's remains. "Dat's der dandy," he spat as he retrieved his weapon. "Need der edge fer der rumpuz."

Gaiseric fumbled for words to express his gratitude to Helchen, but she waved away his overtures. "You put yourself into that fix to help the orc," she said. "I'd like to think you'd do the same for me." There was just a hint of severity in the way she said it. Helchen was a perceptive woman and well aware that witch hunters were far from popular. The disruption of the Order's authority meant, in turn, that her own authority wasn't as absolute as it had once been.

Gaiseric felt uneasy. He considered Helchen a friend. He also considered her vocation a menace, perhaps not as overwhelming as that of the Black Plague, but for anyone who fell within the Order's purview, every bit as deadly. Rather than respond, he decided to shift the conversation. "If there was any doubt that Mournshroud could destroy the undead, I think we've done enough work with it now to put those questions to rest."

Helchen nodded. "Still, it would be best not to tempt fate too far." She indicated the decaying corpses all around them. "I think it is too much to believe our run-ins with these zombies are mere accident." She locked eyes with Gaiseric and expressed one of the rogue's own fears. "The orcs who made Mournshroud, I believe, made its power two-fold. It not only destroys the undead, but it also attracts them."

"Orcs do love a fight and don't always have the patience to wait for one," Gaiseric said, looking over at Ratbag as the warrior dabbed at his cut chest with an old rag. "They'd probably see that as a winning combination."

"For us, it means we have to be careful about using it," Helchen said. "The more we sound the drum, the better the zombies will be able to converge on us."

A feeling of frustration swelled within Gaiseric. "Then all of this has been for nothing!" he snapped. "A relic that destroys zombies but also draws them to you isn't going to do much good for Korbara." He sent a dark look Ratbag's way, wondering if the orc had known about this aspect of the relic when they set out from the monastery to find it.

"It's a dangerous combination," Helchen admitted. "Against spectral walkers, it might be the only option. Better than standing helpless while they slaughter everyone, at least."

Gaiseric examined the torn edges of his cloak. It had been a fine garment. Now it was just a ratty rag, stained with zombie putrescence. Annoyed, he pulled it free, tucking its golden clasp into a pouch on his belt. He could feel the buccaneers' eyes on him, almost smell the greed rolling off them. It didn't matter how much loot they'd already found, there was a common sentiment among all thieves, whether on land or sea. 'Enough' was always 'just a little bit more'.

"We should be moving," Gaiseric said, doing his best to ignore the covetous pirates. "There's always the possibility this mob had a few stragglers limping after it." He nodded at the decimated zombies.

"We need to find Alaric and the others," the witch hunter

stated. "Now that we've found Mournshroud, the sooner we leave Yandryl's island, the better."

"That," Gaiseric told her, "is the best idea I've heard all day."

The best chance for finding the others, Helchen decided, was to head back toward the spire where Doran thought the dragontaming crystal was kept. The battlemage had warned that if it wasn't there, they'd have to investigate the other towers, but at the very least it was a place to start.

A few straggler zombies disturbed them as the witch hunter led her group back through the lavish halls of Yandryl's apartments, but nothing like the mobs they'd encountered before. Helchen was beginning to think that perhaps they'd exterminated all the orcs and goblins Skargash brought to the island. She was a bit unnerved when Ratbag chopped down a human zombie, for it suggested the Black Plague could be passed from the orcish undead to humans. The reason they hadn't encountered any before, she realized, was because of how destructive the orcs were. When they killed a human, they usually didn't leave enough to be reanimated by the necromantic plague.

Ratbag, anxious as ever for a fight, rejected Helchen's efforts to keep him in the middle of their entourage. The orc wasn't sympathetic to her argument that they needed to protect Mournshroud. She needed the renegade's brawn to manage the relic, however. It would take three of the humans to cart the drum around while the orc could just about carry it without even noticing the strain. Against her better judgment, she had to indulge Ratbag, mitigating his recklessness by keeping herself and Gaiseric close to him. At least if another big pack of zombies showed up, the warrior wouldn't be caught alone.

The orc was just a step or so ahead of her when Helchen saw a flash of steel strike out from the doorway he was approaching. Ratbag blocked the stroke with his scimitar. With his free hand he caught the wrist behind the blade. Snarling, he dragged his attacker from concealment. "Ratbag ain't no cadava," he warned.

"My mistake," the attacker said. Sylvia dangled from Ratbag's hand as though she were nothing but a child. Her eyes had widened with fright, so large they looked to completely fill the sockets of the skull inked across her face.

"Been a while since we saw a living orc," Ursola grumbled as she stepped into view. "You can understand how someone might make a mistake."

Ratbag gave the dwarf a stern glance, but did release his hold on Sylvia. "Get ya sum cheatas," he growled, tapping his eye.

Alaric and Doran appeared behind the dwarf, the other buccaneers from The Demoness following behind them. The knight had doffed his helm, his face bearing a look of relief when he saw Helchen. "Is this everyone?"

Helchen nodded. "I'm sorry, but we lost Korsgaard," she said, turning to Sylvia.

The pirate captain simply shrugged. "Sooner or later, we'd have had to cross swords, so whatever happened to him, maybe it's better that it did." Sylvia gave a questioning look at the corsairs with Helchen. "Whatever you found, we divvy up by shares," she said, her finger tapping the blade of her cutlass. The men returned eager nods of agreement.

"Ratbag killed Skargash," Gaiseric told the knight. He coaxed the big orc to turn around, displaying the hideous drum lashed to his back. "We also found Mournshroud."

"Which means we can leave, if you dealt with the dragon," Helchen stated. She didn't like the somber look Alaric and Doran exchanged.

"Flamefang's not a problem anymore," Alaric said. "But we've another problem now. Gogol's here."

Sylvia stamped her boot against the floor. "My crew deserted us when that ghost ship hove into view. We saw it happen from the tower!" She swung her cutlass through the empty air. "If I ever get my hands on that slug Mendoza…"

"Gogol's sending his zombies to the castle," Alaric interrupted the pirate's tirade. "He must have well over a hundred of them."

Helchen bit her lip, trying to hide the worry she felt. Over a hundred? And it was a surety they'd be spectral walkers, immune to anything that wasn't magical in nature. Too much for Doran's spells and Gaiseric's sword to handle. Too many even if she again resorted to magic. "We've already seen that Mournshroud works against other zombies. Looks like we'll have our chance to see what it can do against Gogol's horde."

Doran had stepped forward to inspect the relic. He raised a warning finger when Helchen described her intentions. "I don't imagine the Order taught you overmuch about the way of enchantments. There are arcane rules that govern anything that has been endowed with a dweomer. In some respects, a magic object is a living thing and requires sustenance. Re-vitalization when its powers are invoked." He pointed at Cryptblade. "Sometimes, like Gaiseric's sword, the very use of the device is also what empowers it." The battlemage gestured again at Mournshroud.

"This relic, however, I think can only be called upon so many times before it must be 'fed.'" Doran's face dropped into a scowl. "I hesitate to conjecture what manner of gory rites the orc warlocks performed to enchant this drum, but it is certain that they weren't anything we'd be comfortable emulating." He was contemplative for a moment. "Maybe the templars of Korbara have the stomach for such things. I'd leave that to them."

"Whether we exhaust its powers or not," Helchen pressed, "we really have no choice."

Alaric's voice was strained when he corrected her. "If we hurry, we might reach the forest before Gogol's zombies can get here." Helchen could detect the strain in the knight's voice, the conflict between helping the people at Korbara and getting another chance at the murderer of his family. "Sylvia thinks we can steal his ship and get away. It's something worth trying, at least."

"Then let's get to it," Gaiseric said. "I'll feel a lot better with a sea between myself and Gogol."

Helchen gave Alaric a sympathetic look. "Let's get to it," she said. The protection of the refugees at Korbara had to come before anything else. If Alaric could accept that, she wasn't about to contradict him.

The survivors quickly retraced their path through the citadel, navigating the corridors and chambers they'd first explored. Helchen continued to keep close to Ratbag. The orc might be the bearer of Mournshroud, but she felt as though she were the relic's custodian. She'd assumed responsibility for it: both getting it to Korbara and drawing upon its power, should the need arise.

Ahead of them, the hall leading to the main gate stood empty. The pirates gave a cheer, imagining that they'd won their wager and would soon be quit of Yandryl's castle of horrors. Helchen was more reserved. She felt that something was wrong. A sideways glance at Alaric told her that the knight felt it, too.

Crossing the entryway, the survivors started down the hill, ground blackened by Flamefang's fire crunching under their feet. The forest was near, its dark vastness promising refuge and concealment. A promise that Helchen found suspicious.

"Wait!" she snapped at two of the corsairs as the men bolted for the trees. The pirates ignored her and continued to sprint for cover. They never made it.

Stalking out from the shadows, an ethereal light shimmering around their almost skeletal frames, a mob of spectral walkers converged on the pirates. One man was pulled down instantly, his ragged screams rising to a tortured shriek as he was eaten alive. The other corsair managed to draw his sword and strike at the glowing zombies. The blade rebounded harmlessly, unable to pierce the ectoplasmic aura. All color draining from his face, the terrified pirate retreated back to the castle.

"No choice now," Gaiseric cried to Helchen. "Sound the drum!"

The witch hunter stepped behind Ratbag as the orc crouched so that she could reach Mournshroud. Staring intently at the spectral walkers, she slapped the ghastly skin of the drum. The dull, pulsating boom of the relic rippled through the air. Helchen watched expectantly for the zombies to putrefy and dissolve.

Instead, the emaciated undead turned away from the gory ruin of the corsair and continued their march on the castle.

"It didn't work!" Sylvia moaned. "Mournshroud didn't work on them!"

"How could this happen?" Alaric demanded, turning to Doran. The battlemage gave him a despairing groan.

Helchen clapped Ratbag on the shoulder, motioning for the orc to move. "Worry about it later!" she shouted. "Right now, just run!"

CHAPTER TWENTY-TWO

Gaiseric's blood felt as though it had been spat into his veins by a frost giant. Fear swelled up his throat and made his tongue into a lump of lead. He couldn't have spoken even if he knew what to say. Inwardly, his every thought screamed at him. What he was doing was insane. Certain death. He was a burglar and thief. Leave naive notions like duty and sacrifice to knights like Alaric and get away while he still had a chance.

No. Instead Gaiseric stepped forward and waved his companions back. His fingers tightened around Cryptblade. The sword was enchanted, and they'd all seen it do terrible things to the undead. It should do the same to the spectral walkers. Of course, all of that was also true for Mournshroud, yet Gogol's diabolical zombies were as lively as they'd ever been.

The spectral walkers shambled forward, pirate blood dripping from their clawed hands and rotten teeth. "Loaded dice and marked cards," Gaiseric said as he rushed to confront the zombies.

Cryptblade crunched into the side of a spectral walker.

The very fact that the magic sword was able to connect with the zombie and pass through the phantasmal aura was a good sign, but Gaiseric didn't feel victorious until he saw the already skeletal creature wither further and crumple in a heap at his feet. Not only was the sword potent against the zombies, but it appeared to affect these ensorcelled undead even more quickly than Skargash's horde.

"The sword works! It works!" Gaiseric shouted to his comrades. His celebration faltered when he looked past the zombies coming toward him and appreciated the multitude yet closing on Yandryl's castle. "I'll hold them as long as I can. Get back inside!" He lunged at the advancing enemy, cutting down two more of the spectral walkers.

Suddenly the grim figure of Doran was standing beside him, a scroll gripped in one hand. "How about we all get back inside?" the battlemage said. He closed his eyes and stretched out his other hand. Gaiseric could see the strain on the wizard's face, feel the chill that crept into the air as he invoked arcane forces. A moment later and a blast of wind spread from Doran's hand to the zombie mob. The undead were hurled back, tossed down the forest path like scarecrows caught in a cyclone.

"Move!" Alaric's command rolled like thunder behind Doran's spell. Gaiseric didn't need to be told twice. Neither did anyone else. He joined the frantic exodus as the survivors streamed back into the castle. Just as he turned, the rogue glimpsed Gogol's sinister figure moving along the trail, coaxing his zombies back onto their feet. He wondered if Alaric had seen the villain … and if his friend knight would've quit the battle, knowing his enemy was so close. Likely he would. The knight had shown many times that his obligations took precedence over his desires.

Gaiseric vaulted over the scorched remains of the gates and hurried across the entryway. Having been resolved to stand his ground so that his friends could escape, this call to retreat felt like a new lease on life. One that he wasn't about to squander.

"Did you have any ideas beyond simply getting back inside?" Ursola asked him as they ran through a ruinous parlor they'd searched earlier. Gaiseric tried not to look too closely at the mangled bodies of Yandryl's servants. It was much too easy to start thinking that at any minute he might be just like them. If he was lucky and his corpse didn't rise again as a zombie.

Instead, Gaiseric shot the dwarf a crooked smile. "You should know I'm making this up step by step."

Alaric was ahead of Gaiseric, but when he heard the rogue's words, he stopped and turned to him. "Steps!" He clapped the thief on the shoulder. "There's an idea! Sylvia, lead the way. Take everyone back to the spire."

Jogging along with Gaiseric, the knight explained the plan his flippant exchange had inspired. "If Mournshroud doesn't work against the spectral walkers, we know the sword you carry does. Not much good where the undead can come at us from all sides, but if we lure them into a narrow place where they can only send a few at a time…"

Gaiseric blanched at the role he'd apparently play. He looked at Cryptblade in horror. "Alaric, I'm the least capable of being responsible for everyone's safety. You, or Helchen, or Ratbag… even Sylvia… all of you are better fighters than I am."

"There's no reason for you to do all the fighting," Helchen told the thief, looking to Alaric for confirmation. "We can take it in turns using the sword."

"Thankfully these zombies are slow," Alaric elaborated. "Were they quick like the runners, we'd have trouble, but against walkers we can safely trade positions on the stairs when whoever's doing the fighting tires."

"You'll also have spellcraft to support you," Doran interjected. His eyes locked with Helchen's. It was clear from his next words what he expected of her. "Like the swordsman, a barrage of magic could be set against the zombies if we took things in turns." Helchen grimaced but gave the battlemage a short nod of assent.

Gaiseric frowned. The plan would be sound if they were simply dealing with zombies, but they weren't. He thought of the way Skargash had maneuvered his undead orcs and goblins, directing them in ways the mindless creatures would never have acted on their own. Gogol could be expected to be more devious than the orc had been. "You're forgetting the necromancer. He's not going to just fritter away his horde in a straightforward fight."

"The cutpurse is right," Ursola chimed in. "If he wants to, he could barricade us in and wait for us to starve. Not like he needs to worry about feeding zombies."

The survivors reached the lavish corridors of Yandryl's apartments. The pirates paused up ahead, taking a moment to get their bearings. Sylvia had heard enough of the conversation to add her own concern to the mix. "It's not enough to beat the zombies," she cautioned. "We must get past them. Make it to the ghost ship before they can cut us off."

"Der skull-moll gabbin' straight," Ratbag grunted. "Der bonecalla bein' yeller like'n wolf pizzle. Gogol noodlin' ter get der bump, he gonna leggit ta der watta-wagon."

Gaiseric bit back a curse. "Ratbag says if we do start killing off the spectral walkers, Gogol's sure to take the rest of them and get back to his ship. He'll strand us here and come back with a bigger horde."

Alaric scratched his chin. "We'll just have to be more cunning than he is." He turned to Sylvia. "Do you think your remaining buccaneers are enough to get that derelict moving?"

The pirate considered the matter, tugging at one of her earrings as she thought. "It won't be easy with four of us, but I think we can manage. I've seen no evidence a zombie can swim, so we just need to take her out far enough to the harbor that they can't walk along the bottom and still reach the keel."

"All right," the knight said. "We'll still make for the tower, but I'm amending the plan. Make a quick search of these rooms and grab any ropes, chains, anything that could be cut into strips and tied together."

"What's the idea now?" Gaiseric asked, puzzled by the commands.

"We're still going to fight Gogol on the stairs," Alaric said. He reached forward and tugged Cryptblade from Gaiseric's hand. "At least some of us are. The rest will fashion a line from whatever we can scavenge. There's plenty of holes Flamefang knocked in the side of the tower. While we're fighting the zombies, the rest of you climb down and make for the ship."

Gaiseric glanced at the sword Alaric had taken from him. Despite his own arguments, he now felt ashamed not to be participating in the fight. Helchen intimated the reason for the thief's discomfort. "You're the best climber among us," she said. "We need you to lead the way."

"Besides," Ursola added as the dwarf ripped a tapestry down from the wall and began tearing it into strips, "we need the pirates to sail the ship. So, if anybody were to fall and break his neck, you're the one we can best afford to lose."

Gaiseric sent a smile the dwarf's way. "It's nice to feel appreciated," he said, before joining in the looting of Yandryl's rooms. Ursola's black humor was just the thing to motivate him. If even she could find something to joke about, then maybe there was hope for them after all.

The thief hesitated as he ripped a bellpull from the wall of a bedroom. Hope, yes, at least for those who climbed out of the tower. What about the ones keeping the zombies busy on the stairs? The odds were long for whoever had that job. Especially the one who acted as rearguard for the entire group.

Even as the thought came to him, Gaiseric was certain he knew who'd assume that role. Alaric's sense of duty wouldn't permit him to do anything else. Nor did the thief think there was any argument that would sway the man from his choice.

It was with a decidedly more somber mood that Gaiseric continued his search. The hope of escape was now darkened by the certainty of death. Not his own, but that of a friend.

It took his companions longer than Alaric had hoped to find enough material for a line he judged long enough to reach the hillside. By the time they'd looted Yandryl's rooms, he could hear the spectral walkers in the chambers below them. Once again, he was thankful these zombies weren't as spry as some of the other Black Plague's victims, a slowness he attributed to Gogol's influence over them. With the necromancer to guide the zombies there was little chance the survivors could shake the undead from their trail.

"Up to the tower," the knight ordered the others. He caught Sylvia's eye. The pirate nodded and led them through the deserted hallways toward the guardroom and the tower. Alaric followed behind, the family sword sheathed at his side and Cryptblade clenched in his fist. Though magic spells could destroy the spectral walkers, by their nature such arcane displays drew attention. The longer they could keep Gogol uncertain of their location, the better their chances were. That meant if any of the horde suddenly appeared, it was better they met the subtle bite of an enchanted sword than the sizzling crack of a battlemage's invocation.

The first of their undead pursuers didn't come into view until they were rushing into the guardroom. Alaric glanced back as he heard a crash in the hallway behind him. A marble plinth supporting a jade bowl had been knocked over by a shambling zombie. The creature ambled through the debris, its shriveled face open in a hungry leer. After it, more of the ghastly corpses marched into sight, an unbroken stream that drifted away into the lower corridors.

"They're coming," Alaric hissed to the other survivors. "Get to the stairs. Gaiseric, get that line ready."

The survivors hastened across the guardroom, circling around the carnage left by the earlier fight. Alaric regretted the necessity of smashing through the doors. They'd have been a useful barricade now, even if they delayed Gogol's monsters by a few minutes.

"This way," Sylvia cried out, guiding Gaiseric up the circular steps. The other pirates kept close to their captain, as though convinced their very survival depended on obeying her slightest word.

Alaric backed across the room. Once he was certain the rest were already on the stairs, he started up, keeping one eye always on the doorway through which the enemy would soon appear. He didn't have long to wait, as the spectral walkers emerged from the hallway. There was an intensity about their eyes that he'd found normally to be absent from zombies. When they moved into the room, it was without distraction or confusion. The undead marched straight toward the stairs.

"It's Gogol," Helchen told Alaric. The witch hunter was behind him on the stairs, immediately over his shoulder. Her gaze was every bit as intense as that of the spectral walkers. "He's using his magic to stir what awareness the zombies retain, focusing them on his enemies."

"That means you two more than me," Doran joked from higher on the stairway. "I'm just collateral damage, in a sense. The hapless fox caught between the bear and the wolves."

Alaric glowered at the zombies as they drew ever closer. "If Gogol had any restraint or scruples, they were burned out of him when he was able to draw on the Black Plague's power." The knight clenched his teeth, thinking back to when he'd argued with his father to spare Gogol. The baron had been ready to hang the man for dabbling in sorcery. Alaric had protested that the minor cantrips Gogol had conjured hadn't harmed anyone and certainly didn't warrant ending the man's life. How very different everything might have been had he just let the execution happen.

"Donna bump 'em all," Ratbag growled, the big orc leaning down so that his foul breath rasped across Alaric's scalp. "Noodlin' that Ratbag spellin' ya, bye an' bye."

The knight couldn't help but smile at Ratbag's violent excitement. "Don't worry, I'll be sure to leave some for you."

Then the time for humor was finished. The first of the spectral walkers reached the stairs. Alaric brought Cryptblade chopping down into the creature's desiccated skull, splitting it down to the spine. It was thrown back by the impact, withered still further by the blade's enchantment. The zombies behind it shoved the carcass out of their way and continued onward, heedless of the destruction that awaited them with each swing of the knight's weapon.

"We'll have to go higher." Gaiseric's words drifted down to Alaric from the winding stairway. "The edges here aren't stable enough. They might come apart if we put pressure on them."

"The dragon left plenty of holes," Sylvia told the thief. "Let's see if the next one's more suitable." The knight could hear the clatter of armor and weaponry as the pirates and Gaiseric hurried upward. A grim thought came to Alaric as he played his sword across the chest of an attacking zombie. What if they were forced so high into the spire that their line couldn't reach the ground?

Step by step, the horde advanced. Alaric felt the strain in his arm. It needed only the merest cut from Cryptblade to destroy the undead, but he found it difficult to restrain himself. The zombies were such a horrible affront to every instinct and impulse that he kept venting an urge to see them destroyed utterly. It wasn't enough to just slash them and leave the enchantment to do its work. He had to punish the monsters, as though if he hurt them enough that pain would find its way back to their villainous master.

"Doran," Alaric called up the stairs. At his cry, the battlemage stretched out his hand and a bolt of electricity crackled through the zombies just behind the walker the knight was fighting. As the shocked mob collapsed, Alaric finished his own opponent and retreated upward several steps. Though he was slaughtering them, the sheer numbers of the undead forced him to give ground. If he tried to hold, he was certain to be dragged down.

"Gaiseric's fixed the line," Sylvia shouted down to Alaric. "He'll start out soon."

A bit of good news. Alaric continued back up the steps, a blast of wind conjured by Doran giving him enough space to make his withdrawal. He saw the hole Gaiseric had rejected as too unstable. A few of the zombies were thrown against the compromised wall, knocking free some of the blocks as they hurtled earthward. Another worry, one that blotted out any momentary relief. After all the damage Flamefang had inflicted on it, how much more could the tower endure?

"Gimme der shiv," Ratbag snarled from behind the knight. "Ya get der breatha."

Alaric shook his head and brought Cryptblade slashing through the shoulder of another zombie. "I can stand it," he said. "No need for you to take over."

Lightning smashed down into the spectral walkers, giving Alaric time to withdraw a few more steps. The turn in the stairway now obscured his view of the hole in the wall. However, he soon knew someone else was close enough to see it.

"Climb out! Climb out and come at them from above!" The oily voice was that of Gogol. The necromancer was sending his zombies to climb the outside of the tower.

Rage boiled up inside Alaric. His enemy was near, so near that there was a real possibility of cutting his way down to the man. A few turns on the stairs was all it needed to come to grips with him! Fury burned away the fatigue in his muscles. He threw himself at the zombies, hewing their decayed flesh with brutal sweeps of Cryptblade.

"Alaric! Not that way!" Helchen cried out, but the knight was past listening to anyone. Revenge was too close for that.

Down the steps, Alaric fought, advancing over ground he'd conceded to the undead only moments before. Zombies fell before his flashing sword, but his very triumph created danger. His descending foot, instead of setting down on solid stone, connected with a corpse. The body turned under his boot, and he lost his standing. Disaster struck as the knight slipped and started to slide down the steps. Spectral walkers closed in on him, claws and teeth scratching at his armor as they tried to savage the prostrate man.

"Shove off, cadavaz!" Ratbag bellowed. The big orc lunged down at the mob of zombies. His scimitar licked across the neck of one, sending its head glancing off the inner wall. Another fell with its torso split from its waist. A third crumpled with a gash as wide as its leg in the middle of its chest.

Alaric blinked in amazement. Ratbag's scimitar wasn't enchanted, yet here it was hacking apart the glowing zombies. The reason dawned on him at once. The ectoplasmic aura that clung to the spectral walkers had protected them from

Mournshroud's power, but in doing so that protection had been exhausted. The undead weren't destroyed outright, but now they weren't immune to mundane weapons.

"Helchen! They're no longer invulnerable!" Alaric fought back onto his feet. "Mournshroud dispelled their protection!"

"If that's the case, pull that blasted orc back," Ursola told him. The dwarf had a fire-bomb in each hand and a determined look on her face.

Alaric caught hold of Ratbag's belt and drew the renegade with him a few steps. Then the floor ahead of them exploded into flame. A clutch of spectral walkers was caught in the inferno, their bodies blackening as they withered to the floor. Ursola pushed her way between the knight and the orc, then lobbed the second bomb down into the massed undead.

Alaric heard a pained cry from below. There was only one enemy in that horde who'd cry out in alarm, and it wasn't the zombies. His anger now bolstered by a sense of victory, Alaric charged through the crackling flames, plunging down the steps. Gogol was too close to let the fiend slip away again.

The knight emerged from the burning section of stairway to find several zombies before him. He ignored his own smoldering garments and swept Cryptblade against the creatures. The first went down easily, but the others rushed at him in a mass. He used his shield to batter one and send it careening out the hole in the wall. Another impaled itself on his sword. Alaric was surprised by the deliberately suicidal move, but when the dying creature clutched the weapon to itself and pulled it free from his grasp, he guessed its motive.

Before Alaric could make a move to recover Cryptblade, a black shape flung itself up at him from the steps below. The impact knocked him onto his back, and it was all he could do to put his shield between himself and his enemy.

"Now you die, von Mertz," Gogol hissed at him. The necromancer's visage was pinched into a hateful sneer. "Die and be damned!"

The knight was astounded by the inhuman strength Gogol brought to bear against him. He saw the grotesque arm his foe had used to replace his maimed limb. It reminded him of the mighty abominations the necromancer had set against them in Singerva. Under the pressure of those undead fingers, the steel of his shield was coming apart, fraying as though it were cloth.

"I should never have asked the baron to spare you," Alaric spat at his enemy.

"Mercy is crueler than death," Gogol snapped. "When a man is shown mercy, he gains his life but loses his pride." The necromancer's fingers ripped into the shield and pressed upon Alaric's mailed arm. "Fear not. I'll show you no mercy."

Alaric struggled but knew there was little he could do to throw off his foe. Then, to his wonder, he heard again the dull, grisly boom of Mournshroud. Someone was sounding the drum once more.

Gogol's grip, superhuman a moment before, now lost all its strength. Alaric pushed him away as though he weighed no more than a child. He saw the necromancer's monstrous arm putrefying, fairly dripping off the man's body in a trickle of decayed sludge. Gogol stared at his disintegrating limb in horror, then looked up as Alaric surged to his feet and drew the sword still sheathed at his belt. The sword of the von Mertzes.

"Fear not," Alaric threw the necromancer's own words back at him. "This time, I'll show you no mercy."

Gogol glanced behind him, but the stairway below was still crowded with spectral walkers. His eyes darted back to Alaric, then shifted to the left. Before the knight could swing his sword, the necromancer dove for the hole in the wall. Alaric had a fleeting glimpse of the necromancer's body plummeting to the ground far below, his black robes rippling around him like the pinions of a bat.

"Even in death, he finds a way to cheat me," Alaric cursed Gogol. He had no more time to rue his thwarted revenge. Though the necromancer was gone, his zombies remained. The knight turned to face the resurgent horde as it climbs up to meet him.

The next moment, he heard the boom of Mournshroud once more. Their protective aura already broken, this time when the relic's power washed over the spectral walkers, their bodies rapidly corroded into necrotic slime. With the spectral aura broken by the first intonations, now the drum's power was disintegrating the creatures. Alaric looked back to see Ratbag descending the stairs, Helchen following behind the orc, her hands slapping against the relic strapped to his back.

"It looked like you could use some help," Helchen commented as she neared Alaric.

The knight cast his ruined shield through the hole in the tower. "It did look that way," he grimly conceded, a bitter taste in his mouth. Without Gogol to pursue, he felt hollow inside. In a way, while he had vengeance to accomplish, he felt as though part of his family was still with him. Now that last link with them was gone.

"Fortune smiles on the bold!" Gaiseric's cheer rang down from above. The thief came sprinting down the steps, a broad smile on his face. He clapped his hands as he watched Helchen use Mournshroud to destroy Gogol's horde.

"Why are you so jubilant?" Ursola huffed at the rogue.

Gaiseric smiled and pointed at the disintegrating zombies. "That," he crowed. "That means I don't have to climb down this tower." He looked aside at Alaric. "No offense, but I feel a lot better not having to trust that line you had us string together."

Alaric returned the rogue's smile. "We still have to get off this island," he reminded Gaiseric. "That means we have to trust that derelict will hold together long enough to reach the mainland."

Gaiseric's smile collapsed. "Maybe I could stay here, and you could send another boat back for me?"

CHAPTER TWENTY-THREE

Flames engulfed the mob of zombies lingering within the castle's main gate. Ursola frowned as her hand dipped into the satchel. She only had one more of the incendiaries left. She looked aside at Helchen and told the witch hunter as much. It would be an utter waste to squander the bomb on undead that could be cut down with any old sword.

As the survivors had worked their way back down the citadel, they'd been confronted by the remnants of Gogol's horde. Though many of the spectral walkers had been exposed to Mournshroud, there were some that must have been too far away during that initial rush on the castle. Since the eerie glow persisted even when they'd become vulnerable, the only way to discover if the creatures could be hurt by mundane means was by attacking them.

Doran shook his head at the dwarf. "We don't know how many more times the relic's power can be drawn upon, nor the rites the orc warlocks used to empower it." The battlemage repressed a shudder as he considered that last point. "We must be judicious about using it. It's essential the drum's power isn't exhausted before we return to Korbara so it can

301

be studied by the scholars there. They'll be better able to tell how it can be used to protect the refuge."

Ursola shrugged her shoulders. "Have it your way. That just means we'll need more of your magic to clear the way."

Gaiseric nodded in enthusiastic agreement. "There's only so much I can do with this sword," he said, wagging Cryptblade at the wizard. After his defense of the stairway, Alaric had given the sword back when the thief asked for it. Since then, he'd been quick to rush in whenever an invulnerable spectral walker crossed their path and resisted Ratbag's efforts to massacre it.

"We'll need your sword, too," Sylvia cautioned. The pirate captain's gaze roved across each of the survivors. "We've all seen the condition the ghost ship was in. If Gogol left any zombies to guard it, I don't think it's wise to use spells against them." She bowed slightly to Doran. "Your bolts of lightning, gusts of wind, and sheets of fire are devastating. Too much so. Loose one of them close to that ship and you might turn it into a bunch of flotsam." The warning, given in her cold, stern manner, didn't need to be repeated.

Ursola patted the almost empty satchel. "No need to warn me," she said. "I've only the one bomb left, and I'll give it a lot of thought before I use it."

The dwarf followed along as the survivors cautiously descended the hill. With Ratbag carrying Mournshroud, the task of scouting ahead fell to Gaiseric, a role the thief adopted with a fatalistic shrug and an appeal to whatever fickle spirits governed the nebulous whims of fortune. Ursola had to admit that for her almost instinctive loathing of burglars, the man had proven himself most capable. Certainly, his wariness served him in good stead and if he were to suddenly encounter zombies, Cryptblade would make quick work of them – an overall improvement, in her opinion, to the bloodthirsty bellowing of Ratbag when the orc stumbled on the opportunity for a fight.

The way things transpired, the forest was devoid of zombies. Any left behind by Skargash appeared to have been dealt with by Flamefang, and the horde that arrived with Gogol had followed their master into the castle. Ursola was beginning to think the fighting was all behind them when they emerged from the greenery and were staring down into the harbor.

"The swine did leave a rearguard," Sylvia cursed, drawing her cutlass as she looked toward the beached derelict.

The deck of the decrepit ship teemed with zombies. Ursola judged there must be at least forty of the creatures, all of them aglow with the phantasmal aura of spectral walkers. They stood unmoving, their vacant gaze staring out across the island. It was impossible that they couldn't see the survivors, yet the undead gave no sign that they did.

"What're they waiting for?" Ursola grumbled. "Why don't they come down and fight?"

Doran peered at the zombies, his brow knotted in concentration. "Some command given to them by Gogol before he left," he suggested. "Likely they have orders to guard the ship and nothing else."

"Nice'ndandy," Ratbag said. "Noodlin' a shiv bein bumpin' der cadavaz." He hefted his scimitar, waving its serrated edge at the ghost ship.

"Let's find out," Helchen said. She stepped away from the orc and raised her crossbow. Slowly, foot by foot, she advanced toward the beach until she was within range, then shot a bolt at one of the undead. The shot glanced off the spectral walker, repulsed by the ectoplasmic light that surrounded it.

"Wait." Alaric held his arm out to block Helchen's way as she went toward Ratbag. "Even if we sound Mournshroud, the zombies will still be aboard the ship. The one place we have to be careful about fighting them."

"We need to draw them away," Sylvia stated. "Get them to come down to us."

Helchen bore a tense look when she replied to the pirate. "That would mean figuring out exactly what Gogol told them to do. Figuring out precisely what'll provoke them."

"So, one of us shows himself and makes a lot of noise and gets them to chase him." Gaiseric rubbed at his forehead. "I don't like the idea, so of course I'll be the one to do it. I've more experience with having something chasing me."

"They can see us now, but none of them are moving," Sylvia said, gesturing with her axe at the derelict.

Ursola pointed at Doran. "Maybe he has the right of it. Maybe they're supposed to guard the boat." She smiled at the others as they turned to her. "I mean, he probably didn't want to be stranded here any more than we do. He probably told them to make sure nothing happened to that scow."

"So, if we climbed up there and tried to steal it…" Gaiseric started to say.

"No good," Sylvia cut him off. "The zombies would stay aboard and do their fighting from the deck."

"Agreed," Ursola nodded. She clapped her hands and rubbed her palms together. "But what would happen if it looked like we were going to demolish the boat?" She drew the last fire-bomb from her satchel. "I can lob this thing so close that it'll seem like I'm trying to torch that hulk. If that doesn't motivate that rabble of worm-chow, nothing will."

Alaric displayed his faith in the dwarf demolisher's specialty with a nod of assent. "Do it," the knight told her.

Cautiously, Ursola picked her way down to the shore. She knew she'd be all right as far as Helchen had advanced. After that, each step was taken with a tinge of trepidation. Even though it was her objective, her heart hammered at the idea that she'd be close enough to provoke the zombies.

The undead remained still. They might have been true corpses for all the activity they showed, but Ursola wasn't taken in by appearances. She pressed her luck just as far as she could take it. She walked just near enough to the ghost ship to be certain of her aim. Then, arcing her arm back, she tossed the fire-bomb at the derelict. The incendiary sailed through the air and shattered against the ground. The resultant burst of flames was so close to the derelict that she heard a horrified gasp rise from her on-looking companions. The dwarf knew the vessel was in no danger, but the momentary panic of the others was reassuring. If she could fool the quick, she was certain she could fool the dead.

The spectral walkers descended from the derelict with ungainly, mindless action. Ursola was reminded of a colony of burrow-beetles swarming from their nest, such was the bedlam of their activity. Zombies lurched off the deck to crash to the shore, heedless of the violence of their descent. The eerie glow that protected the creatures proved effective against recklessness as well as enemy blades. None of the shriveled, skeletal limbs were broken in the fall, though the undead made no effort at all to protect themselves.

Ursola observed in horror as some of the zombies threw themselves onto the fire, using their own bodies to smother the flames. The rest of the mob turned toward her, their eyes absent of emotion but now possessed by a new intensity. They knew who had started the fire. They weren't oblivious to the dwarf's presence now.

"A little help," Ursola called out as she backed away from the shambling horde. Her hands tightened about the heft of her warhammer, but she was only too conscious of how little use it would be against spectral walkers.

"Your plan worked. Leave the rest to me."

Ursola shifted her gaze and found Doran standing a small distance away from her on the shore. The battlemage was poised at an angle from the ship, perpendicular to the zombies now on the beach. He held a scroll in his hands, and from this he rapidly spoke a stream of arcane words.

The gusts of wind Doran had invoked before were as nothing beside the tempest he now conjured. A gale of hideous fury swept outward from where the wizard stood. Ursola felt the merest tug of that elemental rage as it rushed past her, stinging her eyes and whipping her flesh. The zombies, caught in the full magnitude of its force, were sent hurtling along the shore, scattered like fallen leaves. The winds lashed at the spectral walkers, hurling them into the abandoned buildings, smashing them against the pilings that supported the jetty.

"That… should… serve…" Doran gasped. The battlemage crumpled to his knees, sucking deep breaths into his lungs. There was a physical toll for harnessing such powerful magic.

Alaric hurried over to the weakened wizard, drawing him up to his feet and supporting him as he led Doran across the beach. "Hurry!" he enjoined the survivors. "There's no time to lose."

Sylvia directed her buccaneers in a mad dash to the derelict. "Let's be aboard and away before any of those things come back!"

Ursola jogged after the pirates, seizing one of the ropes they cast down after they'd scrambled up the hull. "Looks as seaworthy as my grandfather's tomb," she griped as she clambered onto the deck and gazed across the decayed, barnacle-ridden fastenings. "But anything that gets us away from the elf witch's cursed island is as good as gold by my reckoning!"

"How much water can two blasted boots hold?" Gaiseric complained as he tried to wring out at least some of the dampness from his footwear. The leather felt as though it had soaked up half the harbor, easily trebling their weight. He'd needed Ratbag's help to haul him over the gunwale and onto the deck, a circumstance that grated on the burglar's pride and independence.

"You'd rather be back ashore?" Alaric challenged the thief. Like Gaiseric, he was drenched almost from head to toe. The knight, always refusing to spare himself, had helped to shove the ghost ship off the shingle and out into the harbor. Those who'd assisted in the exercise – everyone who wasn't Ursola or a member of Sylvia's crew – had that same bedraggled, half-drowned look about them. It had been hard work and for a terrible moment, it had seemed the waves would be over their heads before the keel was floating free.

Even so, they'd managed to get the ship away and when Gaiseric looked back at the beach, he was certain wet boots weren't the worst that could happen to someone. Spectral walkers prowled along the shoreline, filing back in ones and twos from wherever Doran's spell had thrown them. Gaiseric's blood went cold watching the undead walk to the exact spot where the ghost ship had been. Then, without the least hesitation, they started walking out into the water. For a brief moment, even after they were completely submerged, the ectoplasmic glow could be seen beneath the waves.

"They'll try to retake the ship," Helchen advised, following the direction of Gaiseric's gaze. "They'll follow as long as they can, or at least until the imperative Gogol imposed on them loses its potency."

"It's insane," Gaiseric objected. The zombies couldn't swim, so they couldn't rise up from the deeps to latch onto the hull. All they could do was walk along after them on the bottom. Eventually even the ragged derelict would put the creatures far behind.

"Neither sane nor insane," Doran said, looking up from inspecting his backpack and the arcane scrolls it held. He'd tossed it aboard before rendering such help as he could in freeing the ship, but it was obvious he wanted to make sure none of the pirates had taken advantage of his absence. "A zombie has no mentality, so what it does can't be judged in such terms. You'd not call a rockslide insane, or a typhoon."

"Please," Sylvia shouted down from the quarterdeck, annoyance in her voice. "No talk of typhoons. This derelict is miserable enough to steer as it is." She had her hands clamped to the wheel, but Gaiseric felt she was trying to achieve a delicate balance between force and gentleness as she worked the wheel. She needed the ship to behave, but she was afraid to demand its obedience.

"Can you get us back to the mainland?" Gaiseric asked, rushing the words lest his nerves render him too timid to say them.

Sylvia's eyes roved about the derelict, at her pirates trying to fashion some manner of rigging for the tattered sail they'd found below. At last, her gaze returned to Gaiseric. "Let's just say it might have been a waste of time to wring out your boots."

"I thought you said you could sail this thing?" Ursola demanded. Panic and anger mixed in the dwarf's voice as she glared at Sylvia.

"She looked more seaworthy than she is," the pirate admitted. "Maybe Gogol was using some kind of magic to keep her afloat."

Gaiseric dashed over to Doran, clutching desperately at any chance. "Do you…"

Doran shook his head sadly. There was resignation in his voice when he answered, "A battlemage is trained to harness magic with only one purpose in mind. If you want me to scrap this barge, I can do it like that." He snapped his fingers. "But keeping her from sinking? All I can do is bail water with a bucket."

"And we don't have a bucket," Alaric said. He looked toward the island. "We're about a mile out. Think we can make it back to land?"

Sylvia shrugged. "Bringing her about is probably what put too much strain on her hull to begin with. Try that again and she could break up completely."

6

"From this far out, we could make a swim for it," Gaiseric said. Was it only his imagination, or was the ghost ship riding a bit lower in the water than it had been a moment before?

"Ignoring what awaits us ashore," Helchen said, waving her hat at the spectral walkers still moving along the beach, "we'd never be able to get something as cumbersome as Mournshroud onto land. We'd have to ditch armor and most of our weapons, too."

Gaiseric crossed his fingers, wishing he could ensnare some wisp of their fleeting luck. Drowning at sea. Such an end would have seemed ridiculous to worry about when he was a child in the village of Mertz tending his father's pigs. Now he was minded of the old bit of doggerel about the man who ran to the very edge of the world to escape death only to find that it was already there waiting for him.

"Wotun," Alaric invoked his god, dropping to one knee and leaning upon his sword. "Deliver us from our travails. Not for our sake, but for the salvation of those who depend upon our return."

Gaiseric wasn't a pious man. He'd robbed a few too many temples to believe the gods were terribly attentive to the mortal plane. Even so, he was moved by the sincerity of Alaric's prayer. The knight truly was what nobles claimed to be, a man who cared more about his duty than himself.

Feeling himself unworthy to observe the knight's devotions, Gaiseric turned away and stared out across the harbor. As he did, he spotted something rounding the encircling cliffs. It took him a moment to realize what it was. By the time he did, one of the buccaneers up in the rigging hollered down in a voice that crackled with excitement.

"Sail ho! She's The Demoness!" The pirate fairly flew down from his perch on the mast, relief shining from his face. Everyone aboard the ghost ship bore the same look of jubilant relief.

"Swell," Ratbag grunted when Gaiseric explained things to the orc. "Get ter dumpin' der bentcar. Weren't aimin' ter take der dip." He stared over the gunwales at the rolling sea and for just an instant Gaiseric saw a look of apprehension on the renegade's fanged face.

The prospect of rescue made the situation on the derelict even more tense as far as Gaiseric was concerned. Knowing that safety was near, the prospect of disaster became steadily more dire. Though Sylvia gave up steering the vessel and contented herself with just keeping it on a slow, steady course The Demoness could easily overtake, Gaiseric fretted over every wave that washed into the hull. He continued to study the roll and tilt of the deck, trying to estimate if they were sinking deeper into the water. By the time the pirate ship did come up alongside them, he was almost maddened by his efforts.

"Pardon us leaving," Mendoza called down from The Demoness. He smiled at Sylvia and gestured at the ghost ship. "When this one hove into sight, there wasn't anything to do but run away. Mister Korsgaard took a piece of the ballista, and we had no way to fight the zombies if they tried to board us. So we ran." The florid first mate doffed his hat and smiled. "But we kept an eye on the harbor. It was lucky we realized you were in command of this ship and not the necromancer."

Sylvia's face bore as broad a smile as Gaiseric had ever seen her display. "All is forgiven, Mister Mendoza, the moment I'm standing on the deck of my own ship." She waited while her first mate barked orders to the pirates to cast down ladders and assist the survivors in boarding The Demoness.

Though his heart was racing, and he was eager to be gone from the ghost ship, Gaiseric lingered behind to spare a word to Alaric. "That was a fine prayer you made. I'm tempted to believe Wotun was listening."

The knight gave Gaiseric a reproachful look. "The gods are always listening, we're just too proud to accept when their plans aren't the same as ours."

Gaiseric was surprised by the emotion in Alaric's voice. But then, he supposed it must be difficult for a man of faith to reconcile that faith with the tragedy he'd suffered, the misery he continued to see inflicted on the kingdom by the Black Plague. There had to be a rationalization, trust that the momentary evil was toward a far greater good yet to come.

"I'll help you get aboard," Gaiseric told Alaric, changing the subject to something far more immediate than gods and prayers. "With all that armor, if you missed a step you'd drop to the bottom like a mill stone."

With the help of the crew, the survivors were all soon standing on the deck of The Demoness. Gaiseric glanced over at the ghost ship. There was no question now but that the derelict was foundering. A shudder passed through him as he considered the nearness of their escape.

Sylvia made a quick report to her pirates, explaining the loss of Korsgaard and the rest. The buccaneers who'd gone ashore sheepishly displayed the loot they'd collected, to which Sylvia added several choice pieces of jewelry she'd availed herself of. It seemed likely to Gaiseric that all of them, the captain included, had held something back from the common share. Such was simply the unwritten reality of the Jolly Brotherhood.

"Bring her about, Mister Mendoza," Sylvia ordered the first mate. "Our port of call is Korbara. I want to put as much sea between ourselves and this island as fast as possible."

The pirates executed Sylvia's commands with gusto. Gaiseric judged they were making good time as they sailed away from Yandryl's island. But he was quickly to learn that their escape wasn't fast enough.

A horrified scream rang out from the crow's nest. Gaiseric shielded his eyes and stared up at the main mast. It seemed to him there had been a word at the core of that shriek. When the lookout repeated his cry, he understood both the man's speech and his terror.

"Dragon!"

All eyes turned abaft. Gaiseric felt sick when he saw the dark shape winging its way from the island. He looked over at Alaric. "You said you'd killed him," the thief groaned. There was no doubt in his mind that the dragon could only be Flamefang.

"I thought we did," Alaric protested. "We shot a lance into his chest, and he dropped into the forest."

"One thing every dwarf knows is dragons need a lot of killing," Ursola spat, shaking her fist at the distant shape. "It was wishful thinking to believe one shot from a ballista could finish off Flamefang."

Helchen spun about and pointed at the quarterdeck where The Demoness boasted her own ballista. "Surely there's a way to use that against him."

Mendoza gave the witch hunter a solemn look. "Mister Korsgaard fixed it good. He knew what he was doing."

"I should have remembered," Helchen berated herself. "I should have checked him after the troll…" Her voice trailed away. After the grisly way the abominatroll had dealt with the quartermaster, nobody had been of a mind to search the corpse.

Gaiseric laughed. "It's fortunate then that somebody had the presence of mind to relieve Korsgaard of this before he met the troll." He removed the cog-like mechanism from a pouch on his belt and proffered it to Mendoza. "Korsgaard didn't seem like the kind of person to trust with anything valuable."

Sylvia broke out into laughter. "Picked the pocket of a pirate! I knew you had itchy fingers!"

The pirate captain turned and snapped orders to the surviving artillerists. "Get the ballista back into condition and hurry! I've seen what that dragon can do. Give him half a chance and it won't be a question of survival but whether we burn or drown!"

The pirates scrambled into action. Gaiseric watched them as they repaired the weapon and cranked back the heavy wire. His eyes darted back to the approaching dragon. There was no longer any question that it was Flamefang or that the wyrm was making straight for The Demoness. "Faster," the thief called to the corsairs.

Doran drew back the hood of his robe and squinted at the soaring reptile. "There's another choice," he said. "We make Flamefang slower." Walking to the ship's aft, he extended his hand and read from the arcane scrolls he carried. Gaiseric recognized the tempestuous incantation he'd employed on the beach.

A fierce gale billowed upward from the battlemage's outthrust hand. The winds buffeted Flamefang, causing the wyrm to dip and weave in the air. Straining against the effort of maintaining his spell, Doran shifted to match the dragon's maneuvers. The wind held the beast back, arresting his forward impetus. If the magic wasn't strong enough to knock Flamefang back, at least it was slowing his progress.

"Can't... do... this..." Doran suddenly wilted to the deck, exhausted by the spell. Helchen and Gaiseric rushed over to the man, helping him away from the aft while Flamefang soared nearer. The dragon opened his fanged maw. Gaiseric braced himself for a fiery death.

Instead, there rose a monstrous shriek. When the thief looked upward, he saw Flamefang spinning through the air. The dragon's chest already bore a raw, dripping wound, the effect of the lance shot into him at the castle. The wyrm had clawed that missile out, but now a second skewered his shoulder, just beneath the left wing. Scalding blood gushed from the torn, scaly flesh, steaming as it struck the sea.

Flamefang bellowed once more, then dropped into the rolling waves. Cheers erupted all across the ship. Somehow, Gaiseric was incapable of joining in. He couldn't shake a sense of foreboding.

Celebration abruptly ended when the sea began to bubble and churn. "Dragons need a lot of killing," Ursola whispered, her awed voice almost thunderous in the stunned silence that reigned over The Demoness.

Gaiseric gazed in mute horror as the spot where Flamefang had hit the water exploded upward and the dragon lifted himself back into the sky, his great wings snapping at the air as he climbed.

"Oh, now he's really mad," Gaiseric said as he looked up at the wyrm. Behind him, he could hear the artillerists frantically reloading the ballista. Gaiseric didn't think even the most degenerate gambler would take odds on them landing another shot before the dragon reduced the ship and everyone on her to cinders.

CHAPTER TWENTY-FOUR

Flamefang dove down upon The Demoness, his mouth agape, ready to spew his deadly breath across the ship. By instinct, Alaric lifted his arm to guard himself against the attack, a doubly futile move. Even if it could have protected him from the dragon, his shield had been ruined by Gogol's undead talons and was lying abandoned back on the island.

Sylvia had a more practical response, if just as ineffective. "Archers!" she shouted. The bowmen among the pirates hurriedly took aim and loosed arrows against the diving reptile. A target as big as Flamefang was practically impossible to miss but the missiles lacked the strength to penetrate the dragon's scaly hide. The shafts snapped as the arrows struck the unyielding scales.

"Ballista! Loose!" Mendoza yelled. The crack of the enormous crossbow launching a shaft boomed across the deck. Flamefang was watching for such an attack, however, and turned his dive into a midair twist. The lance went speeding past him, missing the dragon entirely. The leathery wings beat rapidly as the wyrm climbed once more to gain sufficient altitude to dive at the ship again.

"Doran," Alaric called out, but one glance at the reeling battlemage was enough. The wind he'd set against Flamefang had exhausted him. He'd need to recover before he could draw on his magic again. Helchen and Gaiseric attended the wizard as they tried to find him some sort of cover.

Helchen! The knight dashed over to the witch hunter. "We need you to cast a spell on him," he said. Alaric grabbed her by the arm and turned her around so she was facing the descending wyrm. The deep-set repugnance toward magic even now made her reluctant to draw on its power. To break her hesitance, he resorted to the same reasoning that compelled him to keep fighting. "Everyone in Korbara is depending on us."

The witch hunter nodded. Pulling away from Alaric, she opened Hulmul's grimoire, turning it to the page she'd marked. Sweat beaded her forehead as she spoke the incantation and pointed at the dragon.

Alaric could feel the air around him growing colder. He saw the cloud of frost that formed each time Helchen exhaled. The knight lifted his eyes, watching for any sign that the spell was affecting Flamefang. As the wyrm dove lower, he could see that the scaly muzzle was no longer a livid crimson, but had a patina of bluish ice forming over it. The arcane frost struggled against the heat of the dragon, steaming when the wyrm's fiery blood was too strong, advancing down the face when Helchen coerced extra power into the spell.

It was a tug-of-war between conjurer and dragon. A struggle, Alaric realized, Helchen would lose. Perhaps with proper instruction in wizardry she could have made a better fight, but she was relying upon an innate facility for magic and such theoretical understanding of its rules as taught to her by the Order. The blast of frost, capable of freezing a mob of zombies solid, didn't stop Flamefang's attack.

"Down!" Alaric cried, pulling Helchen to the deck. Screams rang out all across the ship. One pirate, mad with terror, threw himself into the sea. Flamefang took no notice of the scrambling crew or even the witch hunter who'd tried to encase his head in ice. When Alaric peered up at the wyrm, he saw that the beast's attention was fixated on the ballista. The gaping maw was turned upon it. The next moment, the knight was certain a sheet of immolating fire would engulf the weapon and its crew.

Instead, the dragon's body convulsed, writhing in a pain so great that Flamefang struggled to keep in the air. A bilious, reeking froth burst from his jaws, heaving a wretched spew across the deck. Instead of exhaling a gout of fire as he'd intended, the reptile instead disgorged the contents of his stomach. Alaric could see horribly suggestive shapes in that reeking spume. More horrible still, some of those shapes were moving, lurching onto their feet.

Being entombed in the guts of a dragon hadn't been enough to extinguish the abominable power of the Black Plague. A half-dozen zombies now stood upon the deck, their decayed bodies further corroded by the acids in Flamefang's belly, bile dripping off their ghastly shapes. The undead faced the horrified pirates around them. Without hesitation, the creatures moved to attack.

One of the zombies, a horribly putrid orc, shuffled toward Helchen, its stump of an arm reaching for her. Alaric intercepted the walker, swinging his sword at the thing's head. The skull exploded like a piece of rotten fruit, whatever integrity it had possessed subsumed by Flamefang's digestive juices. The headless body splashed against the deck, disintegrating into pulpy mush.

Across the deck, Ursola and Gaiseric were helping the pirates cut down the loathsome zombies. Though a few of the crew had been dragged down, it looked to Alaric that the undead would soon be cleared from The Demoness. At least if Flamefang didn't vomit more of them onto the ship.

Perhaps it was that threat that caused Ratbag to act. While the ballista crew were frozen in horror, the renegade snatched up one of the enormous bolts the weapon used. Hefting the cumbersome ammunition as though it were a harpoon, the orc charged across the deck until he was as close as possible to the hovering wyrm.

"Der shiv fer ya, ya dopey lizard!" Ratbag hurled the bolt at Flamefang. Alaric knew there was no way the orc, for all his strength, could match the power of a ballista. So, too, did Ratbag. Instead of trying to pierce the dragon's scales, he cast his throw at one of the leathery wings. The missile slashed through the membrane on the right wing, ripping through it as though it were sailcloth.

A pained hiss rattled from Flamefang as, for the second time, the dragon plunged from the sky. This time the wyrm's descent wasn't so uncontrolled. Alaric thought he could see the reptile's eyes gleaming with viciousness as he careened, not into the sea, but down onto the ship's deck.

The mainmast snapped under the dragon's mass, throwing the lookout and several other pirates into the sea. The broken remains sagged against the hull, torn sails drooping into the water. Flamefang's plunge carried him down to the deck, where his clawed feet smashed buccaneers and zombies alike into gory paste. His tail lashed out, splintering the steps up to the quarterdeck and hurling wreckage over the side.

"He's too heavy!" Sylvia yelled as she tried to maintain her footing near the wheel. "He'll sink us!"

From his place near the aft of the ship, Alaric could see what Sylvia meant. The bow was pitching downward into the waves, letting them wash over and spill down into the hold. The gunwales were almost level with the sea and at each swell, water poured over them. The dragon's weight was pressing down on the vessel. Concentrated in one spot, Flamefang's mass alone was enough to send The Demoness to the bottom.

The crew appreciated their peril. While screaming their terror of the beast, they rushed at Flamefang from all sides with whatever weapons they had. Axes and swords rang off the dragon's armored hide, spears were blunted as they were driven against the impenetrable scales. Ursola alone had better luck. Swinging her hammer high, she brought it crashing against the reptile's tail, putting a definite kink in the extremity as the impact dislocated the bones inside.

Flamefang roared in pain but whipped his tail back around to protect it from further harm. Instead, the dragon glared at the dwarf and opened his massive jaws. No fire exploded from the beast's throat, but the nauseating sight of a half-digested zombie pulling itself from his maw caused Ursola to recoil in disgust. The undead flopped down to the deck almost at her feet. Before it could rise to attack, Ratbag burst its rotten head with a swing of his scimitar. As he did, a swell of water knocked him off his feet. Only by the narrowest margin was the big orc able to avoid Flamefang's stamping claws as the reptile tried to grind him into the deck.

"We've got to get that monster off the ship," Alaric swore. He hadn't come so far, survived so much, brought their desperate quest to the verge of triumph only to have it all undone now.

"A fine idea," Gaiseric said, arching an eyebrow at the knight. "How do we do it?"

"We throw everything we have at him," Doran proclaimed. The battlemage was breathing heavily, but despite his exhaustion, he was drawing a scroll from his bag. "Dead is dead," he said when he noted the worried look Alaric gave him. "Whether I expend myself by casting spells or end up as a snack for a dragon. At least this way, something good may come of it."

Helchen stepped beside the wizard and rested her hand on his shoulder. "Perhaps if we were both to share the burden..."

Doran smiled and nodded at her suggestion. "Yes. What fire and ice alone cannot accomplish, perhaps they can achieve together." The gleam in his eyes showed that the battlemage had some sort of idea. "If we were to strike the same spot, rapidly, the extremes of heat and cold might weaken Flamefang's armor. Create a vulnerable point."

"It would need careful coordination," Alaric advised Doran.

"Just follow my signals," the battlemage told Helchen. She hesitated only a moment, then bowed in agreement.

"What about me?" Gaiseric asked. "What do I do?"

Alaric pushed the thief toward the wheel. "Steer the ship

for a bit and tell Sylvia I need her to rally those artillerists. They need to be ready to shoot the moment Helchen and Doran weaken Flamefang."

Gaiseric hurried away and soon had Sylvia rushing to the ballista. Alaric stood by Doran and Helchen as they readied the magic that he hoped would be the beginning of the end for Flamefang. He resisted the urge to leap down and join those already battling the dragon on the main deck. If something happened, if the wyrm suddenly attacked while they were conjuring, he had to keep himself available to meet that contingency. Give his friends at least some chance of defending themselves.

"Doran! Helchen! Whenever you're ready!" Alaric cried out. Below, Flamefang had seized a corsair in his jaws, the blood gushing from the man's body sizzling as it struck the wyrm's forked tongue.

Poised between the two, Alaric first felt the surge of heat as Doran loosed a fiery sphere against the dragon. It burst without effect against the red scales. A heartbeat later, the air chilled and the knight could see that the same spot was briefly caked in frost. Then it was Doran's fire once more, followed soon after by Helchen's frost. Always the same spot on the dragon. Flamefang shifted about, roaring, agitated by the battery of spells stabbing at his body. As he turned, Ratbag rushed at him again, stamping on the kinked section of tail. The dragon whipped back around, but as he did so, Ursola swung her hammer into his muzzle, cracking several of his fangs.

"Again!" Doran enjoined Helchen. Spells of fire and frost continued to batter the reptile, but each time he started to turn, Ratbag would attack the injured segment of tail and draw the wyrm's wrath.

Alaric blinked his eyes, incredulous at what he saw. The continuous extremes of heat and cold had turned a patch of Flamefang's side brittle. He could actually see shavings flake away from the affected scales when the dragon moved. Here, he knew, was the spot the pirates had to aim for.

"Sylvia! Now!" the knight shouted.

Across the quarterdeck Alaric could see the skull-faced pirate directing her corsairs. "I told you to get off my ship!" she snarled before making a chopping motion with her cutlass. The ballista shuddered as it sent a shaft speeding into the dragon.

The battered scales on Flamefang's side shattered like glass as the huge bolt struck him. The dragon reared onto his hind legs, wings fanning out and sending a pair of buccaneers over the side. From what Alaric could see, the lance had pierced deep into the wyrm's body, deep enough to hit organs.

Flamefang lashed his tail, bowling over the combatants around him. Then, with a tortured howl, the beast started to take flight, his torn wing making the effort ungainly. His shifting weight broke the tenuous grip maintained by the snapped mainmast and it careened into the murky depths.

Alaric felt enraged as he saw the dragon trying to take flight. If he broke free, Flamefang would return to the attack. The wyrm was too vindictive to let them go. And the next time he attacked, he would do so in such a way that those aboard The Demoness couldn't retaliate.

Firming his grip on his sword, Alaric leapt from the quarterdeck just as Flamefang began to rise into the air. He caught hold of the lance Sylvia's crew had just put into the reptile's body. Hanging onto it with one hand, he stabbed his sword into the edge of the wound.

"Alaric! Don't!" Helchen's shout rang out from what seemed to the knight an impossible distance. When he looked down, he felt his stomach drop. Flamefang's ascent might be ungainly, but it had been swift. Already he was some hundred or so feet above the ship. Helchen and the others were only discernible for a few moments, then they became like ants in his sight.

"You're not getting away," Alaric hissed through clenched teeth. He worried the point of his sword in the dragon's flesh, widening the wound.

Flamefang screeched and brought his claw scratching across his side, trying to reach the crazed man stabbing him with a sword. The claws struck sparks from the crimson scales as they scraped down the reptile's flank, but such was the spot Alaric held that his talons couldn't reach the man.

"You're not getting rid of me," Alaric swore. His blade bit deeper into the wyrm. Scalding blood bubbled up, his mail presenting no protection whatsoever from its searing heat. He bit his lip to resist the pain, forcing his mind away from the relief of unconsciousness. Too much depended on him. There was no one else now who could slay the dragon.

"For the quest," Alaric growled. The sword bit deeper into Flamefang's body. To the red of blood, now there was added a sickly yellow fluid that stank of sulphur. The knight twisted his head as a spurt of the yellow filth penetrated his helm and burned his face. He could feel the stuff biting into his eye and cheek, burrowing into him like acid.

"For my friends!" the knight exclaimed, thrusting the blade still deeper. He felt the dragon shudder, imagined he heard something inside burst.

The erratic, sidelong flight, the snarling, hissing voice of the wyrm, the clawing motion of Flamefang's legs, all of these abruptly ceased. Alaric could see the dragon's head twist around. For one fleeting instant, he held the reptile's baleful gaze with his remaining eye. Then the serpentine orb lost its luster, as though an inner light had been extinguished. Alaric knew he no longer gazed upon a titanic beast of malevolent power, but simply a hulk of lifeless meat.

The wings folded as the motivating force that drove them went out. Alaric felt the wind rush about him as he hurtled downward with the dragon's corpse. He could see The Demoness sailing away, carrying his friends and the relic to Korbara. A smile worked itself through the knight's pain. He could die content knowing that his death was not in vain.

Flamefang's body struck the sea with the force of an avalanche. Alaric had one momentary impression of water exploding around him.

Then there was only oblivion.

CHAPTER TWENTY-FIVE

"Turn back?" Sylvia looked as though she wanted to laugh at the suggestion. "You have to know that won't do any good."

Helchen glowered at Sylvia until any note of humor on her face was extinguished. She waved her hand, indicating the area where Flamefang had crashed into the sea. "We have to make sure! I have to make sure!" Both sickness and panic slithered through her body, a cold nausea that stirred her very soul.

"Sylvia's right, and you know it," Gaiseric told the witch hunter. She looked up as the thief walked over to her. His face was heavy with sorrow. Seeing his emotion somehow made the tragedy even more real for Helchen.

"He's survived…" The witch hunter choked on her words, feeling how hollow they were even to her own ears.

Gaiseric put his arm around her shoulders. "Alaric's gone." He didn't mince words. "Even if he survived the fall, the weight of his armor would have dragged him to the bottom." The rogue plucked at the mail he was wearing. "A knight might wear this stuff like it was a second skin, but that doesn't make it any lighter in the water."

Helchen met Gaiseric's gaze. She struggled to maintain some degree of composure, to drive back the sense of loss that threatened to overwhelm her. "He didn't have to sacrifice himself."

"Maybe he did," Ursola said. The dwarf shook her head. "Certainly, Alaric thought so. If Flamefang had escaped, the dragon would probably have come after us again. Wyrms are a vindictive, unforgiving breed."

The last part of Ursola's speech almost broke through Helchen's sorrow. She wondered if the demolisher understood that most people said the same things about dwarves, that they were a folk quick to anger and slow to forgive.

"Der buttons wuz der mezz," Ratbag said. The big orc's savage features had an almost wistful quality as he stared out at the sea. "Ya wuz allreet, nah kibitzer. Alla der moxie." The warrior stepped to the gunwale and made a shallow cut across his palm. Clenching his fist, he let blood drip into the water.

Gaiseric watched Ratbag and clucked his tongue in wonder. "Rare to see an orc show respect to anyone, much less someone who isn't another orc."

"Alaric von Mertz was a remarkable man," Helchen said. She felt like the knight had helped draw her away from the narrow confines of what she'd been taught by the Order, widening her perspective. Teaching her that what she fought to protect was more important than who her enemy might be. She'd learned much about what duty and honor really meant.

"Alaric died to ensure we'd make it back to Korbara," Doran declared. The battlemage sat against the railing, the macabre Mournshroud resting on the deck beside him. The wizard tapped his finger against the relic. "We know this can destroy the undead and at least weaken the spectral walkers. It's vital we bring it back to the monastery where its enchantment can be studied." Doran gave Helchen a reassuring smile. "Alaric made that possible. The victory belongs to him."

Helchen couldn't quite see things so optimistically. "A battle won, perhaps, but the war goes on. The Black Plague yet lays waste to the kingdom."

"Mournshroud may be a clue to how to fight back." Doran emphasized his point. "Force of arms alone cannot prevail against black magic. Magic can only be undone by other magic. Opposing magic. The enchantments the orcs invested into Mournshroud are antithetical to necromancy."

There was little the witch hunter found reassuring about that. "The ones who made that drum were orc warlocks. As you yourself said, there's no knowing what barbaric rites they employed to create the thing or what will be necessary to maintain its powers." Helchen pressed her concern home. As much as Alaric had broadened her viewpoint, in some things she still felt the Order was right. "This isn't benevolent magic opposing necromancy. We've resorted to a power every bit as malignant."

"But there is a chance now," Doran persisted. "We know at least that there are such forces that can be used. Through careful study…"

Helchen scowled. "There isn't time for careful study. The zombie hordes are destroying the kingdom now." She looked back at the island, thinking of the dead sorceress Yandryl and the many evils attributed to her. "Desperation may make monsters of us all." She nodded at the gruesome drum. "Do you think there aren't those who'd try to save themselves by creating more of these relics, no matter how murderous the orcish rituals might be?"

"Maybe that's better," Gaiseric interrupted. "At least some people would be saved. What if the only alternative is for the undead to kill everyone?"

It was a revolting idea, but Helchen was realistic enough to know that there were many nobles and leaders across the kingdom who'd prefer anything – no matter how despicable – to the certainty of death. She tried to imagine what Alaric would do, given such a choice. Would he compromise ideals, surrender the few to save the many? After a moment of consideration, she realized she already knew the answer. Yes, he would, but the knight would insist on being one of the few who was sacrificed. Was that heroic, or was it simply a way to justify something monstrous?

"We'll see what the templars in Korbara think," Helchen declared. "Let them determine if this relic is a vessel of hope, or simply a harbinger of doom."

Ratbag had listened intently during the discussion. Now the orc warrior spoke. "Der tomtom gimicked fer der tribes. Ya wanna chewdatover, noodle up der tomtom, ya gonna leggit fer der orcturf."

Gaiseric followed Ratbag's guttural speech. The thief grimaced as he deciphered the orc's words. "If we want to learn more about the relic, the place to do so is in the orc lands," he translated. "That's where it was made. That's where its secrets will be found."

"Der orcturf crawlin' wid cadavaz," Ratbag grunted. "Skargash weren't der only bonecalla."

Helchen didn't need Gaiseric to interpret the rest. Ratbag had spoken before of the wilderness beyond the frontier, the regions claimed by orcs and goblins. He'd said those lands were afflicted by the zombie plague even worse than the kingdom. Now, after encountering Skargash's horde, they all had a better idea of the kind of undead that infested that territory. The very kind of enemies they would have to fight their way through if they needed to trace Mournshroud back to its origins.

"Let's hope it doesn't come to that," Doran said. "There are many wise scholars and magicians in Korbara and certainly many more who've survived and are scattered elsewhere in the kingdom. They'll certainly be able to solve the secret of how Mournshroud works and how to keep it working."

The witch hunter felt a chill pass through her. "Pray it will be so. Otherwise, we may find the knowledge we need guarded by such a horde of undead never undreamed of."

"Aye," Ursola said, shaking her head. "A horde of zombie orcs. A Green Horde."

"Sufficient to the moment are the evils of the moment," Sylvia told the survivors. "My promise to the people of Korbara was to bring that drum back. That's been ordeal enough. Take some satisfaction in that achievement and worry about the troubles of tomorrow when they come."

Helchen doffed her hat to the pirate. "Wisely said. It's important to maintain perspective." She glanced back in the direction where Flamefang had sunk into the sea. "Alaric would have been the first to recognize the worthiness of saving even a single life."

Sylvia smiled at the witch hunter, then spun about and shouted orders to her crew. "Mister Mendoza! Chart a course for Korbara! The quicker The Demoness makes port, the sooner everyone gets their share of the plunder!"

EPILOGUE

Bloated, its flesh nibbled at by every fish in the harbor, the once vibrant crimson scales faded to a bruised purple, the yellow belly decayed to a putrid green, the gigantic carcass floated toward shore. A devious smile pulled at the face of the lone observer on the beach – at least, the only observer with awareness enough to appreciate the sight. A rabble of zombies stood motionless in the surf: hulking orcish walkers and nimble goblin runners, remnants of the horde Skargash had brought to the island, and which had been scattered throughout Yandryl's castle; a few undead that wore the tattered remains of the elf sorceress's livery; many of the withered spectral walkers that had withstood the vibrations of Mournshroud and the battlemage's spells. A motley horde, but all bound in mindless obedience to Brunon Gogol.

The necromancer's fall from the tower hadn't been as lethal as his enemies hoped. After all, the chief aim of necromancy was to extend the life of the practitioner. It would take far more direct methods to separate Gogol from the mortal coil.

The necromancer raised his new arm, unsettled by its leathery green flesh but overjoyed by the raw strength he felt within it. Mournshroud's enchantment had corroded the other limb into a mush of putrescence, but fortunately he'd found a suitable replacement in Skargash's corpse. It would have been dangerous to animate the orc as a zombie – there was too much chance his spirit would take control of its former flesh – but harvesting Skargash's arm was a step Gogol felt comfortable taking. A limb already initiated in the harmonies of black magic would be even better than the one it was replacing. Besides, to the heightened might of undead flesh was now added the natural brawn of an orc.

Yes, Gogol considered as he worked the clawed fingers, he'd have made short work of Alaric von Mertz with such an arm. Under his guidance, his zombies had done an admirable job attaching it to his body. His enemies would be in for quite a surprise when next they had the misfortune to cross his path.

Gogol uttered a cruel laugh and his eyes fixed on Flamefang's scaly corpse. Soon the dragon would drift near enough to shore for his zombies to wade out and guide it onto the beach. Then the real work would begin. A feat of necromancy of such magnitude that an entire cabal would balk at attempting it. But Gogol would do much more than merely attempt. He would succeed. With the corruption he already sensed in the wyrm's flesh, he would reanimate it. Flamefang would rise again, an undead leviathan. A necromantic dragon that would spread the terror of the Black Plague into the furthest reaches of the kingdom.

Let the fools put their trust in their little relics, Gogol sneered. He would show them how useless it was to defy the doom that had been decreed for their land. Perhaps those who bowed down and submitted would be spared, but for the rest there would be only death. Death... and the eternal darkness of undeath.

Gogol's eyes roved across the draconic carcass, savoring the sharp teeth and vicious claws, the thick scales and massive wings. He thought of his enemies and pictured their destruction when he let loose an undead dragon against them.

"You will meet this creature again," Gogol vowed. "And for you it will be your Angel of Death."

ABOUT THE AUTHOR

Exiled to the blazing wastes of Arizona for communing with ghastly Lovecraftian abominations, C L WERNER strives to infect others with the grotesque images that infest his mind. Cinephile habits acquired during a stint managing a video store have resulted in a movie collection that threatens to devour his domicile. An inveterate bibliophile, he squanders the proceeds from his writing on hoary old volumes – or reasonably affordable reprints of same – to expand his library of fantasy fiction, horror stories and occult tomes. When not engaged in reading or writing, he is known to re-invest in the gaming community via far too many Kickstarter boardgame campaigns and to haunt obscure collectible shops to ferret out outré Godzilla memorabilia. He is the author of forty plus novels including *Marvel Legends of Asgard: The Sword of Sutur, Marvel Legends of Asgard: Three Swords,* and *Zombicide Black Plague: Age of the Undead.*

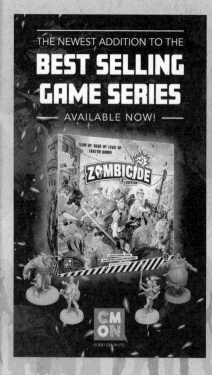